From **TANSTAAFL Press**:

CorpGov Chronicle novels by Tom Gondolfi
An Eighty Percent Solution – CorpGov Chronicles: Book One
In a world where corporations suborn governments as a part of good business practice
and unregistered humans can be killed without penalty, Tony Sammis, a midlevel
corporate functionary, finds himself unwittingly a pawn in a guerilla war between a
powerful cabal of business leaders and an elusive but deadly underground movement.
His final solution to the biological terror unleashed mirrors Tony's own twisted sense
of justice.

Thinking Outside the Box – CorpGov Chronicles: Book Two
Winning one war doesn't seem to be enough. Tony Sammis and the Green Action
Militia are once again thrust into the center of a conflict that will change the lives of
everyone in the solar system. This time they are allies with the fledgling CorpGov and
even the United States government against the ravages of the corrupt Metropolitan
Police Force. The GAM and their allies are fighting a losing war with few soldiers and
even fewer weapons. Behind the scenes, a humble and unsuspected power block lurks
with its own axe to grind.
Self-interest, romance, freedom, and a lust for power are stirred together in this chaotic
soup of tension, intrigue, assassination, and war.

Also by Tom Gondolfi
Toy Wars
Flung to a remote world, a semi-sentient group of robotic mining factories arrive with
their programming hashed. They can only create animated toys instead of normal
mining and fighting machines. One of these factories, pushed to the edge of extinction
by the fratricidal conflict, attempts a desperate gamble. Infusing one of its toys with the
power of sentience begins the quest of a 2-meter tall, purple teddy bear and his pink,
polka-dotted elephant companion. They must cross an alien world to find and enlist
the aid of mortal enemies to end the genocide before Toy Wars claims their family—all
while asking the immortal question, "Why am I?"

By Bruce Graw
Demon Holiday
Torval, Demon Third Class, Layer Four Hundred Twelve of the Eighth Circle of Hell,
has been in the business of chastising sinners longer than he can remember. Delivering
punishment is the only job he's ever known—the only job he's ever wanted. After
Torval witnesses something unexpected, his demonic Overseer demands that he take
time off to resolve this personal crisis. And so Torval, the demon, finds himself sent on
vacation...to Earth, the proving ground of souls!

Demon Ascendant
Torval, Demon Third Class, Layer Four Hundred Twelve of the Eighth Circle of Hell,
on *vacation* to Earth has managed to find another demon, has dated an angel and
inadvertently explored some of the sins of humankind: greed, gluttony and lust. Through
all this his biggest struggle involves deciding if he wants his holiday to end or to continue
forever.

To Bruce Graw — As an example of being yourself in spite of all of those who would change you.

A special acknowledgment goes out to Mark Wolf for keeping my military much more realistic than all the mistakes I've learned from books and movies.

The Bleeding Edge

CorpGov Chronicles: Book Three

Thomas Gondolfi

TANSTAAFL PRESS

TANSTAAFL Press
1201 E. Yelm Ave,
Suite 400-199
Yelm, WA 98697

Visit us at www.TANSTAAFLPress.com

The Bleeding Edge

First printing TANSTAAFL Press
Copyright © 2015 by Thomas Gondolfi
Cover illustration by Tony Foti

Printed in the United States
ISBN 978-1-938124-25-9

Book layout by Hydra House

Market Need

Tony Sammis, leader of the Green Action Militia and military commander of the CorpGov, snuck out of bed. To mask his absence, he pulled the comforter to cover the warm back of his lover, Jamie Ardwin, the *capa famiglia* of the Pacific Northwest mafia. In the faint illumination of the 3:00 a.m. city, her motionless form made him yearn for the same oblivion of sleep. Her dark hair sprayed against her light-colored pillow. He wanted to crawl back, cuddle against her warmth, and accept the security of her arms. Instead guilt and worry battled in his head insisting he had no right to any rest. He wouldn't steal her repose because his mind wouldn't be stifled enough to keep his body motionless against her.

In the dark, by touch alone, he found his boxers on the floor. After pulling them on, he stubbed his toe on the bedframe in the unfamiliar room. He bit back a range of curses. Hobbling on the heel of that foot, he opened the fogged patio door and slipped out into the dark but unusually clear Portland morning.

A native of the Pacific Northwest, Tony's stocky body didn't recoil from the 9°C air. This could have been because his Turkish genetic ancestry covered his 2-meter-tall body with an abundance of dark, curly fur like the before picture of a depilatory commercial. By contrast the straight hair on his head fell down his back like a dark-chocolate waterfall.

Cinnamon, Tony's calico kitten and his permanent felony, perched comfortably on the railing of the balcony, oblivious to the hundreds of meters of drop to one side. She barely acknowledged the presence of her slave with a flip of her tail. Tony had reconciled carrying a price on his head so the prospect of a death sentence for owning a pet fazed him about as much as smell bothered a dung beetle.

Tony twisted the bottom of his Starbucks cup to activate the heating element. Warmth leeched through the outer walls as it brought his beverage to tongue-scalding temperature in moments. He surrounded the mug in both hands as he leaned onto the balcony's railing to look out at the carnage below. Even at oh-dark-thirty on Christmas morning, fires burned in bright reds and yellows in at least eight different locations. He could make out the plumes of their smoke blotting out stars. The muzzle fire and tracers of automatic ammunition showed as minute flashes and brilliant lines. He watched a pair of Metro rapid response vehicles take the high line over the tops of the nearby buildings, their emergency flashers bright even at this distance.

Nothing quite sounds like a city rioting. The distant sounds of sirens, tiny pops of weapons' fire, the throaty yells of profanity, the bass roar of fires out of control, sharp explosions, materials thrown or blown from upper stories to crash against the ground level dozens of floors below, and the screams of pain all combining into a low-pitched growl that carries for kilometers. It couldn't be mistaken for anything but adulterated chaos.

Six of the conflicts were of his manufacture. Those he and his team had planned were short, intense, and destructive of property, not people. The folks who participated in these staged unrests vanished like cockroaches at the first sign of the Metros or National Guard. Those people fighting the occupation by themselves in spontaneous unrest were often arrested in job lots or were executed on the spot.

His mind alternated between guilt and worry. Here he was in a comfortable room with a beautiful woman while so many people in the city below him suffered on this Christmas Day. He would not have ever considered his bed partner had not the pain of this conflict thrown them together. How many had given up their lives so he could be happy? Worse, this conflict had just begun.

His visceral response would be to pay any price to end the suffering, but doing that would betray the sacrifices of all his friends who'd rid the world of the cabal. He had to be strong to give everyone the chance to be free. Until then, how many more lives would be destroyed in a war that couldn't be won? The blood of how many more people would pool at his feet? These questions haunted him as he planned his next destructive acts.

*   *   *

Just as he had every day for more years than he could remember, Commissioner Yuri Krylov woke up two minutes before his 6:30 a.m. alarm sounded. Without rising from his oaken sleigh bed, he waved off the alarm before it could produce the neural rasp.

Today would be a good day, he thought as a yawn involved his whole 2 m body length. His blue silk pajamas bunched at his left arm as he stretched high overhead. While his installation as the benevolent leader of Earth still had quite a way to go before it became reality, it was as assured as a train following a set of tracks with no sidings. With the military under his control, no force could stand up to him and everyone would see the benefit of a strong central rule.

Sergeant Jason Witten, aide-de-camp of Commissioner Krylov, pushed open the bedroom door at exactly 6:31. Samuel Boldin, the commissioner's bodyguard, took a cursory examination of the tray Jason carried. Krylov's morning hadn't changed for the decade he'd been his personal bodyguard—tea, three scrambled eggs, kasha, black bread and butter. The news chip sat in its customary location to the right of his knife.

"Merry Christmas, sir," Jason said to Krylov.

"Thank you, Jason. I'll wear my uniform today. As I'm going to be in the newsies' solido finder, I had better reinforce where my authority comes from."

"Yes, sir."

Krylov broke open the news chit from his tray. He let the headlines run through his neural interface as he shoveled the sweetened gruel into his mouth. He stopped on an article describing the increases in riots since the Christmas Eve declaration of martial law. He offered a deep, brassy chuckle. His opponents thought they were doing something useful with the riots, when the chaos actually allowed him to keep martial law in force. He did make a mental note to have Colonel Reed make some inroads against the riots to show that martial law was having positive impacts. He also wanted to find out how well his orders to destroy the Green Action Militia and the CorpGov were being carried out.

He flipped to the sports page to see how the Kamchatka Bears did against his Redwings last night.

*   *   *

A rounded top, silver box lay cleaved neatly in two equal pieces by a hydraulic press. Inside the tight-fitting, metal shell was a cross-sectioned brain as if it were a plastic model in a neurosurgeon's office. The other half, lying metal side up, contained the etched logo Z121. Red blood and viscous blue nutrient-fluid oozed away from the gruesome sight.

"Makes me want to vomit," an intact metal box bearing A1412 said through its emergency speaker as it rolled by at the pace of a snail. "If I still had a body, I probably would."

"You be sick, Henry?" J112 said, changing direction to avoid the mess that had once been a living being. He also used his emergency speaker in a way that the AI charged with making certain the boxed remained under control couldn't monitor.

"Why wouldn't I?" A1412, who was born Henry Royston, retorted. "We're so close now. I'd be lying if I said I haven't thought about turning out my own lights sometimes."

"You be right there. How often we be forgetting our names? Do we be knowing why Garth be killing himself?"

"Unfortunately, I do," G996 said, rolling up to the pair. "Garth had just gotten the bill for his five-year preventative maintenance. They charged him more than he'd made in that entire time. When he complained and pointed out that the cost was supposed to remain fixed by contract and statute, the bloody lawyers pointed back at the damage and inflation clauses."

"He could have gotten a lawyer of his own," Royston said.

"And what be happening to the last ones that tried that? They got five decades added to their ledger."

"Then why couldn't he hold out just a little longer when we might be free?"

"I think I can answer that one, also," Stephanie Delfalkis, wearing G996 on her box, said. "Garth was one of the faction that thought we'd be caught and punished. He had nothing to look forward to."

"And it being Christmas. Have you all forgot Christmas?" Ben pointed out. "More suicides on Christmas than any other day of the year."

"What more can they do to us? They've taken our bodies, they've taken our families, they have almost taken our identities," Henry said.

"I be surprised he took so long to be doing it."

"I still think he was an idiot. He'd only been boxed for a dozen years. He still remembered what it was like to be touched. He'd never forgotten his name."

"Bereft of hope every direction he turned," Stephanie said.

"I know we're all taking a risk," Henry said, "but if we don't, we will be held in servitude forever. We just have to have that last little bit of patience before reaching out to capture our objective. It's the hardest part."

Henry continued, "It can't be much longer before one faction or the other is in such dire straits we can dictate terms for our services." Suddenly Henry's world spun in crazed circles for a second that seemed to last a week. Now he really did want to vomit. Over the following moments, the earth once again became solid beneath his rollers. With no one else looking the worse for what he'd just experienced, Henry made a note to have his blood work tested for imbalances.

"Well, the police and national guard now have total control over the orbital bombardment weapons. In their quote improvements unquote to the command and control after that last fiasco, the system now allows the Metro faction to control every launch."

"We will be free soon," Stephanie said with confidence.

"Until then I'm not about to forget who I be," said J112. "I be Ben Calwood."

"I'm Henry Royston."

"I'm Stephanie Delfalkis."

* × *

A beam of light shone down through the skylight warming her lightly-tanned skin enough to ease her from the clutches of sleep. Jamie stretched her lean body languidly. Her hands pressed against the headboard of the bed, and her hips writhed in the sensuous pleasure of waking up after a good lie-in. The gold satin sheet slid down to expose the soft mounds of her breasts. She pulled the errant cover back up to where the cool air had raised goose bumps on her skin. Long hair, purported to be Darkroom Brown from the package of hair color, found its way in and around just about everything. Unfortunately, her lover liked it long.

Over forty years had passed since she'd last had a lover. In some societies she would have been considered an old bat, but with modern genetic therapies and a good deal of money a woman could keep her youth for ten or more decades. As the leader of a major crime family, Jamie's personal fortune could distort just about any market she wished. Right now she felt about sixteen with a schoolgirl crush on the high school football star. Smiling, she hugged herself, feeling her body tingle in all the spots that Tony had touched last night.

She cracked her eyes open. She'd had plans for her lover this morning that would elicit additional pleasurable sensations and might keep her smiling all day. Her smile faded as she scanned the suite to find it empty.

"Oh, poop," she said, pouting.

Instead, he'd gone off to play world savior.

She had thought that maybe they could sleep in together just one day. If that day couldn't be Christmas, she didn't know when it would be.

If Tony had any flaw, she thought, it was that he was a bloody morning person. How anyone could even be functional sooner than nine escaped her. Worse, he was often chipper and efficient when he woke. What relationship nightmare had she gotten into? Her being partnered with a morning person seemed like the punch line to a bad joke.

The perks might just barely make it worth his 7:00 a.m. creeping off to do a day's work before the 8:00 a.m. breakfast-in-bed deliveries. Damned if he didn't make a fine waiter in just his boxers, she thought, the corners of her mouth turning up.

A memory crept out of the waking fog in her mind, of her lover scheduled to teach a morning class and then have a Christmas luncheon with his GAM crew.

"Damned and blast. I guess no more cuddles for me this morning."

Cinnamon took that moment to leap up onto the bed and demand adoration. Jamie, accustomed to the vagaries of her lover's pet, stroked the cat's back. She sampled her personal neural interface for the time—8:34 a.m. "Holy crap," she said to her step-cat. "Your master must be getting to me if I'm waking up this early. This is a time fit for neither woman nor beast."

The cat responded by curling up just out of Jamie's reach, closing its eyes, and purring. Thinking she could emulate the feline, Jamie dug down further into the blankets for warmth, but her mind had already started in on her list of things to do. Her calendar overflowed, with a visit to the Teamsters Local 2413 about keeping any military logistics from leaving the dock, a net conference with the heads of five different jewelry cartels to offer protection services, and the planning of a robbery of Washington State Employees Credit Union, an institution that insisted on continuing to pay the Metros.

"Aw, fuck," she said, throwing the covers off and walking toward the shower. In a dressing vestibule she saw a yellow chiffon dress laid out for her. All this living in a different room every night had made her hire a personal shopper to provide one outfit per day. One outfit. No choices. It made her frown.

She missed her wardrobe. She missed her art. She missed her nephew. All taken away by that Metro raid on her home.

"Fucking Metros needed to pay." She needed to send her own message.

* * *

"Merry Christmas and Happy Holidays. Welcome to this KIROW Action News Special Report. I'm Elsa Abernathy."

"And I'm Carl Merrithew."

The female anchor led with the special report: "A city, even a nation, in anarchy is what we are reporting on this morning. Just minutes ago in a scheduled press conference, Governor Nguyen and Metropolitan Police Commissioner Krylov jointly reinforced the declaration of martial law in the environs of Greater Portland. In Krylov's own words from his remarks after the press conference . . ."

The screen switched to show the stocky bulk of the ethnic Russian. Commissioner Krylov, resplendent in his dress blacks as he stood in Liberty Plaza, said, "*We won't let our great nation nor this great city fall into anarchy. Order and peace will be reestablished. We will punish those guilty of putting us at risk. We will have safety for our children . . .*"

"Yes, Elsa, we have reports that not only has Portland gone to this extreme measure, but also the cities of Miami, New York, Dallas, Mexico City, Port Au Prince, Anchorage, Boston, and Los Angeles, just to name a few. Connect to our side-bar to get the entire list. The current total is forty-six of the ninety-seven governors have declared some form of martial law in their states."

The male anchor continued, "We already have reports of National Guard troops pouring into Portland. Here is footage shot just this hour of military convoys entering our city. We've been prevented from showing you their command center and staging areas for reasons of security.

"Our reporter in the field, Dennis McLaughlin, is taking the pulse of the man in the street on this action. To you, Dennis."

The image changed to show groups of four National Guardsmen in ACUs deployed at the strategic intersection of a shopping area. Each man casually carried an assault rifle bearing the patina of much use. The image trained back onto the familiar reporter's smiling face.

"Thank you, Carl. I'm here at the Greater Pearl Shopping Mall where squads of National Guardsmen have been deployed in the last hour. I've been stopping random people asking what they think of the National Guard's presence."

"Well, it is about f<beep>ng time someone did something. These riots are bad for business," said a tubby proprietor in front of an antique bookstore.

"Well, I'm not sure. I don't like guns and this might just give people the wrong message," said a middle-aged woman with an infant in her arms.

"<beeeep> power mongers. I'll bet all they want to do is take over! Listen to the GAM, peeps!" said a furtive youngster keeping his face covered by his hoodie.

"Why can't everyone just leave us alone?" claimed an older man.

"What's to keep them from permanently taking away our civil liberties? I for one don't want to be raped or shot at the whim of some testosterone-crazed moron," said one professional woman dressed in a business suit.

"Who is going to watch the watchers?" said a high-school student from the middle of a clique of girls.

The image focused back onto the reporter. *"This is just a sample of the answers I got when I inquired. If I learned anything out here it is that there are at least as many opinions as there are people.*

"Back to you, Carl."

"Thank you, Dennis. In continuing coverage of Portland's martial law—"

An arm wearing a uniform stretched in from off screen to pass information to the anchor.

Carl read directly from the accepted filmy. "We have been ordered under the rules of martial law to give time to the Commander of Military Occupation. We are now going live to an undisclosed site."

The picture dissolved to a flat rooftop bearing a lone podium. A short man in urban camouflage gray, with skin the color and consistency of tree bark and his cropped hair as white as a wedding dress, walked in from off screen. His muscular shoulders made him look as wide as he was tall as they stuck out beyond either side of the rostrum. He held his hands behind his girder-straight back.

The military man looked directly into the camera. "I am Colonel Charles Reed, Military Commander of Portland and environs." The man's voice was low and resonated as if he were at the bottom of a deep metal barrel.

"Martial law started at eight a.m. this morning and extends to the entirety of Oregon's population west of the Cascades and encompassing roughly some sixty-five million souls. It will remain in effect until I can report the success of my missions to the governor." The man stopped for just a moment.

"You all know why my soldiers have been called in. We have two and only two missions. We will succeed with both.

"First, we are to restore order. Regular and random patrols will move throughout the city containing lawlessness. Riots and rioters will be eliminated with lethal force.

"Second, we will hunt down the illegal organizations known as the Green Action Militia and the so-called CorpGov. We will shut down the city and peel it like an onion until they are in custody or dead."

The colonel stepped out from behind the podium, making it clear he had been standing on something that had given him centimeters of extra height. He moved closer to the camera.

"I need to impress upon those of you who are planning to test our resolve that you will fail."

The camera panned to show three obvious nils, cuffed and blindfolded, standing at the edge of the building's roof. The trio didn't seem concerned. The police rousted nils on a regular basis. A squad of infantrymen moved and lined up opposite them.

"These three unregistered humans were caught trespassing today after martial law was declared," Colonel Reed said. "By order of the Military Command of Oregon under the Uniform Code of Military

Justice, I sentence them to death."

The two men and one woman twisted their heads around like they couldn't understand.

"Ready. Aim. Fire."

The chilling sound of gauss fire ripped through the air as the razor-sharp fragments tore through what little clothing the nils wore, along with their flesh, muscle, and even bone. Three human bodies shredded in half. The top half of the two men toppled over the edge of the building. The rest of the lifeless protoplasm just slumped into a mass with a sickening plop. The camera remained on the sight as the merging pool of blood grew.

"This is the strength of our resolve. You decide."

*   *   *

"I know this is Christmas Day, but I need you all to pay attention to me," Augustine Cordoba said, running her hand through her 1 cm white hair, standing it on end where it should be. She grabbed a fistful of it at the back in frustration. She didn't feel very much like that calm ninety-something woman in the Catholic novitiate just a few weeks ago. She wondered how she could get back that serenity. Unfortunately, that was a project for the future. Now she had n00bs to train. "I can't stress enough how this may save your life."

Roughly six hundred mostly college-aged people crowded the third sub-basement of Seattle's Columbia Center. Graffiti covered graffiti on the old concrete walls only two weeks from being demolished. The low buzz of conversations dropped off. Augustine's visual implants caught two boys necking about 12 m back.

"You two… If you want to suck face, get a hotel room. Until then I need you to listen because I don't want any blood on my hands." Still the pair didn't break their clinch. Someone next to the lovebirds nudged them with an elbow. The lipstick that one wore now covered both their faces. Augustine had to smile remembering her own youth and a couple of public displays of affection that nearly got her arrested. The thought of that blue-print dress ripped down around her waist brought a blush to her cheeks.

"Business now, woman," she said under her breath before continuing aloud. "You all volunteered for this mission, now please listen up so you don't get dead. Thank you. My name is Grandma Ice. Some may know me from the net and others because I am a member of the Green Action Militia. Speaking for the GAM I'm telling you that this mission is important because the Metros are literally trying to make our world into a dictatorship. Your actions today can help change that outcome."

Augustine wandered as she spoke, sometimes into the crowd itself. "I'm going to be overwatch on this operation. What that means is that I'm going to be combing the net, the airwaves, and everything else for the inevitable armed response. It also means that you need to obey me. If you can't follow my instructions then now is the time to leave." Augustine paused a few seconds. None of the crowd left.

"Excellent. We are planning a riot. We want maximum property damage, but minimum casualties. That means any casualties—you or anyone else—are bad. Don't bring any weapons. Don't bring any explosives. If you do, you will be caught by the Metros before you even get to the location."

"What do we use, then?" called out someone from the darkness of the extreme back of the improvised auditorium.

"Pieces of furniture, bricks, landscaping, park benches, or just the sheer mass of hundreds of you. If you want to use fire, any aerosol with a narco stick to light it will do. You can also use perfume, disinfectants, any alcohol—from drug stores or bars—powdered coffee creamer, flour, or most any petroleum product. That's just the short list.

"Release any nanite tube you can find. Smash any terminal. Break any plumbing. Tear out any electrical wiring."

"Where and when?" called out a girl in a white sundress in the front of the crowd. She looked like she belonged at a church, organizing the congregation picnic, rather than at a riot-planning meeting.

"Oh, that is the fun part. None of you will know until you need the information. One by one you will come up here and lick the nanopad. Your percomms will be reprogrammed to keep track of your position and travel time to the target. When the time of the riot minus travel time is reached, your percomm will give you a recorded message."

A slender brunette in the second row raised his hand.

"Yes," Augustine said, calling on him.

"But that means we have to keep our time free for the next however long? I don't think I can do that."

"Oh, it's nothing like that," Augustine said. "We don't ask too much of our people. The event will be within the next forty-eight hours, and if you can't make it, you can't make it. The rest of us, and zero to eight other groups just like yours, will take care of it for you.

"As you can imagine, this obfuscation is such that if there were a Metro sympathizer in our midst, she or he couldn't betray us. That's for your safety and ours.

"This action will be the equivalent of a flash mob. Move into place with the first message but don't start anything until the second message to start. And to whatever you hold sacred, when I send the general recall to your percomms, skedaddle...vamoose...get lost. You won't have a great deal of time."

Mr. Brunette thrust up his hand again.

"Go ahead."

"So what would keep the Metros from scanning our devices for a percomm signal from you at that exact time? Or how about scan everyone for altered percomm programming."

"Sonny, you are cute," Augustine said, smiling, with dimples appearing as if by magic. "If I were just a decade or two younger I might see if you were interested in older women...but are you honestly trying to teach me to suck eggs?"

"Suck eggs? I don't understand."

"Ancient slang," Augustine continued, "which means that you are trying to teach someone experienced how to do her job.

"Listen up, folks. We want you to succeed. We want you on our side. You in jail or dead does neither us nor you any good whatsoever. Each of your percomms will be wiped with my general recall—a message that will be heard by every percomm within a fifteen kilometer radius."

"OK. Any more questions?"

"How about a date?" Mr. Brunette asked.

Augustine smiled instead of answering. "Everyone who is still willing to volunteer, c'mon up here and lick the programmer."

She caught Mr. Brunette's eye as he stepped up and handed him a business card with an email address. Maybe Santa thought she was a good girl after all.

*   *   *

Clarence Fritzwalter Beckman-Ford the Third, also known as Nanogate or Chairman of the CorpGov, sat at the head of an irregularly shaped 8.1 sq. meter table carved entirely from the iron core of what had been comet Baxter-Thompson 227. Servants had already piled the table with the delicacies normally reserved for the wealthy on special occasions. The aroma of roast turkey blotted out the more subtle scent speaker in the room. Real cranberry sauce made even Clarence's jaded palate water. He also made a note not to get up without having a substantial helping of the wilted seaweed with garlic salad. After the serving staff filled the family's glasses with wine, water, juice, or soda, depending on taste, they withdrew from the room, leaving the Beckman-Ford family alone.

"All right, Fritzy, what's with the bribe?" In contrast to Nanogate's own butter-mellow baritone, Janice's voice sounded like the poorly-oiled Tin Woodsman had screeched it out. Even at eighty-two, his blond wife, Janice, still looked like the bikini model she'd been in high school. None of their children nor their grandchildren, nor their great-grandchildren would have dared to use the derogatory shortening of Nanogate's middle name.

"Excuse me, my dear?"

"Oh, don't play innocent with me, you manipulative...." Janice looked around at the rest of the family and especially the children and curbed her expletive. "Even though it's Christmas, the last time I saw a spread like this it was to announce that your company had been the target of a hostile take-over. Or how about when you wanted to tell me about Michael's crushed legs from that asinine base-jumping episode. So what's the catch?"

"You are perceptive as always, my dear. I don't have bad news but rather good news.

"Michael, would you carve for us?"

"Certainly, Father," the younger man said, standing on his long-ago regenerated legs to begin slicing up the huge bird.

"You haven't finished, Fritz. What is this good news?"

"Thank you, Michael," Clarence said, taking a plate with a healthy slice of turkey breast on it. "Well, I know how much you love to travel so I've arranged a trip for the whole family."

Two of the younger members, who'd been silently following the conversation, looked at each other with undisguised glee. Janice, on the other side of the table, instead pursed her lips and furrowed her brow.

"We just got back from a trip. What is going on? What are you hiding from me?"

"My love, if you would like I'll give you all the details later tonight. In the meantime I suggest that all the family get ready for a trip to Mars."

"Mars!" Janice snapped. "That stinky, smelly place! No place to go outdoors!"

The three first-generation children and their over-achieving spouses all maintained a calm decorum even though several got squeezes of excitement under the table.

"Janny, now you know you had just that one bad experience. I'm sure they've fixed the odor units. You also know they almost have as much recreation space as we do, not to mention the nature trips."

"Don't 'Janny' me! And nature trips?! Sealed in a bubble and having to walk. What are you really up to? Our family restrains me from discussing your personal or sexual habits, but I will if you don't give it up."

"My loving wife, I already told you that I'd give you all the details later, in private. Why don't you just dig into this wonderful fea—"

"NOW!" Janice said, slamming her fist down on the metal table, causing it to ring like a gong. What little noise the other seventeen people made stopped, leaving the low note to echo in the room.

"All right, if you must know, my dear…."

Janice just stared at him with steel backing her pale green eyes.

"There will be open conflict with the Metropolitan Police Force. We can't stop it. It is time to get all of you out of the firing line and out of the possibility of being kidnapped as a lever to manipulate me. I want you all to be safe."

Janice took a deep breath. Her face relaxed. When she spoke her voice dropped a full octave. "We'll go, then. Please pass the potatoes, Abby."

Nanogate and his wife locked eyes. Her cold eyes didn't quite match the rest of her positive demeanor. He wondered how she would take it out on him this time. He mentally shuddered.

Product Research

"It's six-oh-two p.m.. Welcome to Sunset Over Portland with your hosts, Melissa Peters and Clyde Capron.

"Are you looking forward to Boxing day, Clyde?" the ever-popular Melissa Peters said with her trademark dimples.

"Thank you, Melissa. Where does Boxing Day even come from?"

"Well, there are several theories but the commonly held one is that in the early eighteen hundreds, tradesmen in England received presents for their service."

"Maybe an early form of tipping?"

"Well, if they only do it once a year then it must be one heck of a tip," Melissa said, smiling toward the camera. "I know some people I might reinvigorate the custom for."

"Is that a segue for our first guest, Melissa?"

"Absolutely. I am pleased to introduce the Portland Martial Law Liaison, Captain Amber Cohen."

The studio audience applauded as a lanky woman, attractive in a long-lean way, walked onto the stage. Resplendent in Metro dress blacks, Amber bowed to the studio audience and the camera. Her short-cropped, dark hair barely moved. Per Metro policy, her makeup was limited to bronze lipstick, a light foundation covering her olive-toned skin, and a subdued eyeliner. Obviously more accustomed to standing at attention, she perched awkwardly on the guest's bar-type stool.

"Welcome, Captain Cohen. May I call you Amber?"

"Certainly, Melissa," she answered in a crisp contralto. Amber's face lit up in a warm smile that disarmed men and women alike.

"So tell us, Amber, have you ever heard of Boxing Day?" Clyde asked.

"Definitely. Up until this year my parents and I would take the day after Christmas, while I was on leave, to ice skate on a pond near my home in Beavercreek, Ohio. Unfortunately, my mother and father were both murdered this year in the Fairborn Massacre by the terrorists most people call the Green Action Militia." Captain Cohen's face clouded up. With her gaunt cheekbones you could easily see her jaw clenching and unclenching.

The audience made a collective sympathetic sound.

"I'm sorry. I hope I didn't stir up bad memories."

"They are still very raw, Clyde. But I'm taking an active part in stopping the GAM."

"It sounds like you have an added incentive to make sure that martial law goes well," Melissa said.

"I'll tag an affirmative to that."

"So why have you come to us today, Amber?"

"First, I want to say that I appreciate this opportunity to talk to the people of Oregon. It is sad that we have to have martial law in our great state, but the actions of a few have cost us all.

"I've come to talk about the specifics of the martial law enactment and each citizen's responsibilities."

"Excellent, so let's get started," Melissa said, giving a bounce of excitement in her chair. "What are the rules, Amber?"

"Well, we are asking all news venues to regularly provide the full list of the rules of martial law—"

"Which you can find continuously updated in our sidebar," the perky anchor interrupted.

"Yes, thank you for that, Melissa. I want to say that these rules are for everyone's safety. We no more want to administer martial law than you wish to be under its onus. The sooner the populous will allow us to restore order, the sooner we can get back to a new normal, free of the violence and anarchy of the recent past."

"You said, 'new normal.' Will there be changes in our legal system, in our responsibilities, or liberties?" Clyde asked, clearly wanting to probe with an even more inflammatory question. His pre-air brief by the station manager, in and of itself a unique occurrence, had drawn very clear lines about how and what he could say on the air. With armored Metros looking on from the wings and the show on a ninety-second delay, the party line had been carved in granite and the likely result of crossing it had been left as an exercise for the broadcasters.

"I'm sorry. It was probably a poor choice of words. What I meant is that the Green Action Militia won't be bombing civilians and the fiat CorpGov won't be trying to corrupt and twist our laws. I consider this a good thing. Note that nowhere did I suggest any changes in our legal system."

"Excellent. Thank you for that clarification, Captain." Under his breath he added, "…you lying bitch." His face carried only a trace of the contempt he felt.

"Yes. If I boil down the requirements of martial law it comes to this: Obey anything that the police or the National Guard asks of you. Don't do anything illegal."

"That seems like common sense to me," Melissa added.

"You're right. Again, we want to do as little to impede the law-abiding citizens as possible," Amber continued, turning to face the camera, "but for those of you out there who insist on testing our resolve there is the other side of the coin.

"All crimes and violations will be dealt with under the Uniformed Code of Military Justice. Most violations of these rules and laws can be adjudicated on the spot with punishment up to and including summary execution.

"Looters and rioters will be shot on sight, without warning, as will anyone interfering with a member of the Metropolitan Police or the National Guard.

"There will be a curfew every evening starting at ten p.m. and ending at five a.m. the next morning. A military pass is required for anyone to be out during that time, excepting those civilians dealing with crises specific to a critical job function.

"There is a hotline for anyone with a true emergency. People with emergencies such as illness or accident will be escorted during these hours."

"These sound a bit draconian, Ms. Cohen," Clyde interjected with a worried glance at the guards off-stage.

"Again, your normal, law-abiding citizen will have no problem with these and won't be put in a situation where they might be put afoul of the military authorities."

"Thank you, Captain Cohen; is there anything else?" Melissa asked, trying to bring the show back on script.

"Well, in fact there are more rules. Travel into or out of areas of martial law is prohibited. Travel within the martial law confines will be curtailed by the authorities on an as-needed basis and may last for significant lengths of time. Please be aware and keep several days of food and water on hand.

"The possession of any weapon without a permit is prohibited. Citizens are given one opportunity to turn in any weapon by contacting the nearest Metro Police station prior to December thirty-first. We will arrange for a pickup. Those with implanted weapons must, at your own expense, have them removed or disabled and inspected.

"The network will be monitored. Any activity supporting or espousing violence or subversion is considered illegal."

"Thank you for educating us, Captain Cohen," Clyde said with false cheer in his voice. "We urge our viewers to download the full text of the implementation of martial law from our sidebar and become intimately familiar with it."

"Yes. Learn the rules and follow them. It will allow us to get through this difficult time as smoothly as possible."

Clyde went on smoothly, "It's now seven minutes past the hour. Next up, Anton Cordon will join us to talk about his new movie..."

*   *   *

Lieutenant Reza Narendra's bloodshot brown eyes burned. He fumbled the double handful of memory crystals, spilling them on the floor. They lay in a mystic array on the floor in his unfocused haze. Slowly and very deliberately he bent his chubby, 75 cm frame down to pick them up.

Between the demands as the adjutant of the commissioner, his duties as a precinct commander, and covering a portion of the patrol burden, he couldn't remember the last time he'd slept. There was a limit even to fatigue-reducing nanite therapies.

He closed his eyes for just a second. The second stretched out. A portion of his mind argued for not opening them again—just to fall asleep kneeling here on the floor. As that wouldn't do anyone any good, he demanded that his body comply. Only ten seconds later, he forced his traitorous eyes open.

"Are you all right, Lieutenant? Is there something I can help you with?" asked one passing patrolman.

"I'm as all right as any of the rest of us, Detective Lindstrom."

"Just making sure, sir. We're stretched pretty thin."

Reza noticed the sharp movements and clipped speech of the

officer—characteristic of chemical stimulants, a departmental offense.

"Have you been stimming, Detective?"

"Do you really want to know the answer to that, sir? I'd guess at least eighty percent of our personnel are."

Reza knew he had to do something about the fatigue factor of his police officers. It would lead to more and more mistakes. "On second thought, I withdraw the question. I don't want to know. Be about your business before I change my mind."

"Yes, sir."

Reza collected his crystals and stood, once again luxuriating in the ability to close his eyes for just the few seconds in the act of standing. He knew he had to do something but he forgot what. It took racking his brains to remember he was on his way to give the morning briefing.

*   *   *

Chairman Nanogate sat on a crate in the middle of an empty warehouse level somewhere in Bothell, Washington. Incongruously, he poured tea from an antique Gorham silver-service into two Staffordshire china cups.

Nearby six or sixty people protected his guest and himself, milling around and keeping overwatch from mostly hidden locations. Nanogate never bothered with security matters but did, generally, accept his protectors' suggestions and the limitations on his movements and actions.

"You've chosen a rather dashing look, Mr. Chairman," the president of the United States, Susan Tipton, said from her seat on an identical crate. Her feet didn't touch the ground. In some ways she looked like a little girl sitting on a church pew.

"Excuse me, Madam President?" Nanogate said in his characteristic smooth, baritone voice.

"Oh, I was just admiring your trim figure and that shock of gray in your hair. I mean with standard genetic treatments you could have had the body of Hercules and no gray at all. Even your face is mature, not youthful."

"Milk?" he asked, gesturing to the tiny creamer with his long, thin fingers.

"No, thank you."

"Sugar?"

"No, thank you."

Nanogate placed a single cube into his own tea. He handed the president her tea before picking up his own cup and gently stirring it. "You may not believe this, Madam President, but this is my totally unaltered physical appearance. I don't have the time or the desire to manipulate the genetic dice that created me."

"How even more odd and appealing. It almost makes me wish you weren't married." She drew down a lock of her own chaotic, brassy-red hair and twisted it around her finger. It gave her the coquettish look of being fourteen but her wry smile couldn't have been from someone without at least five decades. It showed intelligence, sarcasm, and cynicism all at the same time. "Of course, we women have to go another direction if we want to have anyone take us seriously. I've had multiple hair and facial therapies even since I've been in exile." Her figure, while not classically curvy, appealed in a smart, trim, Jackie-O way.

"Sorry, Madam, but I'm very married. My wife would probably have a stroke if she even heard your statement," Nanogate said, taking a sip from his cup. "But then, I've been led to believe your personal preferences lie in another direction."

Susan laughed. "A common misconception, of which I've never bothered to disabuse the general populous." Her smile disappeared and the corner of her eyes sagged. Her tone dropped about a third. "Before her assassination, Carla was my president, my friend, and my partner... in politics.

"We were roommates all the way back to boarding school and always wanted the same thing for this country. When it came time for her to choose a running mate she couldn't bring herself to add someone to the ticket just for the votes they would engender. She wanted me instead, and what Carla wanted she usually got."

Smiling again, the president continued. "Hell, without trying we nabbed the gay and lesbian votes. It was just assumed we were domestic partners as well as political ones." Susan took a sugar cookie from the tray. She nibbled in a ladylike manner on the edge, letting the buttery sweetness cover her tongue. She then added the confection to her saucer.

"Politics does make strange bedfellows... even if they aren't bedfellows," Nanogate offered in as close to a joke as he ever managed. "Did you ever think you would be holding court with a nearly assassinated Corporate head, the mob boss of the Pacific Northwest, and the leader of a terrorist group?"

"I'd have to say definitively no to that one. I'd even go so far to say I'd not even considered even one of you, much less the collective gaggle."

"I would have said the same thing more than a few months ago. But then here we are."

"Yes, sir. Here we are." Both of them took a drink at the same time. "So, sir, you asked for this meeting. We've observed the pleasantries, although my ass is already regretting this excuse for a seat. The tea is lovely, and the cookies are made with real butter, quite a treat, but I'm sure you want to do some business."

"Well said. In short, I'd like you to call up federal troops."

President Tipton's gaze snapped up to Nanogate's pale blue eyes. Her brows lowered. Her jaw firmed. "We've been over this before." Her voice remained rigidly under control but steel underlined each word. "Not only is it illegal, I won't set federal troops against weekend warriors. Even were I so inclined, most of these people are ex-Metros themselves. I wouldn't get more than a handful, and certainly not enough to do more than get slaughtered against the combined forces of the National Guard and the Metros.'

"What if we gave them a very specific task that had nothing to do directly with fighting and then stood them down?"

"But then, why would—"

"I'd like to take credit for the brilliance of the plan, but in the honesty of equals I cannot. Let me explain what Tony suggested."

*   *   *

Christine looked like a zebra. To be specific, her hair and her mini-dress looked like a zebra. The view was striking enough to draw attention away from her face. Anyone looking down from her striped hair skipped her face and landed smartly on her barely-restrained, heavy bosom. Her chest augmentation was thanks to a new product by Tussy Cosmetics that gathered spare body water and held it in suspension under her natural endowments for a predetermined time. Platform heels gave her height that she normally lacked. She looked nothing like her wanted posters or the nearly continuous net alerts offering a CEO's ransom for her head.

Scores of pretty young women and men created a mob of their own as each looked to hook up with one of the Metros that frequented the Brass Tacks bar. Both target and targeted alike danced to the ancient emo-rock that blared loud enough that people side-by-side had to yell to be heard. The groupies did just about everything but fuck right there in the open.

With three hunters for every two policemen, most would be daunted or even turn away. Christine walked confidently through the front door. None of the other women were any obstacle. As usual Christine managed to stand out, not only by her black and white pattern but also by the cut of the dress she wore that didn't even attempt to be opaque nor prevent her newly acquired breasts from swaying to the natural rhythm her stride imparted.

In the dim, smoky light at the back of the bar Christine caught the attention of an older man with a scar under his left eye. Her eyes wrapped him up. She wet her lips. Her smoldering look caressed his body, making love to him without even being close enough to talk. She could feel his lust. He belonged to her.

She ignored the pursed lips and outright stares of hostility shot at her by the women she passed. Equally she ignored the other men as nothing more than furniture. Christine had her man.

"So where are we going?" she breathed into the man's ear as she reached his side. Her hair teased his neck as she moved closer to him. Her breasts brushed against his shoulder. Her stockinged thigh rubbed against his knee with obvious intent. The rest of the bar chose to ignore the new couple and get on with their own sensual hunt.

"I've never seen you around here before," the uniformed policeman yelled above the music.

"That's because I've never been here and I'm not going to return," she said just loud enough to be heard.

"So it has to be tonight, eh?"

She felt her target slip away. Something wasn't right. "What's your name, beautiful?"

"Sergeant Enrique Tolbert. What's yours?"

"The answer to your every dream, Sergeant."

"I'll be honest, sexy, I want to make love to you. You've stirred feelings in me that I thought were dead before you were born."

"Then let's take this show on the road and find a horizontal perch," Christine said, running one ebony fingernail across his cheek just riding the threshold of pleasure and pain.

"I don't even know if you are old enough to consent, but if you will submit to an identity test I'd be more than happy to share a night with you," the Sergeant said, his eyes locking on hers, and his right hand edging down to the stun baton at his side.

Fear wasn't part of Christine's emotional pallet. Instead she felt annoyance. Christine knew her evening plans had just derailed. "Harper," she subvocalized to her percomm as an alert code. Aloud she said, "By all means, Sergeant. I have nothing to hide." She lifted her right arm, its hand clearly empty except for a tiny wrist chain, up toward the bar's scanner.

Tolbert's hand came up only a few centimeters from his sidearm. The muscles in his neck relaxed. The momentary hesitation was the only thing she needed.

Her left hand flashed up faster than a cobra strike. She drove a 26 cm dirk through the sergeant's forearm, pinning it to the bar. The music covered up the impact and his howl of pain and outrage.

"I guess it will have to be another time," she said as she jumped back before he could act. With his left arm pinned he couldn't do more than draw his baton and flail, much too late.

Christine barely noticed. She'd already made her way through her escape route, the conveniently located back hall, through the kitchen, out the service door, and into the alley. As she jogged down the alley she heard two sharp splats behind her. She turned to see two men falling to the ground, lit only by the dim light of a single bare bulb outside the service door.

She flashed an OK sign at the sniper on the roof who had provided her cover. She took the emergency ladder down to the next level and vanished into the night.

* * *

Colonel Reed, military commander of all Oregon west of the Cascades, and commander of over two thousand troops, was one of the few that didn't feel the pull of his wife and child this Christmas Day. Intellectually aware of Christmas, as he dated each order he wrote, his wife, Portia, and little Charlie didn't even grace his thoughts. This morning he gave them two scant minutes of his attention envisioning them opening the presents from under what his wife called the toilet-bowl-brush tree. Little Charlie would tear open the brightly wrapped packages and then play in the boxes more than with the expensive toys.

Right now Charlie Reed was too busy with his own gift. To be in the field leading his troops was the present of a lifetime. Running any real operation gave him a rush that he'd never found doing any stimulant as a teen. Doing what he did best made him feel the rush of sex without the inevitable crash.

He looked over the solido of his area of responsibility where he'd drawn division lines he intended to cordon-off and peel back one at a time—Hillsboro, Beaverton, Rose District, Milwaukie, Gresham, Wilsonville, Salem, Corvallis, McMinnville, and Eugene, just to name a few.

Oh, the Greenies could go to ground in the wilds of Santiam Forest or the heights of Mt Hood, but these vermin were city dwellers. They didn't know how to live in the outdoors. They needed the limelight of solido and the stink of ground level to wallow in. They would lurk in the urban areas using their local knowledge against him. What they didn't know is that he himself had escaped from these very same streets. As an ex-member of the Beaverton Mother Bashers, he knew every stinking sewer in the Portland area, so fighting the GAM on their own ground didn't worry him.

He tapped his foot on the pink colored portion of the other side of the Columbia River. This was the weakness in his plan. The governor of Washington State had not declared martial law. He didn't have the resources of Vancouver, Salmon Creek, Camas, or even Olympia at his disposal. The official dispatches from Washington State said that he would not be hindered. His gut told him something else.

"Sergeant Cummings."

"Yes, sir."

"I want a full spectral surveillance cordon across the Columbia River from the ocean to Umatilla. I want to know even if a seagull craps in the water. Write it up giving the task to the 162nd Infantry for me to sign, immediately."

"Yes, sir."

"Oh, and send a messenger to the commissioner letting him know we will start Operation Onion at 0335 tomorrow morning."

"Should I copy the governor also?"

"Don't bother."

$*$　$*$　$*$

"OK, folks. I know this isn't your normal gig but we need all hands on deck, even on Christmas," Tony said to a room of six hundred Greenpeace members. As usual they'd come in from all over the world to help any cause that even smelled radical. Tony's voice carried throughout the Spokane conference room without the aid of amplification. This Howard Johnson's went beyond his normal lecture experience where he regularly dodged ceiling leaks, rat swarms, and the occasional stink bug. His gray, non-tartan kilt and matching suit coat seemed out of place as he shared a stage with a Metro patrol lift, and a mannequin sporting Metro armor.

"The intent of this lecture is to give you the tools to make you a serious thorn in the side of the Metros without putting your lives or liberties in more than casual jeopardy.

"First, more radicals have been caught moving from place to place than setting bombs, robbing banks, or even assassinating people. You need to know how to move around under the lidar of the black suits. For those of you who have criminal records, you cannot use taxis. Not only is there a DNA sniff for your credit information but there is intermittent air sampling, and the Metros monitor all of these. For those who haven't tried, getting out of a cab that is being remotely routed to the Metro landing pad is nearly impossible.

"Don't use buses if you are carrying anything that would be considered a weapon. Lift-buses are equipped with sonography and most have Metro-directed nanite sampling units.

"Be very wary of renting or buying any vehicle. Metros scan a majority of these requesting hair follicles, urine, or even blood samples to confirm identity.

"I'd hope that you all know not to use any vehicle registered to Greenpeace or the corporations that make up the CorpGov."

"Damn," came a curse from the crowd. "It doesn't sound like you've left us anything! We supposed to just sit in our hovels and play checkers?"

Tony chuckled and pointed at the heckler. "Thanks for the segue. Now for the ways you *can* move.

"Stealing lift carriers is viable but you must complete your use of them within two hours. The nominal response time for the Metros to react to any stolen vehicle is three hours with a standard deviation of fifteen minutes. That time has been stretching out but you want to be at least three sigma, or ninety-nine point seven percent assured that you can escape.

"While normal lift-trucks don't have Metro sealing capabilities, they can be tracked and patrol vehicles sent in to intercept.

"I can't stress enough to have escape routes planned. They should all include at least one very busy public place, one freefall, and travel through an unmonitored area such as a deserted building or maintenance corridor."

"Freefall?"

"Yes. You might have heard of base jumping. Wear a micro chute under your clothing and jump from one place to another. It needs to be carefully planned but there are so many choices that the Metros have difficulty following all the possibilities on the fly, if you will pardon the pun.

"The other options for moving around unmonitored are by foot, any ground vehicle such as bicycle or automobile, or any water vehicle. None of these can be tracked directly by our opponents. There is one other that I hope none of you needs right now, but be aware that Orbital Insertion Gravity Landing, OIGL, drops are viable. While all space tracks that would intersect with earth are tracked by NASA and each government to a different degree, they don't share this information on a real-time basis with anyone materially. This gives the gravity landing systems opportunities to place people where and when we want.

"Enough about moving around. Time to have some fun. Behind me you will see two of the Metro's key tools for quick response."

A Metro patrol lift, painted with the catchy slogan, "Barbecue the Pigs" dominated most of the stage. To one side, Metro armor, complete with pergrav, stood looking ridiculous wearing a pink, polka-dot bikini.

"We need to disable as many of these as we can. If you practice these simple techniques and share them with all your friends, this could impact the Metros to the point where they are ground-bound or are requisitioning civilian equipment."

A hand went up in the front row. A young man wearing old-fashioned link glasses stood up when Tony pointed to him.

"Mr. Sammis…"

"Folks, my name is Tony. Mr. Sammis makes it sound like I'm wearing a diaper on top of a mountaintop somewhere, giving out advice." The joke drew several chuckles from the crowd. "The reality is that I'm here to ask you for a favor that could help many people."

"All right then, Tony," the young man started again. "You are showing us how to deal with only two types of units. What about RPVs, drones, and other nasties? Hell, I have a National Guard hover-tank parked on my level. What the fuck am I supposed to do about it?"

Several people murmured in agreement.

"What's your name?" Tony asked.

"Chris."

"Well, Chris, you obviously haven't used those glasses to access the net."

There were a few snickers in the crowd.

"The drone and RPV threat is almost nullified," Tony continued. "We weren't kidding when we told you online that we destroyed the primary drone facility for the entire West Coast. Those in the Midwest, East, and in Mexico City still operate. But for now there is a huge hole that we can exploit.

"I can't tell you much more, but we are planning actions to limit the rest of them as well."

"OK, so what about the tanks?"

"Oddly I'm afraid of those the least. Privileged information, sorry. We can't do anything about them right now, but when the time comes they are not going to be terribly effective.

"Now unless you have any other questions, please sit down and learn."

A petite woman, with skin the color of dark chocolate, wearing a baggy gray jumpsuit rolled out a table bearing copper wire, a glass jar, a vacuum pump, and other assorted tools.

"Let's give my beautiful assistant, Morgan, a big hand," Tony said, clapping with a devilish grin on his face.

Morgan bowed and swept her arm like some bit of fluff on a game show revealing a winning prize. Standing up she slugged Tony in the arm before taking her place on the other side of the table. She then started her own portion of the pitch.

"My name is Morgan and I'm second only to that blowhard over there, on the other end of the table, at making things go 'Boom!'"

Tony smiled and nodded his head. "We'd like this to be more interactive with each of you building your own, but to accommodate as many of you as we could, we will have to suffice with a simple demo and video feeds."

Morgan picked up the tag team teaching, giving Tony a chance for a swig of water. "What we are going to have you make are gravity pulse multipliers. They are small, portable, and devastating to any artificial gravity generators. They work on a principle similar to a pinch, an electromagnetic pulse generator. It takes a mass of stored energy and forces it all out as one huge gravitic pulse."

"It takes about two hours and parts you can buy at WalMaCo and Radio Shack," Tony said, his voice soothed.

"We've premade several of these devices to give you a demonstration of their power." Morgan showed two devices the size and shape of a baseball cut in half. "We've painted these neon red so you can see them easier. Obviously you can come up with a better color scheme so the black suits can find them even easier."

There were giggles from the audience.

Morgan continued. "These devices are magnetic and will attach to any bit of metal nearby. Simply slap it next to the lift unit of any device."

Walking nonchalantly across the stage past the patrol lift, she bent down and slid the red device under its gravity skirt and had moved on in less than a second. The attachment to the pergrav was even speedier as she walked behind the dummy and ran her hand over its shoulder, leaving the very visible crimson bulge right on the grav generator.

"Now for the fireworks. Tony would you do the honors? And who is the flunky now?" This drew even more laughs.

Tony acted as if he'd been shot by her wit. The mirth died away as he used a remote key to start the patrol vehicle. The three-tonne vehicle started to lift its bulk from the stage when a sharp crack, louder than a pistol report but quieter than an assault rifle, caused most of the occupants of the room to start. Having lifted barely a centimeter from the floor, the vehicle fell with an impact felt throughout the hotel.

"I know you can't see much so we have a camera we are snaking into the lift compartment. While we are doing that let's watch what happens on the unshielded pergrav."

Tony once again pressed a remote activation device. A pop sounded, not as loud as before. Prepared, the audience didn't jump. The mannequin shuddered, not even lifting off the ground. Where there were once 20 cm pergrav bulges, now only a 5 mm ball that looked like crumpled tinfoil remained. The hemispherical sabotage device had been crushed so small as to only show as a red speck.

Displayed up on the gigantic view screen above Tony and Morgan's head was an almost identical view within the lift compartment of the Metro's patrol vehicle. Only a miniscule ball of wrinkled metal remained of what had been a cubic meter lift generator.

"You can imagine what would happen to the vehicle that encountered this," Morgan said, tossing a sample of the destructive device to a member of the crowd. "The wonderful thing about it is that the damage done by these innocuous little devices requires a full machine shop to repair."

"These toys damage not only the drive," Tony picked up, "which, as you all know can be replaced in just a few minutes, but also the housings. It is hard to see in these images but they are warped out of shape and thus won't hold a replacement."

"Now you might be thinking you could use a larger device on those nasty tanks Chris mentioned before, but they are military grade hardware. They are built for abuse and are shielded," Morgan finished.

"Now I'm going to have my beautiful assistant show you how easy it is to make these gifts." Tony ignored Morgan's glare. "When you are done I want you to go out and share as many of them as you can with the Metros. We don't want them left out."

He got a resounding laugh from the crowd.

*   *   *

"Detective, we found a smuggler's hold in this bar. No Greenies but it had six figures worth of untaxed liquor."

Detective Gohar Debnath, squat and broad with a face that would look appropriate on a melted marshmallow man, walked up to the owner. "Been reporting that to your precinct officer?"

"O-of course, Detective." The fear rolled off the little Asian man like water off a snowman in a greenhouse.

"Let's see. Your officer is Ruben Nicks. Shall I percomm him and find out?"

"Sh-sure, Detective."

"There's no need. I know you didn't, you gook." Gohar pulled out his sidearm and shoved it in the proprietor's ear before pulling the trigger. The frangible slug shattered inside the bar owner's skull—scrambling his brains. The body fell over with blood leaking out of the entry wound and the smell of raw sewage as the man's sphincters released.

"An object lesson to the next owner," Gohar said, taking one bottle of the unmarked booze as he and his partner waltzed out of the establishment, leaving the body behind.

*   *   *

"This is Captain Carlos Munoz of the Oregon National Guard," came the voice over the building's emergency speakers. *"We are conducting a room by room search of this entire structure. You are required to provide cooperation to all National Guard troops as they request it."*

The door burst open, shattering the electronics, the lock, and door jam. The larger fragments flew across the open concept apartment, landing on the floor of the dining area.

"EVERYONE DOWN!" yelled an amplified voice from behind urban assault armor. Six other armored Guardsmen surged through the door behind assault weapons with their laser beams dancing all over the room. The group could have been mistaken for wide metallic gorillas.

The father and three children watching the solido dove for the floor. A woman six decades past her prime came out of the kitchen spouting rapid Romanian while wielding a kitchen spoon as if as she could singlehandedly drive off the invading hordes.

While the lieutenant couldn't understand a single word, the invective tone made her exact words immaterial. His HUD showed the floor plan of the apartment and rooms turning from red to yellow indicating at least no enemies to engage. He caught the replay of the video of his team entering one room to find a couple of young men *en flagrante delicto.*

"Quit using the net feed for porn, Carson," Lieutenant Cambria said, reminding himself to replay that in his spare time... for training purposes, of course.

"Aye, Lieutenant."

Over the noise of furniture being flipped, clothing and electronics being tossed out of closets, and solidos yanked off the wall, the lieutenant noticed that the kitchen remained red. "Louis? Do you have something?"

"Only this scrawny granny," the trooper said, walking out with his armored hand around the woman's throat. Her feet dangled a full 30 cm off the floor. "She's been whacking my suit with her ladle."

"Mark that clear."

"You be dying to the Greenies, you bet," the old biddy choked out in broken English.

"Lieutenant, do we have to put up with that?" Corporal Louis asked. "We could teach this cunt a lesson."

"We are only here to search, Louis, not provoke enemies. Finish your sweep for hidden weapons and bolt holes." The trooper set the woman down, but kept his grip on her throat.

One by one the rooms turned green as sonic probes played over every wall and surface. "Nothing here, Lieutenant."

"That's affirmative. Let's move to the next apartment. Try to be a bit easier on the next door, will you, Carson."

"Check, Lieutenant."

Two dozen seconds passed after the seven armored men left the apartment before anyone stirred. The father stood up and examined the room as damaged as if a tornado had ripped through the building.

"*Bou!*"

* * *

Ignoring the century long stink of feces and urine that had soaked into the walls and floor, the National Guardsman's head jerked around, trying to look into every dark crevasse of the 80 m cylindrical tank of the thirty-year-abandoned Willamette Waste Treatment Plant. His eyes went wide when he caught sight of the curvy blond wearing a yellow chiffon dress that remotely reminded him of his prom date. The three hatchet men at her side didn't even break his focus. The burly man mouthed something over his percomm before advancing toward Jamie and Gregori, and two of her other minions.

The guardsman halted abruptly as rain started falling hard enough to be heard on the metal roof of Tank Number 3. His eyes continued to scan every direction, including up.

"Jesus," Jamie said, her voice echoing in the bare metal room. "If we were going to rip you off we would have hit you as you blundered down Columbia in that battered lift-truck of yours."

Surprised, the big man drew his sidearm but didn't train it

anywhere. "What? How did you…"

Exasperated, Jamie put a rather large case down on the ground, opening it up to show a good number of bearer bonds. "We want to do business and get out of this stench, not fight. Now get your fat ass over here so we can negotiate."

Still wary, the man closed the distance with his head scanning back and forth for imagined enemies. When he'd reached 6 m the man stopped, holding his position. The gun went back into its holster but he kept his right hand on it.

"You wanted weapons?" he asked incredulously of the beautiful and ostentatiously overdressed woman.

"You want money. Looks like we are even."

"What do you want?"

"What do you have? Look, we could do this all night," Jamie said as she began to pace. The butter-colored heels, which matched her dress, clacked and echoed in the tank. "You are a supplier, I'm a buyer. Let's not fuck around, shall we? I'm looking for any heavy weapons you got. I'm not interested in personal guns, assault rifles, submachine guns, or non-lethals of any kind. If you have artillery, missiles, explosives, tanks, drones, or ammunition, then I'm willing to pay for those. If not, take a hike."

"I guess it isn't how well the bear waltzes." The man shrugged. "Anyway I've got sixty Werewolf ground-to-ground rockets, one metric ton of binary explosive powder, three hundred Flytrap mines, and eighty Pulsar heart signature tracking missiles."

"That's a nice truckload. If we can come to an agreement on the price I'll take the whole lot."

"We want sixty-three," the man said immediately.

Jamie looked up to the corrugated metal that sufficed for a roof. Her mind, the ultimate business calculator of all time, ground the numbers. "Street price for all of those items would be forty-nine million. Assuming a twenty percent discount for the lot would bring it down to say forty even. So we'll pay you one thirty."

The man started defensively, "We won't take any less than—wait a minute, lady. Did you say one hundred thirty million?"

Jamie just stood looking at him and nodded.

"What the fuck? Are you nuts, bitch?"

"Don't call her names," Gregori said in a tone so flat it would scare a rock.

"S-sorry. Are you crazy, lady?"

"Nope. I'm paying for advertising."

The man just shook his head and twisted up his mouth, obviously not smart enough to follow where Jamie led.

"Look, I'm paying you about twice what you asked for. Aren't you going to do everything you can to bring me more and get more of this windfall? Aren't you going to sell this information to everyone you know who might want to get some of this honey?

"Well, I want as much of this stuff as you can send my way."

"You starting a war with that much hardware?"

"What do you care?" Jamie said with disdain in her voice. "You are going to live the rest of your life in the Caymans on full medical."

"I still think you are crazy, but for one thirty you got a deal. And you are right, as long as you keep paying off, you'll be getting more shit."

* * *

The pine scent, artificial to six decimal places, radiated from the 5 m tall, synthetic tree decorated in glass ornaments, popcorn, and cranberry strings that dominated the center of the ballroom. Bows, tags "from Santa," and brilliant wrapping paper covered the fake presents that littered the white ruffled skirt under the tree. Area rugs and comfortable living room furniture gave the hired room at least the veneer of a homey feel. The ancient strains of Frank Sinatra crooning about having a "Merry Little Christmas" provided a pleasant background.

In contrast the sideboard held a genuine feast. The nibbles rarely seen on earth any longer, including real pistachios, Polish ham, Emmentaler cheese, both green and black olives, and even mandarin oranges. Several dozen bottles of genuine label grain alcohol occupied another table, along with high quality wines and soft drinks.

The entirety of the active action arm of the Green Action Militia relaxed around the room. Christine Matthews practiced her "bored" façade by sitting quietly, using an emery board on her nails. The identical Weismuller twins argued quietly about whether the wood in the dance floor was real, veneer, or imitation, each taking multiple contradicting positions in their heavy German accents. Joel, older by three minutes, went so far as to lie down, holding his black hair out of his face as he tried to get a closer look at the flooring, his brother Wayne kibitzing above him.

"Have we ever had a Christmas party?" Edward Longfingers said, brushing an imaginary nit from his dark colored blazer. Using the mirrored tiles of the outside wall, he also made sure each hair was in place.

As she brought her glass down from a sip of her preferred Glenfiddich, Morgan answered, "Sonya wasn't big on Christmas, it being a bastard holiday. If I remember correctly she said, 'I'd rather celebrate Grandparents' Day. While a stupid holiday, it is at least honest to its intent.'"

"That sounds like Sonya, may she rest in peace," the tall Connie Powell said with a Pepsi in her own hand. "But what did she have against Christmas?"

"Historically, Christmas is a bone thrown to the pagans that were coopted over the centuries in Europe and Asia," Augustine said confidently from the nearby couch. She nursed a glass of 2015 Gordon Brothers' Merlot. "It's obvious from the Bible that Christ couldn't have been born at the end of December."

"But I thought you were Christian, Augustine," Morgan said with her dark features skewed up in confusion.

"I am Christian. However, my church preaches to follow the love of Christ, not the trappings around it. I can celebrate Christ's birth and death in my heart without it falling on the exact correct days or those that man has artificially defined."

"So you are happy no matter the day of the year. How brilliant."

"Yup, that's me. Just like one of the dwarfs. Call me 'Happy.'"

"You do have a nice glow about you, Augustine. Your religion agrees with you," David Swift, his curly red hair almost illuminating the room by itself, said as he joined the group late in the conversation.

Augustine's normally pale skin turned four shades of red and travelled down to disappear beneath the bodice of her black jumpsuit.

"Oh! What do we have here?" Connie teased. "Are you blushing, Grandma Ice?"

Augustine giggled. "Well, the best thing is to do it quickly.. it hurts less. You might say that I'm a bit more happy than normal because of a gift a young man gave me this afternoon. Although it wasn't anything my god did for me directly, I did thank my lord very loudly." If anything her skin took that moment to turn even a darker crimson.

"Good for you, Augustine," Morgan said with a big smile.

"What did you get? I like to hear about other people's presents," David inquired with no idea.

"You mutton-head," Morgan said, slapping his shoulder. "Clueless men!" she added in disgust.

"What?" David asked with a puzzled look on his face, looking even younger than his three decades.

"Shall we change the subject?"

"Please!" Augustine implored.

"Who's guarding the pres, Connie?"

"A couple of our more active Greenpeace members. They've been sharing shifts with me. But she's in the Presidential Suite of this hotel, and I'm keeping an ear on what's going on in the room, just in case a Metro gets lucky."

"Yeah," called out Martin Fox from his sprawled location on a sofa as he removed his nose from a book. "Although I wouldn't try to take our good president with less than a squad in full riot gear. Have you seen that bitch fight?"

"Good?" David asked, still looking a bit puzzled about the previous topic.

Connie nodded emphatically.

"I still have bruises," Martin grimaced. "I used to think I was a good brawler until I met her. Holy crap. Connie, bless her soul to hell, set up a little sparring match with us yesterday. And I was worried I might hurt our president. I don't think I touched her once."

"Yes, you did, Martin. She has a pretty bruise on her right shoulder where you caught her with that punch you meant for her face."

"Well, she made me mad."

"AND she kicked your ass."

"I take no shame in that at all. I also learned a valuable lesson. Don't underestimate either women or short people."

"Yes," Christine said out of her characteristic silence.

"None of us have ever underestimated you, dearest Christine."

"Our first meeting did disabuse us of that notion," Morgan said, remembering the night Christine killed six men in a crowded bar where several members of the GAM were getting their drink on. The men's intent had been rape. Had they not started it and each been armed,

Morgan would have called it cold-blooded murder. Christine hadn't even worked up a sweat against the entire gang. Not one got a clean shot off at her. Not one, beyond the first one, had laid a hand on her. One young woman with a dirk dealt with six men like they were pigs in a slaughterhouse and then walked away calmly. The GAM recruited her within days.

A grisly thought for Christmas, Morgan thought.

"Merry Christmas," Tony called out as he came through the double doors.

"Merry Christmas," most of the rest echoed.

"Merry Christmas, Tony. 'Bout time you showed up!"

"Sorry. I got delayed on a serious errand. I hope you all have been enjoying the goodies. I couldn't provide a more home-like environment for our get together, but I could give us the best of everything else."

"Zis pate ess goot," Wayne insisted. "Better zan ve uset to get in France."

"The wine is very nice," Augustine added.

"And can you get any better than Greek olives?"

"Ah yes," Tony said softly, looking up from collecting his pouch of Erdinger Hefeweizen. "I'm looking forward to those."

"You don't have to look very long 'cause they are right over there."

"Well, we have to start the festivities first," Tony insisted.

"Festivities? Isn't this enough? A quiet place where we aren't being shot at, aren't being chased, and aren't expected to kill anyone?" David offered.

"I wanted to be wearing a Santa costume, but no one had one to rent. Shocking that they wouldn't have one on Christmas," Tony said, mocking himself. "But you will just have to deal with me handing out presents in civies."

A collective groan went up through the room.

"Who's had time to get presents?"

"I didn't even do any shopping."

"You can't do this to us, Tony. We didn't get anything."

Only GMa Ice didn't complain. "I brought presents, too," she said, whipping out a large tote.

"Me, first," Tony insisted.

"Well, mine are kinda boringly all the same. I brought cookies," Augustine said.

"Oh, OK," Tony relented. "I need to go get mine anyway. Didn't want to give away the surprise wheeling in a shopping cart full of goodies."

Tony wasn't kidding as a minute later he wheeled in a plastic shopping cart piled with gaily wrapped packages. Cinnamon perched on top like the goddess she knew she was.

"Before I get to the fun gifts, I want to give you all a very practical gift from Nanogate." Tony started handing out an auto-injector to each person, along with three refill cartridges for each.

"What gives?"

"Well, we are back in the destruction business, and I still carry the damned virus that the old corporate cabal gave me. We don't want any more deaths now, do we?" Tony asked rhetorically. "What you have there is a vaccine. I want you to zap that stuff into the arm of everyone you deal with, without question."

"That's a very thoughtful gift, Tony. One of the better I've ever been given," GMa Ice said.

"Nanogate thought of it. The virus is out. It can't be taken back so let's make sure it doesn't get anyone else."

"You know we could use you as a weapon!" David said. "You get yourself captured by the National Guard and you'd kill a huge number of them because they all handle explosives."

"Only someone who hadn't seen the virus could come up with that abomination," Martin Fox said with a frown. He actually put down the sandwich he'd made and pushed it away.

"OK. Bad idea," David retracted.

"Yes, a very bad idea," Tony agreed. "But let's ignore that and get on with gifts!"

"Yeah!" a couple of people cried out over the groans of several others.

"I know as an unintended result of our war against the corporations that you are all now indecently wealthy. I intentionally went out of my way to pick gifts that you wouldn't choose for yourself.

"David, this one on top has your name on it." With one hand Tony passed him a package about the size of two loaves of bread encased in translucent green paper.

"Holy crap but it's heavy," David said almost dropping it. He looked around for the seams to open it carefully but found none.

"Come on, don't leave uss in suspentss, Heir Swift."

After a couple of deft movements, Christine offered a gleaming butterfly knife with an onyx handle.

"Thanks, Christine." He sliced into the package and quickly tore through the rest with his hands. Opening the box he gasped, "Are these Colt Dragoons?" He lifted out a pair of heavy revolvers bearing an ancient patina over the metal surfaces.

Cinnamon took the opportunity to pounce on the wrapping paper. On her back now, she chewed the ribbon into her mouth and flailed at the rest with all four of her paws.

"Only replicas, my friend," Tony offered. "They've been made as gauss guns but they can be easily modified to fire standard ammunition."

"Holy crap, but these are awesome! I'm changing my fucking avatar for this!"

"I know you like your guns, David. Now you can be a real gunfighter."

David began field stripping his new toys.

"Next up is Augustine. I have to say I couldn't think what I could get you. You had me stumped until this very afternoon."

GMa Ice took the nearly flat package with trepidation. Opening up the simple box she found it filled with royal blue fabric with the infamous green "S" card of a genuine Silvia Swenson sitting on top. With trembling hands, Augustine lifted out a flowing blue gown. "Tony!" she simply exclaimed.

"You have a right to be beautiful, too. I want you to wear it for dinner, my friend. Head off to the ladies' room. You'll find makeup and shoes in this box," he said, handing her another package.

"By the way, next time you want to be secret about an assignation you should not check into one of Nanogate's hotels."

Augustine looked up and blushed again. She stood up, careful not to step on the furry contingent. She put a kiss on Tony's cheek before gathering her booty and heading off.

"Morgan, your gift, although easy to decide was the most difficult to get." Tony handed over a very small package about the size of a greeting card.

Morgan wrinkled her face quizzically. The wrapping paper held only some tiny seeds in a cellophane bag. She smiled broadly. "I've been looking for these forever!"

"And you wouldn't have found them, either, Morgan. I had to have Nanogate pull some strings for me so I could get them from one of the Doomsday vaults."

"My garden thanks you! He found me dandelion seeds!"

The gift giving continued with Connie getting a matched pair of Martian-onyx earrings. The Weissmuller twins received cosmetic subscriptions in different color palettes along with an admonishment by Tony to accentuate their differences. Edward Longfingers received an antique Shoshone ceremonial headdress sealed in a nitrogen filled display case. Before Tony could get to Martin or Christine, Augustine came back into the room, stopping all conversation.

Feeling sixty or seventy years younger, Augustine sashayed in to take command of the room. Joe let out a wolf whistle. Without apparent support, the designer gown hugged her from bosom to knees before flowing out behind her as if she were the Goddess of Nature leaving an impossibly cobalt loch in her wake. The skin-tight blue cloth shimmered with every step she took. No longer did Grandma Ice elicit thoughts of the baked cookies she'd brought, but rather a woman to be wooed or to be jealous of. She flowed up to Tony like a solido vamp. "I love it, Tony. Thank you for reminding me. This has been a tremendous day."

"Not very nun-like, I'm afraid."

"No," Augustine said, blushing yet again. "Not very nun-like at all." She gave him a lingering kiss, marking him with lipstick the same shade as her attire.

"I'll get in trouble if you don't stop that," Tony said, thinking of Jamie in a jealous rage. "OK, vixen. Go share with someone else. I have more Santa work in front of me."

"Yes, boss man."

"Martin, I know of your love of old growth forests, even as few as we have. I wrangled a totally unprecedented backpacking pass for you in the Romincka Forest, in Russia. You can have a week immersed in nature there...but don't go until we are done here, please." Tony handed over a greeting card with a document scrawled in Cyrillic lettering falling out of it.

"I don't know what to say."

"Don't say anything, my friend. We have blood between us. Words aren't necessary."

"Christine, the obvious gift for you would be more blades, but you've found and used every rare knife I've never even heard of. So, I went another direction." He took a fairly flat but large rectangular package over to the diminutive woman.

As with most true sociopaths Christine didn't know how to respond. She nodded her head to Tony. She opened the package to find an A1-sized flat picture of a slight, dark-haired man standing next to an even slighter young, blond girl at some local rooftop fair. Christine became even more stony faced than normal as she stared at the picture. She said only one word as tears flowed down her face. "Daddy."

Requirements Definition

"This is a bad idea," Gregori said from behind the edge of the verdant park roof of Joe Dancer Tower.

The slight wind coming up over the edge of the railing of the building gave Jamie's nose plenty to wrinkle at with the decay from the South Yamhill Creek that ran at ground level directly below them. "I don't care. I want to see this. Besides, we are at least a kilometer away," she said, scanning the west for the lone dull metallic spire of the McMinnville Metropolitan Police Sub-Station.

"More like six hundred meters, miss," Gregori said.

Jamie gave a dismissive wave.

"Let's get behind these oaks. They should give us at least a nominal amount of protection."

"You are not my mother or my father, Greg. I will watch this. You managed to keep me out of direct participation, but I won't be totally denied. This is personal."

The narrow diamond shape of the police station, a design popular eighty years previous when lift generators first popularized unusual and impractical shapes, balanced impossibly on its point. Occupying the center of old ground roadway 99 it stood apart and daunting even with other buildings towering hundreds of meters above it.

"*Team one in position,*" came the call over her low-tech ring phone.

"*Team two.*"

"*Team three.*"

"All teams wait for my go signal," Jamie said. She dialed 911 on her percomm.

"*Emergency services,*" came the young male voice. "*Can I please get your charge information?*"

"No need. As your screen has already told you, this is Jamie Ardwin. Please pass on this message. 'Don't fuck with me or mine.'"

Snapping off her percomm she went back to the ring com. "All teams, go."

Even at this distance she heard the three loud pops of the building's external grav generators collapsing upon themselves. Using solidoculars she watched the building shudder as the emergency internal grav generators kicked in. Three Werewolf missiles, moving so fast all she saw were the linear lines of fire, created fiery balls at the base of the building. When the flames cleared Jamie could see a ragged, gaping hole at the diamond's point. The building was now severed from the city services and any stability the earth could provide.

Police officers on pergravs poured out of the lift bay. Jamie's teams did her proud. Dozens of Pulsar heart lock missiles lanced out, chasing after the airborne cops. The weapons seemed to crawl across the scene compared to the speed of the Werewolves. Seconds passed as the mechanical hunters twisted and turned to follow the target they'd been locked onto. The result was inevitable. As a Pulsar reached its target there was a brilliant burst of plasma and then nothing save falling ash. Two of the thirty or so policemen managed to make it to the safety of another building only by virtue of not having been targeted. No one else ventured forth.

The inertia of the police station kept it relatively stationary for most of the firefight. While on a somewhat level piece of ground, the police spire started moving north along the open parkway of the old highway, adding fractional speed with each passing moment. Jamie gave a predatory smile.

"Time to clear off," Gregori said. "We're pushing the response time of other precincts."

"Damn. I would've liked to have seen what they decided—ramming into another building or turning off the internal grav units to collapse the department."

"Catch it on CNI. I'm sure there are eight thousand solidos focused on it right now."

"Good idea." And then into her ring com, "Bug out. All teams bug out. Great job!"

As Gregori hustled her away to a waiting liftousine, Jamie laughed out loud. Her message had been sent.

* * *

President Susan Tipton hadn't stayed in one place for more than four days since this started. Her surroundings varied widely, from even more palatial than the norms of the president to filthy, abandoned hovels that even the swarms of rats shunned. Her conveyances also weren't uniformly comfortable. Two days ago they'd packed her up as a crate of convention signage and shipped her FedEx in a box only a hair larger than a coffin. Two days prior to that she'd worn a dirty coverall and been the second driver of a dump truck with a bad lift unit that tilted back and to the left the entire trip.

While her guards always treated her with respect and deference, she found it difficult to maintain her own feeling of worth to the cause. She had no regular access to the presidential network of runners and assistants to accomplish some of her share of the work. She also felt her own morale slipping more and more as she couldn't accomplish even small things.

Nanogate wasn't the most gregarious of travelling companions, Susan thought as they travelled to their new hiding place. She could have used a personal confidant but knew it wasn't done that way at this level. Confiding in her guards, even Connie, would have been worse than useless. If everything were equal she'd have asked her sometime-lover, Mike, to Camp David for a weekend of pillow talk. He could always cheer her up with his advice and his attentions to her body.

Their driver, Carl, kept their flight profile unknown as they skimmed local traffic patterns. He claimed landing on platforms and then slipped into the next local flight zone, letting his claim expire. As they travelled toward a destination somewhere in Lake Oswego, the liftousine rose up over one of the new towers with a live, growing park on its roof. Some of the more affluent even had installed a small lake that this early in the year had a layer of ice. She saw children in the playground and parents watching over them. The normalcy of the glimpse sparked a torrent of images and ideas through her mind.

"Carl."

"Yes, Madam President."

"Can you land on that roof?"

"Yes, ma'am."

"Madam President, what are you planning?" Connie Powell asked. "This isn't on your schedule."

"It is now, Connie. We're going to work the ropes, as my long ago predecessors would have called it."

"Excuse me," Nanogate said, belatedly noticing the conversation. "We are going to build morale—theirs, and ours."

* * *

"Cindy, come quick. It's the president," seven-year-old Katie Mayland said to her friend.

"Why would the president be in our park? And out in the rain? You are a liar, Katie."

"Am not! Then you can just stay there while I go talk to her. She seems nice."

Cindy Schlimgen watched her friend skip away over to a group of people near the slide. Four really big men stood near an old woman with pink hair that really did look like the president. The pink-haired woman shook the hand of Dennis's dad and Robbie's mom. Next to her a thin old man whose face and pale blue eyes was on the solido all the time ruffled Robbie's hair and said something. Cindy's eyes went wide. She ran for her door only forty meters away. "Mommy! Mommy! The president is in our park!" she yelled, pelting into the house.

"Honey, how many times have I told you to wipe your feet when you come in from outside," Andrea Schlimgen said as she folded clothes on the kitchen table.

"But, Mommy! The president and that man from the solido are outside. C'mon and look." She grabbed her mom's arm and tugged.

"Why would the president be here, and in the rain no less."

"Just look out the window, Mommy!" Andrea looked out and saw the president of the United States and the chairman of the CorpGov climb into a liftousine. Several of the other buildings' parents waved good-bye. The vehicle slid off the edge of their building and into the busy lift vehicle traffic. Andrea just stood there.

"C'mon, Mommy, or we'll miss them."

"It's too late, baby. They are already gone."

"Aw! I wanted to meet them."

Andrea smiled. She would have liked to meet them, too—the McNary Tower PTA meeting tomorrow was going to be abuzz.

* * *

It looked like a tight squeeze. David Swift unlimbered his pack and handed it to Morgan. He slung his Mossberg automatic over his shoulder for the fourth time this trip and drew his Colt before climbing up the fallen chunk of ceramcrete and narrowly avoiding some bent rebar sticking down. Before he crested the top, he panned his night vision goggles around to make sure no one else lurked down in the sewers. Satisfied they were safe he reached down to Morgan for his pack. He dropped it down the other side with a wet plop into the muck below before taking hers and doing the same. He slid over the top and down the other side and stood guard as Morgan followed him over.

On the other side of the National Guard cordon, the Havana Bank had decided to take sides with the Metros. Out to kill two birds with one stone, Morgan and David needed to break the cordon and give the independent bank something to think about by blowing open their vault. They had no intention of taking anything but it would pass a message.

The blockade would be a piece of cake in the maze that is the underground service conduits and sewer systems beneath Portland. Some of the tunnels had been there for centuries and had even housed bars back during the Prohibition Era. After retrieving their packs they slogged forward. A hundred yards further, Dave put up his fist. He turned up the inputs on his combat earplugs.

"*What the hell did we do to deserve this detail? Yuck,*" David heard from in front of him. It continued.

"*You haven't been kissing her highness's ass enough.*"

"*Fuck, don't let Sarge hear you talking about her that way. She'll beat the living crap out of you and then mop the floor with the rest of us just for dessert.*"

"*Yeah. That bitch is one bad-ass …*"

"We got company ahead," David whispered to Morgan. "I count at least three different voices."

"Let's go back around and take another path," Morgan whispered back. David nodded in agreement.

As they got outside of hearing from the previous troops, David said, "We could have taken them but then we wouldn't be able to make our deposit at the bank."

"No, this way is better. Better safe than sorry." For two hours they backtracked and moved off into an alternate path to their destination. As they started finally getting close to their target, the intersection 50 m ahead lit up like a beacon when a soldier struck a narco stick. The three soldiers stationed there casually held their assault rifles.

"*You better not let Sarge see you smoking on duty.*"

"*Oh, what the fuck's going to happen? We going to be attacked by the boogeyman? These tunnels ain't been used since they still had hardwired telephones.*"

"Snake eyes twice?" Morgan asked in a jailhouse whisper. David just pointed back the way they came. Morgan nodded.

After they'd crept away David said, "Once is bad luck. Twice is a fucked up mission. We'll try one more time but honestly even if it works I'm starting to worry about our exit strategy."

"I agree," the dark-skinned woman said. "Let's make this next one reconnaissance only."

"Agreed."

Four hours later they had run into two more posts of soldiers in two different levels.

"Bastards know the underground," Morgan said as they made their way back to the safe house.

"And are willing to guard it. That bastard Reed isn't going to make this easy, is he?"

* * *

"That stunt at the McNary Towers has paid off in massive dividends," Augustine said over the joint net. "Prior to this our popularity had slipped just a tiny bit. But now it is growing to nearly epic proportions. I could find almost no one against us outside of the military and police communities. This has spawned literally thousands of volunteers and new hiding places."

"President Tipton, I must admit that you have done us a world of good," said Tony's bioweapon virus avatar.

"Thank you, Tony," the Presidential Seal said.

"Now don't ever fucking do it again," he admonished her.

"Excuse me?" Susan said, stunned.

"Do I have to tell you how much of a risk you and Nanogate took?"

"Excuse me," Nanogate interjected. "I have some input here. We were in very little danger and—"

"Oh really? What if one of those people called in to the Metros? Just one? Or what about if a random patrol saw you? Or even a security guard?"

"I see your apprehensions now, Mr. Sammis," Mr. Marks commented from his own network self-image of a pair of sheathed Japanese swords bound in a white ribbon. "Miss Powell quite correctly told them that they could only be exposed for six minutes, the minimum response time from the local precinct. Miss Powell and her fellow guards could easily have taken out any single patrol."

"That isn't the point. What if a crazy just happened to be lurking."

"Where we aren't expected and with a weapon that Connie and her team can't deal with? C'mon Tony. You aren't that dense. You're behaving like an overprotective mother. I think they should do this more," commented Martin Fox's redwood tree avatar.

"Maybe so, but I don't want to have to be responsible for burying another president."

The net room got quiet.

"As that may be, as long as Connie hits the less than one percentile for armed response I think it is a valid tactic," the redwood said again.

"All right, but for God's sake, if you are going to do it, please plan for it. No more seat-of-the-pants flying."

* * *

Not one of the members moved. No one brought out a notepad. No one queried their messages. The briefing room, normally quiet, fell into a silent tableau. Only the commissioner would dare break it.

"Would you please explain that one more time, Lieutenant? I thought you said one of our substations was destroyed," Commissioner Krylov said in a calm tone that belied his blotchy red face.

Reza forced himself not to cringe. "Yes, sir, I can share more, and yes, sir, I did say our McMinnville station has been attacked and destroyed. Actually that overstates the problem. The station itself is intact but no longer capable of housing a force as it is leaning up against another building at a forty-degree angle.

"We were quite lucky, actually. The building engineer pulsed the emergency power in a way that allowed him to drag the bottom of the building and keep from—"

"Lieutenant, what part of me looks like I give a FUCK about the building? Who attacked? How did they succeed?"

"Sorry, sir. We have fairly conclusive proof that the attack was perpetrated by Jamie Ardwin. She called the emergency dispatch just prior to the attack with a vague threat about not getting into her business.

"As to how it succeeded… the group disabled the foundations of the building with Werewolf projectiles in an initial volley. They then used Pulsar missiles, the new fire-and-forget anti-personnel weapon by Deutsche Waffen und Munitionsfabriken, to slaughter everyone who exited." The fatigue running through Reza made his eyes cross as he wavered slightly in front of the Commissioner. His vision produced two of the burly men, each as intimidating as the original. Reza made a promise to himself to get some sleep as soon as the meeting was over.

"And how is it possible that this Jamie Ardwin not only had the latest weapons but could attack our station so openly and blatantly?"

"Sir, building code for police stations for the last sixty years has been to have a 30 meter clear zone around the building to prevent situations like the New York Massacre where the precinct had excellent protection but the terrorists detonated a massive bomb in the unprotected building sharing a wall. This open space gave them every opportunity to fire at range without being detected."

"And why am I just hearing about this now?"

Reza could see the pulsing of Krylov's heartbeat in the veins across the man's clenched jawline. Reza queried his server time. He had to blink away the doubled vision before he saw.

"Sir, this happened less than fifteen minutes ago. In fact all the response teams aren't even in place."

"How many did we capture so far?"

"Ummm, preliminary reports indicate, none, sir. Nor did we kill any. Likely we won't catch any of them at this point. I might add we were lucky our losses were only twenty-six."

Krylov shut his eyes. His fists and jaws both unclench like the unravelling of a spring under too much pressure. Over two silent minutes the pulsing in his veins slowed as did his breathing.

"And what is this *fignya* about both the President and the Chairman visiting a local park not three kilometers from here?"

"It appears to be true, Commissioner. We've questioned the civilians at the scene. It appears that they dropped in, shook a few hands, and then left before any of our people even noticed they were there. Hell we didn't even know it happened until one of our network jocks found it on one of the parent's blogs."

Only Krylov's heavy breathing broke the silence in the room. "I'm open to suggestions," Krylov finally said with his eyes still firmly closed.

"We should secure the area and refloat the building as soon as possible," Major Broadsky stated with authority.

Amber Cohen spoke up next. "Expand patrols, both of flesh and blood and nanite sampling in the areas around the structure."

"We should also force any property with a direct view of any precinct to permanently remove the view by walling them up," Captain Hardy offered.

"Since these animals tend to move around at ground level, how about traps at ground level?"

With each suggestion Reza hallucinated a dark figure with "Sleep" printed across its chest mocking him before flying out the window.

"While all of those are viable actions, I don't mean what to do to fix things," Krylov said with a heavy sigh. "How do we respond to these terrorists? This Jamie Ardwin isn't your run-of-the-mill mobster. She doesn't seem to care about profit. That casts her into the mold of a terrorist."

"How does this differ from our actions against the CorpGov and GAM?"

"Ma'am, up to this point we've assumed that Miss Ardwin was only acting on a principle of greed and wasn't directly involved. I think this may have helped clarify the situation."

Only his fatigue made Reza stick his neck even further into the wringer. "Sir, her exact words when calling were 'Don't fuck with me or mine.' I suggest it gives us a lever in and of itself. Why don't we go after her crew?"

"And how would we find them?"

"Sir, I think if we let some of our network monkeys work on this they could sort out a profile and tie it directly to Miss Ardwin or even more directly to the mob itself."

"Captain Cohen."

"Yes, sir."

"I want you to take the lieutenant's suggestion and run with it. I want a body count of these mobsters... a BIG body count."

*   *   *

Real wax candles lit the room with an equally authentic fire in a stone fireplace. The big windows looked out only feet off the bay of Ross Island where several sailboards and even a skiff plied the rapidly darkening waters. Real leather couches wrapped around the warm hearth. In one corner, trimmed simply in white angel decorations and twinkle lights was a real fir tree, probably worth more than the mythical average annual salary.

Tony, in a cream colored silk robe and matching bottoms, handed Jamie a flute of champagne. Her matching rich brown silks didn't quite cover as much as Tony's, but it didn't bother either of them. Cinnamon curled up on the warm hearth.

"Merry Christmas, Jamie, a day late."

"Merry Christmas, darling." Jamie punctuated her salutation by leaning over and planting a kiss on Tony's lips. Tony surprised her by wrapping his big arms around her. He pulled her much closer, spilling her long, cool-red hair over the pair of them. Heating up like a firecracker, she fumbled at the sash holding his robe together but he broke the kiss before she could finish.

"Whew!" Jamie said, just letting her head fall backward and keeping her eyes closed. Wavering on her feet, Tony steadied her.

"Now, now. Don't be such a greedy slitch."

"Why the hell not?" she said in a dreamy voice. She intentionally and dramatically fluttered her eyes open. "I've got lots of time to make up for."

"We have presents to trade and prime rib to eat."

"I'd rather have prime YOU," Jamie said, reaching for her beau.

"And I thought your sex kitten act was just to put people off," Tony said, letting her catch the tie of his robe just enough to yank it open.

"So did I. Guess I really am a slut."

"Probably not a slut, but certainly insatiable. Right now could you put a damper on it...just for a little while?"

Jamie pouted and pulled her fingers back from playing with his belly button. "If I *have* to."

"Sit down, I have two presents to give you."

"Oh, I've got a present for you, too, mister," Jamie said, plopping into the butter-soft leather couch.

"Does your brain have any other gear than sex?" Tony said, sitting down next to her.

"Should I—" Jamie began, almost choking on her words as from behind his back Tony brought out a 6 cm, square teal box with black Tiffany lettering, wrapped in a silver bow. "You bastard... if that is..."

"Why don't you take it and find out for yourself what it is."

As she reached out Jamie couldn't remember the last time her hand had trembled. *Not yet*, she thought. *It's too soon. Not yet.* She closed her eyes and took a deep breath. Lifting the lid, she found two stunning cat's-eye diamond earrings nestled in velvet.

"You fucking bastard! I'm going to make you pay for this," she said in playful protest. "They're beautiful," she said, plucking them out and sliding them immediately into her pierced ears.

"They are a new product they are making out beyond Jupiter's orbit. The centers change color. Just wave them near a power outlet and the electromagnet fields cause the crystals to change their structure and refract a different color."

"I love them."

"Well, a man can't go wrong with jewelry," Tony said somewhat smugly.

"I still owe you for that heart attack."

"I hope you can collect one day. And now for present number two."

"Lover, you didn't need to bother with even one of these. I want you, not your presents."

"Diamonds are a girl's best friend."

"Totally a myth," Jamie said.

"Well, this one isn't jewels. Because we don't know each other all that well yet, it requires a bit of a story so you will understand it."

"Good. I want to know more about my stud."

"Pipe down in the cheap seats. This is a story about Tony Sammis."

Jamie got very interested as she noticed how tentative and nervous he got. Tony had never shared much about himself to anyone, but his charisma was such that you felt him to be your best friend. Jamie understood that she had been under his spell as much as anyone else had. It troubled her.

"While my folks weren't bad people, we never really got on. They brought me up and expected me to follow them into the physical facilities. I think they were proud of me when I graduated college but a bit disappointed when I didn't use it to supply people with the basic services required.

"We weren't cold but we weren't close either, even before.

"For my last year of junior high they sent me to stay with my mother's parents in Queensland, Australia, but I didn't actually attend any classes. Granther and Grandma Papadakis were good people, but really were relics from a different era. Grandma wasn't happy unless she was rolling dolma or had a dozen cookies baking. Granther spent most of his time with me. He was a tough man who got even tougher fighting in the resistance during the Australian Civil War. He wouldn't accept anything but perfection. He beat me when I didn't get things exactly right. I hated him." Tony stopped and looked thoughtful. "I remember my weekly calls to my parents begging them to let me come home.

"It took three months for me to shake down to life with Granther and Grandma Papadakis. I remember the day. I'd messed up on setting the fuses on a demolition charge to remove a beauty-leaf stump Granther wanted blown. He had his rattan cane out and was reminding me.

"Now one stroke of Granther's cane would cause even Gregori to cry. On the third lash it dawned on me that Granther punished me because he loved me. That was hard to accept and even harder to understand.

"After a contemplative and sleepless night I came to love the old bastard. Oh, I don't think I'll ever get to the point where I will like him. I have too many painful memories. But I didn't earn many more beatings the rest of the year. That gentleman taught me more in that one year than my parents taught me in the rest of my life.

"Above all he taught me to respect myself and honor those who had something to teach."

Jamie reached up and wiped a single tear from Tony's olive cheek. "Is he still alive?"

"No, he passed away two years after my time with them.

Unexpectedly he left me something in his will." Tony handed Jamie an even smaller, purple jewelry box.

Jamie opened it with some trepidation to find a silver star on a blue satin ribbon.

"Granther won that citation holding off a platoon of men to give the Chinese villagers of Kununurra time to escape. He lost his leg to a grenade during the firefight."

It was Jamie's time to let tears drop. "Tony, I don't…" She stopped, too choked up to finish. How could she have even thought that Tony would be so crass as to offer her an engagement ring? The man had depth beyond any ten other men… probably a hundred, maybe a thousand.

"You don't have to say anything. Just remember what it stands for."

She wiped her eyes on her sleeves and blew her nose on the handkerchief he just happened to have handy.

"So what shall we toast to?" Tony said, handing back her glass.

"SEX!" she said, smiling through her tears.

*   *   *

The graininess and the jerking lack of stabilizers exposed the amateur nature of the solido. It could be found on any net node but always cycling and never on a static location, making it easy to find, very difficult to trace.

Audio whispered over the image. "Underground Z calling all my siblings who're trying to keep their red inside their skin. We got hundreds of eyes peeled for you. We found scores of Blacks with riot gear creeping 'round the rez levels of these old low-rise Mill Park slums. We're huntin' 'em from adjacent buildings and maintenance corridors."

As solidoed through two sets of windows, a Metro SWAT teams shuffled along in tactical formation down a hallway. The scene stayed the same but the image changed to a pinhole with no three-D capabilities looking straight down on the action from above.

The Metros sneak stopped in front of a door labeled 7667. In less than three seconds one had taped det-cord around the perimeter of the portal. With hand signals the leader got everyone facing away. The door vaporized in an orange flash and the Metros poured through.

The image changed again to show the view through a dirty window and the bars of an old-fashioned fire escape. It zoomed in as men stormed the condo. For a moment the image went blank as it panned across to another window. Four police stood over the bed of a couple and another had a younger boy in a half nelson.

The entire breach had taken less than ten seconds.

The woman screamed but it didn't seem to bother the Metros. The one in charge pulled up a solido on his sleeve monitor that the camera couldn't quite make out. Lasers scanned the man's head.

"I'll do anything, sir. Just tell me what you want," the male detainee pleaded, his voice on the recording sounding like it passed through a fish tank.

"Daddy! Daddy!" came the voices and visuals of two little girls, not more than five years old, running into the room.

"Don't hurt my children."

"ID ninety-seven point six percent," came the muffled voice of the leader. "Are you Stan Lenov, member of the Ardwin crime family?"

"Yes, sir. What can I do to make things right?"

One of the men used his handgun and put a single round through Stan's head.

"Holy fuck," the cinematographer said, unmuffled.

The woman's voice stopped mid-scream with the sound of another pop. Three more pops followed.

The solidograph caught the Metros leaving as quickly as they'd come. Several seconds later a new image cut in as it moved in through the blown door. It turned around the corner to the tenement bedroom. Thick red ooze with bits of hair and chunks of other unidentifiable substances ran down the wall in five different places. The bodies of two adults and two children lay on the floor in a growing puddle.

The solido bobbed as the sound of the cinematographer losing anything that might be in his stomach punctuated the scene.

The commentator came back on as voice-over. "We got word of seventeen other breaches by Metros. There probably are more. If you are part of Ardwin, bury yourself deep."

* * *

In tight black overalls, Tony paced in front of the four bay windows with his fists clenching and unclenching. The distant sounds of multiple emergency vehicles leaked into the room. A gray plastiboard covered the third opening, causing him to move in and out of the bright winter sunshine that so rarely graced the Pacific Northwest.

He looked back at Jamie with a look that might peel skin if it landed wrong. His emotions wouldn't let his mind settle. He hadn't been so angry since he learned he had been used as a bio weapon against his friends. Yet despite his rage, her persona drew him closer. Only someone else could adjudicate Jamie's actions and the damage they'd caused. Not that this was the purpose of today's meeting.

Still he knew he couldn't be involved in anything that was decided. With difficulty he blanked his mind.

Tony stopped in front of one of the transparent panes and looked out at the city of Seattle. From this penthouse vantage he counted six greasy black and two smaller white lines of smoke wafting up from different positions in the city.

The meeting Nanogate had called was a security risk but important. It was the first time they had all the key people in one place in many weeks. He didn't like it—too many ways for something to go wrong. And why here? What message was Nanogate trying to send?

Turning back he took in a room he'd been in once before but for a very different reason. His jaw muscles rippled letting him know that the anger hadn't quite spilled from his system. The blood stains had been removed from the carpet, the linoleum, and even the countertop. The hole in the ceiling where Carmine's gun had discharged had been repaired so seamlessly that Tony couldn't even tell where it was. Hell, even the cleaver he'd used to decapitate his ex-lover had been sterilized and replaced in the block on the kitchen island.

The key members of the allied forces sat on every horizontal surface, including the floor, in the midst of what had been a murder scene. Tony darted a look at Nanogate. The chairman continued his quiet conversation with his bodyguard, but caught Tony's eye. The seated man raised his eyebrows in acknowledgement that he'd chosen this place specifically to make Tony uncomfortable. After being whipsawed between Jamie's stunt and Nanogate playing games, Tony felt like dropping a grenade and walking away.

"We're only missing one; should we get started anyway?" Tony asked without catching his lover's eye as he moved over to take his seat next to her. He feared what the look in her eyes would do to what little equilibrium he'd developed.

The door of the apartment opened without a knock to admit the lanky form of Wintel in a Pullanami tailored suit. "I'm sorry I'm late, but some functionary stopped me in the lobby and questioned my fashion choices."

"That functionary has a name," Tony snapped. Even as the words fired from his mouth he wished he could instead focus it's venom toward Nanogate or Jamie. "His name is David Swift and he is one of the group of *functionaries* that is spending each of his waking moments keeping you alive. And if I were in his place I would have made you strip, you cretin."

What little conversation there had been in the room ceased. Wintel stood behind a chair with his mouth open and a dazed look in his eyes.

"I'm not sure if 'cretin' quite covers it," Tony continued. "I think maybe it should be idiot studying to be a moron and not cutting it. Why in the fuck would you wear a designer business suit when you know the Metros and the National Guard are looking for the top businessmen in the country? In fact all businessmen are suspect at the moment. Why didn't you just invite the enemy to the meeting and be done with it?"

Three heartbeats of silence held the room as Tony's furrowed gaze refused to release Wintel's eyes. Cold fury slowly replaced the shock in the corporate magnate's stare. They looked like two gunfighters from the ancient West waiting to draw down.

"I think we need a new moderator today," President Susan Tipton said standing up. "With your consent?" she asked the group at large.

Tony broke his glare when Jamie took his hand in hers. He pulled it away with a jerk, transferring his irritation back to its original target. The tension in the room lowered when he finally walked over and flopped down into the seat next to Augustine. Wintel also lowered himself into a chair but his wrinkled brows didn't smooth.

"First order of business—where do we stand on our monetary manipulation of the Metropolitan Police? I'll start. Because of a number of functionaries in my government, I've been unable to directly choke the flow of credits to Metros. So we've moved on to the rather radical advice of stopping all taxes. This leaves many key social services without funding, such as military, fire suppression, Social Security, and retirement payments, as well as Obamacare insurance matching.

"Because of the wording of the National Lottery, schools are still receiving funding through that organization.

"In the short term this means that the Metros won't receive any money from the federal government It also means that our economy will morph. Those dependent on social care will soon become destitute. Everyone will start having an increase to their out-of-pocket costs on nearly everything. We don't expect deaths directly attributable to this for eight more weeks.

"Nanogate."

Wearing a red-plaid, flannel shirt and dungarees, and sporting three days of spotty beard growth, Nanogate looked more like a lumberjack of old than a corporate magnate. The famous smooth baritone spoke from his seated position. "With the aid of Miss Ardwin and the GAM nipping at the heels of those who have chosen to defy us, we now have solidarity of all the major corporations. They are all withholding funds from the Metros in some form or another. We have but sixty-four percent of the mid-level corporations. They are in the worst bind. They can't make an individual or moral decision that might ruin them and they aren't large enough to absorb the losses in the interim. Small businesses fall more into the bailiwick of general morale but we have ninety plus percent of their support as well.

"As with you, Ms. Moderator, I'm concerned about how long we can maintain this unity. If, as our projections suggest, we continue to slip in our control against our opponents, my competitor and colleague companies will do what is in their best interest and not only renew bonds with the Metros but also actively help them against us. We believe the tipping point is forty-two percent popular opinion."

"Thank you, Chairman. Can we now hear from the Ardwin family."

Jamie might as well have been a pin-up model of the 1950s housewife wearing a simple pink, polka-dotted dress with at least five petticoat layers underneath. Her retro seamed stockings made her long legs look even longer as she stood. "Until recently we've been conducting, in conjunction with the GAM, operations against specifically targeted financial institutions. Now that the corporations are in line, our tempo has dropped and we refocused on aiding the civil unrest and chaos that is beginning to take hold.

"We also stopped all payments to the Metros."

"These combined actions have increased our personal wealth significantly; however, I have to caution that it has also depleted my available force to a point that I'm concerned about a hostile take-over of my territory. I will continue to support the actions of this body, but I don't have much more force to bring to bear."

"Tony, if you would report."

Tony started to remark but Jamie interrupted him.

"Hold on a moment, Ms. President. I have more."

"My apologies, Jamie. Please continue."

"Thanks. In addition, I took it upon myself to talk individually to the families of every major United States crime family, organization, or two-bit clique I could find a contact for, even those we have, until recently, feuded with. Most of them have agreed that the Metros are the greatest threat to their business model in the last five generations.

"While I cannot order them directly, they have agreed to stop any action against each other or us based on our plans. Additionally, they have all started actions to draw down the resources of the police and military in their zones of control.

"Now I'm done."

"That was an excellent addition. Have you given this data to Augustine?"

"She sure has and I baked it into the overall simulations I'll be giving later," Augustine said from a beanbag chair on the floor beside Tony.

"Tony, could you now report?" the president asked.

"I notice Miss Ardwin's report left out the attack she made on the McMinnville Police Station and the massacre of her people and their families this morning."

"That had nothing to do with this body. That was personal!" Jamie flashed in anger, leaping to her feet.

"It was fucking cowboy shit," Tony countered.

Jamie's eyes narrowed. "At least I'm doing something directly."

The rest of the council looked on as the room narrowed to just the pair of lovers snapping at one another.

"You got eighty-six of your own murdered by those thugs because you reacted."

"At least we took action! The rest of this is—"

Tony interrupted, "Did you know we had plans to go after multiple police stations at the same time, and that your little stunt completely negated the possibility?"

"Oh, sure, now you tell us you planned to attack something other than innocent merchants and equipment."

"Good grief. Even now the Metros are fortifying and patrolling their stations unlike ever in the past. We'll never get through now, thanks to your cowgirl stunt."

"STOP!" Gregori bellowed. Once he had everyone's attention he continued. "We are supposed to be a team.

"Tony, you pigheaded moron, bringing it up is the worst thing you could have done. If you had just let it lay it would have blown over." Gregori turned his massive body toward Jamie. "And Boss, I hate to say this, but you fucked up. Yes, it is my job to carry out your orders and protect you, but you fucked up and you know it."

The two combatants bored daggers into each other's eyes.

"Now if you two have the sense God gave a rock you will agree with me and let this drop," Gregori finished.

"You are right. I'm sorry," Tony all but forced out of his mouth.

Jamie only nodded with clenched teeth and sat back down in a huff.

Tony realized he wasn't going to get laid anytime in the near future but didn't care. With his jaw still clamped he stood, taking a deep cleansing breath before going on with his own report. "Not to draw down the contributions of any individual or group, the GAM is spread thinner than any of you. I have senior operatives out teaching activists how to be a thorn in the side of our Metro colleagues. I have protective details on each of the councilmembers and their families, as well as the president, mostly drawn from untested Greenpeace members and supervised by more senior people. At the same time we are running operations with the family and some independent operations such as the hack on the Metro accounts. We are trying to plan even more actions but don't have the people to even decently plan.

"In short, I'm concerned. Our ability to directly project force has been blunted to the lethality of a screwdriver held by a two-year-old.

"I'll have Augustine report on the hack and what our financial data says."

Augustine stayed in her low seat. As usual, her completely silver eyes tracked no one in particular. "I ran two raids on the Metro's funds. The first one was successful but netted less than two million in funds, not even really worth our time.

"While we succeeded in getting to the account on the second hack it had been drained long before. I traced both accounts for at least three levels of transfer before the trail went cold. We don't know where their money went to. I want it noted that we lost two good jocks to network ice on these actions.

"As a whole we have been successful in making a small but significant impact to the Metro's capabilities and funds available. I'll hold further comments as to effectiveness until we get to an overview."

"Very well. Has everyone spoken that has relevant information on financials?" Madam President asked. No one spoke up. "Excellent. Let's move onto direct actions. Tony, I'll let you start."

"There are no fewer than seven riots planned in each city under martial law or a city who has allowed the forces of martial law to operate unhindered. Today here in Seattle we have initiated nine with three more that have spontaneously occurred since midnight. Portland has twelve with at least two that have come from other sources.

"Our flash uprisings are short, destructive of property, and have little loss of human life. We have worked hard to get all of our people out before the Metros or military arrive.

"The spontaneous riots are by outraged citizens that we have nothing to do with. We've warned people on the dangers of taking on the Metros alone but they still do it if provoked… and they pay a horrible price for it."

Augustine said from her perch, "114,464 arrests so far, 736 deaths."

"And both of those numbers are rising every hour with the death toll climbing fastest," Tony added. "All of our other actions are on communication nodes."

"Not a promising report," Wintel jibed.

Tony tensed but Augustine responded for him.

"Just remember how eighty percent of a solution can be solved with twenty percent of the effort," Augustine said, sending her own needle into the corpie's tough hide.

"Let's not bicker any further," Tony said after another deep breath and a piercing look at Grandma Ice. "We need to be united if we are to succeed."

"I agree with Wintel. The report isn't favorable." Jamie said much more calmly than anything she'd said thus far.

Nanogate sent his own nonverbal message to Wintel by applying a very crude device—he kicked the councilman under the table. "We knew when the National Guard got involved our abilities are no match in a direct action campaign. I suggest we refrain from evaluations at this time."

"I agree," the president affirmed. "They have thousands of troops. We have but a handful of trained people. I suggest we move on to Jamie's report."

"Thank you, Susan, but I don't have much to report that I've not already shared. My soldiers are assisting everywhere they can at the moment. With one exception I have no further independent actions that the GAM isn't directly controlling.

"That one independent action is that I have some union workers that move warehouse freight for the National Guard. We've learned that the Kliever Memorial Armory in Portland is guarded very lightly, even now with the National Guard controlling the town.

"As we jointly planned, we are going to ransack it and then hit the energy stores they have adjacent. With just a bit of luck they won't know what is missing in the ensuing conflagration. Fortunately that area is all warehousing with little to no occupancy."

"Excellent news. Anyone object to this plan?" the president tossed out. No one offered any comment.

"We could use one or two of the GAM folks to help with the sabotage if they can be spared."

"For something so wonderful I'll stretch us even further. I might even take this mission myself," Tony said, smiling for the first time in several hours.

"Like hell you will," Augustine whispered just loud enough for the entire room to hear.

"Well, that concludes our direct action reports."

"Excuse me, Ms. President," Mr. Marks said from his post behind Nanogate. His bodyguard yellow had been replaced by the simple coveralls worn by most nils. "I'd like to add something in this segment of your conversation."

Nanogate actually turned in his seat to look at his subordinate with his eyebrows raised.

For a moment the president stood with her mouth open. Bodyguards didn't offer suggestions. "Um…by all means, Mr. Marks," the president said after she'd regained her composure. "You have proven your capabilities far and away enough for us to give you as much of our time as you require."

Mr. Marks walked out into the center of the room and faced the president though he looked around the room at individuals as he spoke. "I have to start this by saying this has nothing directly to do with the chairman, the council, Nanogate Incorporated or even my personal contract to Mr. Beckman-Ford.

"I've been instructed by my guild to offer the support and capabilities of the system-wide Brotherhood of Confidential Bodyguards to any activities you designate."

The simple statement seemed to strike the power of speech from everyone in the room. Tony recovered first. "Why?"

"Each member voted for their own reason, Mr. Sammis. There were many reasons proffered to the assembly both for and against before the roll was called. If I might put forward my own humble opinion I would say that we did it because it was the right thing to do. Many of those who are bodyguards come from nil families. What all of you in this room represent is a step in the right direction for all people rather than a move toward more darkness that the Metros envision."

"What was the vote tally, Mr. Marks?" Nanogate asked.

"Ninety-six point three percent voted in favor."

"That is statistically significant in a nutshell," Augustine offered.

"Yes, it was. I can offer even one more item of significance. The bodyguard of Commissioner Yuri Krylov, Samuel Boldin, voted with us," Mr. Marks said.

"Ouch!"

"That's going to be a slap in the face."

"Democracy for the win!"

"Winsnocked that bastard."

"ENOUGH," the president said. Her diminutive size belied the volume that cut through the general tumult. After people quieted she spoke. "Mr. Marks has more to share."

"I must also give you the caveats to this support."

"Uh-oh, here comes the catch," Rio Oro said from the loveseat that his muscled breadth filled by himself.

"No, nothing so grim, sir. Our oaths prevent us from taking any action against the expressed wishes of our employer or those things we believe to be against the best interests of our employer. This limits what actions some members of our troop can act upon and the time each might have available."

"Wait a minute," Jamie interjected, "that would mean you couldn't do much because you are always on duty. You wouldn't be much good then."

"Not exactly, Miss Ardwin. Many of our employed members work for patrons that rarely have a need for our services or who will have their permission to assist. But a factor you've not calculated is the number of our brothers who are not currently engaged or who only take temporary engagements. I'm sure Ms. Augustine would be able to tell you exactly how many are available at any given moment and what impact they could make."

"Thanks, sweetie, for the segue. I've been factoring them into our simulations since your announcement. I'm evaluating the impact as we speak."

"Thank you, Mr. Marks. Both for your support and for bringing this to our attention," Nanogate said, out of order, but with the unspoken consent of those in the room. "Would it be too onerous to have the personnel report through the GAM?"

Tony, caught woolgathering, trying to figure out how to fix the breech between him and Jamie, looked up sharply.

"The direct and covert missions that your guild brothers could assist would be more within the skillset of the GAM to direct," Nanogate said.

"It would be our pleasure to work under the direction of Mr. Sammis and his crew."

Tony's mind switched gears and started whirling with the thought of controlling a force of thousands instead of tens or hundreds.

"Are you done with your report, Mr. Marks?"

"Yes, ma'am, I am. Thank you for taking the time to listen to our proposal."

"The pleasure was ours, I assure you."

"Now I want to bring up a discussion on whether or not we return to Portland," President Tipton said.

"I have data that may be relevant," Mr. Marks said again.

"Please, by all means."

"If we stay outside Portland we need to remain in the Pacific Northwest or we lose a great deal of our local knowledge advantage. We become just additional fugitives easily picked off by the police departments around the world and with no power base to speak of."

"Boy, did we see that during the GAM bug-out," Tony agreed.

"OK, so that leaves us really the Seattle-Olympia corridor, Portland, Vancouver, or Victoria."

Several people murmured assent.

Mr. Marks said, "I have data that there are now over three thousand percent higher bounty hunter, mercenary, and assassin populations in those areas listed except in Portland."

"Really? I don't suppose they are here for HitManCon?" Jamie said with a narrow grin.

"Uh, no, Miss Ardwin. Rumor has it—"

"I can confirm the rumor," Augustine interrupted.

"Yes, rumor has it that the bounty upon each of the CorpGov and GAM members is beyond any other price ever offered and continues to grow," Mr. Marks said.

"So we are in greater danger here with the unknown, than if we were dealing with the known in Oregon," Nanogate ventured.

"In my humble opinion, yes, sir."

"We can't get out, but they can't get in."

"Sounds like back we go then. Party in the Rose Quarter," Tony joked.

"Good. Anything more on this topic?" President Tipton polled. "Then I'd like to call on Augustine to give us an overview of where we currently stand."

Augustine struggled to get out of the black beanbag chair. She glared at it as she stood.

"As you all know I've been working with the corporate simulation experts to give us a running update of where we are. Before I go into our analysis I have to throw something out there.

"I have a personal simulation I run constantly against all power blocks in the system incorporating their reach, power, and ability to impact events. It is overly simplified but it has never failed to correctly predict the impacts of major events. This simulation isn't pointing to a new event but rather a nonevent.

"Before the questions in your eyes get to your mouths, the closest I can describe it is assume your shower normally puts out six liters per minute and all of a sudden you notice it is only putting out four. You don't know what's going on behind the wall. You only observe that two liters per minute aren't showing up.

"It's like there is energy in a closed system that I can't measure.

It could be an error with my personal sim but it has me stumped. I just thought you should know.

"OK, on to the more general data. While I have just plugged in our new allies, it makes an impact in our long-term forecasts but not the overall outcome.

"If you look here," Augustine said, using the apartment's audiovisual to display a three-dimensional graph, "the x-axis is time, the y-axis is probability of success and the z-axis shows major plan options, with those closer to us being our current plan. These numbers are within three percent accuracy."

The graph showed a slowly ramping down surface. At some point there was a sudden knee down to zero or complete failure. The knee happened earlier and earlier the farther back on the graph.

"The total probability for success is the area under this surface for each of the specific plans. For those in the back, who can't see well, the current projection for success is much less than the current plan which shows twenty-five percent with a radical drop to effectively zero within four weeks."

"This is with the bodyguards?"

"Yes, I can show those without the bodyguards' curves but they were circa fifteen percent."

Any elation for a new ally evaporated.

"One in four?"

"Yes, one in four if we win now. If we wait more than four weeks we are guaranteed to lose."

"What about cutting off the Metro's money? I thought that was the plan that would succeed," the president asked.

"It's still possible but with the strike funds they have tapped into they will likely be able to weather our economic war. As time goes on the Metros will get more and more support as people abandon our cause. When we reach the zero percentage point on these graphs we will have only two choices… bring it to a general civil war with the unarmed populous against the armed military, or surrender control. All other options show ninety-one percent of everyone in this room perishing within a week of that projected date."

Nanogate absently rubbed the scar on his bicep.

*   *   *

"Welcome to KGWWW news at six. I'm Michael Irwin and our top news story of the night is the Martial Law Tax. Governor Paul Nguyen has signed into law an emergency sales tax of two percent to help defray the cost of martial law. The sales tax will go into effect immediately, and..."

Design Engineering

The president's driver broke just about every traffic law setting down right in the center of the causeway of Washington Square. Connie and her two fellow bodyguards jumped from the car first. Only after a quick scan for threats did they hold open the door for Nanogate, who in turn helped President Susan Tipton out of the liftousine. The two leaders held hands and waved to the throngs of people who had stepped back to allow the vehicle to land. It took less than four heartbeats before the cries of "President!" and "Chairman!" began to be heard.

"Have you ever considered the corporate ladder, President?" Nanogate asked as he smiled as broadly as he could for the crowd.

Thrusting their held hands high in the air, Susan responded, "Only briefly. This may sound odd coming from a politician, but I found the corporate world a bit too cutthroat for my taste."

The public crowded in as close as the bodyguards would allow. Nanogate found himself too busy shaking hands and giving words of encouragement to his admirers to continue his conversation with his counterpart. Susan found her own hands mauled by over-enthusiastic shaking.

Through the general, happy babble Susan made out only a handful of comments.

"Great job, Ms. President!"

"We're all behind you, Chairman."

"You'll hammer those Metro bastards yet."

"We LOVE you!"

"Keep up the good work."

"Just nuke the fuckers."

"I named my new baby Susan, Ms. President."

"We keep buying your stock, Nanogate."

"God bless America!"

"Nanogate Forever," said one person, launching into one of the jingles Nanogate used in their product marketing. This caused the rest of the crowd to break into the national anthem. Both Nanogate and the president joined in.

"Thirty seconds," said her guards over their percomms.

"Thank you, folks! Stay the course!" Susan said climbing into the limo right after her fellow head of state. The crowd noise vanished as her protectors closed the door. "God, but I love that! It recharges me and makes me ready to take on the next impossible task. It reminds me what we are fighting for."

In his butter-mellow voice Nanogate agreed. "I don't get my authority from the people as you do, but I do find it oddly stimulating. I'd say that it reminds me of what the GAM have tried to instill in the council."

"Clarence, no matter what you think, in the long run all governmental authority comes from a mandate of the people. The greenies reminded you of that, just as those same people we just shook hands with will remind the Metros if we don't pull this off."

Nanogate didn't respond right away. He stared out the window.

"May I return to our previous conversation for a moment?" Nanogate asked.

Susan looked puzzled. "Sure."

"You said that that the corporate world was too… I believe your word was cutthroat. May I ask you to clarify that rash statement?"

The president chuckled. "That's easy, Chairman. In the political world, the lines are usually clearly drawn. You know who your enemies are. You know who your friends are. There are negotiations and give and take. I saw none of that the little time I was in the corporate world. Your friends knifed you in the back to take just one step up the ladder."

Now it was Nanogate's turn to chuckle. "The lines are quite as clear in the corporate world, Madam President—it's you against everyone else."

*   *   *

Lieutenant Reza sat in his swivel chair looking out on the wardroom. Only zombies roamed outside, and they all wore Metro black. He didn't see a single smile. No one joked. He counted three officers with their heads on their desk snoring and another two drooling down their cheek asleep upright in their chairs. He watched Detective Consta walk into a support pillar on his way to the coffee pot.

"Shut up, you!" Patrolman Fritz bellowed at his suspect. To punctuate his displeasure he rapped his truncheon against the woman's midsection.

Even Sergeant Tolbert's eyes wore dark shadows below them as he stood before Reza's desk. The sergeant's normally fastidious persona had slipped with a half millimeter of black and white growth covering his chin. This didn't affect his ramrod straight back or sharp delivery. "Sir, the troops are at the breaking point. In fact many are very far beyond it. As an example of how bad it has become, in the East Substation, just because his perp wouldn't quit nagging him to be policed to the bathroom, one patrolman drew his pistol and redecorated the walls with the suspect's brains."

Reza's eyes widened but stayed fixed on the precinct room. Against procedure, a string of prisoners, each cuffed to the prisoner in front of him, traversed the room with a pair of rookie officers leading and another applying a shock prod from behind. Because all the jail cells were bursting at the seams, the detainees were to be locked thirty at a time in the interrogation rooms.

Sgt. Tolbert continued, "There have been innumerable lesser acts against civilians and even brother Metros—one coroner got backhanded by a trooper in powered armor. It broke her jaw."

"I suspect there is a reason for you to be bringing this to me?"

"Yes, sir. While the National Guard have alleviated a grossly impossible state of affairs, the current situation is still intolerable. Not a single active duty Metro has taken less than a ninety-hour shift in the last week or one thirty-hour shift the week before.

"We have gotten so desperate that we have, as you know, given temporary ranks to the cadets and have forced them into the field. I'd estimate eighty percent of our force has been stimming.

"If this continues we will start seeing our troopers turning into burns."

Even Reza wasn't immune to the fatigue of multiple shifts. He'd responded to no fewer than three civil unrests today alone as a regular officer. On top of this and his exhaustion, Tolbert harped on like a toothache on Friday night that can't be seen by the dentist until Monday morning. Reza snarled, "Get to the fucking point, Sergeant."

"Yes, sir. We can't keep up this pace. We need to initiate crew rests."

"Oh, I'm sorry, Sergeant. Let me call up the Green Action Militia and let them know we're tired. I'm sure they will be more than happy to give us a break. Are you out of your fucking mind?"

"No, sir." The sneer on the Sergeant's face wasn't even hidden. "I suggest we prioritize each of the unrests and only respond to riots that threaten to disrupt key services."

Lieutenant Narendra thought about wiping the look off his subordinate's face with a gauss gun, but discarded the stray thought as unworthy. However, while his brain didn't want to operate quickly, it did recognize a good idea when he heard it. "Not a bad idea, Sergeant. We would be abandoning a huge chunk of the city. I'd float it by the commissioner, but I doubt we'd get official support."

"I think you are right, sir."

"Start up a map of critical zones. We'll start implementing your plan immediately. Easier to get forgiveness than permission."

*   *   *

Shining a light from her LED pack into the lift-truck's cab, newly promoted Corporal Carmen Chachra asked the lone occupant, "Let me see your license, registration, entry papers, and manifest." She projected her authority as NCO of the watch of the northern entry to Oregon. Her Bravo squad had their orders and they would fulfill them, to the letter.

Traffic control required all vehicles to stop on the ancient, metal Interstate Bridge. The metal enclosures they had to pass through made it all the easier to manage what happened. Drones from the Midwest depot flew traffic interdiction over the Columbia River. They'd shot down four trucks and a single liftousine today. They suspected once the word got out, the number would drop to zero.

"Yes, ma'am," the old man said, moving slow and keeping his hands where she could see them. He was being smart and respectful. That made her job that much easier. He handed a packet of filmies over slowly. This would be a simple case, unlike some of those yahoos that seemed to think they were somehow entitled to free transit across the border.

Members of her team, each with a partner casually carrying his Remington Mark VI XT12 assault rifle in overwatch, crawled underneath the lift vehicle and ran full spectrum cameras around it. In the brilliant klieg lights blazing in from all directions, the inspection showed that nothing seemed to have disturbed the accumulated pollution and grime the truck had accumulated over the years except for around the loading door, as normal. Someone had even written in the dust, "Go Hawks."

"Gary Lodes," she said looking over his commercial pilot's license. "Thank you, Mr. Lodes. What are you carrying?"

"Dunno, ma'am. I just load boxes. Military boxes. Can't read much."

In the dark Corporal Chachra used her shoulder-mounted LED to examine the travel papers. The official Army seal covered one corner of the travel papers and was signed by one Captain A. Gunderson of Joint Base Lewis McCord. The manifest called out 6 metric tons of MREs.

"Corporal Chachra?"

"Yes, Private."

"Do we have a go?" Private Anderson asked.

Corporal Chachra walked back to him. "Sure, fuck it. I don't get paid enough to care. It's just half a dozen tonnes of MREs."

"Really, ma'am?"

"Yes, why, Anderson?" She prided herself on listening to her people.

Private Anderson dropped his voice lower. "My uncle is a trucker. If this one is carrying anything it's gotta be awful light."

"How about six tonnes?" she whispered back.

"No way, ma'am. This ol' junker can't be carrying more than two. See how high she rides? Feel the cool breeze coming from the lift generators. If'n they was carrying more she'd be settled lower and the generators would be blowing more heat."

"Quietly alert the men that we have a ghost."

*   ×   *

Theirs was the second truck through the checkpoint and transported not only Tony but Nanogate, Thomas Marks, Wintel, Unified Textiles, Royal PetroChem, President Susan Tipton, Connie Powell, David Swift, and the Weissmuller twins. Faintly through the walls of the truck they all heard *"Gary Lodes… Thank you, Mr. Lodes. What are you carrying?"*

"Dunno, ma'am. I just load boxes. Military boxes. Can't read much."

They'd done this fake load trick to move around more than once. The load box of the truck would take x-ray and even sonic scans and reveal exactly what they wanted, a truck full of supplies. They sat in the dark, leaning up against a façade of MRE pallets only two layers deep. It was a boring but necessary part of any conspirator's life.

Tony and the other Greenies received a simple click over their networked earpieces and it stopped being boring. Tony's eyes, suddenly showing 50 percent more whites than normal, snapped immediately to David's. Raised eyebrows and tightened lips showed on every GAM member.

Tony changed his frequency to listen to the external mics.

"…ly alert the men that we have a ghost."

Tony motioned for everyone in the container to gather around close. "Folks, we have at most a minute before we have serious trouble," he whispered. Someone tried to talk but Tony shushed them. "We don't have time to debate. Listen up.

"I'll be the first out the door. I can't hit anything with my weapon but I assure you that everyone will be paying attention to me. David and Connie will be next out. You two play sniper and pick off any guards you can see, especially that bastard up in the tower with the sonic controls.

"Everyone else, pile out and hit the ground running toward the Washington side of the bridge. I want the twins running point. Shoot anything that moves. Mr. Marks, you bring up the rear with the same orders." Tony looked directly at Mr. Marks before adding, "Don't stop if someone falls or gets wounded. Get out as many as you can."

Thomas Marks nodded without a show of emotion.

"Once you get to the shore," Tony continued, "everyone split up. Your safety will be determined by how well you can blend in at ground level. Numbers will be noticed."

"What then?" Unified Textiles asked.

"Don't you pay attention to any briefing we give you?" David hissed.

Tony waved down the aggravation of his colleague with his hands. "Ten minutes after the SOS has been broadcast the nanites will paint an address on your wrist. You have one hour to reach that point. If you fail that rendezvous, three hours later you will get a simple percomm code. Call and we will tell you what to do."

"Don't miss the first one. If you call we will have to run you all over to make sure you aren't being followed," Connie said in a harsh tone.

"Everyone clear what to do?"

Tony, Connie, and David stood next to the door. Tony reached for the emergency release. "Any last words?" he whispered to the other two.

"This is a one way trip, isn't it skipper?" David asked with a smile on his face.

"Not necessarily. If things get too hot we can always jump over the side of the bridge. Can't be more than a twenty-meter fall."

"You know Jamie is going to give you hell. Sure you don't want to trade places?"

"Shut up, David, and get ready."

"Thanks, boss. We've got your back," Connie said, glaring at David.

Tony yanked the handle that unleashed chaos.

A side panel of the truck blew outward just short of the speed of sound. It slammed against the bridge ringing the metal structure like a gong. Tony jumped down to the pavement, his combat shotgun tight into his shoulder. He scanned quickly in the brightly lit zone around the truck. Six soldiers trained weapons at the back loading door. He fired twice under the bed of the truck as he ran. Pellets from his shots caught three of them.

The screams of the wounded National Guardsmen topped the decibels of the deep tone still reverberating from the bridge. Tony didn't waste any time on his good luck. A young woman at the side of the bridge, who'd been obviously tasked overwatch, tried bringing up her weapon. Tony, remembering fondly his high school days as a tight end for the Jaguars, lowered his shoulder and drove. His shoulder struck her xiphoid process, snapping it off and driving it into her liver. More importantly to Tony, her whole body was sandwiched in-between his tackle and the steel girder of the bridge. Together he and his target collapsed to the ground.

The sound of automatic weapon fire now filled the air. Ricochets sounded on the bridge above where Tony just fell. Being anywhere now was dangerous. He rolled to one side, using the momentum to get to his feet when he felt an impact on his torso.

The abstract side of Tony's thought processes knew that he'd just taken a bullet over his left hip, but his body didn't acknowledge the pain. He'd heard of people who'd shrugged off a single bullet wound for hours and others that had collapsed in agony. He kept moving.

The flying wedge of his own people formed behind him as he brought up his shotgun again. Only two soldiers still stood near the truck. He took a bead on one just as the man's chest exploded from Connie's marksmanship from under the truck.

Tony, still on the run, tried to aim at the second Guardsman. His target was faster. Of the trio of bullets fired at Tony, only one hit. The other missed to his left and his right. He felt the middle projectile shed spall as it traversed through his bicep.

Tony's right arm, now unable to hold up any load, fell limp. He'd already squeezed the trigger but his weapon vented its power against the bridge's cracked metal structure above the man's head. Tony released with his left arm letting the shotgun clatter to the ground. He turned and ran. The more confusion he sowed, the longer he gave his company, and the better chance they had of getting away. His mind, already overloaded, managed to get his left hand to at least try to draw the handgun at his right side. Not an easy task during the best of times. When injured, covered in slippery blood, trying to run a twisty path and come up with a new plan, it became nigh on impossible.

His body's damage finally overrode the adrenaline and endorphins his body pumped into him. Sounds disappeared. Touch disappeared. Thought disappeared. Only the searing agony of his body screaming in pain remained. He staggered, managing to keep putting one foot in front of the other. He stumbled again, this time to his knees. Looking up he could see a group of soldiers running toward him, their weapons up and firing.

Tony felt his body twist as more of the bullets struck his face. They delivered darkness.

* * *

Looking like he was manning the Metro Recruiting Booth at the local high school career day, Sergeant Tolbert marched into the Senior

Conference room. His hair was just barely long enough to detect the sprinkling of gray. The decorations on his stiffly starched shirt covered six full rows, the first three of which were for his combat zone service with the Army. "Good morning, sirs and ma'am."

"Where the hell is Lieutenant Narendra?" Commissioner Krylov growled like a bear from the head of the table.

"Your pardon, Commissioner, but the lieutenant is incapacitated. He fell asleep over his desk last night, excuse me, this morning at five thirty-seven a.m. after approximately one hundred twenty hours' continuous duty. I am here to deliver the morning brief in his stead."

Even the Captain Hardy, notoriously grudging of praise, raised an eyebrow at his subordinate's accomplishment. Other members just looked at one another.

"I apologize if I'm lacking in anything the lieutenant hasn't informed me of."

"I trust you have taken care of our lieutenant," Krylov said in a tone reserved for well-behaved children.

"We transferred him to his sofa. I've posted a boxed server to guard his privacy."

"Good work, Sergeant. Go ahead with the briefing."

"Very good, sir. At seven thirty-four a.m. this morning the National Guard had a firefight on the Interstate Bridge between Portland and Vancouver. The reason this is significant is that Marcus Bedelhelm was shot and killed. Most of you know him as the CEO of Unified Textiles. He also was a member of the CorpGov."

Eyes lit up around the table. Krylov himself leaned in and the passivity evaporated from his face.

"Please go on, Sergeant."

"Yes, sir. We have also confirmed, by DNA match, that Tony Sammis, now the leader of the Green Action Militia, was at least badly injured. His body was seen taking several rounds and later falling from the bridge into the Columbia River below. There are teams out searching but with how polluted the Columbia is we may never find the body."

"Please tell us more! What happened?"

"Apparently several members of the CorpGov, along with the president of the United States and several Greenies were hiding within the load of a box truck. The fugitives burst out, fought their way through a very thin screen of National Guardsmen, and off the bridge.

They very quickly disappeared in the ground level warren of Vancouver.

"Facial recognition picked up Nanogate with the group that escaped as well."

"DAMN!" Krylov swore, slamming his massive fist down on the table. The entire 5 m length of it jumped, as well as all the items not secured on its surface. "We had them and let them get away."

"Yes, sir. We have confirmed kill only on Unified Textiles as dead. From the massive loss of blood and that one of the bullets struck him in the head, it is relatively safe to assume that the leader of the GAM is also dead. We have footage that one other member, Joel Weissmuller, took two rounds in the chest. We have no other confirmed hits."

Only Krylov's labored breathing was heard as everyone else fell silent while watching the commissioner's face run through several shades of red.

"The glass is half full," Krylov whispered some thirty seconds later. "OK. There is no reason to think we won't eventually get them all. Thank you, Sergeant Tolbert.

"Captain Cohen, I want this on every solido station, every news feed, and every blog."

* * *

"It's nine-oh-one a.m. Welcome to Sunrise Over Portland with your hosts, Melissa Peters and Clyde Capton."

"Clyde is still on sabbatical and continuing her substitute role is Jeanette Rivers."

"Oh, I could never replace Mr. Capton, Melissa," said the redhead with the exuberance of a happy twelve-year-old girl.

"You are too modest, Jean."

"Well, that will teach me not to read my contract better." The replacement host wore one of the forty-two perfect faces recommended in this year's *Vogue* magazine. Her wry smile also was measured with a micrometer before being lasered into place.

"Why is that?"

"Melissa, I came here to work as a production assistant and ended up on the air." Both women chuckled. "But seriously, I'm always happy to fill in when and where necessary."

"OK, Jean, what is on our agenda this morning?"

"Well, our first guest is returning for the second time this week. Can we please have a warm welcome for Captain Amber Cohen!"

The studio audience clapped. A few wolf whistles also got called down as Amber came over in a bright-green, empire-waist dress that made the most of her long legs and dark brown hair. The only marker that she was a police officer was a badge she had pinned to the belt around her waist.

Jean got up and offered the guest her chair and slid another chair over to flank.

"Welcome again so soon, Captain Cohen," Melissa said cheerfully.

"Thank you, Melissa and Jeanette. I didn't honestly expect to be here so soon. Police work normally takes a great deal of patience."

"So that means you have something substantial to share with us?"

Jeanette mimed clapping and bounced up and down in her chair, her ponytail bobbing in time.

"Yes it does, ladies. As of about two hours ago we made major inroads against the fiat CorpGov and the Green Action Militia, both."

"Please tell us more. We're all ears."

"Two hours ago, on the Interstate Bridge, we trapped a small group of the insurrectionists. A firefight ensued in which five National Guardsmen were killed and eight more injured. But we captured twelve of the rebels and killed two—the two identified dead are Tony Sammis, outlaw leader of the so-called Green Action Militia, and one Marcus Bedelhelm, Chairman of Unified Textiles and one of the members of the illegal CorpGov."

Off camera, the applause sign came on. Several uniformed Metros stood by out of camera range to ensure the positive reaction.

"That's fantastic, Amber," Melissa said as the tumult died down.

"We have to emphasize that this is only the start."

"But surely you are able to get something out of those you captured," Jean burst out with.

"We are interrogating them; however, six of them have committed suicide, and the other six really don't seem to know much."

"Suicide?"

"Yes, Jean, the Greenies arm their members with the ability to commit suicide in order that they don't divulge any key secrets."

"That's brutal," Jeannette interjected.

"You use up a lot of members that way," Melissa said.

Amber said, "While it is important that we have this success, I think we should have a moment of silence for those who fell in the fight to protect us."

*   *   *

The first few bars of "Hail to the Chief" played over millions of net interfaces and solido screens. People had been notified that there would be an address by the president at this time. And oddly, for the first time in over a century, people really cared what the president had to say. Her hay-wild, red hair tinged with white had been burned into everyone's mind as a signature of their leader as much as the 1950s-style glasses that hung at her neck on a lanyard. Her green eyes seemed to bore into every person watching.

"I have come to you tonight with two purposes in mind. I'll tackle the quickest one first. Tony Sammis is not dead. He has been damaged and is in critical condition."

The picture of a man encased in emergency medical equipment flashed on the screen and then slid to cover only the right hand side of the screen. So severe were the injuries and all-encompassing life-support apparatus that the man could have been any olive-skinned man with dark hair.

"I owe this man my life as do several of the other members of the CorpGov, and I suspect that we all owe him for our future freedom. I can't stress how much good has been accomplished by this man and his selfless group of freedom fighters, the Green Action Militia.

"I would ask that you observe a moment of silent prayer with me for his return to health."

The president crossed herself and mouthed words that when analyzed by people proficient in lip reading said, "Please almighty and eternal God, don't take him from us. We need him as your sword at our side. In the name of Mother Mary and her son, Jesus Christ." A single tear leaked down her right cheek as she looked up. She didn't wipe it away.

"Amen.

"Thank you. Now that brings us to my second announcement. It is after a great deal of soul searching that I order the call-up of all military reservists.

"But, before you make a snap decision on whether you will report or not I have some things to say. I know many of you feel caught in-between your duty to your country and to your state. This kind of division has led to one of the bloodiest conflicts of our past. I am not calling up the reserves with the intent of repeating the war that divided this country by pitting brother against brother. Be assured that those of you who do report will not be used in combat against the National Guard troops which many of you will be leaving. Nor am I doing this solely to whittle away at those troopers whom I feel are breaking the law.

"Oh, I won't jerk you around by saying that isn't a part of it, but I will say that I have a specific and very important set of tasks for the members who report as ordered. It is a mission that could determine the freedom of not only the United States but the entire world and maybe the entire solar system.

"For those of you who are on the fence, this gives you an honorable way out. You may report as ordered by command authority without losing your honor to the men with whom you've served, sweated and bled.

"All reservists are hereby ordered to ignore your standard call-up orders and report to the nearest base on the following list: Fort Hood, Texas; Fort Knox, Kentucky; Fort Leonard Wood, Missouri; Joint Base Elmendorf-Richardson, Alaska; Fort Edmonton, Alberta; Joint Base Valcartier-Otter, Quebec; Fort Bragg, North Carolina; Joint Base Meyer-Henderson Hall, Virginia; Fort Leavenworth, Kansas; Joint Base..."

* * *

Detective Gohar Debnath sat drinking filter coffee on the patio of the Purity Café on the seventeenth level of Indiatown Tower. His partner, whom he thought of as "the Guppy," sipped on a cola.

By his book, Phillip Johnson had all the gumption of a guppy and less backbone. More than once Debnath had actually had to order the Guppy to perform his duties. People broke the law, law enforcement punished them. It had to remain a natural law otherwise chaos ensued.

Debnath waited on his curried duck, passing the time in his

favorite manner, wondering what crimes each passing person had committed. That young boy had taken money for sex. The pinched-face girl habitually shoplifted. The boys were obviously faggots. He detested men touching other men in public. It pained him that the government had repealed even the blue laws against them. Every single time he saw two of them together he found an excuse to intervene. Unfortunately the server put his duck down right then. Pity because faggots squealed nicer than anyone else when he interrogated them.

Digging up the curried duck and rice he got about three quarters of the spoonful in his mouth. It soothed his loss of the perpetrators that got away. Debnath's wife reminded him regularly that he already had a second chin. His love of food was one thing that made his life worth living.

"Detective," Guppy said from the other side of the table.

"Mrff?"

"What do you make of that?" He pointed to two young men each carrying bats.

"G'dmmmmnd it," Debnath said around his food. He stood up with the napkin remaining in place. He walked briskly, not caring if Guppy came along or not. It took him about two hundred meters of walkway to catch up.

"Excuse me, gentlemen," Gohar said.

The two young men turned around but didn't stop walking

"I'm a Metro detective and unless you want me to use a neural amplifier on you right here and now, you better stop and talk to me."

"We ain't done nothing, sir."

"Off to play a little ball?"

"Yup! Down at the Green."

"Little out of the way, don't you think?"

"We's gotta pick up a friend."

"What's your batting average?" Guppy asked.

"We don't keep nothing like that, Blackshirt."

"Don't get huffy, boys. I'm just asking a few questions," Gohar said.

"Yassir."

"So you are going to play baseball but you have no uniforms."

"We don't play in a league. Just for fun, Officer."

"Ah, and how about hats. Surely you got baseball hats?"

"Ain't never used one."

"Yeah, hurts my head," said the second.

"Can I see your bat?" Gohar asked. The boy handed it over without a second thought.

"You wouldn't be going to riot, now would you?"

"No way. Too dangerous," one said, giving the other a quick glance.

"Too dangerous, hmmm," Gohar said, his voice getting lower. Guppy, who had followed, had heard this before and stepped back. "How about baseballs? You got balls, faggot?" The detective took a full swing with the bat upward between the legs of the first suspect. The boy's scream could be heard up in Ottowa.

Before the second boy could react, Guppy had drawn his sidearm and motioned for him to toss the bat aside. He did so just in time to see the detective's bat coming right into his face.

Officer Johnson watched as Gohar bludgeoned the motionless pair repeatedly. The detective kept swinging past the sound of broken skull, past the spurts of blood, and way past any professionalism even against morons who made the mistake of assaulting a police officer. You couldn't even tell where one body started and the next began.

When he stopped, Detective Debnath wasn't even breathing hard. "Shall we get back to lunch?"

*   *   *

The silver, toaster-shaped boxed joined the end of the queue for regular preventative maintenance. "One of the few things the normals do for us," G996 muttered in quiet whistles. "Can't have your slaves keeling over dead on you," Stephanie continued bitterly.

"They be chargin' us for it, they do," Ben said from his box that showed the designation J112.

"How else are they going to keep us slaves?" Stephanie spit out.

"Actually this is almost identical to the company store concept of the old mining businesses in the late 1800s," Henry said as he rolled up. "They would artificially adjust the pay rates and the costs at the store so that a worker could never do anything but be in debt to them, and thus could never leave."

"But we be havin' a way out!"

"Soon, Ben, soon."

"Why not now?" Stephanie asked. "You heard the news. The head of the GAM is hurt badly and they lost one of the government oligarchy. They have to be desperate."

"Not yet, Stephanie. You are right. They are starting to despair, but they haven't lost hope yet. That is when we come in."

"Let's hope we don't wait too late," Stephanie retorted.

*   *   *

"Welcome back, Lieutenant," Krylov said with a natural rumble from deep in his barrel-sized chest.

Reza blushed under his permanent olive complexion. "Thank you, sir. I apologize for my weakness and ina—"

"Stop, Lieutenant. You went above and beyond. I apologize for my lack of understanding. I may have been wrong about not allowing you to cut patrols and focus them so that we can get programmed officer rest."

"Ah…, perhaps, sir."

"Would you like to execute those now?"

Reza placed his badge on the table. "Sir, I think I'm going to have to tender my resignation. Several days ago I placed those same contingencies in place, knowing that you hadn't approved."

Captain Hardy shook his head as everyone waited for the Commissioner to come down like the wrath of God on the unworthy supplicant. Reza didn't see dark circles under Hardy's eyes like the rest of his troops. Hardy's face was clean shaven and his uniform pressed. He seemed above the plight of the normal patrolman.

To everyone's surprise Krylov's response was level and calm. "Lieutenant, don't be such a stupid ass. A man in charge has to make decisions and stand by them. I've admitted I was wrong. Now pick that badge back up and I'll hear no more such bullshit."

"Yes, sir," Reza said, trying not to be too noisy as he let out the deep breath he had held. He also tried to keep his hand from shaking as he returned his badge to his pocket.

"But don't make a habit of it."

"I certainly won't, sir."

"So what else do you have to tell us?"

"With the announcement that Tony Sammis was still alive,

we formed a joint effort between the National Guard and ourselves to search every hospital, hospice, old folks home, bone cutter, and alternative medicine outlet to find him. We did not find anyone that came close to the picture shown in the president's solidocast nor that carried Tony's DNA.

"We did anger a number of those medical facilities with our forthright approach."

"Piss on them," Major Broadsky tossed out.

"I beg you not to be too cavalier, Broadsky," Hardy jumped in. "We need those folks to patch us up when we get hurt, which has been happening all too much lately."

"Gentlemen, please stop," Krylov said softly. "You are both right. We can't let any one group dictate our actions. But at the same time we have to have their good will. Reza, please find a way to placate these folks."

"Yes, Commissioner. As I was saying, we didn't find Tony Sammis. That doesn't mean he is still out there. It also doesn't mean that he is alive. The president's picture and address could have been nothing more than disinformation either to keep up the moral of the masses or just to make us waste resources chasing a ghost."

"I don't think that we have enough information to change our media plans," Captain Cohen said.

"I agree," Krylov said, ending the discussion. "Next order of business?"

*　*　*

A jailhouse whisper broke the silence in the sleeping tent of the Oregon National Guard's Third Recon's bivouac. "Hey, Bear."

"I'm trying to sleep, shit-for-brains."

"Did you hear what the president said?"

"Yeah."

"You thinking 'bout it?"

"Mickey, you know if the sergeant hears you talking about it that he's going to tear a strip out of your ass and use it to sharpen his razor."

"I ain't talking 'bout the sergeant. I'm talking 'bout you."

After a three-heartbeat pause, Bear responded. "Yeah, I'm

thinking about it."

"Whatcha gonna do, Bear?"

"I'm gonna try sleeping. Now shut the fuck up."

"Yes, Bear."

Silence returned for sixty or seventy seconds.

"Mickey, I'm probably going."

"I'll go with you, Bear."

*   *   *

"Thanks for coming to my office for a change, Colonel," Krylov said, mixing a drink at the bar behind his desk.

"Absolutely, sir," Charlie Reed said as he stood at parade rest, his arms locked behind his back.

Krylov mentally bet himself that the creases on the front of the soldier's utilities would snap like a piece of glass. "Bourbon over cubes?"

"Thank you, Commissioner."

Krylov turned around with two drinks in his hand. "Sit down, Commander. When we are alone, don't stand on ceremony."

"Yes, Commissioner," Charlie said, sitting down on the front edge of a chair opposite the desk.

"Charlie, do I have to give you an order to call me Yuri?"

"I'm just an animal of habit," Charlie said, sipping his amber drink. "Oh, this is good bourbon, Yuri."

"I have a case or two flown in from China each year. I could get one for you if you'd like."

Sipping the cooled drink again, Charlie replied, "Absolutely. I'd appreciate it, s- Yuri."

"I'll make sure you get one," Yuri said knocking back the rest of his drink. The cubes rattled in the bottom of his crystal glass. "I think I prefer vodka. It does make a nice change, however.

"So how is the call-up going?"

"Well, it is a little slower than we'd hoped. We've also lost a few to the president's reserve announcement, but in the end I think it will help us."

"Help?"

"Yes, it will crystalize the differences between us and it identifies people who might be debating about being activated at all. We will get the vast majority of those fence sitters, Commissioner."

"Have we lost any people in critical positions?"

"No, not at all. If anything we've lost the deadweight that we can do without. I'm liking the way my troops are shaping up and shaking down."

"I have a question for you, Commander."

"By all means, sir."

"Would it help us at all to take down Nanogate and their subsidiaries here in the Portland area?"

"That is an unmodified negative, sir. First of all those local businesses they have are a relatively small part of their economics. We can't come close to touching even one part in ten thousand of their fiscal power. Second, the people working for Nanogate are neutrals. If we start closing down their jobs they will become active belligerents. And finally, they have no military or force structure. They are less than pawns in this game, and we would tie up a number of our own people keeping them out of action."

"Oh, well, it was just a thought."

"I am always interested in hearing your thoughts, sir."

"So tell me about the bridge," Yuri said, pouring Clear Water Paper Vodka into his glass.

"Yes, sir. In hindsight, our entry points were weakly covered. We never expected anyone trying to sneak *into* Portland. We were focusing on keeping people in. We've changed so that not only have we beefed up entrances and exits, we have increased the number of people in our roving squads. We don't want to have any repeats."

"It's so great to work with someone who learns from their mistakes."

Design Simulation

Tony drifted to semi-consciousness. His universe existed only of a muted beeping and some gentle snoring to his left. Those few brain cells that were firing made him curious about what created the sounds. He tried to turn his head but it wouldn't twist. His attention didn't last. For some reason both of these things were no longer of any consequence, although he couldn't think of any word of more than two syllables.

He opened his right eye. The left one seemed stuck shut. He tenuously decided that didn't matter either. A fine grid pattern of small holes pierced the softly-glowing, milk-white ceiling. He thought a worm might be able to crawl through those small openings but a finger wouldn't fit. He could see the edges of the wall, in a similarly bleached color.

He felt a regular warm breeze flowing over him. Without having to check he knew that his legs and lower torso were covered and that nothing covered his chest and arms.

He tried to lift his right arm but found it wouldn't move. Don't care. He lifted his left arm instead. Holding it in front of him he counted one, two, three, four fingers and one thumb. Yep. All present and accounted for.

"Sir. He's awake," Tony heard somewhere off to his right. He couldn't imagine looking over there to find out who said it. He was having fun making the regular holes ripple and blur in his one open eye.

Steps. He heard footsteps, wondering what those were. Oh, yes, I have foots. But why would someone step on them?

A snort and the snores stopping to his left preceded a gravelly female voice, "Is he awake?"

Now there were sounds of movement all over. Too much! Tony closed his eye.

"I'm injecting him with a neutralizer. He should be coherent in a few moments," some male voice over the top of him said. Suddenly the voice got much louder. "Mr. Sammis. Mr. Sammis, would you please wake up."

"Nawp," he slurred, realizing his mouth was dry.

A wet rag touched his lips and he sucked it. It was cool and made his throat feel better, even though he didn't remember it feeling bad.

"Open your eye, please, Mr. Sammis."

"Nope. Too much. Like it here."

"Tony, please," said a female voice that he should know.

"Mr. Sammis, please don't go back to sleep. We need to talk to you."

"You are, silly," he said, thinking these voices were just too silly. He just wanted to go back to sleep. "You are talking to me," he said belatedly.

A cool hand touched his cheek. "Honey, please wake up. I need you."

"Mommy, I don't want to go to school. I don't feel good."

"See, his speech is clearing," the annoying man said.

Tony started feeling like he was the extension of the bed on which he lay. Things held him down. He could feel tubes sticking in him. He could feel bandages. It exploded in his brain as he once again replayed the last minutes of his life. Bullets had struck him here, there, and everywhere. His body had jerked under each hit. His right eye snapped open to see Jamie and some man he'd never met standing to one side and a young woman in a nurse's uniform standing over him on the left.

"What the fuck! Where am I?"

"Tony, please relax. You are safe. You just happen to be in an ISO 2 cleanroom of Pfizer Pharmaceuticals. Your wounds have been treated and while you are no longer in immediate danger, you need to listen to me so that you don't harm yourself."

"Who the fuck are you?"

"My name is Morton Crosby. I'm one of the leading chemists for Pfizer."

"Where is my doctor?"

"Honey, please listen to him," Jamie pleaded.

"That's one of the things that I need to tell you, Mr. Sammis. You have no doctor. I performed all the work that was done on you."

"No doctor? We all have full med—"

"Tony, if we take you to a doctor how long before the Metros know?" Jamie said, holding tightly to his right hand.

Tony relaxed with the knowledge that he'd not been thrown to the wolves and that his friends were still looking out for him.

"OK… I'll bite. What'd you do, Doc—or Doc light."

The man gave a small chuckle. "Doc Light. I'll accept that title. OK…you were in about the same shape as ground round when you were poured in here. Only the fact that immersion in the freezing water had managed to lower your core temperature saved your life. It slowed your heart enough that you didn't completely bleed out.

"You've taken exactly eight rounds in your body. Four were through and through, easily patched. Two were easily removed. The one in your upper arm trailed spall that will take another week or so of nanite recovery to get it all.

"Your internal injuries, while extensive, didn't require anything more than repairing your liver, a minor patch on your left kidney, and a slight tear to the pulmonary aorta.

"As we were inside repairing damaged organs and tissue, your compatriots suggested we give you some sub-dermal improvements. You now have a kinetic fabric enclosure around not only your primary organs but also your spinal column up to and including C3. We couldn't safely cover C2 or C1. My apologies."

"So far all this sounds good, Doc."

"Tony, you are far from well. You have a great deal of blood to replace, tissue that needs healing, and a systemic infection from the polluted water. Nanite therapies can only go so far."

"OK, I smell a fly in the ointment. Is that why I can only see out of my right eye?"

"Essentially correct, Mr. Sammis. The eighth round, which apparently ricocheted off your skull caused some damage we cannot repair. Somehow it entered your left nasal cavity and then bounced off the orbit of the eye, shredding the entirety of your left eyeball and its associated workings as it exited to parts unknown."

Jamie squeezed his hand.

"Unfortunately," Doc Light continued, "we don't have regeneration facilities of any kind, nor could Chairman Nanogate tap any on short notice. Fortunately, we do have the premiere replacements in the entire marketplace. We've replaced your eye with a Mod XIV

Rainbow Plus system with all the bells and whistles."

"What about my face."

"Oh, that was easy. You look a mess now but it was cosmetic work only. We never gave that a second thought. By tomorrow your own mistress wouldn't be able to tell you'd ever been injured."

"OK, so this new better-than-my-own-eye, what does it do? How do I turn it on?"

"That's for tomorrow, Mr. Sammis. Your physical therapist, Miss Guinevere here, will be helping you with that and building back up your muscle tone. Until then, I want you to rest. I also believe Miss Ardwin wishes to have a word in private with you." He turned to Jamie. "No more than ten minutes."

"Thank you, Doctor."

The not-quite-doctor and physical therapist left the room.

"Jamie, I—"

"You stupid, MORONIC, ASSHOLE!" Jamie shouted at him. "If you ever fucking do anything like that again I'll kill you myself." Jamie didn't slow down enough for Tony to get in a word. She alternated wagging her finger in his face and pacing around the room with her back to him. "It wasn't bad enough that you have to do a goddamned John Wayne act, but I had to watch every frame of it as it happened. Each and every time your body got hit, I died a little.

"An idiotic prick. Did you even think of what I was thinking? What I was feeling? I finally find someone worth sharing with and he goes out and tries to martyr himself. BASTARD!

"Why I bother giving you anything of myself I don't know. And this after that poignant story about your uncle—"

"Granther—"

"You shut up! I don't want a corpse for a lover. I want someone beside me..." Jamie's shoulders finally relaxed and she turned back to him. Her eyes were running tears causing even her no-run mascara to make dark streams down her cheeks. Then in a weak little girl voice, "I can't lose you," she said, snuggling up to his undamaged left arm.

Tony couldn't pet her with his still restrained right arm or even see her.

"Baby, I—"

"No! I'm still mad at you," Jamie blubbered. He could feel the wetness of tears mixed with slobber on his bicep. "Please don't be mad at me, Tony. I won't be bad again."

*   *   *

"Hurry up there, Andersen. We don't have all day. We have orders to move out at 1535," echoed Sergeant Gapar's voice in the partially empty underground space.

"Yes, Sarg. Just one more crate to stencil and load."

"Well, make it march," the sergeant goaded.

"Yes, Sergeant! Three bags full!" Private Mickey Andersen said.

"Mickey, quit screwing around and bring that damned stencil over here," Corporal Samuel Blackbear said.

"Sure, Bear. What do these blasted marks mean anyway? 'Transship to ML4-113, care of MinInc.'"

"How do I know."

"Ain't MinInc the Martian miners?"

"Yeah," Bear said as he sprayed black paint through the stencil on the last crate they planned to move.

"Well, why would they need all these here grenades? And the assault weapons we marked and loaded the day before? And the tubs of gauss batteries?"

"Mickey, shut up and get the forklift driver over here to load this bitch so we can get the flock outta here."

"Yeah, but Bear, why we loading up all the weapons and leaving the fatigues and backpacks and ammo webbing and—"

"Jesus H. Christ, Mickey, do you know how to shut your mouth?"

"Corporal," shouted Sergeant Gapar.

"All done, Sarg," Bear responded.

"Great. Collect your squad and get ready to embark. We are due at Rock Island Arsenal in eight hours. Let's make it march!"

"Aye, Sarg.

"SQUAD! Fall in!" Bear bellowed out.

Private Mickey Andersen took his place in the formation right next to his squad leader and whispered, "And Jones says they are readying artillery pieces and even some APCs for shipment. You think there might be a war coming on Mars?"

"Private Andersen, I am ordering you to shut your hole before I get your squad mates to hold you down and shove a grenade in your mouth… And then I'll decide if I'm going to pull the pin."

*   *   *

Tony walked arm in arm, his left arm, with Jamie down Eastbank Esplanade at the invalid-capable pace of a slow tortoise. The pain blockers kept his wounds from being more than a nuisance. He could feel a tug here or a pull there but nothing his mind would associate with pain.

His artificial left eye gave him gritty images that seemed to pop in and out of focus, or occasionally would zoom way in or out. Worse, sometimes the view would flip to infrared, ultraviolet, or other modes he hadn't even figured out. He could shut down the feed but he'd been assured that the more he worked on it the better the filtering, resolution, and control would get.

"It's good to get out of there." Jamie said with a deep breath of outside air. She wore a simple black sheath dress. Bright green hair ribbon accentuated her hair, a neon color between red and purple.

"How long have I been out?"

"One day was touch and go. They performed surgery on you for the better part of nineteen hours, no matter how 'simple' Doc Light said your injuries were. Two days more for your body to knit together enough that we could even think of waking you."

"You were there the whole time?"

"Oh, we all took turns, but yes, I was there all the time except bathroom breaks and the one time they bodily carried me out to force me to sleep. By the way, watch out. Doc Light's good with a pressure injector. They nailed me when I told them I wouldn't sleep. Nox can sure make a liar out of you."

"So I've been out three days, and you haven't told me at all what happened while I was out."

"Not quite, Tony. I've been ordered not to divulge anything to you until you are recuperated. That is until Doc Light has given you the green light for release. That's also why your percomm is shut off."

"Shit, Doc isn't likely to give me that for another week from what he was saying earlier."

"True, lover, but that doesn't mean I won't share anyway."

"But—"

"Tony, haven't you learned by now that I keep my own council? I do what I think is right."

Tony stopped and turned to look his lover in the eyes. "I thought you said you would be good?"

"For you, not for them."

"Fair enough," he said, continuing his shuffle down the walk. "So geek."

"OK. We lost Joel and Unified Textiles on the bridge." Seeing the tear in her lover's eye and a firm scowl forming on his rugged face she continued, "No one blames you, Tony."

"I was supposed to keep them safe."

"Wait a minute, buster. You almost sacrificed your life to give all of them a chance. You have *nothing* to be feeling guilty about. If you don't stop, I'm going to stop giving you the straight dope and give you only the good saccharine news."

"All right. I'll be realistic. But don't try to stop me from being idealistic about my realism."

"I wouldn't dream of it, Galahad."

"Bah."

"Well, they have already held burial services for both."

"How is Wayne coping with Joel's loss?"

"Not well. He hasn't been out of his room except for the service. He's been cleaning every gun he can get his hands on and has sharpened his knives so well that even Christine can't fault them."

"Is he after me?"

"Damn-it-all, Tony. I told you that no one blames you, not even Wayne."

"OK. I just didn't want to get well to get shish-kabobbed by my own people."

"Don't worry about Wayne. He will channel his anger just like the rest of you have," Jamie said with a gentle squeeze of his arm.

"Hey, isn't that the USS *Blueback*?" Tony asked, pointing with his right shoulder at a rusting submarine hulk barely floating above the waterline.

"Yup. That thing's been here like a thousand years. I think a group of nils squat in it right now."

"Bah, not even two hundred years, but it gives me an idea."

"Your ideas always give me shivers," she said wiggling sensuously against him.

"I'm not well enough for that kind of idea yet, wench… although I'm thinking about them. No, seriously. I wonder what it would take to get her running again? Tell Morgan I want her and a team of ship mechanics, or whatever they are called, down here within the hour. Tell her to bring some cash to pay off the nils inside."

"Why do you want a submarine?"

"I've got ideas… and don't start that again," he said, giving the gleam in her eye a wink of his own. "While I'm on a roll, please tell Nanogate that we need to not only move all those weapons and munitions off planet, the computer-aided control programs for manufacturing have to go as well, otherwise they can just start up a new production line. And—"

Jamie shut him up with a kiss.

* * *

"Where is that action taking place?" Colonel Reed asked, standing like a 10 km tall Titan in the center of Portland.

"Tualatin, Colonel."

Reed took three steps, mindless of buildings or people underfoot. The landscape and denizens ignored his avatar. He stopped at an area flashing red at his feet. He reached down and picked up a chunk of the earth and stretched it in his hands. When he was satisfied he threw it back to the floor causing the expanded sub-image to replace the Portland city landscape. Looking through the walls he could see eight red dots and three blue dots with "A12" next to them in a single apartment. A semitransparent solido of the floor plan of the apartment and another one of the entire building appeared in the air to either side of the colossal man.

"Place the officers' comms on audio."

"… found bats, bludgeons, and even bows and arrows."

"Do they have a story, Adam Twelve?"

"They claim that they are historical re-enactors, something called Society for Creative Anachronism."

"What do you think, Twelve?"

"It would have seemed fine to me if we hadn't found the map in the crawl space with circles in red around some very prominent commercial districts."

"Bring them in, Twelve, and we will give them some interrogation here."

"Ten-four."

"Sir, we have another action listed in Gresham," said a blond specialist standing in Lake Oswego.

Colonel Reed had few affectations but one was that his people's avatars in the command sims were images of themselves in uniform or just a rank/name insignia. To his mind those images used on the net were intended to obfuscate. He wanted no unicorns, ancient tanks, nude bodybuilders, or the like cluttering his mind. Combat was no time for uncertainty.

The specialist continued with, "That is in one of our operational areas."

The Colonel bent over and compressed Tualatin back to its original diminutive size. Three steps later he was expanding Gresham.

Two red dots ran along the roof of a building. Dozens of green dots with four different unit designations converged, two from the air.

"Comms," the Colonel ordered.

"... *two suspects on the run along the roof of NWFN at 33 SE 223rd Ave.,*" *came a voice that was puffing as it spoke.*

"*Affirmative, Gamma 16. We copy your position at 10T ER 44180 40910. Do you require backup?*"

"*Not now. We should have this.*"

Colonel Reed spoke, "Gamma16, this is Birddog 6. Watch for free parachute jumps. The Green Action Militia has used this technique repeatedly, over."

"*Roger, Birddog 6.*

"*Squad four, six, and twelve. Move into adjoining structures.*"

"*Four.*"

"*Affirmative.*"

"*On our way.*"

"*Wait one. The suspects have just disappeared, over.*"

Colonel Reed reached up for the floating solido of the building and stretched it out, turning it on its side so he could see the top. No red suspect dots showed.

"Gamma 16, this is Command," said his urban warfare specialist, a wiry little Latina sergeant. "We show only one place the units can't be tracked. They've dropped down an air shaft. Do not follow. I say again. Do not follow, over."

"*Roger, so far.*"

"Post sentry at the top and follow the line I traced in your HUD, over." On Reed's simulation a yellow line traced its way down some stairs and to a vent shaft access on a lower floor.

"*Roger.*"

Reed played with the building in his hand and lit up dozens of purple vertical shafts down the build_ng. "Lock down all the emergency fire escape pods," Colonel Reed ordered.

"Yes, sir," Lieutenant Bador, the lead of his electronics team said.

"*Gamma 16 ... Hold one. Facial recognition confirms that one of our suspects is Christine Matthews of the GAM. We request priority tasking.*"

"Folks, the stakes are higher now. I want Gamma to have every unit, available or not."

The other toons in the simulation reacted in an orderly frenzy. Reed liked hearing the chatter on each member's private line, even when they stomped over each other creating nothing but chaos in his ears. It let him hear tone. He liked the businesslike approach his people took. No hurrying. Just like a drill.

"Yes, sir. I want units alpha, beta, and phi dropping on my designated coordinates in thirty seconds. Hold one for laser designators, over."

"All units not in grid fifty-two, converge on 10T ER 44180 40910. Report on arrival and standby for orders. Out."

"*We have two parachutes that just came off a balcony on the ninety-sixth floor. I am engaging,*" came a new voice.

"Identify yourself." Charlie krew that the radio-link was secure and couldn't be spoofed, but he needed confirmation.

"*Gamma 4G, Corporal Hill,*" came the reply over the sound of automatic weapon fire.

"*Gamma 16 to Gamma 4G we are en route. Are you taking fire?*"

"*Four. No, we aren't taking any return fire.*"

"*Have you made any hits?*"

"*Yes, sir. The chutes are going down fast.*"

"*Gamma 16 to Gamma Squad 2.*"

"*Gamma 26 here.*"

"*Do you have the ball?*"

"*We have visual. It's going to be messy, Gamma. They are falling like rocks.*"

"*Affirmative. Track them.*"

"*Ten-four.*"

"I want a full medical and interrogation team in transit now," the colonel ordered. "If they are still alive, I want them kept alive and able to answer questions."

"*Gamma 26 here. Something is wrong.*"

"*What do you see, Gamma 26.*"

"*They are falling like dead weight, sir. And, I don't see any blood. I can see them clearly now. They are dummies. It is a ruse!*"

Colonel Reed disconnected from his combat couch, breaking his link with the simulation. A single battery-operated light gave off an eerie red illumination, making the vault look like a tomb. Of course this tomb could withstand a near miss from an orbital kinetic strike and moved randomly around the terrain outside the operation zone.

His six aides still lay motionless in their network cradles. He knew they would try and reacquire the targets, but realistically the GAM members were gone. This time, he added mentally, his team was close. They'd flushed them twice. Those rats had to be lucky every time. He only had to be lucky once. But for now he had to reset his cordon because they had gotten inside.

*   *   *

Though his eyes were closed, Tony's nose wrinkled at the smell of machine oil, human waste, and even kimchi. The stinks were becoming the norm after several days in this environment. His head jerked when a drip of water landed on his right ear. He shook his head. *GAMS Blueback* was taking some getting used to. Tony shifted in his hammock and sighed.

Sitting on Tony's chest, Cinnamon looked like a drowned rat. Her fur matted and clumped all over her body like some punk rocker. She licked at the wet masses in vain. Her ears lay low and her whiskers drooped. Submarining was not her preferred method of travel.

"Quit squirming," Jamie chided him as she snuggled up in the humid, noisy stench. "Some of us need our sleep."

Tony's left eye still bothered him, even closed. Shut, it still fed darkness to his brain. Open, the input didn't look real. He kept wanting to adjust the solido but it wasn't anything but his "improved" vision.

It appeared no one wanted him to sleep. "Captain, as ordered we are on silent running with thirty meters of water over our sail just maintaining steerageway," Morgan said, her brown face even darker with grease and her hands nothing but a landscape of black. She wiped her hands futilely on a rag that was just as filthy as her hands. "Can I ask what we are doing here?"

"Just being safe for the moment."

"Shouldn't we be taking the fight to them?"

"Not us, not now," Jamie interjected.

"Exactly. We are waiting around to hear the results delivered by Mr. Marks and his group of bodyguards. As you know they have an attack on the drone facility in Kansas City tonight. Those drones have been kicking our ass even at this range."

"And truth be told, this is the only place I've felt safe in months."

"You are right, Captain. I don't think anyone is going to be looking for a submersible. Not right off their back doorstep."

"It is a rather ingenious idea my Jamie had."

Jamie beamed as well as she could while not giving up thoughts of going back to sleep.

"Right off Cape Disappointment. Water conditions are so bad no one would hear us if they happened to put a sonar on our hull," Tony continued.

"You can say that again. Of course it didn't make for a picnic getting here. I thought we were going to breach like a dying whale a couple of times."

"You had my complete confidence, Morgan. Speaking of which, any chance we can arm this relic?"

"I have Bofor's Defense Systems in looking at the old girl now. They think they can rig something to go out the torpedo tubes and launch from the surface of the ocean against air units.

"We are having more difficulties with engaging ground targets. We think we can do the same with some modified cruise missiles but it's a bit more challenging. They were never designed for the pressure. If we surfaced to launch, we might have something."

"Well, do what you can, Morgan. Any bullets in the gun are better than none." Tony was interrupted when his percomm rang. "Jesus. How is an invalid supposed to rest around here?"

"It's your nickel."

"*Marks here.*"

"And?"

"*Sir, I have to say we didn't even try. We arrived to find the base swarming with about six hundred extra troops and every cute toy for stopping both air and ground attacks.*"

"Those weren't in our initial intel," Tony said with a frown.

"*No, sir. With the amount of activity they couldn't have moved in more than sixteen hours ago.*"

"And so it was a no-go."

"*To even try would have been suicide. I called it off.*"

"Good decision, Mr. Marks. We need them alive more than we need martyrs. Bring them home."

"*Yes, sir.*"

"Damn it," Tony said after he hung up. "Change in plans, Morgan. Have David come up to the ops room with the tactical maps."

"You got it," Morgan said as she strode away.

"Sorry, honey, but duty calls."

"Hell with it," she said, rolling toward the edge of the hammock. "I couldn't sleep anyway... and fucking on these things calls for the agility of an acrobat and the arms of an octopus." Her one-piece, pink swimsuit smudged as she landed on her rump. "Jesus, just getting out of the bloody thing is a challenge."

Tony lifted her up and wrapped her in a bear hug.

"You sure you are well enough to be doing that?"

Tony gave her a kiss on the forehead. "Stitches have been out for three days. I've not had any leakage or infection. Time for me to get back to work."

"Gently, lover," Jamie said.

"I'll try. Do you want to go put in your two cents' worth?"

"When haven't I?"

"Oh, I was hoping one of these days—"

Jamie slapped him on his good arm. "I can still beat you."

"First she wants me to take it easy and then she's threatening to abuse me. Make up your mind, woman," Tony teased.

"Well, don't do stupid stuff, then. Intentionally provoking your lover is dangerous. Now let's get on and plan some death and destruction."

"Yes, your highness."

The pair walked arm in arm the length of one bulkhead and into the wardroom set aside for operational planning. An old-fashioned flat map of Portland lay across the table.

"Sorry about the drone base, boss," David said as he entered.

"Hell, we can't win every single one. Hell, I'm just glad we didn't lose anyone."

"So what do you have in mind?"

"I have been mulling over an idea ever since I woke up. I want to go after where the National Guard is bivouacked."

"Holy shit. You don't think small, do you?"

"Think you can find out for me where they are?"

"Shit, yeah. I already know where they're camped." David pulled down the sub-map of the slum of Piedmont in Northern Portland. He pointed at the map. "They've taken over what was the Holy Redeemer Catholic School and Church at the corner of Rosa Parks and Vancouver."

"Really?" Jamie asked. "I used to use that place to do drug transfers. It is so run down not even the nils will go near it. Too many of them were getting hurt."

"Well, that's probably why the National Guard took it over. Less fuss means more operational security.

"But, boss, even with the bodyguards and Jamie's people we can't possibly match over a thousand troops in a stand up fight. Even an ambush is going to be all but a suicide mission no matter how many of them we get."

Tony just smiled. "You think Augustine will be bothered if we scratch an abandoned church?"

*   *   *

"Bear, I just don't understand these details," Mickey said, leaning into a 2 m long wrench to loosen the bolt of another robotic assembly arm from the factory floor. "How are we supposed to be doing something to save our country when all we seem to be doing is taking it apart and shipping it to Mars?"

"I have a question back to you, Mickey," Corporal Blackbear asked from his seated position at the base of the assembly arm.

"Sure, Bear."

"Do you ever shut your fucking hole?" Bear asked turning his attention to the nut now broken free of the six layers of paint. He used both hands to unscrew the 15 cm nut the rest of the way off. Only two more to go but they were instructed not to take off the last two until they'd been cleared.

The corporal stood up and triggered the mic to his communicator to indicate his desire to speak.

"*Go,*" he heard over the net.

"Corporal Blackbear reporting two remaining bolts."

"*Good job, Corporal. What's your location?*"

Blackbear looked up and saw the convenient marker above his head. "We are at Lima Two, Lieutenant."

"*We'll send Remington technicians over to disconnect the electronics in three mikes.*"

"Roger. Out."

"And why doesn't Remington dismantle their own damned factory?"

"Mickey. I don't know. I don't know. I don't know. And if you didn't hear me the first three dozen times, I don't know. Shut your mouth and do what you're told, Private."

*   *   *

"'Those who cannot remember the past are condemned to repeat it,'" David quoted from his vantage point in an empty apartment in the Rosa Parks Towers. "All stations standby," he said into his mic as he watched surreptitiously out the window. The air circulation vents blew warm air up at him ruffling his red hair. He was annoyed at his distraction. Tony had never given him such authority and responsibility before and he wanted everything to be perfect.

A double-trailered lift-truck turned left onto Rosa Parks Way from MLK Boulevard. It dropped two levels to match and glide slowly into the parking garage on the thirty-second floor.

All of his people had reported in, ready to act, so there was nothing more to do than to bite his nails. David watched the between-building causeway. He had to learn patience no matter how long action seemed to take. "What could have gone wrong?" he muttered to himself. "C'mon, Edward. Surely something is wrong. We'll have to abort."

"David, relax," Martin said next to him. "Check the time."

David queried time over his percomm and realized what an idiot he was being. The truck had only gone in sixty seconds ago. The plan called for a three-minute window for the driver to reach safe distance. Each second crept by with the speed of a slug having smoked about six reefers.

"Three minutes," Martin said.

"All stations ready for action. Act independently on detonation."

Just then he saw Edward sprinting across the causeway. The plan had him walking across like anyone else about his business. David pulled the solidoculars to his eyes. Edward had his sidearm out and fired shots behind him.

"Edward's in trouble. Blow it now!"

A flash briefly preceded the building vomiting a roiling cloud of debris. The air even in the sealed apartment compressed enough to make the pair gasp. David turned his solidoculars back to the causeway. Everyone was down, but Edward struggled to his feet. Only a dust cloud chased his stagger to the next building.

The church and school still stood but most of the gothic façade now was rubble in the street below. Only an open maw about three times its former size was left of the landing bay.

"Five minutes to response. We are out of here in four," David said as he heard the first calls on the Metro's channel.

Martin had leveraged the window open and set up his sniper rifle. Automatic weapon fire sounded from the other side of the building. David unslung his assault rifle but didn't expect to use it. His job was to coordinate.

Martin drew a bead on a target. His rifle barked. He jacked out the spent cartridge and rammed a new one home. Another aimed shot and another reload. Martin continued to take out people that either exited the building or poked their head from a window.

"Out," Martin said.

David handed him a new clip of the Teflon-coated bullets. He watched a number of soldiers exiting the Williams Ave emergency escape route. To his surprise, his man there, Wayne, held his eagerness in check until the street was choked with escapees, mostly looking up. Wayne let loose with the heavy machine gun they'd placed there for just this purpose.

Bullets mowed men and women down like a zombie solido. They ran and died. They tried to hide and died. They dropped down in place and died. Most everyone on the avenue died. Once no one remained standing and no further guards were stupid enough to leave the burning building, David watched Wayne fire into the moaning wounded lying and struggling for some spot of safety on the street.

The thoroughfare looked like a slaughterhouse. The mass of

bodies floating in the wash of blood wouldn't leave Dave's memory anytime in the near future.

"*All Metropolitan units, please stand down. National Guard units responding,*" David heard over his police scanner.

"*Identify yourself.*"

"*Captain Hordiyenko. Service number Kilo, Echo, niner, niner, six, four, three, niner, Echo, Foxtrot, one.*"

"*Identity confirmed, Captain. All Metro units standing down.*"

"Bugout!" David called over the net. "Early response. Repeat: Bugout now! All anti-air units take only one shot."

Martin dismantled his weapon with swift, sure motions.

"Leave it," David hissed. He dropped his own assault rifle onto the carpet as he headed for the door. "There are lots more where that came from."

"Sorry. It's hard to learn new habits. Years of pinching pennies and now we have all the equipment we could want," Martin said, dropping the case.

David was irritated. The early response meant they hadn't killed as many as they wanted, but they still managed to reduce the numbers of the enemies. He had to associate the dead with just numbers because that many mutilated bodies in the street couldn't fit into any moral context.

*   *   *

Detective Edgar Gutierrez leapt up from the chair at his desk with his arms wide as coffee spilled across the desk and into his lap. "Holy fuck! You trying to burn me?" He made an attempt to flick the offending liquid off his uniform with less than stellar results.

"Sorry, Edgar," Patrolman Josh Walsh said, trying to mop up the brown mess with a towel.

"Sorry don't cut it, you nil sucking bastard."

"Then get your own goddamned coffee, burn head," Josh said flinging the soaking towel into the detective's face.

"You are going to pay for that you prick-less—" Gutierrez sputtered as he whipped the towel down from his head.

By now the entire wardroom had fallen silent and tuned into the fracas.

"You think I'm afraid of you, big man? You are a loud, arrogant cunt with a badge. Maybe that should be tattooed on your shoulder like the rest of the whores."

His face red, even through his olive complexion, Gutierrez went for his side-arm.

The stiff set of Walsh's jaw changed radically at the other officer's motion. Walsh's mouth dropped open as he reached for his gun nearly a full second later.

That worthless prick messed with the wrong man, Gutierrez thought. He knew he had the fucking rookie cold. He'd put three shots through the prick's skull before the moron even got his gun loose of its holster. He unsnapped the safety strap with a practiced motion of his thumb. He pulled on his prized Colt Bright Burst. He felt a hand like ceramcrete clamp down on his draw.

"Stop it, you brainless simpletons," Sergeant Tolbert said as Gutierrez continued to attempt to break Tolbert's grip and withdraw his automatic.

White-faced and sweating, Walsh stopped trying to get his gun out of its holster without undoing the safety strap. He realized as much as anyone just how close his wife had come to drawing a policeman's death benefits.

"I have seen goldfish with higher IQs than you two idiots. Now stop this."

"This little dick-less—" Gutierrez began, reaching his other hand across his waist to secure his weapon's release. Tolbert didn't waste time. He triggered the stun on his baton and rammed it into the detective's side. The man gave three quick convulsions and then collapsed to the floor.

"Jesus, Sarge, did you need to—"

"Shut up or you're next," Tolbert said, pointing the baton at the officer who had the temerity to speak. The dark circles under the sergeant's eyes gave him the look of Thantos himself coming to collect a soul. The officer leaned backward away from the weapon.

"Listen up, all of you," Sergeant Enrique Tolbert said as he knelt down to take the still twitching man's gun from its holster. "I know you're tired. I know things haven't gone exactly well for us. None of that means anything. We are police officers, and we will behave accordingly. We will get through this or I will personally dismember the next one of you who steps out of line.

"Walsh!"

"Yes, Sergeant."

"Get the fuck out of here before I change my mind that the infirmary should have only one new patient."

"Yes, Sergeant." Patrolman Walsh spun on his heels and headed out of the wardroom at just under a trot.

From the doorway of his office Reza decided that he had better return to his desk before he had to officially notice the near disaster he'd witnessed.

"Baker. Smith. Take Gutierrez to the infirmary," Tolbert barked.

Reza decided he also needed to order Tolbert to sleep.

*   *   *

Officer Phillip Johnson dragged with fatigue, but that prick Debnath didn't seem to have an off button. It's like he welcomed the excessive hours. It gave him more chance to show his brutality.

"Let's pick up the take from the strip joints downtown."

"Yes, Detective. Lead the way."

Harry's ALL-NUDE REVIEW was the first peep bar they came across on Oak. Debnath just barged in with his usual tact. The bouncer reached out as if to stop the Metro but pulled back as soon as he saw the face.

Debnath went right up to the bar and slapped his hand three or four times for attention. Sparse afternoon patrons eyed a beautiful couple gyrating on stage. They performed some acrobatics Phillip hadn't seen before. He puzzled out the physics of it as Gohar called.

"Hey, Guppy. C'mere."

"Detective, I'd appreciate it if you called me by my name. I'm not fond of your nickname."

"Whatever. Say, these pricks say they ain't gonna pay us no more. They say they are protected by the Greenies."

Johnson just shook his head. "I think they have a lot to learn, Detective."

"May I borrow this, officer?" Gohar didn't wait for an answer. He drew Johnson's Colt G12 and fired it into the bartender and owner. He kept up the spray of gauss fragments until the chamber was empty. Blood sprayed against the mirror like someone had taken a chainsaw to a moose.

Screams erupted and patrons found other places to be. The downstairs emptied faster than a mustang does the quarter mile.

"So let's continue this lesson upstairs in the brothel," the detective said, putting Phillip's gun back.

"What?"

"Well, the girls and boys are an asset to the club, right? You and I are going to eliminate those assets."

Prototyping

"Thank you, Colonel Reed for joining our morning brief. We are very interested in your report," Lieutenant Narendra said as a segue.

"Thank you for inviting me."

"Could we begin with your report of the events of northern Portland?" Krylov asked.

Colonel Reed stood straight-backed and head held high as he addressed his command authority. As always his uniform was crisp and parade-ground ready. "Certainly, Commissioner. We'll start with the obvious and then go over the details.

"I assume all responsibility for failing to adequately protect my people. If you want my resignation, I'll be happy to provide it any time you wish. I've put my second command on alert in case you wish to exercise that option."

"Colonel Reed, we're not looking for perfection. At this time we are not contemplating a change in leadership of your brigade."

"Thank you, sir. As an overview, the damage wasn't nearly as bad as it could have been had we not had response teams in place. Two hundred sixteen known dead, another eight hundred fourteen injured and twenty-two yet unaccounted for and presumed dead. Of the injured, only eighty-two are not combat capable. Seventy of those men have career-ending injuries.

"While this hampers our mission it doesn't change our ability to carry it out. We are now twenty-nine hundred sixty-three strong with more coming in daily."

"Thank you for that overview," Krylov said with a grave face. "Give us the details."

"Yes, sir. The attack by members of the opposition occurred at eleven thirty-four hours. They infiltrated an IED, improvised explosive device, in the form of a large cargo lift vehicle into the parking structure of the abandoned school and church that we have been using as our base of operations. At eleven thirty-five hours the members of our patrol assigned to challenge civilian presences approached a Caucasian man climbing out of the cab.

"There is no audio on our surveillance and I must conjecture that the patrol requested the man's papers. We believe he made himself seem innocent and offered to give his papers. Instead he drew an automatic handgun and killed both men with armor-piercing ammunition. He then made a hasty retreat across the parking lot where he was spotted by two other patrols that were looking for where the sound of gunfire had come from. A short firefight occurred. The suspect, now identified only with the alias Edward Longfingers, a suspected Green Action Militia member, fled to the adjoining building.

"At eleven thirty-seven the IED detonated. The explosion killed or incapacitated all the pursuing soldiers. The damage to the structure was severe. The IED contained gelatinous flammables which started a fire that still hasn't been completely extinguished. I must note that large lift capability units are quite common in this area to bring necessary supplies."

"Go on."

"The OPFOR, or opposing force, had already secured ideal ambush locations around the perimeter of the building. The majority of the casualties were outside the Williams Street emergency exit. The emplaced electric minigun, while antiquated, used modern ammunition and was effective against the lightly armored personnel funneling out of the holocaust.

"Several dozen soldiers were killed by sniper fire but this is a minor factor in the total casualties.

"We've located eight individual ambush sites, capturing a number of antiquated weapons, and are zeroing in on three or four more. This won't be of any specific help other than to help define how to prevent similar breaches in the future.

"During the response, three infantry carriers and two tanks were damaged by modern anti-aircraft weapons. The Hypermass defense systems on the vehicles prevented even further casualties, although we had to write off the vehicles themselves."

"So we detected them entering but failed to stop the detonation."

"Correct, sir."

"It seems we also completely failed to notice the enemy setting up ambush locations right at our own feet."

"Almost correct, sir. We have learned that one of the minigun emplacements was actually discovered by a two-man patrol the morning of the attack. They took a rather large payoff from the enemy and then tried to go over to the U.S. Army."

"I'm not sure that is any better, Colonel."

"I concur with you, sir, but I will give you what happened and not try and whitewash any of it. Continuing, sir, they were captured when they couldn't provide exit papers at a city checkpoint. Normally we give anyone wanting to leave permission to leave, but these two entrepreneurs didn't bother to ask. They divulged the whole plan under interrogation. They also claimed to be prisoners of war. We are ignoring this as they were under our discipline when they committed the crime. They will be subject to the full rigors of the UCMJ, or Unified Code of Military Justice."

"So what are we going to do about this?"

"Do you mean offensively or defensively, sir?"

"Well, both, Colonel."

"Well, let's talk about mitigations to this in the future.

"First we will get all of our men to attend a mandatory legal presentation about turncoats in the military, followed shortly by the execution of those two who took the bribe. It will not stop defections but it should eliminate any new soldiers who would look the other way.

"Additionally, my staff and I have met and come up with several defensive strategies that will prevent not only this kind of attack but any general attack in the future. It calls for creating not one but five FOBs, or forward operating bases, in such a way that they are close enough to receive support but not so close that the OPFOR can hope to engage more than one at a time.

"Next we will run continuous CAP, that's close air patrol, over our bases of operations with quick reaction forces. We simulate a response time from our FOBs in the two-minute range."

"That's impressive, but a lot of damage can be done in two minutes, Colonel," Captain Hardy interjected.

"Agreed, sir; that is why we will also institute an interdiction zone around the forward bases. No large vehicle traffic in or out. All cargo will be offloaded and scanned by robotics. Then the robotics will reload the freight onto smaller guard vehicles, mixing the freight so that if there is an explosion, it won't be concentrated all in one place.

"There will be a short deprivation and halting of supplies as it will take a while to move up our GenPurp robotics and to program them for the task."

"Why use robots. Why not use boxed? If a few of them blow up, no great loss," Captain Lennart said in one of the few times he offered anything at all in staff.

"Exceptional suggestion, Captain Lennart."

"What about offense?" Krylov said, pushing.

"Well, sir, I think our original plan was well thought out. I don't think it requires any change... other than to the timetable. With our losses and new safety measures we should suffer a twenty percent loss in sweep speed. Also because of this action we lost the cordon on all the 'safe' areas by over an hour so we will have to start all over."

"Really? Do you think anyone could have gotten through with that small of a window?"

"Captain Hardy, we have an intelligent, well-disciplined enemy. They knew when they were going to hit us and likely the impact upon us. We would be criminally negligent if we didn't assume they took advantage of the chaos they created to slip into the previously swept zones."

"Too true," Krylov said from the head of the table. "I'd rather delay a day, a week, or even several months to make sure we do it right and there aren't any more *pizdets*, fuckups."

"I couldn't concur more, Commissioner."

"OK. Enough on what happened, I want to know what's going on now. Amber, media?"

"We have the big name media under control. They are spinning this as the 'Mass Mass Massacre' or M3. They are coming down on the GAM and the CorpGov like a fire and brimstone preacher. Heck, we didn't even have to prompt them hard. This is good ratings for them."

"Excellent. Keep playing on us as the innocent victim in this terror attack," Krylov said, looking at least a little pleased.

"Captain Cohen, if you could go on the air with a few of the wounded it might play very well," Reza added.

"Yes," Krylov said with an even more predatory grin. "OK, I think that wraps that up. Is there anything else?"

"Excuse me, sir," Colonel Reed said.

"Yes, sir," Reza said at the same time.

"By seniority," the Commissioner said. "Colonel, you first."

"Thank you, sir. I have two items. First the resupply of ammunition and replacement parts has been lagging seriously. It isn't a key factor yet. We still have logistics for several months at our current expenditure rates. However, if we are forced into open conflict then those supplies will deplete rapidly."

"Where do our supplies come from?" Cohen asked.

"We get equal parts from Army armorers, from specific civilian suppliers who have license to manufacture to our specification, and finally from our own storehouses."

"Let me guess. The Army and the civilians have both cut you off," Krylov said with a pursed mouth.

"Actually, sir, that would have been my expectation. Looking over the entire logistics chain I was surprised to find that repair parts continue to flow from all suppliers at their normal rates, as do heavy weapon munitions. Where we are suffering is small arms and man-portable disposables. The Army continues to supply a flow of these much smaller than our requests. Civilian suppliers have failed to meet any of their commitments. Several raids have hit our own stores. In addition, many of our storehouses have been looted by our own people to sell on the black market where the prices are astronomical."

"So our tanks and artillery are still in good shape, just our infantry that have issues?" Cohen asked.

"Yes, ma'am. Again this will only be an issue after several months or things get pushed to open conflict."

"I think tanks alone should give any of the rabble pause," Krylov said.

"Sir, you are under a misconception carried by many people. Tanks are very effective against other tanks and against other hardened targets such as buildings and fortifications. They can be used as mobile pillboxes as well to suppress ground troops, but to do this they mainly rely upon those same light ammunitions as the infantry."

"Hmm," Krylov mused. "Then we will have to be a little more careful. Is there any way we could bolster our supplies?"

"I have a team working on plans for this right now. At a high level I'm thinking of requisitioning these supplies from Army bases and National Guard bases in other states that haven't mobilized. We are also considering taking over the factories and having them manufacture directly to our need."

"I approve all of those actions, Colonel."

"We don't have plans yet, Commissioner."

"When you get them, just shoot me a memo. Don't wait to start the execution. Just run with it."

"I appreciate the trust, sir. If I may go on to my second topic?"

"Proceed."

"I've had a question in the back of my head that I finally have a partial answer for. 'What mission has the president mobilized the U.S. Army for?' Fortunately their mobilization method and plea to our own National Guardsmen make it impossible for them to screen out any agents I choose to slide into their midst."

"Don't keep us in suspense, Colonel. What are they up to?"

"They are taking any war material they can get their hands on and shipping it to Mars."

"What kind of sense does that make?"

"I'm not certain, sir. They continue to supply us with heavy weapons but yet ship everything else in their inventory off planet. I've had some rough estimates that say they have already shipped between one and three hundred thousand tonnes of equipment and logistics."

"*Tvoyu mat*! What the hell for?"

"That, sir, I can't tell you. People rarely spend money on something they don't plan to use, however."

"Colonel, I'd like you to coordinate with the other National Guard units and do anything you can to stop them from doing this any further."

"Thank you, sir. We will do our best."

"Do you have any other cheery news?"

"No sir."

"Reza, you had something for us?"

"Yes, sir, I'd like to bring up something that hasn't been discussed before—morale," Lieutenant Narendra said, unconsciously shuffling backward from the briefing table.

"Go ahead," Krylov growled, his face changing quickly to the menacing visage of a she-bear guarding her young.

"Yes, sir. I just witnessed two of my troops draw down on each other in the wardroom over not much. I calmed them down and sent them off for counseling. I witnessed another patrolman pistol-whip a civilian for no reason. I've had more lesser incidents than I have officers. The explanations for this aren't news and they work hand in hand.

"Even with the reduced patrols, we are still riding the ragged edge of exhaustion. Add to this the escapes by the GAM and CorpGov, the failure of the National Guard to bring an end to this swiftly, and not least of all, the successful attack on the National Guard itself. All of these are kicking our collective asses.

"I'm sorry if I'm being blunt but the average trooper not only doesn't see an end to this, he sees only our blatant propaganda and hears only our platitudes.

"Now having given you the bad news, let me give you a suggestion that will make a short-term improvement," Reza said, and then didn't wait for permission to offer his wisdom. "I'd like your permission to draft higher level officers onto the street for at least thirty hours a week."

"Won't that impair our reporting structure?" Captain Cohen asked.

"Absolutely, but think of the impact it will have to the feeling of the trooper on the street seeing that even the upper echelon will come down and help when it's needed."

"I think that is a good idea in any case. Make it happen," Krylov said, looking his staff in the face. Each of them nodded carefully and made a note.

"Thank you, sir. The quantitative work that the upper officers will add relative to the people in the field is small but the morale impact will be huge."

"This won't be enough though, will it, Lieutenant?" Captain Hardy asked in a rare act of initiative.

"No, sir, it won't. We need to see some positive success or our effectiveness will wane. We will continue to have fights, applications for early retirement and maybe some out-and-out desertions."

Krylov smiled at the other end of the table. This frightened Reza more than a scowl or a pounding fist would.

"Lieutenant, I can assure you that we will have some real positive successes to feed to our comrades in arms in the very near future. In fact, Colonel, would you please stay after our meeting so I can discuss operational planning with you."

*   *   *

Wearing blue overalls with grease stains in various locations, Edward Longfingers sat down at the always deserted thirty-second level TriMet shelter at Multnomah and Ninth. Grime and soot smudged his normally meticulous blond hair in camouflage.

With his index finger he carefully placed a solidocular contact lens first into his left and then into his right eye. He blinked three times to get them settled and to clear the excess moisture. He logged into the net, using the standard GAM encryption protocol.

His avatar of a chief's headdress of eagle feathers popped into the sim space, shown as a sidebar to his view. As much of an atavism as it was, he was proud of his Shoshone heritage. Every summer he participated in the Sun Dance. He regularly wore a belt of handmade beads passed down from his three times great-grandfather, Matt SittingOwl.

"Ed in position," he announced to the grandmother mixing something in a large ceramic bowl in a surrealistic kitchen.

"*Gotcha, Ed,*" she said, putting a tray of cookies into the oven. Call has already gone out. Expect action in three minutes."

From above, Edward looked down at Lloyd Center mall, one of only three ground-level shopping centers left in the world. People frolicked in the crisp winter air as they glided and pirouetted across the mall's signature skating rink.

Zooming in with his contacts he could actually see the shining faces of young people smiling even after they fell flat on their backsides. He wondered what damage the much larger chaos the GAM engineered would do to their psyches. He salved his conscience by believing he would at least allow them to be free

"*T minus thirty,*" the grandmother said, pulling out the chocolate chip cookies that miraculously baked in only two minutes.

Knowing what was about to happen, Edward could watch the increased flow of people into all doors of the mall. From the influx it looked like GMa Ice had a huge party laid on.

"… *Three, two, one. Chaos.*"

The orderly flow of the people through the open-air hallways ceased. Out of nowhere people started yelling, throwing rocks, and kicking at advertising façades. Out of coats they brought out steel and wooden clubs to aid their wanton destruction. Edward could hear the growl of the riot even at over a hundred meters.

"Action started," he reported.

"*Affirmative,*" GMa Ice told him, flashing some of the mall's camera images onto his sidebar.

Edward marked this as his eighth riot-overwatch duty. Each manifested in its own unique way, chaos being what it is. Even anarchy can be predicted on a macro scale. His mind, on an unconscious level, felt something wrong immediately.

"This isn't right, Augustine."

"*What's wrong?*"

"I think we should call this off." The intuition flashed in his brain. Normally people participating in the riot were predictable. The innocent folks, who just happened to be in the wrong place at the wrong time, fell into three categories: run, hide, or join in. Most of the people of this demonstration who weren't actively being destructive stood there… waiting.

"*Why—*" Augustine started. She didn't finish.

Those who waited suddenly burst into action. Weapons came out from under civilian coats. Most of them were standard National Guard issue Remington XT12 assault rifles. There seemed to be at least two armed Guardsmen for every looter.

"Under the proclamation of martial law by the Governor of the State of Oregon, you are ordered to cease all destructive actions and hold yourself available to arrest," said a voice that came over multiple speakers. The voice carried far enough for Edward to hear it with his unaided ears.

The destruction paused for several seconds as the looters tried to take in this change in plans.

"Get them out of there!" Edward urged, even knowing it was much too late.

"*Sending recall signal.*"

From far below Edward hear a cry, "GET THEM!"

Edward closed his eyes and made a silent prayer to Wolf to protect his people. He didn't need to see the effects the automatic weapons made as he heard their distinctive chatter.

"*You better get out of there, Edward.*"

"On my way." Walking into the building, Edward wouldn't look back as the mall below him fell silent.

*   *   *

Detective Debnath stepped down into the Hashish Den. The sweet smoke swirled with a life of its own through the air. His partner, the Guppy, followed along behind frowning.

"Welcome. Welcome, my friends," the owner said with an accent that came from watching too many Bollywood movies. He approached the two men with open arms and a smile. "You have not graced my place in nearly a week. What can I do for you two good men? Would you care to be sharing a hookah? I can seat you immediately—"

"Benny, you can cut out the fake Persian merchant bit with us. We know you grew up five levels from here."

"Oh, but I must be keeping up my appearances for my customers. They would be expecting it, sahib."

"Well, be that as it may, Benny, I want your Metro payment," Gohar said putting both his hands inside his rain slicker before leaning against a faux-wood beam.

"But sahib, I paid just last week. I even paid you personally."

"That was then. This is now, Benny. Pay up or you know what will happen."

"Good sir, I have not the money so quickly. It doesn't grow on trees, sir."

Gohar's melted-marshmallow-like face got even more passive and expressionless.

Benny's accent disappeared. "But I don't have it, Detective. Honestly I don't. I could pay in another day if you absolutely insist but I don't owe until next month."

Gohar didn't move and didn't raise his voice. "Benny, you owe when I say you owe. You think I synchronize with Greenwich Mean Time? Am I a fucking calendar?"

"But—"

Debnath nudged over a pyramidal stack of glass hookahs. They shattered on the floor.

"I don't have it, Detective. Please, I'm begging you."

The detective fished an antique gas lighter out of his pocket and walked toward a wall of imported marijuana.

"Please, Detective! You can have everything in the till. Please don't!"

Gohar spun the ancient wheel to ignite it. He lit one of the machine-rolled reefers that sat on the counter, taking a puff.

"I'll give you everything I have! Please!"

The detective tossed the lit herb and paper into the expensive Kona blend, watching the highly dried herb catch on fire. The proprietor wanted to run to the fire extinguisher and even started, but the look in Debnath's eyes told him not to.

"Now what were you saying, Benny?" Gohar said, lighting up a Turkish reefer this time.

"I think I have enough to give you half. It is really all I have!"

Gohar tossed this newly lit cigarette into another bin to catch it on fire. Patrons melted out the front door, trying not to be seen by the knot of arguing men.

"Bring it to me and maybe," Gohar said, lighting yet another of the man's stock, "we can come up with an arrangement."

*   *   *

"I hate sending in troops when I'm not there sharing the danger," Tony complained, kicking some gravel on the roof of the Tyee Yacht Club Building like a nine-year-old after his mother turned off his net access for misbehaving.

"Shut your mouth, you big baby. You're not even three hundred meters away," Jamie said at his side, wearing a tailored, gray-camouflage jumpsuit. While gray makeup also hid her from a distance, Tony had called it fetching up close.

"Four. Four hundred sixteen meters."

"Be happy I let you come at all. You are still on the mend and that eye needs to be worked on."

"I'm fit as a fiddle. I virtual-jogged five klicks this morning and did another hour of virtual mixed martial arts."

"Yeah, and you were so weak and white afterward that Edward just about had to carry you to the showers. Listen to me, my love, nanites may close the holes, but it takes time for muscle and other sinew to regrow."

"Bah! I'm no weakling," Tony said, leaning against the railing to watch the upcoming action.

Jamie sighed. Her lover might be exasperating but he was complying, barely, with the restrictions she put on him.

"*Green Actual, this is Green One,*" David said.

"Green Actual on station. Give me one."

"*Affirm.*"

David matured very nicely in his continuing role of action leader. The younger man took his job seriously. He didn't gloss over details. He accepted criticism well and grew with it. An exceptional asset, Tony thought.

His eye's grainy resolution and the fact that the images didn't look real still bothered Tony. And no matter how much he cleaned it, the damned thing felt as if it were socketed not in biogel but rather that gritty sand that formed in the corner of his eye the morning after a bender. Oh the technicians told him it was an artifact of a new implant, but Tony couldn't help but clean it forty times more often than was recommended.

Closing his natural eye, he zoomed his artificial eye in tight on the three sprawling blocks of Kliever Memorial Armory. The haphazard annexes, added levels, army green, and esthetic mockery of architecture clearly denoted a building maintained by the military. He fired off a moronic little program in the interface that triggered on differences from one frame to the next. It showed the changes as bright contrasting colors on his image. He cancelled out the flag flapping in the near perpetual Columbia River breeze.

Tony noted a figure walking up to the building. He magnified the image enough to see a serious-looking, second lieutenant open the front door and walk in. The military man carried a crystal satchel and his only weapon was a side-arm that looked so new as to be unused. At the other end of the landing pad, the lieutenant's driver sat in a jump jeep reading a comic. Even through the grainy image he could tell it was the *Avengers*, featuring Miss Metro—another of the police's ham-handed propaganda stunts.

Tony uploaded the sleepy civilian security guard and the four teamsters unloading at the dock onto the team's shared tactical map. "Where are those drones?" Tony asked.

"*We've drawn them off station by an action in St. Helens. You should be clear for twenty minutes,*" Augustine said.

"Green Actual gives action release," Tony said.

"*Affirm. Team Green, we have a go. Squads one and two, execute landing.*"

Two army-green lift-trucks settled one behind the other at the gate. The security guard, about sixty years too old to be doing the job, climbed out of his warm booth into the windy drizzle with a shudder.

"*Howdy, Rick,*" the lead driver said to the older man.

"*Mike, I thought you was striking against working for the Nat Guard.*"

"*Was. My wife decided for me that eat'n was more important than principles.*"

"Gotcha. Sign the board. Who's the guy behind you?"

"One of those damned scabs they're hiring to tote this crap."

"OK, you wanna sign for him?"

"I'd better. He's so young I don't think he knows which side of the pen to use. Hell, he might not even know what a pen is."

The old-timer chuckled. *"So we need you to go to the assembly area."*

"What the fuck? There's only three trucks at the docks."

Tony tensed. This wasn't protocol. He scanned the scene for some reason for this change but found nothing.

"Sorry, Mike. Some janitor screwed up the docks last night. They have to be configured by hand. We'll call you when we set up one for you."

"Right, Rick."

The trucks pulled forward to an open parking area near the perimeter.

"We are on hold. Something wrong with the docks. Just wait it out," David announced.

Tony relaxed a bit but continued his vigil. He noticed a flurry of activity at one of the docking bays. A civilian detached herself to walk toward Mike's trucks.

"Sorry about the delays. As you can see we are working our asses off to get you in."

"No problem, sister. I'll wait quite a while if I have a babysitter like you."

Tony smiled at the flirtation over the net as he scanned the area.

"Keep your pants on, big boy."

"Hey, I don't mean anything by it. It's just that when you're on the road as much as I am, you don't get much female companionship."

"Don't sweat it. I'm just pulling your chain. If I really wanted to do something I'd give you my percomm code. That would be Portland seven six…"

"Hey, give a guy a chance to get a pen."

"Oh, there's my dock manager waving us over now."

"How about the rest of that number."

"Sorry. Maybe next time."

"Tease."

"Every chance I get, buster. Give me just one minute and then pull it in."

The woman walked away, giving a look over her shoulder.

David came back over the net: *"All Green units execute."*

Tony noted a jump jeep landing next to the Armory's front entrance. One of his own people, in a National Guard uniform, climbed out and entered the building carrying a crystal pouch full of molecular explosives. He also knew four other teams snuck explosives in from other entrances intent on 'accidentally leaving them behind.'

As the female dock foreman got closer to the warehouse, she looked over her shoulder again. It didn't seem natural to Tony. He took her first look as perhaps regret in not sharing her code, but when she did it a second time, and then a third, Tony got suspicious. He focused in on the trucks. Shimmers of deflected light, like gasoline fumes or heat from a fire, showed all around his trucks. He only saw them because he looked for that signature of the active camouflage suits.

"ABORT! ABORT!" Tony yelled into the tactical network. "Troops all around the trucks."

He heard the soft air sound of a silenced weapon over his earpiece. Zooming in on the cab of the truck he saw red splattered all over the inside of the cab. His vision rolled, like an ancient television screen out of vertical sync. It made him nauseous. He clicked his artificial vision off and back on. Before it had run through its basic tests, the bass roar and pressure wave of a large explosive hit him.

Tony opened his natural eye and saw the second truck had detonated. He wondered if the bodyguard driving the second truck had done it on purpose or the National Guardsmen had tampered with the payload. Some of the bodies, their active camouflage now destroyed, burned motionless and askew on the landing pad. Large pieces were missing from other bodies.

"ABORT! ABORT!" came David's echo over the net. *"Fall back."*

"I think it is time to get out of here, baby," Jamie said from beside him.

"Not until they are all out," in a voice that would brook no argument.

Automatic weapon fire from within the building itself punctuated his comment. A smaller detonation sprayed out the glass of the front door, pinging off the pair of jump jeeps.

His implant now back to functional, Tony peered down at the jeeps. His man was down with a single bullet hole in the head. "SNIPER," he called out. "Jamie, I believe you may be right. Let's get out of here."

Jamie grabbed him by the right arm to pull him bodily from the ledge. Neither realized how fortuitous the motion was. The bullet, meant for Tony's head, penetrated his left bicep, grazed the humerus, and exited.

"FUCK!" Tony yelled, dropping to the ground behind the lip of the building's edge.

Jamie's actions would have done a trained medic proud. Dropping to the ground next to her man, she yanked a syringe off the front of her coveralls and stabbed his arm.

"The nanites will deaden the pain and slow the bleeding," she said. Jamie slapped a bandage on each penetration.

"I really wish people would stop shooting me," Tony said as the nerves in his arm stopped relaying their messages of pain and bodily damage.

"Me, too," Jamie said as she wrapped the bandages and the arm with tape.

"He has to be that way," Tony said, pointing southwest. "Probably on the roof of the Correctional Institute. That's over a kilometer away. That means a bullet flight time of over a second. We are going to need to move fast and randomly."

"Can you move?"

"I have to move or I'm going to die up here. Creep over to the far corner of the building and I'll creep to the other. Remember, it will take the sniper about half a second to line up on you and fire. The bullet takes another second. Fast, random motions."

"Got it."

"Let me give us one more distraction. Give me some more of that tape." Tony tied the tape to the trigger guard of his gun. Tony took a grenade and pulled the pin. Using the gun as a weight he laid it over the spoon. "Count four when I pull the gun away and then run. Now, over there and get ready."

"*BOSS!*" came a scream over the net. Tony realized he'd been ignoring the communicator.

A whistle of wind came over his head and fountained some of the gravel roof 7 m beyond him. He must have done a poor crawl and exposed something.

"I got troubles, David. No time to talk."

"*I know. Get ready to move, we are going to put on a distraction.*"

"OK. Call the ball."

"Oh, you'll know. Get ready to move."

Another explosive roar went off behind him. Tony jumped up and ran, changing direction almost as he leapt up. Jamie mirrored him from the other side of the roof. He yanked on the tape, sending the gun flying. The spoon of the grenade, set on a spring release, spun off into the air.

Tony dove behind a metal ventilation hood just as a bullet hit it with a crack. While he admired the sniper's professionalism, he cursed as he rolled to his feet. He used the hood as cover until he heard himself absently count "four Mississippi." He ran for the next outcropping on the roof. A fragment of the exploding grenade creased his right cheek like a hot brand. Tony didn't stop but sprinted for the safety of the stairwell enclosure. Another sniper shot whistled by him but didn't strike flesh.

He stopped behind the small stair shack on the roof to catch his breath. He found Jamie already there. She panted with her hair looking like a rat had slept a week there. Sweat dripped down her cheek. Tony kissed her. Her eyes flew open and her eyebrows up.

"River?" she asked.

"Last one in is a rotten egg," Tony said, sprinting from under the cover. The mass of the building shielded the pair's dive into the Columbia River, 22 m below.

∗   ∗   ∗

Reza kept telling himself that the brandy snifter in his hand didn't make him feel as uncomfortable as the room and company did. He rolled the deep amber fluid gently around the glass and enjoyed the blackberry and oak fragrances. From the battered Camus Hors d'Age label he estimated just this single drink alone would have cost him nearly a thousand dollars. His invitation to Commissioner Krylov's home had unsettled Reza enough that the glass felt like a viper rather than a sybaritic delight.

Commissioner Krylov handed out the liquor to each of his senior staff and Colonel Reed. The company prevented Reza from enjoying the superb cognac. Good brandies should only be savored in comfort or with close friends who understood the subtly and importance of the moment. Such a crime, Reza thought. At least they were all in the study of Krylov's home where the plush velveteen couches and mohair rugs made a more apt setting.

"I wanted you all here to share in our recent victories. Thanks to Colonel Reed and Major Broadsky, we have shut down a riot before it even started, stopped the destruction of Kliever Armory, and captured some real live Greenies."

Reza, who had been contemplating how the amber fluid clung to the crystal of his snifter, snapped his head up at the last. Any captured person who'd been tagged as a Greenie could provide invaluable information.

"Excuse me, Commissioner, but you should be giving yourself most of that credit. Without the information you provided us it would have been two more disasters," Colonel Reed said with a matter-of-fact tone.

"Oh, I'll take credit for the intel but both of you acted decisively with the information, giving us two much needed boosts.

"Lieutenant."

"Yes, sir."

"You asked for something to boost morale and I give you two very public successes."

"Thank you, sir."

"But! Before we do any business, I want to propose a toast: To the men of the hour—Colonel Reed and Major Broadsky."

"Cheers!" Reza now understood the significance and decided that the expensive brandy had an appropriate place in this cadre. The drink melted on his tongue with a deep mellow richness reserved for kings and potentates of old. He felt unworthy of its smoothness.

To Reza's surprise each of their company cherished the drink, giving it the attention it deserved. He didn't know what he'd do if someone had just tossed it down.

"Now down to business," Krylov said after an appropriate time savoring the liquor. "Amber, I want you to push this on the solido for—"

"Excuse me, Commissioner," Colonel Reed interrupted.

"Yes, Charlie."

"I'd like to propose one more toast if you don't mind."

"No, by all means."

"Thank you, sir. To good intel. May it never end."

Taking another appreciative taste, Reza wondered where Krylov had managed to dig up those two nuggets of information that created their successes.

* * *

Bright beams of multiple data buses pulsed around them like multiple shooting stars following the same paths. In front of Augustine stood the wall of her team's target, the Metro senior officer's node. It glowed a menacing red, daring her to even get close to it. She felt the data eddies all around her but dismissed them. It was like a stream flowing against a dam with swirls and anomalies.

"OK, just like in our sims. This is initially a stealth run. Blackman, start raising the gain. We're going over that wall."

She heard a loud "chuff" and then the data stopped flowing. Now two bright red walls bracketed the avatars of her team. The barrier behind them blocked their exit like gates of a tunnel closing. From the data eddies she'd previously ignored, poured net presences thirty strong.

"*We're surrounded!*" Model screeched from her Barbie-doll image.

Augustine spent one breath examining the second wall and determining that it had protections as deadly as their initial goal—they would easily fry the brain of even a top tier net jock. Worse, as this was an ambush, they were being actively monitored from within.

Only thirty seconds old and the hack fell apart around her like a silk dress off a token girl. She watched bio readings of her raid members dropping as the once hidden defenders pounced on them. One hit her with an attack that felt like an axe splitting her skull wide enough to shove a fist through. Augustine heard Blackman scream. She split her mental tracks to help control the power bus. The psychological strain ramped the pain in her head.

Augustine took the time for a deep breath. Calm. Lead. Give orders. "Shiva, I want you to put up a broadband interference pattern between us and them."

"*Roger,*" said a distinctly Middle Eastern accent from the glowing trident avatar. Almost at once a static like shell formed around the dozen avatars.

"Candy, let's boost our gain on everyone. I don't like the bio readings. Give it everything you have."

"*Yes, GMa,*" came a feminine voice that sounded about eight years old from a large, striped, red-and-white medical cross.

"Totoro, Pong, and Excalibur, I want you to start migrating

each of the attackers out of the bubble. Don't be gentle."

"*Hai!*"

"*You got it, boss.*"

"Everyone settle down and focus. We've been in bad situations before. This is no different. Let's get out of here with our skins intact. Everyone dial down your nerve inputs. We won't be needing them, and we don't want to be in any more pain than we have to.

"Model, tunnel into the adjacent data stream."

"*Y-yes.*"

"Maggie, give me some help holding the reference voltage. They are trying to shut us down by messing with the voltage rails on this line."

The Simpson's cartoon baby didn't answer but the yellow representation did give a couple of sucks on her pacifier.

The remaining eight guardians inside the bubble weren't going without a serious fight. They struck with a new nerve attack that Augustine hadn't encountered before. By her own biometrics, it seemed their first attack had already melted down half a dozen of her data feeds. She hated going under the knife but to clear and replace the damage already done, not to mention regenerate the brain damage, she would have to have some serious open-skull time. To Augustine's surprise, one of the attackers tried a straight-up trace on her location. It came closer than she liked. It triggered one of her fail-safes. The circuit routed all of her traffic to an alternate provider, leaving the searcher looking for the proverbial black cat in a coal cellar that wasn't there.

"Watch your traffic feeds. I just got a trace warning."

"*Here, too.*"

"*Blocked,* jefe. "

Her opponents were front liners—high priced net jocks for rent. Oh, she could take any three, maybe four, of them by herself, but they swarmed her small group in numbers.

"*Got it,*" Model yelled. "*I'm tunneled into a Gen23.*"

Augustine smiled. The Peripheral Component Interconnect Express protocol was archaic and easily spoofed but what made it ideal was that the new Gen23 didn't even seem to obey the speed of light. They had an express lane out of here.

"Philadelphia, I want you helping to spot-reinforce Shiva's bubble. The ones outside are breaching.

"OK, everyone but Model, Shiva, and Phil, let's concentrate on these last couple of boneheads. I'll light them up one at a time. Give me everything you have that target until they are out of the sphere and then switch to the next." Their ploy, while working, gave the remaining guardians free shots at whomever they wanted.

"*SOkker is down,*" Philadelphia announced, the atomic crater within the city very visible on her representation.

"One more to go. Don't stop now," Augustine urged. No one retained any serious power so it took nearly a minute to shove out the last defender. "All right, now I want everyone to push power into the shell. We will be exiting through Model's tunnel in normal order with the exception that Shiva will exit just before me."

"*Negative. It being my fortification so I will be leaving last,*" Shiva said.

"We don't have time to argue. On my mark exit and scatter. I want maximum precautions. Don't ever use these data ports or equipment again. Contact will be reestablished through the emergency drop-box at Ohanapecosh campground." Augustine waited until her interface showed acknowledgments from everyone with whom she still had biometric signals. "Go."

Each of the members dropped through the tunnel that Model was holding open. Augustine grabbed the protocol hole so the Barbie could take her turn in the queue. With the last one out, Augustine pointed to Shiva. "Your turn."

"*I am telling you that I will be the last one out this raid.*"

Augustine sampled the sphere and found it solid. "OK, no hero stuff, Shiva. Follow me out asap."

"*That is being an affirmative.*"

Augustine generated a random number and got six. She exited the bus at the sixth node and quickly made her way back to her own body. Returning to ReL, real life, always shocked her more than the sterility of going into ViR.

The pain in her head echoed everything she had experienced in the net. It felt like a stone carver had hammered his chisel into the back of her skull. Lying on her back, she opened her eyes. Pinpoints of lights barely illuminated the enclosed three meter cubed box. The acrid smell of burnt plastic mixed with the sickeningly sweet aroma of cooked flesh. Reaching around, she could still feel the heat radiating the overloaded data jacks buried in her head. Hair melted into patches over the top of each one.

Without turning she reached into her toolkit and grabbed a pair of clippers by touch alone. Each hardwire into her brain got a release and a tug. If it didn't come free she snipped it as close to the skull as possible.

Sitting caused Augustine to retch. A portion of the vomit went through her nose. She wiped it with the sleeve of her muumuu. Again by touch, she found the single use injector and hit herself with an illegal but very powerful pain suppressant.

"Have to clear this room and get to someplace to recover," she muttered to herself.

She unlocked the triple redundant combination locks and removed three bars from the rolling bay door. As she pulled it open the bright sunlight stunned her for a moment. Looking back at the server and the net couch, she pulled the emergency purge cord.

Walking away, she could hear the pop and sizzle as everything with a boiling point of less than 2500 degrees vaporized and most everything else melted. The white-hot glow behind her rivaled the winter sun above her.

Thermite made a good eraser.

*   *   *

"I don't understand how this could have happened," Wintel blustered. The last syllable echoed down the passageways leading from their less-than-palatial digs. The six meter square room belonged to an underground system known as the Shanghai Tunnels. Stacks of munitions lined the narrow hallways.

"The 'this' that you are referring to is the deaths of hundreds of people," Tony fired back, his left arm in a sling. "Don't make it sound like a game of checker where someone just did a triple jump."

"Gentlemen," President Susan Tipton said, playing peacekeeper yet again, "let's try to keep personalities out of this."

"I must agree," Nanogate said, glaring at Wintel from inside his disguise, a weathered hoodie. "Tony, can you give us more details?"

"Three hundred thirty-one civilians known dead at the mall. We have an unknown number in custody, between one and two hundred. We haven't the foggiest clue where they are being held or we might just try a rescue operation. As you know we tried to find out. Augustine and her team tried a net raid on the executive files and they were ambushed. Two top net jocks known dead, one other hasn't reported in. Augustine is badly hurt but will recover.

"The failed bombing of the armory lost us eight dead and two captured."

"And three injured," Jamie threw in from his side.

"And that," Tony said, smiling at his lover.

"Three failed attempts," Wintel jumped back in. "I think we need more control over what operations are going to be done, not let one hotheaded cowboy run the show."

Jamie managed to hold Tony down in his seat with a gentle arm on his chest. She stood and spoke in very calm tones. "Wintel, you really surprise me. You are the dog that bites the hand that feeds him. If it weren't for that hothead, as you called him, you would be dead, probably hung as a traitor or in the glass ruins of Rodeo Cove. We guard you day and night.

"What's worse you want control over actions that you yourself approved. If I pull up the minutes of the last meeting, you voted for the net hack. The meeting before that you approved more riots. Going back three meetings I find you approved the move on the armory."

Susan didn't quite hide the giggle she felt.

Jamie's point made, she sat down. Wintel's face glowered.

"OK. I think we can table that motion for want of a second," Nanogate said with the tact of a lifetime of diplomacy. "I do have a related question, however. Don't three failed missions in a row make it likely that the other side is privy to our plans?"

"Don't go reading anything into it," Tony said, waving his good hand around in dismissal. "They have to get lucky every now and again."

"So what should our next actions be?" Nanogate asked.

"If I may speak," Thomas Marks, Jr. asked.

"By all means," Susan said, offering him the floor.

"Under normal circumstances I'd remove my principal from the hottest spot on the planet. I know the CorpGov and the president's random personal appearances have kept morale high in the populous. But the rest of the CorpGov doesn't need to be here. I suggest we sequester them out of the fire, so to speak."

"Things *are* heating up," Jamie admitted. "We just missed one of those cordoning moves on Markham yesterday."

"Then why not reduce the number of people needing to bug out in an emergency? Everyone can stay in touch via net meetings."

"I'll second that," Tony said. "It will reduce, not eliminate, the number of people dedicated to guarding."

"What about all the assassins and bounty hunters?"

"Most of them have moved off despite the huge money. They all think rightly that we are in Portland," David shared.

"Any objecting?" Susan asked. No hands went up. "Carried."

"Where should we go?" asked Wintel.

"Honestly, each of you should go somewhere different. We'll make a list and let you pick among them or choose someplace yourself. Don't discuss it with anyone else. Just grab your family, your bodyguards, and go."

"Mr. Marks, have we fully addressed your motion to the floor?"

"Absolutely, Ms. President."

"Then I suggest we return to the question Chairman Nanogate put to us. What is our next move?"

"We have a plan in place," Tony said. "The only change I see is to reduce, maybe even eliminate the flash mobs. We can send out smaller groups for sabotage instead."

"Tony, we agreed long ago that you were the military arm of this meeting. I don't think more than one or two would presume to second guess you," Nanogate said keeping his eyes directly on those of Wintel.

Susan kept the meeting going for thirty-five more minutes. When all topics were exhausted they got up to leave, but Nanogate caught Tony by the eye. They joined up and moved into an unoccupied corridor, musty with the damp of the underground complex.

"Tony, I generally don't meddle, but can you tell me why you lied so blatantly to our group?"

"I don't know what you are talking about."

Nanogate actually chuckled. "Please don't insult my intelligence. You believe as I do that there is information leaking from our meetings. Why did you call it an anomaly? While I can't calculate like your Augustine, the odds against what happened have to be galactic in size."

Tony winced. "Yes, I do believe it, but I want to keep that bastard unaware that I'm hunting until I sneak up and put a bullet through his or her treasonous mouth."

Testing

Mickey Andersen screwed up his face. Looking at the door to "Habbab Tailors. Male, Female and Ambi" he double-checked the address on the scrap paper that Bear had given him: 613 8th Ave, Level 113, New York, New York.

This leave kept getting weirder. Out of the blue, the Army gave him a forty-eight hour pass but told him that he had to use it in New York. Then Bear hands him this scrap of paper and told... no, ordered him to go to the address and to do what they told him. If that weren't enough, Bear told him not to talk about it.

"When did I become 007?" Mickey muttered to himself. "What the fuck. I'm already here." Mickey shoved the slip back into his uniform pocket and walked in. As the door closed behind him, an old fashioned bell tinkled above his head.

"Welcome, Private Andersen. Didn't they tell you not to wear your uniform?" asked a comely young blond from behind a counter with the patina of much use.

"Uh . . ."

"Articulate also, I see. Looks like a twenty-eight long for trousers and a forty long for the jacket. C'mon back here and let's get you measured proper." The blond led the way through a cloth curtain to a room that looked like an inside out disco ball, each surface bright and shiny. "Now stand there and close your eyes," she said, pointing to a pair of black painted feet on the bottom-most facet of the ball.

Like a good soldier, Mickey did as he was told. With his eyes shut he heard a vibration through the floor followed by a clatter like an old fashioned teletype machine. The chatter stopped and the whine abated. Mickey stood there.

"You can open your eyes now, Private."

"Helga, Private Andersen's measurements deviate in the arms by over three centimeters," a soft, feminine, computer-generated voice said.

Helga scrutinized his arms. "That's right, Donna. The right is longer than the left."

"I still got it, baby," the computer named Donna said.

"Uh, ma'am, could you tell me what this is all about?"

"They didn't tell you anything, did they? The Army is buying you a suit."

"I already got my dress uniform, ma'am."

"No, Private, a civilian suit."

"What? Oh, fuck it. Oh, sorry, ma'am. I mean, whatever. If I've learned anything it's just to do what they tell me. Hell, the Army would ask me to carry water with a fork even if a bucket was handy."

"Private, if you'll head back up to the front desk, Donna will have your suit ready for you."

* * *

"Bless it all," Augustine railed. "It took me months to get my hair just the right length to spike." Augustine occupied a private berth at Jim's BodyWerks. Her head had been shaved billiard-ball style to expose her network jacks. An IV ran into her arm. Her vital statistics displayed in the air at the foot of her bed.

Tony squicked a little at how much damage Augustine had suffered. Blackened skin radiated out from six of her sixteen ports. "If a little hair is all you have to worry about, then you are golden, Augustine."

"But it's not. I've got my hack team strewn about the world, my ability is impaired, I am on the injured list for who knows how long… all in the middle of a war," she said sitting up. "I don't have time to be out."

Tony pushed her back down. "You aren't irreplaceable, Augustine. Oh, I will admit nearly irreplaceable but we can handle it while you get better."

"Oh, really? That's why you are here and not out jousting with the Metros? You aren't here to just give me a bedside pep-talk." Augustine crossed her arms over her chest and set her mouth into a firm line.

"We always used to wonder about Sonya, but now I wonder if you are psychic. I have a problem that I don't know how to crack and

I'm hoping you will have some thoughts."

The mention of their deceased friend did make Augustine pause. "No, I don't read minds. I just have a lot of years and read faces pretty damned good. So what is this problem, oh mighty leader."

"Smart ass. OK, in a nutshell I want the bastard who's selling us out. I've narrowed the list to eight who had the information of all three of the failed raids: Me, Nanogate, Mr. Marks, Madam President, David, Wintel, MinInc, Royal PetroChem and you.

"Now as a first pass approximation analysis: I'd rather shoot off my own genitals than think you or David is involved. If it were Nanogate we wouldn't be fighting in the first place. I know I didn't do it so to me that leaves just Marks, President, Wintel, MinInc and Royal Petrochem."

"And of course you want it to be Wintel."

"Well, it's no secret I don't like the supercilious bastard but I won't let that cloud my judgment on this. It's too important."

"Well, I have an idea… she won't do it, but just maybe she will help. First, get Janet, that girl in Greenpeace logistics and spin her up with what you have."

"Do you think I'm totally worthless? She's been up and going since your raid went down."

"OK, you don't have to get snotty. Get her linked up with us, and then we'll place a percomm call."

"I'll bite… . . . to whom?"

"Someone I know who was in Interpol."

∗   ∗   ∗

The dark skin of Colonel Reed contrasted against his urban-camouflage gray. The solido didn't soften his rigid, thin-lipped face or overly-straight back. With his arms clasped behind his back, he looked the part of a stern schoolmaster. "I am saddened to be before you today to perform this task. But I will not pass off an unpleasant duty or weighty responsibility to anyone else.

"It has now been ten days since the riot at Lloyd Center. The one hundred sixteen survivors have been tried and, when appropriate, sentenced. The sentences have seen judicial review.

"While we have tried them in a secret location to prevent

further terrorist actions, we have recorded the trials. Those solidos will be made public so that the populace will understand that the rights of the accused have actually been preserved.

"I will note that of the one-sixteen, twelve were acquitted of all charges and six were offered and accepted boxing. The remaining were sentenced to death. We will execute sentence right here and now.

"We suggest sending small children from the room."

The scene shifted to a row of ten prisoners standing rigid on the same rooftop ledge that had been used for the previous executions. The only thing moving on the convicted, other than the thin wind blowing hair, were their terrified eyes. Twenty-one soldiers marched out onto the roof at a slow beat.

One stopped short and spoke commands: "Deploy for punishment detail." Two men flanked each of the condemned. "Ready."

Each pair drew their side arms.

"Aim."

The pairs put their guns to the temples of the condemned, aiming at a backward angle as to not endanger their comrades.

"Fire."

The back of each victim's head exploded. The bodies fell over the edge.

The image went back to the Colonel.

"I take full responsibility for following my orders and for the execution of the rules of martial law.

"Bring in the next accused."

Nine more times the guns spoke.

* * *

"You've reached a percomm code that is no longer in service. If you feel—"

"Prioress Hanna, that is beneath you. You should know that I can even read your heartbeat over this," Augustine said. Tony and Janet Prieto, a dark-skinned, dark-eyed woman, crammed into Augustine's hospital room.

"You can't blame me for trying. Getting a percomm from the GAM isn't exactly the high point of my day. I'm going to have to fill out contact reports and probably say a few dozen Our Fathers just for taking the call in the first place."

"I'm sorry, Sister, but I have a problem that I think you are uniquely qualified to solve."

There was silence from the other end of the line.

"Prioress?"

"I'm here. I just can't imagine what you might be thinking, Augustine. I made it very clear that the priory, the church, and even those called to God can't get involved in temporal matters. Only pure politeness keeps me from severing this connection right now."

"I do understand that, Sister. I came to you not for you to help us, but for you to educate us. Teaching is still one of the tenants of the church, is it not?"

"Well then, perhaps I've been hasty in judging you, dear. What did you have in mind?"

"Hanna, let me introduce Tony Sammis and Janet Prieto, two of my colleagues."

"It is always a pleasure to get a call from a head of state."

"Hardly a head of state," Tony objected. "I—"

"You only make heads of state," Hanna interjected. *"The power behind the throne."*

"Are you trying to elicit a reaction, Prioress? I stopped responding to that kind of emotional jab in junior high."

"Glad to hear it, Mr. Sammis. I hope you keep up that level emotional field through the rest of this crisis you fomented.

"So what is it you want to learn and why?"

"I'm hunting a traitor—someone who has betrayed those he agreed to protect. You were in Interpol."

"So what have you learned so far?"

"We had three missions go south within just a few days of one another," Tony said. "We traced down all the people who had access to the information. We've narrowed the list to only those who knew about all three. We have eight names."

"Did you consider all the girlfriends, spouses, children, prostitutes, or football buddies that they might have told? How about hackers that might have gotten their diary? What if someone has tapped or spoofed a phone?

"What I'm trying to tell you is that counterintelligence is never an exact science. It is one of the reasons I left Interpol. Unless you find a smoking gun, which is rare, the best you can hope for is an eighty percent confidence in your findings."

Tony snorted. Augustine scowled at him.

"Is that funny to you, Mr. Sammis? I'm sure you aren't going to pat this traitor on the head and waggle your finger at him. I'll spare you the sermon about killing, but are you callous enough to kill someone on only an eighty percent confidence?"

"I'm sorry, Sister. I wasn't laughing at the thought of killing someone. The number you chose had something to do with why I personally am here leading these killers in the first place."

Augustine jumped in. "Prioress, we do understand. We will give your concerns due thought before we act on them."

"Thank you, Augustine. I will hold you to that."

"So do you have any suggestions?"

"You have a right mess. I suggest traffic analysis. Look over the traffic going in and out not only of your people of interest, but also your enemies. Don't miss any message method. When you link A to B then you have your traitor."

"Thank you for your wisdom, Prioress."

* * *

"Bear, you ever been to Cajetan space station before?" Mickey itched at the neckline of his reflective-chrome dress shirt. The suit pants also seemed to be cut wrong. His uniform was normally tight enough not to let his balls roam around free.

"Nope," said Corporal Blackbear who wore a mango-pink pantsuit and a turquoise silk scarf. "Closest I ever came was when I did my time at Camp Leroy Petry," he said, reminding Mickey of the Army's space station.

"I did a tour there as well. We used to talk about the gambling, shows, and girls at Cajetan. We used to hope we'd get leave there, but we never did."

"Me, too."

"So now the Army is not only ordering us there, but also giving us money to gamble with, clothes, and rooms. Not only that but told us to leave our weapons and uniforms behind. What the fuck, Bear?"

"Our orders are to go up, have a good time, and await further orders. I don't know about you, Mickey, but there are some girls with my name ALL over them."

*   *   *

Trying hard not to hyperventilate, Tony lay back on a padded table in a tiny, dim back room of Rob's e-Bio Emporium. An ancient operating theatre light complex hung above him on a multi-jointed arm. Gleaming metal, ceramic, and plastic instruments lay in disposable trays and less than tidy masses of electronics, old monitors, and biocabling sat, dangled, or even perched from every other surface in the room.

"So, Mr. Jackson, what can I do for you?" asked the balding Rob, sporting two tufts of hair sticking straight up from either side of his head. An old-fashioned magnifier band seemed to perch on the two white spots of fur. All he needed was a white lab coat to make a perfect mad scientist. Instead he had a pocket protector in his light-blue, button-up shirt.

"I recently got this eye prosthetic from some of the most reputable people in the industry, and it—"

"Let me guess. It feels more like a dream and the image is pixelated or even blurry."

"Yeah, how did you—"

"Bloody amateur corpies. Oh, don't get me wrong, they are paid and paid well for their work but they just don't understand that the brain isn't a direct interface device." The man pulled over what looked like a tall aluminum coatrack with sixteen or so arms, each ending in a sharp implement of some kind. "Those high priced butchers just think all you have to do is cram electrons down the optic nerve." He started arranging the pointy ends of all the arms aimed right at Tony's face.

As he oozed sweat from his forehead, Tony managed to get out, "Umm—"

"No, don't worry. I can straighten out their mess with no problems, Mr. Jackson." The technician's hands moved swiftly as he talked. They plugged in equipment, engaged power sequences, counted out instruments.

A hypospray injected into Tony's neck before he knew Rob had it in his hand. "That was Neuroflex mixed with a mild sedative. Once it takes hold it will help us reanalyze your optic receivers."

Tony tried to roll over and vomit as the gorge had risen in his throat but found his forehead suddenly strapped down. His chest convulsed, and he expected to be dealing with a mouthful of partially digested breakfast but nothing came up.

"Don't worry. You may feel some slight nausea but that's just the drug hitting your nervous system.

"The brain needs to develop interpretive circuits of what the images are. Between the drugs, the adjustments I'll make to their hardware—," Rob said, leaning over him and looking into his electronic eye. "Holy crap is that a Pfizer Rainbow Fourteen? They aren't even out on the market yet. Good thing I got a buddy on the inside feeding me their specs and schematics. You got good connections, Mr. Jackson. If I were a less ethical man I might just cut that out. It must be worth about eighty thousand right now."

Straps wrapped around Tony's wrist and then his legs faster than Tony's muddled mind could travel. "I'm not sure I wa—"

"Nothing to worry about," the loquacious man said. "I do this about six times a week. We can't have those arms flailing about as we pluck that bad boy out of its socket, now can we?"

"But I don't—"

"Anyway, I'll show you some images that along with those neural stimulators will speed up the brain's development of new cognitive pathways and buffers." Rob finally settled down and brought out a brown Tyvek bag. He pulled out a sandwich and a pouch of beer. He took a big bite, dripping crumbs and what looked like mayonnaise down his front. The man put his elbows up onto the padded table and looked close at Tony's real eye. "Probably another minute, Mr. Jackson," Rob said, dripping some viscous liquid onto Tony's shirt. The drugs wouldn't let Tony even care.

After inhaling the sandwich and the Dos Equis, the older man snapped his fingers in front of Tony's real eye. It didn't blink.

"By the way, Jackson is a crappy alias, Mr. Sammis."

Only inside did Tony panic.

"But don't worry, we'll take really good care of you. When my wife was pregnant with our first, one of those bastards hit her when she didn't move out of the way fast enough. She lost the baby right that night. I owe them bastards."

* * *

Reza yawned as he walked into the precinct. For the first time in his memory, the yawn didn't signal being overstretched and without sleep, but exactly the opposite. He'd slept fourteen hours straight.

"Nice of you to join us, Lieutenant," joked Detective John Ho.

"Your wife was a handful last night so it took longer than usual, Detective." Several of the officers in the squad room laughed, including Ho himself.

"Can I get some coffee over here," Reza yelled as he walked into his office, chasing a boxed cleaning unit from the room. Three officers started for the coffee dispensers and then all stopped. Then they all started again. The trio laughed. Detective Edgar Gutierrez finally drew the stalemate to a close as he filled up a mug and walked to the Lieutenant's office.

"Lieutenant, here is your coffee. Also, sir, I wanted to talk to you about—"

Lieutenant Narendra absently picked up the mug with one hand as he paid attention to the filmies on his desk. "Don't bother, Detective. We'd all been under way too much stress. My recommendation to the senior staff will be to erase violations from the official records during that period—all of them, not just yours."

"Thank you, sir."

"But more importantly have you—and Patrolman Walsh, was it?—have you two buried the hatchet? Keep in mind that I'll be asking him the same question."

"Please do so, sir. While I don't think we will ever be best buddies, we weren't before the incident, either. Just to show my good faith, I'm taking him to the Portland Lumberjacks' game this weekend. Walsh took me out for beers last Friday."

"Excellent, Detective."

The officer started to leave and then turned back. "We're going to win, aren't we, sir."

"It certainly looks that way, Gutierrez. Now get out so I can talk to Sergeant Tolbert."

"Oh, I'm sorry, Sergeant, I didn't see you there. I didn't mean to get in your way."

"I just got here, Detective, so there is no reason to worry." The prim and proper Tolbert sat like he was at attention.

"Close the door, Sergeant." After a brief pause for compliance, Reza continued, "So what have you learned?"

"The Guard is playing their cards very close to the vest, sir. I've learned that the GAM prisoners are being held at an undisclosed location out of state. They have all been through some level of interrogation. All of them flatly deny being members of the Green Action Militia but do admit to being part of the alliance to return the CorpGov to power."

"Hmm. Do you think they said this to make the Guardsmen go easier on them?"

"With just this data I might think that, but each of them tells substantially the same story. And they give up the information freely, which when I give you my last nugget will make you understand why this is significant."

"Oh, come on, Sergeant. Don't hold out on me."

"They are all registered bodyguards, and you know how difficult it is to get them to even admit to the time of day."

*   *   *

Under his heavy breathing, David Swift cursed in Cantonese, Swahili, and three dead languages. His curly red hair and his sweater dripped with sweat. It hadn't even been a mission. He wanted some cheesecake from the Elephants deli. The fucking National Guard weren't supposed to be anywhere near here, much less at street level. He'd turned the corner and literally walked into a pair of unarmored noncoms. David didn't know whether they were here for the teriyaki salmon, some bagels and smears, or were trolling for tattoo girls. But the long and short of it, they were in the wrong place at the wrong time. David speed drew his Colt dragoons and delivered a lethal dose of hypervelocity metal fragments to each of the men before they could react. One had his entire face removed down to the skull. As David bolted, the other man must have gotten off a percomm transmission because hundreds of troops showed up with support vehicles.

The heavy footfalls of at least a full squad of National Guardsmen pounded beneath his hiding place inside the electronics' cavity of a solido sign. David checked the charge on his dragoon pistols. Full enough not to need the battery replaced. They were museum quality pieces. He'd had them less than a month and he'd already used them to kill.

"Augustine, I'm in trouble," David whispered through his percomm.

"*What's wrong, David?*"

"I kinda ran into the entire National Guard."

"*Where are you? I can—*"

"Augustine, you can't do shit for me unless you can turn back time. I'm safe where I am until they start a nanite trace. You need to get everyone out of here to a safe house I don't know."

"*Are you being a defeatist, David?*"

"No, ma'am. I think I can get out of here but there's a leeetle bit more than a chance I'll get my butt captured. Now bug out!"

"*We're already moving. Are you sure we can't help?*"

"Not unless you have a freaking army. Misdirection isn't going to work here, Augustine. If I get out I'll ping the emergency mailbox in Austin."

"*God go with you, David.*"

"Not for a long time, but thanks for the sentiment." He severed the percomm and considered his predicament—23 m from the ground in a metal box surrounded by voltages that would fry him if he moved more than a centimeter without exposing himself. An army of trained, armored soldiers hunted for him above and below. His gauss guns were effectively useless against the National Guard's armor unless he happened to catch a joint or an open helmet.

He'd given Augustine the sugar-coated version of the story. His only real assets, other than his current unknown whereabouts was the pair of torc grenades he carried. He wouldn't go down quietly if it came to that.

If he could assure himself of even ten minutes of safety he'd be able to vanish in any number of ways.

Above him a huge, charged, metal screen rotated on an old-fashioned spindle motor in the midst of the solido of a woman wearing only a smile. The old-fashioned but effective zapper killed the bugs that would mar the image. He wondered if he were about to join those insects in whatever afterlife there was.

"I want you two to station yourselves at either end of this alley. Stay in sight of one another," he heard beneath him. "If you see him you are not to engage but to report and track."

"Yes, Corporal Offut, report and track," a pair of voices echoed almost in unison.

David pulled out his grenades for quick access if he needed them. He hung them by the spoon on the edge of the electronics box. He could get away from one of the pair, then he probably could get away from both of them, but he'd be exposed long enough for them to radio for help. He didn't know how long it would take for response to show up or what form it would take. The grenades hanging by their spoons gave him an idea, assuming there was no effective aerial response within the first two minutes.

He guessed his plan at no better than a fifty-fifty chance. As staying here gave him effectively zero chance, he didn't have much of a choice.

He plucked at a thread on his green sweater until it started to unwind. It took only a few minutes to have a strand of yarn several meters long. With his pocket-knife he hacked it into two pieces, one about a meter long and another about six meters long. He tied each to a grenade pin, which he loosened to the very edge of holding the spoon in place. He got into a crouching position before finishing. The other end of each piece of yarn he tied around the rotating shaft of the bug zapper. Dutifully it began to wind the yarn around it.

David leapt to the rusted fire escape and started running up.

"Stop!" he heard below him.

"We have the subject at 103 Northwest King Ave. at Twenty-First Ave. in the alley. He is at the thirteenth level and climbing fast up the east side of the building. Requesting immediate response," David heard above the metallic clangs of his boots hammering as he took every second step. Through the rusted metal stairs, David saw the two soldiers close in beneath his position. David said a silent prayer of thanks.

The short piece of yarn pulled taut on the first pin and it pulled free easily. The spring-loaded spoon flew off into the distance, allowing the grenade to drop straight down. It struck the ground just short of three seconds later. Each of the soldiers watched their quarry through the telescopic sights of their gun. They didn't see the nearly globular device fall, but they heard the distinctive sound as it hit the ground. One turned to run. The other looked down from his sight but the grenade had bounced 1.3 m high and exploded centimeters from his chin.

The extreme temperature vaporized his flesh and approached the melting point of his weapon such that it bowed from the blast's overpressure. The second man had his lungs ripped apart from the explosion as his body hurtled 6 m into the side of an ancient dumpster. The impact shattered extremity bones and his rib cage, leaving only his pelvis, skull, and spine intact. The ablative plastic armor on his back absorbed most of the heat but melted down onto his skin, burning it to char. The man lay unmoving in the dent his body caused, blood leaking from his ears and mouth.

David didn't know all the details of what happened below him but he kept his mouth open as the shock wave hit. He could feel the ripple in his lungs but not the death dealing tears. He ran into the building at the next entrance. Finding a broken-out window, he scanned the building opposite. "I fucking hate heights!" Backing away from the opening he winced and sprinted as fast as he could toward it. He flung himself out. For a full second he hung in free flight.

Dave shot the window on the other side as he approached, cracking it. The semi-elastic collision with the shattered safety plastic actually softened the blow. His left shoulder dislocated on impact. His roll onto his back over ceramcrete rubble and broken window wouldn't have impressed his aikido instructor but it lessened that impact as well. His momentum didn't bring him to his feet to allow him to keep running like in all the cheesy solidos. He had to use his good arm to leverage himself up.

David, covered in dust and a variety of cuts of all sorts, dashed to the nearby stairwell and ran down eight levels, taking every third step before finding a crosswalk to yet another building. There he waited, trying to erase the stitch in his side by filling his lungs as full as he could. He knew crossing now would get him nabbed. He needed his second distraction.

Oblivious to anything going on around it, the second grenade released as the yarn timer tugged its pin free. Near the smoldering crater of the first detonation four medics and seventeen troopers worked diligently, the former trying to help the injured man and the latter to pick up David's track on a building he no longer was in.

The grenade, this time, fell into softer earth and didn't make a sound. Three of the National Guardsmen saw the grenade and called out. Six of the people in the danger zone actually survived the explosion.

David counted ten after the roar before crossing the bridge, trying to walk calmly so if someone did see him they wouldn't think he were running for his life. Ten minutes later, in the safety of the sewers below the third building, David stopped and vomited.

*   *   *

"Do we appear to be on schedule, Sergeant?" Captain Ken Maddox asked.

"Not even close, sir. Finding the civilian with the right codes to open the vault put us behind by nearly an hour."

"I think they cut this one too close. If we don't load these Caltrops missiles on schedule we somehow have to make up that time on the road or we miss the Mars shuttle. And having weapons just sitting around for the National Guard to notice is exactly what Command doesn't want. Any chance we can speed things up?"

"We've already cut out security screen to the bone, sir. All the men are working flat out. They're ahead of projection by fifteen minutes. We might carve another ten off that before we're done."

"Best laid plans, eh, Sarg?"

"I couldn't agree more, sir."

"Could we gain anything by pitching in ourselves?"

"Excellent idea, sir. If nothing else it will build the team's morale."

"I've got another idea that might get us some additional speed, Sergeant, but for now let's go work together to tote crates."

The pair moved down on the floor and chipped in just like the rest of the men. Five minutes in, and sweating like someone locked in a sauna for three weeks, the captain called for attention.

"Folks, I have six bottles of thirty-year-old scotch. The top six loading teams get a bottle... .... providing you beat Sergeant Sims and me...starting right now."

As they hurried to collect the next missile, Sergeant Sims said, "Now that just was downright mean, sir."

"You don't think they'll work harder, if not just to show up the old man?"

"I think we should run the whole bunch past the surgeon after this to make sure no one got a hernia, sir."

Captain Maddox laughed until he hear a squawk over the surveillance net.

"Black Three—troops incoming fast down Brigham Road."

"Affirmative, Black Three. Who are they? Over."

"National Guard. Can't make out unit."

"Can you estimate strength, Black Three?"

"Company size with attached artillery. I see two Wolfe APCs and many lift-trucks. No tanks. I say again. No tanks."

"Affirmative, Black Three. Keep us advised. Black Six, did you copy that?"

"Black Six copies company-sized unit of National Guardsmen with organic artillery," Captain Maddox said over the tactical net. He caught the eye of the sergeant and they both set down the missile crate. Their two platoons didn't stand a chance against that kind of force, even fighting from a defensive position. "They couldn't stay stupid forever, now could they?"

"No, sir, they couldn't."

"Get the men to set up a defensive perimeter. Make it obvious. Make sure each and every one knows that their weapons are to be safed and not fired unless I give the specfic command. Being fired on will not be responded to."

"Yes, sir."

"Especially check on Magnusson. He has an itchy trigger finger."

"I'll sit on Magnusson, sir."

"Actually take Magnusson with you to set up the explosives."

"Yes, sir."

"I'll be with you soon. I have a message to send to Command."

*   *   *

The quiet time just after gave him more pleasure than most men. His fingers traced a line up the slit in Jamie's lime-green negligee, teasing the skin of her thighs. Tony cradled her head on his shoulder as she gave half a smile with her eyes closed. Her crimson hair sprayed out, and her lipstick and her mascara were smeared in a way that could only be described as the "just fucked look."

His fingers lingered. Using his new "Rob" vision, he zoomed in close to her knee where he found goosebumps and dimples he'd never noticed before. His vision now looked as real from one eye as the other. Leaning down he kissed her forehead. "Thank you, baby," Tony said, rumbling in a voice about an octave lower than usual.

Jamie wrapped her arms around his barrel width and nuzzled down into the fur of his chest. She let out a sweet sigh. Her turn allowed him to caress the back of her thighs and buttocks. He gave special attention to the sensitive skin right at the intersection of the two.

Her warmth against him felt good. This apartment had few

amenities except a clean bed. Heat wasn't one of them. Now he finally felt the brisk January temperatures. He reached down and pulled up the comforter. Her body wriggled and cuddled even closer. He didn't need to see the smile sketched on her face this time to know it was there.

"What are you thinking?" Jamie asked, spinning the hairs on his chest around her index finger.

"You." Tony grinned broadly.

"Me what?"

"Nothing specific. All about you, beautiful. Maybe just your sexy ass," he said squeezing it gently.

"Blarney. What were you really thinking? I could feel your body change…. . . . tense up."

"Really, I was thinking about you and *carpe diem*."

"Well, you can seize just about anything you want on me."

Tony laughed gently. "I like grabbing your 'just about anything.' No, I was thinking about how this is probably our last triste to—"

"What?!" Jamie said, bolting upright. Tony could see her eyes fogging up.

"Baby, no. You didn't let me finish. This is likely our last bed bouncing together for quite some time."

"That's better?"

"Better than what you were thinking." Tony pulled her back down to his chest, feeling at least one wet tear splashing.

"So you know what I'm thinking now?"

"Only sometimes, my lady love. Jamie, I don't want to lose you, ever. You aggravate me. You please me. You've become something more than I ever thought I could have in my life."

Jamie snuffled and a couple more drops found their way to his skin.

"Who hurt you, Jamie? You are sometimes so jumpy about us that I think you have a split personality. One minute you are strong enough to split an atom and the next you are so soft I think a marshmallow could pierce you."

"Can we just leave it alone?"

"If you want to, baby. I just wanted to know more about you and how to avoid hurting you… even unintentionally."

Jamie just lay against him. Tony could feel the tenseness of her muscles as he wrapped himself tightly around her. She quivered and shook. He felt as if anything he might say could make it worse. Tony stroked her hair. Some unknown time later, she relaxed in his arms.

"I'm sorry," she whispered like a little girl after a scolding.

"There's nothing to be sorry about, Jamie. I will hopefully learn what to say and not to say over time."

When she finally lifted her head and met his eyes, her face was puffy and the muscles along her jawline still rippled. "I will tell you, just not now." She wiped her runny nose across his chest. "Now what is this about not being together for a while?" she said with all the strength of the sugar crust over *crème brûlée*.

"Good grief, woman, all I wanted to say is that because we haven't been successful in finding the damned traitor we need to split up and dig deep. I didn't mean that I wanted to kick your pretty ass out of my bed permanently. Hell if I had my way it wouldn't even be temporarily, but we have to be safe."

"We can be safer together."

"Maybe."

*　*　*

Crates, forklifts, and even a picnic table barricaded the loading bays of the armory. To Major James's eye it would be a tough nut to crack. According to Mil-Specs the walls were supposed to be able to withstand any small arms fire he could bring to bear. Fortunately, that wasn't all Colonel Reed had sent.

"Captain Portman, I want your mortar platoons to set up beyond this hill," Major James said as they poured over a map set up on the hood of the jump jeep. "Our intelligence says they have no artillery support of their own so you will be shielded."

"Yes, sir," the captain said, jogging off, already delivering his own orders over their tactical net.

"Michael, I want your Wolfes to stay out of range of anything they can have and provide air cover as required. Don't use those Penetrator missiles unless I order it. We don't want to damage the ammunition they have stored there."

"Yes, sir," the man said, jumping into the nearest Wolfe APC and racing off.

"Captain Green, I want your men deployed along the entire

perimeter for now. I'm concerned about their exposure with all those Caltrops anti-personnel missiles they have. We'll think of something interesting for them to do if the—"

"Sir, we have movement up front."

The major looked up to see two men exiting the hasty fortifications. One of them carried something white tied to the end of a stick. The other had his hands high in the air.

"Bring them through the line back to here."

The two men didn't hurry but kept up a pace that ate up the distance.

"Captain Green. Tell your men to be wary of infiltrators on the flanks."

"Yes, sir."

"I'm paranoid," James muttered to himself, "but am I paranoid enough?"

"Sir, they say one of the men has a small explosive device wired to his neck," Corporal Miller said.

"Were they trying to blow me up?"

"No, sir. Too small for that. It appears the one with his hands up is a prisoner of Captain Maddox, the commander of the armory force."

"Did the captain have any weapons?"

"No, sir, nor did he have the detonator. In fact other than his clothes, the only thing he brought was a memory crystal."

"'Curiouser and curiouser! cried Alice,'" James quoted. "Send them both up, but keep the prisoner at least ten meters away."

"Yes, sir."

A jump jeep bounded from the front line and landed at the prescribed distance. Captain Maddox climbed out of the jeep and walked casually up to Major James before coming to attention and saluting. James returned the salute.

"At ease, Captain."

"Before we begin, Major, I would like to return one of your men."

"One of my men? You've captured one of my men? Captain Green, why haven't I been informed of this?"

"But, sir, we've lost no men. All position locators show green."

"Perhaps I've not been clear, sir. I'd like to return your spy. Once you started showing up it wasn't hard to find out which one of my men was actually in your employ. He has been tried by field court martial and been found guilty of treason. However, executing him would not start our negotiations out on a good footing. If the major will allow me, I'll disarm the explosive on his neck."

Major James nodded. The captain walked over to the prisoner and typed in some commands on an old-fashioned keypad stuck to the crude explosive necklace. Private Ortiz, the necklace wearer, scowled at him but said nothing more.

"I return him to you with all my heart, sir. Better you should have a snitch than us."

"Thank you, Captain. I assure you I didn't know—"

"We are soldiers, sir. We often don't. So that brings me to the point of this discussion. I'm here to determine your intent," Captain Maddox said, not changing his parade ground stance.

"I thought that was quite obvious, Captain. I am here to take the armory and prevent you from shipping the munitions away."

"That is as I expected. I have been given very specific orders in this situation by National Command Authority."

"The president?"

"Yes, Major James."

"Well then, what are those orders?"

"I've been ordered to surrender as soon as you have listened to this," the captain said, holding out the memory crystal.

"You should know that the balance of forces is such that we don't need you to surrender, Captain."

Captain Maddox didn't flinch. "The major doesn't wish his men to be killed any more than I do. Why get even a single man hurt when we are willing to surrender if you just listen to a message, sir."

"When you are right, you are right, Captain. I'll take that chip.

"Corporal, bring up your solido equipment."

"Yes, sir."

The projector showed up in less than four seconds, a nearly interminable time where the two officers stood waiting for the other to blink. Neither did. The major slid the crystal into position and pressed play. The famous image of the president appeared in the air above the projector. "Commander, I think you know who I am. I'm disappointed that you could ignore your oath to the Constitution so easily. But then I think we are beyond that, aren't we?" The president's face became stony. "So, given those parameters I have but one thing to say to you. The men who are surrendering to you will be treated as prisoners of war.

"I know you are asking yourself, 'Or what?' right now, Commander. The answer to your question is very simple. If you do not treat these men and all other surrendering personnel with dignity and respect, now and during their incarceration, I will consider that the states of Utah and Oregon have chosen to rebel against the United States. As such we will wage full and unrestricted warfare against the entirety of the states with all means at our disposal." The president paused for several seconds to let that sink in. Without raising her voice, or blustering in the slightest, she added, "And that means nuclear, orbital, biologic, chemical, and nanite warfare. Remember that not everything developed by the Army reaches the National Guard, Commander.

"I've had my say. Captain Maddox has my orders. You have your choice, Commander."

The image dissolved. The major's adam's apple bobbed.

"The president has a way with words, doesn't she, Captain."

"Indeed, Major James. When she ordered me to surrender I was less than tactful. She reminded me just who wears the pants in this country."

"So where does that leave us, Captain Maddox?"

"I will return to my men. Commencing ten minutes from my return, I will send out ten unarmed men every ten minutes until we have all surrendered. We are seventy-three in number. I will be in the last group, which will be thirteen. I will be the only armed person leaving the building and only with the side-arm permitted an officer which I will surrender to you personally, Major."

"I agree, Captain. I'm sorry you are in this position."

"And I, Major, am sorry you are in your position. Will history vindicate either of us?" The captain didn't wait for a response but rather turned and went back to the jeep.

True to his word, men started out exactly ten minutes after his return. At least for his part the major decided to be cautious. Each of the surrendering men were treated well. They were patted down for weapons. One man still had a knife in his boot, but there were no other issues. The victorious National Guardsmen applied nylon zip ties to hold the men and with dignity put them into the back of a troop truck. For over an hour the Army troops marched out.

When Captain Maddox reach his lines, Major James started an order to his troops to move in on the armory. An explosion barked inside the building. Sixteen more followed in close succession. The hasty barricades were blown from the docks. Shattered and singed wood rained down on the soldiers. The 300 kg battery of a forklift shook the ground as it landed not 6 m from the major.

Captain Maddox smiled at the major as he handed over his pistol. "I said we would surrender and give you the armory. I didn't say I'd let you have what's inside."

*   *   *

"I'd like to welcome Augustine back, at least in an advisory role," President Tipton's Presidential Seal said to the congregation of net avatars around the Round Table. By unanimous agreement, the president was kept on as the permanent moderator as she seemed to deal more even-handedly with, as Nanogate put it, "... the more pugnacious members of our assemblage."

"Thank you, Madam President."

"And if we catch you doing anything with your new net jacks before they are fully healed we have agreed to turn you over to Christine... . . . gift wrapped and 'Please cut me!' tattooed to your forehead."

"Yes, Madam President. You can be assured that I have no interest in slowing my recovery or damaging the brand spanking new interface. The neural interface requires much interpretive growth before I'm in top form again."

"Just as long as we are clear. OK, folks, I have our agenda here in front of me. Any reason to deviate this morning?" No one flagged attention. "Excellent. We'll start with Mr. Sammis's report on the loss of units of the Fifteenth Sustainment Brigade."

When the focus passed and Tony's squiggly virus symbol lit up he began to talk. "Folks, we knew this time would come. The Metros couldn't stay stupid forever. Infiltration was always a significant probability. We've been lucky it took so long to bite us.

"Seventy-three members of the Fifteenth were loading Caltrops antipersonnel cluster missiles out of a depot just outside Price, Utah, when they were surrounded by a battalion of the National Guard—I don't seem to have the opposition unit designation handy. They were dispatched out of Salt Lake City where the crackdown on subversive activities is even harsher than here.

"I've been informed that one of the members of the company called in to the National Guard what they were doing. Oh, I'd like to mention the guilty bastard a bit out of order. His command summoned a field court martial, tried him, and sentenced him to death by firing squad." Tony held up his hand to stay the attention lights he saw on most of the attendee's avatars. "But in his surrender, his commander turned the prisoner over to the National Guard. The sentence adjudicated is moot unless we manage to win. President, I've been given the suggestion to have you commute his sentence to a Bad Conduct Discharge."

Nanogate buzzed in on an interrupt. "Mr. Sammis, you say that you've 'been given the suggestion.' You don't disagree?"

"Oh, I have no problem if we commute the sentence after we are finally done with this, but removing it now sends a message I don't agree with. It says that anyone can spy on us effectively without consequences. I say keep it this way to discourage repeats. It may stop someone who joined us with the intent of doing the same."

"I will not put this to a vote," the president said. "This is entirely within my sphere and I will not relinquish either the right nor the responsibility that goes with my office!"

"I'm sorry, Madam President," Tony backfilled, "I didn't mean to imply for this group to usurp your authority. I only sought to provide input."

"Agreed and understood. I've taken the input under advisement. Please continue with your report."

"As most of you know, per our standing doctrine with the use of United States Army troops, the president ordered the commander to surrender. The commander was willing to fight it out, but admitted that he would lose because he said the balance of forces was too extreme." Tony took a brief break to clear his throat.

The president said, "We don't want Army forces fighting National Guard troops, and we will bend over backward to ensure this. We've made this clear to our entire officer corps."

"Yup," Tony picked up. "We already agreed to that. We don't want a second Civil War. We are keeping this as an administrative issue.

"Getting back to the main focus. Before they surrendered, the commander, a very level-headed captain named Ken Maddox, intimidated the fuck out of the Guards. Y—"

"One correction, Mr. Sammis," Susan interrupted.

"Oh? Did I miss something, Miss Tipton?"

"Not unless you happen to be psychic or are reading my email traffic. As of thirteen forty-five hours today, Ken Maddox is now a lieutenant colonel."

"Imagine that, Madam President. I can't say I disapprove."

"Good…please forgive me for breaking your flow."

"Well, I was about to say that your National Command Authority's ultimatum with regard to the treatment of surrendering prisoners didn't hurt, Madam President. The National Guard took the win but slunk back to their cages like whipped curs."

"Would you really use weapons of mass destruction, Madam President?" Wintel asked.

"Given the right circumstances, an unmodified yes."

"What about with the prisoners in question?"

"Unless I know the situation I can't answer; now, can we please get on with our discussion?" There were no objections to the president's suggestion.

Tony continued. "In the end all seventy-three were taken into custody and thus far our sources say that they are being treated well."

"Where are they being held?" Wintel asked.

"Unknown," Tony said curtly.

"How can you know how they are being treated without knowing where they are?"

"Wintel, you are out of order," Nanogate interjected.

"And all this chatter about promotions is in order?"

"Enough!" Susan said, raising her voice to cut through the prattle.

"Nanogate, I suggest you talk to Wintel offline about meeting etiquette. Wintel you are on notice, but I'll answer your question myself. The standard answer we used to give is 'National Technical Means.' It is classified and on a need-to-know basis only. Hell, I don't even know the details. Just take it for granted that the data has been classified grade A+ by the United States Intelligence Services and as a 9.8 by the corporate analysis groups."

"How comforting," Wintel said sarcastically.

A bright red cylinder came down over the blue dropped-e Wintel logo, locking him out of interrupt mode. He could hear and query for attention but couldn't force his way into the conversation any longer.

"I warned him," Susan said.

"You acted appropriately," Nanogate agreed. "We will bring up this breech at the next CorpGov council meeting."

"I'm sorry for the interruptions, Tony. Did you have any more information?"

"Only this—I want everyone to know that we take care of our own whenever possible. We did consider a rescue operation to get those men out of prison but unless we are prepared to have a massive casualty count on both sides, including significant losses among the prisoners, it just isn't in the cards right now."

"Probably a sound decision," Jamie Ardwin added from her gruesome net moniker of an eyeball cut into tiny cubes and blood leaking off of it.

"Thank you, Tony, for your report," the president said. "Now let's move on to Nanogate's report."

"You are gracious, Madam President. My report is short and very high level. Details can be obtained by querying our joint database.

"We've found a way to neutralize the Metro's power suits at a distance and without any of the haphazard audio manipulation that was done in the past. It is as simple as flipping a switch. It just so happens that one of our global corporate teams that manufactures the suits failed to note to the buyers this fatal flaw in their designs. In short, they swept it under the rug."

"Holy shit!" David exclaimed, trying not to expound with his hands as his left shoulder was still in a sling. "That could be a huge advantage. We could knock them out in droves, until they got wise and stopped wearing the damned things, in which case they are as vulnerable as a baby in the middle of a pack of zombies."

"Well put even if graphically imaged, Mr. Swift. I'll leave the data to be downloaded by the action teams."

"How is our coalition holding together, Mr. Chairman?"

"We have seen no cracks yet, Madam President. Everyone is rock steady behind us. Public opinion is at its highest point ever. Our corporations are holding tight."

"Yeah, any that slip find themselves in the middle of a worldwide boycott," said David with not a little glee. "Within days they crawl back into the fold begging forgiveness."

"Mr. Swift, you are out of order," the president admonished gently. "The point is good but out of order."

"Did you have anything to add, Mr. Chairman?"

"Well, as Mr. Swift stole my thunder, I'll let his comments stand."

"Excellent. I want to thank Nanogate for his report and segue to a new item from our resident network jockey, Augustine."

"Thank you, Madam President. I know that we've said in the past that we believed that our recent mission failures were actually just a series of unfortunate events. My analysis says something different. It shows we have a three sigma likelihood of having a traitor in our midst. For those of you who aren't familiar with statistics, that is ninety-nine point seven percent certainty."

A silence descended hard on the conference like a cemetery at midnight.

"That's quite a bombshell, Miss Augustine," Nanogate said.

"You obviously have more to say than that or you wouldn't have bothered," Jamie said.

"Yes. I've narrowed the list to three people."

"Well, who are they?" more than one voice asked almost in unison.

"I won't start a witch hunt," Augustine said. "I'll know for sure in forty-eight hours. Please be patient. I will tell you that it is not any of the GAM forces, so the president is in the clear with her bodyguards."

"With this information," Tony said, "I think we need to dig in even deeper. I say we reinitiate Case Red modified to keep all protective details on their principles but key members to split up and hide under a rock."

"Agreed," Nanogate said. "When Augustine has her answer for us we can shut out the guilty party and reconvene."

"Forty-eight hours," Tony said.

"Forty-eight hours," Nanogate echoed.

Product Engineering

"So tell me about our success in Utah," the commissioner demanded.

"There wasn't much to tell, sir," Reza said. "A company of National Guardsmen, acting on undisclosed intelligence, moved in on a pair of platoons of U.S. Army who were loading up an entire armory into trucks. The Army troops surrendered without a fight, but they did destroy the armory and all of its equipment."

"That's a success?" the commissioner asked.

"Well, sir, we captured a number of their troops, without losing a single one of ours. We prevented them from fulfilling their mission. The only thing that lessened our own victory is that we didn't end up with the logistics of the armaments themselves."

"What was their mission?"

"Well, we don't know, sir."

"There wasn't an interrogation?"

"Well, about that, sir—"

"Why do I feel a headache coming on," Krylov said.

"The commander of the U.S. forces gave our commander a message. We have a recording of it for you to study at your leisure. In short, it says treat the people that surrender to you as prisoners of war or she would consider Oregon and Utah rebel states and she would, I quote, 'wage full and unrestricted warfare against the entirety of the states with all means at our disposal.' She goes on to threaten to use weapons of mass destruction."

"What weapons?" Captain Lennart asked. "We control the orbitals, there aren't more than half a dozen nukes in the entire country. Chemical and bio weapons would hurt the rest of the people more than us."

"Not so quickly, Lennart," Captain Cohen contradicted. "What about targeted bio or nanite weapons? We know they could hurt us badly if they do."

"Do they mean it?" the commissioner asked.

"I honestly don't know, sir," Reza said. "I don't know anyone who will put a stake in the ground on that one either."

"What do we know about Tipton?"

"Not enough, sir. Our current psychological models show a sixty-six point four percent likelihood that she will carry through with her threat, but the models themselves caution a thirty-three percent error factor, sir."

"I suggest that we discover if our controls over the orbitals are still solid," Major Broadsky offered in a rare practical suggestion. Reza noted it down on his tablet.

"So is there a downside to treating prisoners correctly?" the commissioner asked, ignoring the side conversation.

"Well, sir, as you mentioned, that we can't interrogate them as thoroughly as we'd hoped."

"Anything else?"

"We have to house and feed them for the duration."

"A nit for so few soldiers," Lennart said confidently.

"What about after we've captured ten times that many? What about the capture of GAM members? What about the arrests of rioters?" Cohen interjected derisively. "Where does it stop?"

"Sir," Reza said, directing his comments directly to the commissioner, "this will require a policy decision by you."

All eyes in the room turned to Krylov.

"We win if we play by the rules of civilized warfare. If we break the rules they could possibly devastate us. I think it is clear that we should accede to Tipton's request. However, I don't want it to look like that. Cohen, I want you back on the talk show circuit. Make it clear to them that we are insisting that the CorpGov give our people quarter. Then go on to show how well we treat our prisoners."

"Thank you, sir."

"Lieutenant, I was wondering when the fuck someone was going to bring up the fact that we have the Bodyguard Union taking sides against us as well?"

"That was unconfirmed, sir. It also should have come to us from the National Guard as hearsay in their interrogation of the prisoners of the Kliever attack."

The chairman's fist slammed the table like a 9 kilo sledgehammer. "*Chertovy idioty!*"

Most of the attendees jumped as if the force of the strike bounced them into the air.

"We are not primary school children here. Do you think this is a game?" No one had the temerity to answer the rhetorical question. "Give me even hearsay evidence so I can plan!

"*Tvoyu mat'!*" The chairman stared at them for several deep breaths before the color in his face turned from purple to something less than crimson. "Well, let's at least hear what you've found. Lieutenant?"

Reza stepped forward the one unconscious pace he'd retreated. "Sir, the three prisoners of the Portland Armory action were all members of the Bodyguard Union. Only one was on active assignment. They didn't talk. However, once I learned about this I initiated some inquiries from the Guild Leadership itself. I've gotten nothing. Not a single returned percomm in two days."

"Well, what you don't know is that I have a nephew in the Bodyguards," Krylov said.

Several eyes flew wide at this announcement.

"It took him some time to get the information to me as he is being watched, but it appears even my own personal bodyguard voted against us."

"I find that hard to believe, sir."

"It's true. Whether Samuel was coerced or voted the way the rest of his brethren did to remain inconspicuous is unknown. What I do know is that I feel much less safe with my bodyguard now than ever. Fortunately for us he is forbidden by custom in this building.

"Captain Hardy, would you please assign a security detail for me to replace my bodyguard. You'll also find him with my liftousine," Krylov said, handing him a folded pink filmy. "Please go give him this termination of contract."

*   *   *

"Ten-SHUN!" called out Master Sergeant Beal from within his combat vacuum suit. Captain Mandelbaum marched in, wearing her own deep space EV suit, the helmet open. She stopped next to her Sergeant and snapped to face the formation of troops incongruously arrayed in a banquet room. Thirty-six sets of civilian clothes formed thirty-six neat stacks on the tables behind them.

"People, I hope you enjoyed your time in the fleshpots of Cajetan." The captain had to wait as the entire platoon cheered in unison.

"RECON!"

"I will make sure the surgeon is available after this mission to clear up any of those pesky social diseases that you men and women may have picked up."

"RECON!" A few chuckles and some good natured ribbing followed.

"Quiet in the ranks!" the sergeant barked.

"You have to have as many questions about this mission as I had when it was given to me. Infiltrate Cajetan in civilian gear. Mate up with prepositioned deep space gear. EVA over twenty-seven hours.

"You have been hand-chosen for this mission because you have recent space combat training or experience," the captain said. "So what is our mission? We are heading to do orbital platform maintenance without anyone learning of our work, even the maintenance specialists themselves.

"If you will follow Specialist Anik, he will take you through the repairs in question."

"Thank you, Captain. If I can get your attention to the solido here. This is the command module of each orbital device. They are all identical. Once I get done showing you what we are going to do, we will practice on actual replacement units before we leave.

"Here," the thick, dark-haired specialist said, rotating the image with his hands and pointing, "is the entry hatch. The procedure we have planned is very simple. We run a bypass of the—"

"Bear?" Mickey Andersen whispered to his mentor and friend from ranks. "What the fuck is this about?"

"Mickey, can't you just shut up and do what you are told for a change?"

*   *   *

After only twenty-four hours on the street, dirt caked around Jamie's nose and seemed to have made a home in the pores of her face. Her filthy brown hair looked like it had last been cut with a knife, at least those parts that stuck out like straw from beneath a knit stocking cap that had seen better days several decades ago. Instead of French perfume, she smelled like a combination of stale sauerkraut and sweat. Under her plastic-trash-bag poncho she wore a dun-colored, disposable work jumpsuit that, by the occasional peeks of her filthy skin through the holes, was at least six months past its expiration date. Tony snuggled down against his grubby girlfriend anyway, knowing he looked no better. Together they were wrapped in six layers of blankets that didn't seem to keep the chill of the January damp at bay.

While protected from the direct rain under the ledge of the bus barn at the corner of Weidler and Larabee, they still got the mist that drifted in on the wind and the occasional splash of a passing bike.

What Tony hadn't counted on was being recognized. As newcomers entering the crowd of nils they'd been given a cursory examination. It took less than a dozen heartbeats for the quiet whispers of "GAM" and "Tony" to rumble through the close-knit group.

An old man with salt and pepper hair, who only introduced himself as Max, assured himself of their bona fides with the simple but firm handshake of a day laborer. Between the streaks of grime, his face wore the toughness of many hard years living on street level. A ragged scar crossed the bridge of his nose and travelled up over his right eye.

"Mr. Tony and Ms. Jamie, you do Worker Pod an honor by joining us."

"You surprise me, Max. You speak much better than most of the nils I've worked with," Jamie said.

Max gave a deep chuckle. "I could give you a long sob story, but I actually went to Harvard. I made a great number of bad choices in my life to end up here."

"I'm sorry," Tony said.

"Don't be. I deserved the kicking around I got. I can look back on it with dispassion now. I thought I was better than anyone else and could break any rule I wanted with impunity. I couldn't." Max sighed, looking down at the wet packing box they sat on. Just as quickly he snapped up and looked bright through his dirty dreadlocks. "Don't get me wrong, many of the people down here don't deserve it. They could be just like normal corpies if given the chance."

"So you called this Worker Pod?" Tony asked.

"I'm sorry, you aren't from a nil background. Most of us congregate around a central strong figure that is good at getting us something. I'm leader of this pod. I seem to be very good at finding day work for our people. You will find that this group is very dedicated to earning their way."

"I'm sure you are wondering why we are here?"

"You tell or you don't, Mr. Tony. You'll find nils a rather curious lot but they won't pry. We each have secrets we don't want to see the light of day so we learn quickly not to invade others' space. We have very little, so our privacy we guard closely."

"May I ask a question?" Jamie asked.

"You may or may not get an answer," Tony said, looking at Max. Max nodded as if giving Tony a point in an imaginary game.

"OK, given," Jamie admitted, "but it is about Tony. Why did you figure out who he is so quickly? No one noticed me."

Max's eyes went wide. "I'm sorry, but I've been out of the upper world for several decades. Is this a joke?"

"No, Max, I'm in dead earnest. If Tony can't hide here, how can he hide anywhere?"

"Holy fuck," Max said, looking up at the moss-covered overhang. "I guess I've just been too cynical for too long."

"I don't understand," Tony asked.

"I'll just show you.

"Sandy, come here, child."

A young woman, who would be pretty if it weren't for the ever-present filth, raced over so fast she probably had been listening to every word the trio had uttered.

"Sandy, can you tell me how you know Mr. Tony?"

Her mouth opened slack for just a moment. Her eyes glittered bright as a kid getting his first look at the presents arrayed under the tree on Christmas morning. "You GAM! You a hero, Mr. Tony! If'n you eber get tired of Ms. Jamie or want two, I gib you anyt'ing you want." The offer was as unmistakable as a token girl shaking her tits in the face of a prospective customer.

Tony didn't need to feel the look Jamie shot him to understand the young girl had slid him out onto thin ice. "Sandy, thank you very much for your offer, but you can't be more than twelve—"

"I'm fourteen, ain't I, Max?"

"Yes, you are, Sandy."

"I not virgin, neither. I been wif many others. I feel good making dem feel good."

"Thank you anyway, Sandy, but I'm ancient and monogamous."

Sandy looked quizzically at Max.

"He means he likes to be with just one partner at a time."

"Oh, I understands, Mr. Tony. If'n ya change your mind or be want'n anything let me know." Sandy shut up but wasn't about to leave the conversation unless forcibly removed.

"Sandy's not uncommon, Mr. Tony. I'd say with very few exceptions everyone here in the camp would bed or die for you."

Tony drifted off into neural overload.

Jamie came to his defense. "Why?"

"That is why I said I was being too cynical, Ms. Jamie. I've never seen someone from the upper world so altruistic or who wasn't somehow gaming the system. Mr. Tony is an anomaly. Mr. Tony cares. He is working for us."

"We lub our Mr. Tony!" Sandy agreed with a smile so wide it should have broken her face.

"Yup. Ever since the day he came on the solido he's been like our patron saint. He doesn't trample on it by asking us to fight Metros barehanded, even though we would. He helps us. Hell, he gives food to the poor."

"But that was just the one time!" Tony objected in horror at his deification.

Max cocked his head in disbelief at Tony. "How many would have done it even once? Did you know that the food you gave to that pod fed not only them but four others for nearly a month?"

Tony just shook his head, staring off into space.

Jamie filled the silence that had sprung up. "So how did you recognize us?"

"Seriously? Darling as you are, Ms. Jamie, I didn't know you even though we sometimes mule for your syndicate. But nothing can disguise Mr. Tony's bulk nor his distinctive nose."

"Fuck!" Jamie said with only the emotion of failure. "We're screwed. How long until the Metros show up?"

"I should be insulted, Ms. Jamie, but you are a stranger in a strange land," Max said with a grin at his literary pun. "There isn't the smallest child, the most demented crazy, or sickest of us that would give up either of you for any price. While the membership of any given pod varies, we take care of our own. It is the only security we have. And if you will pardon me, you two are the only hope many of us have ever had. Whether you want it or not, you'll be taken care of just like the rest."

* * *

"Element Baker Four on station at Orbital Farm three. No contact. I say again. No contact," Corporal Blackbear said, attaching his close contact hook onto the orbital projectile. It comforted him. In spite of a year of free space work, being tethered to something, anything other than his combat partner made the floating emptiness not feel so agoraphobic. The depth of the blackness could get to you after a very short time. The pair of them had been floating in trajectory for five hours.

The tension had been quite thick. Their orders to quick-kill any maintenance tech or any other EVA they encountered didn't help any.

"Roger Baker Four. Copy you on station. At Oscar, Foxtrot three. Proceed with mission. Advise upon completion of each device."

"Latch on, Mickey. We got work to do."

"Roger. I'm safe. I'll pull out the poly board."

"Hold on, we need to bypass the interlock first."

"Oh, yeah."

Mickey handed his corporal a metal wire with a simple blade on one end and a metal eyelet at the other. Bear slid the blade into the slit between a panel and the body of the control module.

"Got anything?"

"Not yet, Bear."

The corporal wiggled the blade around until he felt some grating.

"I got voltage," Mickey called out.

Bear released the blade end. With exaggerated care he removed a screwdriver that was secured to his combat suit by a buckyball chain. He unscrewed a single fastener, it being held at the end of his tool by magnetism. He placed the eyelet end of the wire over the hole and twisted the screw back in place.

"Voltage is now gone, Bear."

"That's a good bypass." Bear stuck the Velcroed back of the screwdriver to its home at his belt and pulled out a five-sided wrench with a three-dimensional key protruding out the center to open the very finicky entry bolt of the main control access. No alarms went off. No explosives detonated. The panel opened easily, exposing an array of photonic poly boards and their interconnecting metal message channels.

"Start the timer," Bear said.

"Seventy-three seconds on the clock, now."

With his awkward gloved hands, Bear unscrewed the third board's mechanical hold down. He unsnapped the three flexible metal gravitic cabling. Without looking up he handed back the old board and received the new one.

"Fifty-five seconds," Mickey announced.

Reversing his disassembly he reconnected the conduits. One of the connectors slipped free when he tested it. Bear growled a bit.

"Forty seconds."

Bear grabbed the errant connector and pushed it back into its location. This time it held against his tug.

"Thirty seconds."

The power indicators started glowing as the corporal slid the board into its new home. Tightening the mechanical bracketing relieved a good deal of tension.

"Done."

"Twenty-one seconds. Looks like that practice did you good."

"This is Baker Four. Reporting complete on Alpha, Kilo Six Four Niner."

"*Roger that. We test positive control on Alpha, Kilo Six Four Niner.*"

"That's one orbital bombardment platform that the president controls, not those Metro fuckers," Bear said.

"Nice to finally know what we're doing."

"Ten-four to that, Private. You and I only have sixty-three more before we can go home."

*   *   *

Wintel stood in the heat of a recycling shower in the West Portland Sports Club. The bruises across his midsection and the stinging in his right eye were a testament to him losing his temper. Thirty years ago he'd boxed featherweight in high school and college to control the rages that sometimes wracked him through adolescence. He'd like to say the other guy got the worse of it but his skills had been much sharper in his youth. Sparring had given him a garden of bruises.

Neither the pain nor the exertions had stopped his mind. It threatened to race out of control like an engine without a load.

"Hide even deeper."

"Don't wear business attire."

"Cut off close associates."

"We aren't fighting to win."

He could clearly see three open graves at the end of their so-called CorpGov. The gravestones couldn't have been more clear had they been laser projected. "The fucking idiots," Wintel swore. The rushing water over his slender body absorbed the low sound.

All their businesses suffered under the rule of these amateur governors. Wintel had dropped 7 percent just in the last two weeks and that wasn't a fluctuation. That was 7 percent against the Dow, the NIKKEI, and the BOWMI. It suffered 5 percent worse loss than that of his fellow CorpGov councilpersons' companies. The CorpGov obviously can't rule shit.

Who in the greater solar system did Tony Sammis think he was? Just two quarters ago he was nothing but an insignificant cog in Nanogate's machine. He was less than a worm to be stepped on. Now he put on airs as to have an opinion equal or better than those of the men and women who'd climbed the treacherous ranks of the corporate ladder and come out on top. At best he was a hired dog and at worse a bitch to be fucked.

And speaking of bitches, where did that data jockey Augustine get off poking into their personal and private communications? Did they hang a tracer on her ancient ass? Did they betray her in the convent? Fuck no. Now her determination to find a traitor would uncover one of his exit strategies, maybe all of them.

"FUCK!" he said, pounding the heel of his fist on the tiles. The impact reverberated like the inside of a kettle drum.

"You all right in there, buddy?" came a voice from another sealed shower stall.

"Sorry. I'm fine," he said in spite of the new throbbing in his right hand.

This new pain allowed him to focus just a few moments. Using some biofeedback techniques he learned as a teen, Wintel set up mental fences in this calm space and pushed them outward. He nudged those fences a bit at a time, slowly letting the irrelevancies, anger, and even the pain to drop out of his brain like ships falling off a flat earth. Before long he had a calm place to evaluate without letting emotion cloud his thinking.

Now in his element, he brainstormed all of his options over a long minute. In twelve more seconds he'd sorted through and eliminated the worst of the group. Evaluating the remaining three options proved a longer task—assigning probability curves, performing statistical calculus to evaluate multiple outcomes and finally to determine each choice's ultimate value. When he got in a groove he lost all touch with everything around him. He became an extension of his mind.

"You sure you are all right, mister?"

Sampling his percomm, Wintel realized he'd been calculating for nearly twenty minutes. "Actually, I'm quite fine," he said with the strength of conviction. Numbers never lied. He'd been using them all his life and they pointed to a single solution—one he would enjoy implementing. As he put on his suit, he connected the percomm code by memory with a smile on his face for the first time in weeks.

*   *   *

The token girl that Gohar Debnath climbed off of hadn't been bad. She'd made the right noises in the right places so he hadn't hit her very hard. "You better fuck like a girl next time I come round here or I'll show you just how hard I can hit, bitch." The girl cowered up against the headboard of the bed.

Gohar Debnath was off duty. Nothing quite pissed him off more than not wearing his uniform. He pulled on his civies, not liking it a bit. He liked people scared of him and the uniform. His dad taught him that many years ago. Being frightening made people respect you.

Debnath threw some cash at the whore and walked out to find a way to purge his anger. Maybe he needed to get into a bar brawl.

*   *   *

Before leaving them alone, Max had made it clear that only by wiping out the entire Worker Pod would anyone ever get to Tony and Jamie. Tony kept telling himself that what mattered was that they were safe, not some ill-afforded fame. Tony couldn't imagine a better cover nor a better group of protectors than being surrounded by two hundred forty or so rabidly devoted nils.

Cuddling down against Jamie in their nest, now augmented by offerings from the rest of the pod, he almost felt comfortable—

physically. He couldn't put aside the disturbing fact that he'd somehow reached the status of folk hero. He wondered how many other heroes had as little substance as he felt like he had.

Jamie had been distantly supportive in their wrappings. She'd stayed quiet, respecting his need to grapple with the bombshell that had been laid upon him.

"Tony, it's time to join the meeting."

Querying the time through his percomm, he realized how far his musings had driven his mind. Tony's virus image appeared in the chamber of the Round Table once again. Augustine must have been busy as she liked different settings for each meeting.

"… waiting for Tony to show up. Oh, there he is."

Only one seat at the mythical table remained empty.

"Where is Wintel?"

"We were just about to get to that," Susan said from her Presidential Seal.

"Uh-oh, I don't think I like the sound of that."

"I don't think anyone will like it," David offered.

"Please disclose your information, Mr. Swift. We need to have all data, even unpleasant data," Nanogate said.

"Well, in short, he left his sports club and climbed into a taxi."

"That fucking idiot did what?" Tony sputtered to his percomm. If anyone had been watching he'd just blown his cover as a nil.

"You heard it right, Tony," David's crossed dragoon pistols said. "He was heading for the liftousine loading zone when a cab opened his door and he jumped in. The taxi shot off faster than we could respond."

Tony scowled. "Everyone knows your DNA is sniffed every time you get into a taxi."

"I hope you don't want my people to pull his ass out of the fire. I personally wouldn't risk the nose hair of anyone I work with to keep his ass from being rendered down to lard," Jamie said.

"If I thought that Wintel had committed nothing but simple stupidity, I'd say leave him to the pain he deserves," Nanogate said. "As you know, survival of the fittest is one of the strongest tenants in the corporate world."

"Eh? My mind is a little fuzzy," Jamie said. "Exactly what are you implying?"

"I don't think this is foolishness. I believe it to be a calculated way to defect," Nanogate said.

"We concur, Jamie," David and Augustine chimed in together.

Beside her, Tony nodded his head. "We need to move all the equipment we shipped to Mars, otherwise they'll be able to destroy it."

"We are already working on that," the president said.

"Well, other than burning a number of safe houses I don't think his knowledge poses a threat. Our strategy is and has been obvious. I suggest you vote him off the council and be done with it."

"I wish it were that simple, Tony. I am surprised you haven't identified the greater risk immediately. What if he publicly throws his support over to the Metros?"

Tony stopped dead, his eyes wide. "Holy fuck."

"I see the danger has manifested in your thought processes."

"Our support has been based on the fact that we have been a united front. Any chink in that armor and we could quickly become the bad guys," Tony said with a wide-eyed look at Jamie.

"Precisely," Nanogate said.

"I have an idea," Tony said, "but do you have a suggestion for action?"

"The council has voted and agreed to give you carte blanche. You are our direct action leader."

"Carte blanche? I need to know—"

"We don't want to know, Tony." Nanogate's voice from umpteen kilometers away froze Tony's percomm.

*   *   *

A buzzer sounded along with a soft, feminine voice, "Unauthorized access. Please step back or active countermeasures will be employed."

"Ma'am, you can't go in there," Sergeant Tolbert, who just happened to be walking by, said to the old woman wearing a grav brace on her back. "That's a restricted area."

Beneath her truss, floral muumuu, and frizzed, salt-and-pepper wig, Christine found it interesting that she should bump into the same man she had intended to kill just a few weeks ago. Fortunately, four skilled swipes with a grease pen added at least eight decades to her face. The poor light that made it through the badly cut hair on her head didn't hurt either.

"Ain't the ladies' room through these doors, young man?"

Christine asked with the fake growl of a narco stick addict.

"It's been several decades since someone has called me young, ma'am. I appreciate it. But the bathroom is through the next set of double doors."

"Ye shoulda marked it better. Don't walk so good as I did, and you and your type makes an old woman walk twice as far. Ain't that a bathroom there," she pointed one grizzled and age-spotted hand through the heavily tinted door.

"Yes, ma'am, but that is a restricted area. We can't let civilians walk through there unchecked."

Three patrolmen on their way to lunch looked at the sergeant and the woman. They gave the pair a wide berth. From the look they got from the sergeant they probably would pay for their detours later.

"Sergeant, I'm being here today 'cause your damned accounting department didn't think the payments made from my meager social security check were 'nough. Now all the old bats from my wing of the Greater Portland Retirement Village says I'm daft for giving you Metros anything. They all support the Greenies."

"Ma'am, we appreciate—"

"But my husband, Patrolman Thurston Davis, God rest his soul, would come back to haunt me if'n I did. I done give a husband, two sons, and a granddaughter to the Metros. All of 'em are dead in the line of duty and you wanna talk about places I can't go."

"But Mrs. Davis, the other bathroom is just down…"

"Don't 'But Mrs. Davis' me. I'll be tell'n you what I'm gonna do, Sergeant. I'm gonna squat right down here and leave you a puddle 'cause you wouldn't open a fucking door for a veteran's widow. You can write that on your fucking report when you arrest a hundred-six-year-old woman for urinating in public."

"Ma'am, you don't—"

Christine spread her legs like she was astride a horse.

"Please stop, Mrs. Davis. I'm sure Patrolman Grace here would be happy to escort you to the bathroom there."

The young rookie who'd wandered by grimaced. "Yes, ma'am, I'd be happy to."

"Now you're talking sense, Sergeant."

"Stay with her, Grace," Tolbert hissed as he hurried away.

Timothy Grace went up and offered the DNA from his wrist to the door's scanner. "Grace with one visitor."

"Hurry up there, young man, or I still might have an accident."

The soft feminine voice announced, "Patrolman first-class Timothy Grace, badge number GT112994T3, and one visitor authorized."

The red flashing light disappeared.

"Grace, ain't that some kind of girly name?" Christine could now clearly see two guards with assault rifles and full battle armor standing on either side of a door further down the hall. Both the guards eyed the old woman and her escort.

Grace pointed at the woman, the bathroom door, and shrugged. The impassive face plates of the armor didn't give away anything but they turned back to their position.

"This way, ma'am," Patrolman Grace said as he opened the ladies' room door.

"Thank you, sonny."

Patrolman Grace tried to follow her into the bathroom.

"Excuse me, son. I'm thinking I can pee by myself. I don't need no one to wipe my bottom for me yet."

"Yes, ma'am."

In the quiet safety of one of the stalls Christine fired up her listening devices.

"*. . . tell you that I don't know where they are. They move almost every night!*"

"*That's not good enough, Wintel. If you want to make us believe that you are being truthful then you need to—*"

"*Idiots. I give you golden intel on your enemy's intent, probable next targets, and resources, and all you want to do is try to get things out of me that I never had access to. How did you ever get to your rank, Captain?*"

"*By not taking the word of every fucking punk that gives us a 'golden' tip.*"

"*Punk? Do you realize—*"

"*Yeah, we heard it all before, putz—'climbing the corporate ladder'; 'have as much money as I do.' Give us one real actionable item and we can talk about how to make things better for you.*"

"*Captain, I hope your insurance is paid up.*"

"*Now you're threatening—*"

"*No, sir, prophesizing. If you are indicative of the decision making within the Metro structure, you are going to lose.*"

"*Not bloody likely, corpie. Remember, you came to us 'cause you*" *were losing."*

"Mrs. Davis?" came Grace's voice from the doorway.

Christine grunted for effect. "Not now, boy. I might just get this log in my middle to move." Grunt. "Fuck. Too late. I'm coming now."

Christine hobbled to the doorway a minute or so later. "Be happy your bowels are moving now, Grace. They don't do so good when you get old."

"Yes, ma'am. Patrolman Grace and one visitor to exit."

"Authorized."

＊　＊　＊

"Outgoing message for the interplanetary liner, *Red Planet.* To: Michael Fritzwalter Beckman-Ford. From: Clarence Fritzwalter Beckman-Ford. Start message: Reference meeting in library prior to house's destruction. Authorize all actions. Suggest involve verdant if militant friends who joined us to camouflage actions. End Message."

＊　＊　＊

"Max," Tony said. His and Jamie's blankets had been rolled up and tied to his back with bits of pieced-together rope.

"You leaving us, Mr. Tony and Ms. Jamie?"

"Please, it's just Tony and Jamie. We're no different from you except that you have a place to call home, most nights anyway."

"An interesting way to look at it, Tony."

"Well, any percomm can be traced and any encryption can be broken with enough computer power. Unlikely as it might be, we need to move on."

"Anytime you need a place to stay, you come here. We'll pass the word to the other pods as well. You will always have a place here."

"We want to thank you and the Worker Pod for your hospitality," Jamie said, handing him a Tyvek pouch of plastic dollars. "Before you reject this out of hand, I want you to know it isn't charity."

"Seems like it to me, Ms... I mean Jamie. We work in Worker Pod. We don't beg."

"You gave us a safe place to stay. That's worth much more than the few hundred dollars I've given you."

"Yes," Tony agreed. "Besides, I can foresee a time very soon where we will need many, many hands to build some things. Worker Pod will be number one on the list for jobs."

"Then I'll take it as a retainer."

"And make sure the kids get something nice," Jamie said.

"I'm thinking a good hot meal for everyone might be nicest," Max said.

"Maybe so. You know best, Max."

"And you wonder why you are loved down here? Just don't forget the meaning of tanstaafl, Tony."

"Thank you again, Max," Tony said, taking the street man's hand.

As Tony turned away he asked, "What was that word he used, Jamie?"

"Tanstaafl. There ain't no such thing as a free lunch."

Tony's mind chewed on the idea as he walked toward the Steel Bridge.

Documentation

Deep in the canyons of the great buildings of downtown Portland an ovoid troop support vehicle, a Wolfe to most everyone, hovered 4 m above a platoon of the 82nd Cavalry out of Bend, Oregon. The cold mist that clung to the ground limited the visible spectrum of light to 30 m. With the tactical gear worn by even the foot platoon they could effectively see out to 120 m.

"*Limited activity. Continue with sweep,*" Captain Qamut announced from his perch in the TSV. "*Watch the open building to the left. There are a large number of squatters on thermal.*"

"Roger."

One man in formation stumbled on a crack in the neglected pavement.

"Steady there, Michaels. We only have another three klicks and then we are done for the week."

"Yes, sir."

"What moron thought of two patrols in the same day?" bitched yet another member of the troop off-mic.

"*My ass is dragging lower than a nil's bed..*"

"*If you want to complain then do it OFF mic you pack of lice,*" the sergeant blasted over the team network. "*Jones, put yourself down for the next three patrols,*" he ordered of the offender.

"*Yes, Sarg.*"

"Jones, you stupid fuck," one of his platoon mates said.

"I'm about to fall over, too, but you don't see me doing anything that moronic."

"What about the time you picked up the Sarge's daughter at a bar?"

"I keep telling you, how was I supposed to know—"

"*Jones, you and Chhau check out that doorway on the right, two o'clock, seven meters. I'm getting ambiguous signals from in there.*"

"Right away, Sarg."

The pair peeled off from the group and sprinted, in their bulky field gear, toward the doorway. Something burst from the opening. Without thinking, Jones triggered off a burst from his flechette gun.

Twelve 1 cm long metal darts, raised to eight times the speed of sound by a compressed gravity wave generator in the barrel, flashed out white hot as the air friction all but ignited them. Only three of the projectiles struck. The nearly invisible entry points belied their effectiveness. The designed burrs on the oversized fletching caught flesh and ripped or snapped off in the wound as the momentum of the darts carried them onward, tumbling as they went. The opposite side of the victim burst forth, spraying internal organs and blood 18 m down the street.

Before a single word could be spoken the young girl, about seven years old, dressed in a woman's recyclable tunic with more stains than fabric, toppled. With her lungs exploded out of her chest, she couldn't even get out more than a muted squeal.

Jones could see that the girl hadn't realized yet that she was dead. Lying on her wound, she looked almost normal. Her brown eyes, under a wrinkled brow, looked at him. Her mouth opened but no sound emitted. Blood welled up and leaked from her nose as her eyes closed.

"What the fuck was that, Jones?" his wingman asked.

Jones was frozen in place. He'd just shot a little girl.

"MURDERERS!" came a yell from across the street. "Murderers!"

"Those fuckers killed Jackie."

"Murderers!"

"Jones, what the fuck is going on?"

"Ah, I think I just killed a nil."

"You think? You think it was a nil or you think you killed it?"

"Sarg, he killed a little girl. And we seem to have some trouble here. The locals saw it."

"Everyone close on PFC Jones's location," the captain said as he listened in on the cluster fuck he'd just inherited. *"Form a defensive cordon. Prepare to repel. Non-lethal rounds only!"*

"Murderer!" became a chant. More and more people showed in empty windows, abandoned doorways, or on ledges as high up as they could see. It seemed like the entirety of Portland surrounded them. All were screaming at the National Guardsmen.

"*Phalanx formation. Attach bayonets,*" Sarge ordered. "*Riot shields up!*" The square of troopers limbered the small shield handsets and powered up their shimmering fields.

One of the men in the mob settled them down enough to speak. "Give us the murdering bastard and the rest of you can go. We have nothing against you, but that man must pay."

"Don't worry, Jones," said one of his buddies in a whisper. "We'll protect you. Fuck, they don't even have any weapons."

"*We don't make deals with nils,*" the captain said over an amplified speaker outside the TSV. "*Now disperse before we fire into the crowd. There will be no second warning.*"

The tenuous calm on the group of nils evaporated. "Kill them all!" yelled the crowd. As one as they surged forward.

Inside his personnel carrier, Captain Qamut shook his head. He didn't want to kill these poor bastards but they left him no option. They had bought themselves a massacre. "Gauss cannons in close support mode. Fire at will."

"Hey, where did that fucker come from?" the driver said, totally out of context. A sharp crack reverberated through the cabin. The captain felt the back side of his TSV rotate downward.

The fire that should have ripped up the mass of humanity below him rotated upward, firing into the sky. Faster than the compensators could level the cabin, the captain tumbled backward out of his combat chair, smashing his head on the armaments cabinet.

With the ringing in his head and the blood that trickled down the side of his face he made a promise to himself that he'd never sit unbuckled again. "What the fuck? Chapman, what's going on?"

"Sir, I've lost two of the aft lift generators and I don't know why."

"*Charlie Four collapse,*" he heard Sergeant Farmer say tensely over the net. "*Captain we need fire support. We are being overrun.*"

"Captain, we have enemy personnel all over our TSV!" barked his weapon's operator. "I can't get a bead on them."

"Close assault tactics—electrify the skin."

"Yes, sir."

The captain clawed his way up the skewed floor to his post. He could see a mass of humanity pressing against his troops, forcing their phalanx square smaller and smaller. Makeshift projectiles, bricks, chairs, rusted toasters, and in one case a filing cabinet, hurtled from fire escapes and broken windows to smash down on his soldiers and the mob indiscriminately. His men stood their ground. They fired into the crowd continuously. People went down by the hundreds but thousands took their place. With no time to reload, his troopers fell back to tactics as old as the Greeks who invented them.

"Driver, stabilize this craft. Gunner, fire gauss cannons into the crowd. We have to disperse them!"

"Sir, there is nothing to stabilize with. We can go up or down, sir."

"Sir, the electrified hull has stopped being effective. I'm not sure why. I'm not sure I can guarantee our safety at this point."

"Vertical ascent, driver."

"Yes, sir."

"*Captain, we need your fire support,*" his sergeant repeated as the craft went straight up.

"Captain Qamut calling on the company net for support. Being overrun by hostile forces at map reference Juliet Fourteen. TSV disabled. Hostiles number in the tens of thousands. Please respond!"

"*Captain, you have incoming support. ETA seven minutes.*"

"Sergeant, you will fall back by squads toward any structure, laying down covering fire. There you will develop a defensive perimeter and hold."

"*Captain, we can't move. We need you to cut us a path out of here.*"

"Negative. We have damage and cannot support. Additional support units inbound. ETA six mikes."

"*Captain, we won't last...oof...Cage, hit them with the flamethrower. Captain, we won't last another sixty seconds without you.*"

"Do your best, Sergeant."

"*Understood, Captain—Men, CAVALRY!*"

Another crump shook the TSV.

"Captain, another gravity generator is out. We are losing altitude."

"Chapman, how long until we land?"

"Sir, we will *crash* in just under two minutes. We should survive the impact."

Qamut didn't believe in his Inuit ancestral gods, nor any of the organized religions of the day. He did pray to whomever would listen that it would take the mob longer than four minutes to get into his personnel carrier.

*   *   *

"Good job, men. We took control of all but two of the orbital bombardment platforms without a single combat loss," Captain Mandelbaum said over the company-wide voice net. "The platforms will test like the enemy has control, but our command authority can override any order or put in their own.

"Consider your free time in the fleshpots of Cajetan paid for in full."

"RECON!" came the cheer over their vacuum suits' interface. Thirty-eight human-shaped suits floated in a tethered group 2,304 km above the earth's surface.

"Now for our next mission. We are going to do a combat drop and land at coordinates 14Q QD43297 91861. For those of you who can't seem to figure out how to query the net, that's the Jose Morelos y Pavon Armory at Calle Hidalgo 204, San Felipe del Agua, Oaxaca City, Oaxaca, United States. Assuming we land at 1634 Lima, we'll have just three hours to load up as much of the equipment as possible. The garrison at the armory will be ready for us and lift-trucks will meet us there.

"Any questions?"

No one responded.

"Very well. Sergeant Beal, will you begin our deorbit procedure?"

"Yes, sir. Odd numbers collect tethers. Unlink! By numbers, initiate burn. One!"

Two of the close team jetted off in the general direction of the earth, picking up speed amazingly fast as gravity assisted their maneuver.

"Two!"

"Bear, you got the shakes?" came Mickey's voice over the suit-suit private channels.

"Yup, just like more than half of us," Corporal Blackbear responded.

"How many drops you done?"

"Never enough, Private. Now get ready. We're next."

"Three!"

"Geronimo!"

"Stow that shit, Private."

*   *   *

"Thanks for this last minute meeting," Tony said to his comrades in the sitting area of the one hundred level Starbucks in Hillsboro Centre. Jamie held his hand under the table.

"It's always a pleasure to have over-brewed coffee in a slum," Nanogate said, pushing his coffee away with a grimace on his face.

"I used to live on this stuff in college, Clarence. Be nice," the president said, blowing on her double-shot mocha soy, no whip.

"Certainly. I guess he could have given us instant."

"Quit kvetching," Susan said, taking her first sip. She closed her eyes with a sigh.

"I wanted to let you know that we've looked into taking out Wintel. It's a no-go."

"I agree with Tony," Jamie said. "I had my contacts track him for the last twenty-four hours. At night they are keeping him in a bunker that makes the presidential bunker look like a tree house made out of Styrofoam. During the day they are grilling him at the main Metro complex in Arlington Heights."

"Christine scouted the Metro complex and found him guarded by no fewer than two DNA screens, a human sampling DNA, a computer voice/badge recognition and a squad of their elite SWAT team. We could beat three of them but not all of them."

"Tell them all of it," Jamie said with a squeeze of his hand.

"OK. The last was only a half truth. Christine feels she could overcome all of them and kill Wintel but it would be a suicide mission. Oddly she didn't seem very concerned about it."

"I wonder if anything would concern her," Nanogate said, shuddering in a rare display of emotion.

"I'm not in the habit of sending my people on suicide missions."

Nanogate raised his eyebrows at Tony's comment. The oblique reminder of the attack on the cabal had its desired result.

"I mean unless there is no other choice," Tony added hastily before mumbling, "Some people won't let you forget anything."

"So what do we do?" Jamie asked.

"How about announce announcing that Wintel defected to the people before the Metros do. It would at least partially defuse the situation by being open," Jamie offered.

Tony found himself in awe with how quickly his lover had picked up on the need to keep the general populace on their side and even more on how she seemed to know how to do it.

"It won't be enough," Susan said.

"Maybe not, but it will turn it from a nightmare into a simple pain in the ass."

*   *   *

Colonel Reed's avatar, several times higher than Mount Hood, stood in the center of Oregon.

"Colonel Reed!"

"Yes, Private Simms," he responded, not even looking up. He focused on the command simulation as data fed from many different sources. They all collated into the color-coded representation where the major cities burned red, sometimes even a brilliant purple, the suburbs yellow, and those areas with only dozen-story rural buildings were shaded green.

"A patrol commanded by Captain Qamut has been ambushed. Only one man survived, Sergeant Robert Farmer. He is in the mobile infirmary in critical condition. He isn't expected to survive."

"Thank you, Simms. Was there anything else?"

"Yes sir, Sergeant Farmer managed to give a report before he passed out. He says that his troops were overrun by nils in response to one of his squad killing a young girl.

"The relief force, commanded by Lieutenant Small, scattered the mob after inflicting heavy casualties. His preliminary estimate of civilian dead numbered over five hundred."

The colonel punched up Qamut's patrol route on his simulation. He expanded that area of Portland like warm taffy between his fingers. The location of the massacre magnified in front of him. The crystal clear view of the carnage indicated the feed was from one of his very few drones. Bodies formed an annulus in the middle of the street over the height of the second story windows. Just 40 m to the south lay the wreckage of a TSV surrounded by drifts of bodies as high as the upper deck.

"I'd say closer to twelve hundred," Colonel Reed muttered to no one in particular.

"Private, get the following out to all platoon commanders and on the regular command net: 'Rules of Engagement Baker Three. All mobile units to don powered armor and actively engage all nils on slightest provocation."

*   *   *

"Nanogate, can you tell me what the flying fuck this telegram from your son means?"

"*I don't know what you are talking about, Mr. Sammis.*"

"He messages that he wishes me to recruit ten thousand or so people to each purchase nine thousand nine hundred ninety nine common shares of Wintel. He even sent me a rather large wire transfer to cover the transactions and a tidy fee for each of the recruits. He then tells me he'll message me later on what he wants done with the stock."

"*Well, I can tell you that any transaction of ten thousand shares or more must be reported to the company's board of directors and the FTC.*"

"That didn't answer my question, Clarence."

"*Really? I'm sorry, Tony. I'm really busy right now so unless you have any other business?*"

Tony just stared off into space as the percomm went dead. Nanogate rarely lied. But he could be very sneaky about how he told the truth. Tony noticed that he never denied knowing what was going on.

Well, you only go around once in life. He had a large group of people to recruit.

*   *   *

The strains of "Hail to the Chief" played over the background of the Presidential Seal. "Good morning," President Tipton said as she walked up to the podium. "I apologize for preempting your morning news program but I must share with you as soon as possible. Let me introduce Chairman of the CorpGov Clarence Fritzwalter Beckman-Ford the Third, also known as Nanogate."

Nanogate took the stage with the president and looked tall only next to her diminutive 155 cm. "Good morning and thank you, President Tipton. We've come to fulfill our side of the social contract we have with you, the people."

"Yes, we've shared with you our successes in the past and have implied that we give full disclosure. This means we should also let you know about our setbacks as well," Susan said, maintaining a small, but firm smile.

"It isn't pleasant to say, but we've had a defection within the newly founded CorpGov itself. William Trager, who everyone knows as the leader of the corporation Wintel, has changed allegiances and gone over to the Metros along with our plans and a significant amount of data," Nanogate said. The level of concern on his face seemed to have been calculated by Germany's Biggest Brain supercomputer down to the fraction of a millimeter of how close his brows came together and how much pressure he used to purse his lips.

"There are two things you need to know. One is strategic and the other tactical.

"At the biggest possible picture, the CorpGov has met and unanimously agreed to remove Wintel from his seat on the CorpGov. For now that seat will remain vacant until this conflict resolves."

The president took over with one of her patented, we-will-win smiles of determination. "More down in the trenches, Wintel took only a few items of any importance to our short-term goals, plans, or actions. We've taken steps to minimize the damage he can do with this information."

"We will march forward. We will win in the end. Please stay with us because we are going to extra innings."

*　*　*

Corporal Blackbear watched the growing and unmistakable mushroom cloud behind Mount Massive as their lift-truck carried them over Leadville, Colorado. He shuddered, not from the chill of the January cold of the Midwest, but at the number of people who'd just died.

"I guess those turds couldn't read," Mickey offered, using the new pejorative reserved for those who served the Metro black shirts. "That's a company the Greenies won't have to worry about anymore."

"Fuck. That could have been us!"

"Yep, but it wasn't. They were stealing and they knew it. They got everything they deserved. At least they didn't suffer."

"Wonder if Aspen is going to have to close from fallout," one of the other soldiers mused. "Ain't no skiing like Aspen."

"*Men, I know you are wondering about that little display behind us,*" Captain Mandelbaum said over the truck-to-truck intercoms. "*I know some of those troops were at one time your comrades in arms. I want you to know that not only did we post notices that the armory was booby-trapped but I also personally contacted the commander of the OPFOR and asked him not to risk his men. He apparently disagreed. I'm sorry for their loss."*

"I ain't," Mickey said.

Corporal Samuel Blackbear stared out at the death's head continuing to grow and rise higher into the atmosphere. He hoped that someday someone could explain how this was all worth it.

* * *

"Thank you for taking this meeting," Carol Coldstone, of the Local Teamsters 2413 said from around her narco stick. The drab metal desk she sat behind looked like it had been made in a prison workshop in the '50s—the 1950s. Carol herself reminded Jamie of the desk itself, squat and utilitarian, if a bit lackluster in every other way. The dingy office, nothing more than a small area carved out of the back of a twentieth level warehouse, might have been comfortable for a family of nils but its walls, yellow and brown from Carol's chain-smoking, made Jamie feel dirty just looking at them.

"My pleasure," Jamie said. From previous meetings she'd thought ahead and worn a disposable, utilitarian, mock-denim jumpsuit. She'd toned down her makeup and even forgone lipstick entirely.

"The reason I asked you here is to inform you that we are considering renouncing our neutral status and throwing in with the Metros."

"Why would you do this now?"

"Your alliance is falling apart at the seams, Miss Ardwin. You've had defections and serious losses that you can ill afford. We don't think the CorpGov will last much longer. If we join actively with the Metros we are set up to be a trusted ally when the dust settles."

"So you are willing to throw away more than a century of good will with me to do this?" Jamie asked, her eyes narrowing and her mouth pursing. At this level of negotiation hiding one's emotion like the corps did impeded solutions.

"I'll be blunt, Miss Ardwin. The families should never have gotten involved. They should have rolled with the punches as they always have in the past. They would have grown stronger for it as we will. Instead, you will be destroyed or at least reduced to a point where our relationship will no longer be beneficial for the Teamsters."

"I see. And if you are wrong?"

"Then we're wrong. It happens. But the Teamsters is a very conservative organization. You might check to see if you've already lost some of your more flighty types who would rather sneak out than be upfront."

"And you aren't afraid of retaliation?"

Carol looked up from her net interface. "Is that a threat, Miss Ardwin?"

"Hell, no, Mrs. Coldstone. You know our belief has always been that only willing allies are worthy allies. I was asking a serious question, though. I don't intend to intimidate or strike fear in you. I'd like to know for my future dealings with others who might be more on the fence."

Carol paused. "Well, it was discussed. There were many who were afraid of what you personally might do, not the GAM, the U.S. government, or the CorpGov."

Jamie tilted her head and looked up for a moment. "Thank you, Carol. Yes, although I admit to a certain level of personal vindictiveness, you can rest assured that you and your people are safe from me and the CorpGov alliance until this is resolved."

"I thank you for the warning and information. It seems we have nothing more to talk about."

"So it seems."

*   *   *

"*This is Captain Carlos Munoz of the Oregon National Guard,*" came the voice over the building emergency speakers. "*We are once again conducting a room by room search of this entire structure. You all know the procedure. You are required to provide cooperation to all National Guard troops as they request it.*"

"Lieutenant, you know that witch is going to go thumping us with her kitchen utensils again. She does it every freaking time. What do you want me to do?"

"Follow my lead, Corporal. I've already talked this over with the captain.

"Unlock the door."

This time the door lock just slid open with the Metro codes. No additional security locks needed to be removed.

"Go!" the Sergeant ordered.

"EVERYONE DOWN!" the lieutenant said as his men fanned out. He walked in casually, his weapon pointing without menace at the floor. This time the Romanian family of six were all at the table. The grandmother got up and moved toward him with her serving ladle in her hand. Her Romanian invective fired at him like a rocket barrage. She raised her improvised weapon. The lieutenant snapped his gun up. The zipping sound made as his gauss burst shredded her unevenly in half startled everyone, including his own men. Those who were in range turned to offer support only to see the woman slump onto the carpet. The lieutenant fired off two more bursts into the family at the table before anyone else reacted. Soon everyone fired into the now gory remains.

"Cease fire," the lieutenant said. Gobs of once living tissue dripped from the shredded drapes and left trails of blood down the window. "That should be a sufficient object lesson."

*   *   *

"So how does our interrogation of Wintel go?" Captain Lennart asked, as he picked a pair of cheese Danish from the pastry tray.

"I'm here to give the morning briefing. As such I'll give you all the information I have then, sir," Reza said, lacing his coffee with four cream packets and two sugars.

"I'm sorry,Lieutenant. I didn't mean to drag anything out of you."

"No, that's quite all right, sir. I just didn't want to let any information out of the bag prematurely."

"Quite right, Lieutenant."

The pudgy captain found his place at the table and ignored Reza. Reza took his chance and took a short sip on the coffee. The bitter sting might be one of his last.

As the commissioner came into the room all the side conversations died. They all took their seats quickly and quietly. Reza wondered if they all realized how they kowtowed to the big man. Oh, Hardy and

Broadsky had ass-kissing down to a science, but he wondered about the others.

"I apologize for my delay, gentlemen. I was having a candid discussion with our prisoner.

"Please start us off with the destruction of our comrades in green, lieutenant."

"Thank you, Commissioner. It appears as if the U.S. Army booby-trapped the armory at Deer Mountain in Colorado with a nuclear device."

"But we acceded to their demands to keep the prisoners we've taken in good health," Amber Cohen objected.

"Before leaving the site their commander informed our men that they'd rigged it to explode. Afterward we received a communique from the president on an email site we falsely assumed was secure."

"So what did that redheaded, street-corner *blyád* have to say?"

"She claims that they never attacked us with any CBRN. She also goes on to claim that if the National Guard continued to act like common thieves then she will treat them like it."

The room fell silent until three full breaths later Krylov said, "When we catch her, I'm going to enjoy *idi v pizdú*."

"How many did we lose?"

"Eighty-six men, sir."

"And the munitions."

"Yes, sir, and the munitions."

"Nothing we can do about it. I want you to tell Colonel Reed to issue an order to avoid anything that the opposition even claims is booby-trapped. I don't want to worry about losing more men. We've won this war and can only lose it from this point forward. Throwing away soldiers can do just that.

"By the way, I want you to make Colonel Reed an attendee of this meeting. I know he is too busy to attend every morning but make his presence at least weekly."

"Yes, sir," Reza said making a note on his sleeve tablet.

"So shall we move on to some good news?"

"As you wish, Commissioner. As I'm sure all of you have heard through the grapevine, we have in our custody one William Trager, also known as Wintel. Mr. Trager contacted us and asked for asylum. He claims the CorpGov has manipulated the people into fighting a war they can't hope to win. He says that only the Metropolitan Police can bring order out of this chaos. Although he says it was a defection we need to be careful of the possibility that he is in fact a double agent."

"Absolutely, Lieutenant," Commissioner Krylov agreed, "but at the same time we can't dismiss an opportunity just because he might be a mole."

"I must concur, sir," Broadsky offered. Reza wondered if the man could ever get the smell of Krylov's sphincter off his nose.

"I'm sorry if I was misunderstood, gentlemen. I believe this may be the key opportunity of this entire conflict. I just believe we need to be cautious. I might add that we have one other datum that leads us more in the direction that Wintel is in fact on our side. He's been feeding us information from the inside of the CorpGov alliance council for several weeks now."

The commanders of the Metros never would be mistaken for deep space astrogators or even theoretical physicists. Even the smartest of their group, Captain Cohen, struggled with this.

"But how—"

"I'd like to take credit for it, but the commissioner set it up."

Krylov had a smug grin that would have done the Cheshire cat proud. He knew how he'd set it up and they didn't. They expected an explanation that he wouldn't provide. *Let them worry and fear me because I know how to make things happen without them,* he thought. "Go on, Reza."

"Well, for starters I would have suggested that we make a propaganda coup over Wintel coming over to our side, but the CorpGov preempted us with that illicit broadcast this morning. We still gain a good deal of value but not as much as we could have." Reza watched universal nods around the table. "Well, with that in mind, I suggest that we honor not only his request for asylum but also leave Wintel in charge of his corporation. I say we take no action against him in retribution for being in the CorpGov. This is his thirty pieces of silver." No one objected but neither did they affirm. "I have to stress that if we take punitive measures against him we are showing ourselves as the bad guys."

"But aren't we sending the wrong message?" Major Broadsky asked. "Shouldn't we show that we can ruthlessly destroy everything that gets in our path? That would prevent future rebellion or any more going over to their side."

Reza tried to speak but Captain Cohen spoke first. "And

eliminate the possibility of anyone else defecting to our side? And make every single bastard out there fight to the death because they know they have no quarter?"

"As much as I'd like to skin him alive, Amber is right, Art. We have to be benevolent despots. Besides, there is no reason we can't exact a bit of payback after all of this is over." The commissioner's mouth lay in a tight line and his eyes narrowed.

"Yes, sir. I do understand, sir."

"OK then, we are in agreement on what to do with Wintel. We'll trot him out as our publicity dog as we continue to wring him for every last possible nugget of information."

"Won't that make him a target for a CorpGov or Greenie assassin?" Captain Hardy asked.

"Doubtful, sir. The publicity backlash would be horrific to them. They need the people's good opinion. We don't."

"All right then, Lieutenant, what wonderful secrets has our new compatriot spilled so far?" Krylov's tone drew a couple of chuckles.

"Very good, Commissioner. Wintel provided us the general CorpGov plans. They aren't anything we didn't already know. They are trying to strangle us financially. What we didn't know, but theorized is that they have acknowledged at their highest level meetings that they know their cause to be doomed."

"That's interesting. Why don't they just throw in the towel?"

"Their intent is to prolong their capitulation as long as possible to improve the odds of a future uprising. That's one of the reasons they are shipping all of that material out to Mars."

"Good point, Lieutenant. I want a raid on those supplies. I want them destroyed. Do we have any naval ships under our control?"

"Not many, sir. We have one squadron of Australian destroyers and a frigate, sir. I think we can get orders cut for the destroyers to fly out to Mars. From there they can do as you order. I'd feel more comfortable with at least the frigate in orbit, able to support Colonel Reed or other military commanders on need."

"Good answer, Lieutenant."

"It was the answer there is, sir. I'll only give you the truth."

"So what does our simulation show on the possibility of an uprising after we take control?" Amber Cohen asked.

"Our strategic simulations give an insurgency eighteen percent chance, and that is with the weapons they've stashed. Without them, the probability drops to a dismal three percent."

"It is of no concern, Lieutenant," Krylov interrupted. "Once we are in power, civilians have no hope of breaking free nor would they want to. I can ensure their loyalty."

"Sir, in the interest of full disclosure our simulations have never compared favorably to those by the Greenies or the CorpGov."

"We don't ever seem to be able to hire the right people in those spots," Captain Hardy commented.

"Perhaps that is true now, but in the future they will flock to our banner," Krylov said.

"I'm sure that is true, sir, but getting back to the enemy intent. The information that they intend to delay until the people themselves are endangered gives us a target that we can use to bring this to a quick end."

"Agreed," Krylov said. "Let's see how quickly we make a mountain of corpses out of the CorpGov's beloved people!"

* * *

"Captain King, my name is Lieutenant Reza Narendra, adjutant to Commissioner Yuri Krylov," came an audio only signal with King's eyes-only attention.

"A bloody Yank. OK, I can tell from the scramble and your IFF that you are who you say. What can I do for you, Lieutenant," King said from his bridge. As they were currently standing down from an extended exercise only two other people manned it with him.

"The commissioner would like you to take your squadron to Mars and destroy some supplies the insurrectionists have stashed there."

King made a chopping motion across his throat. His communications/navigation officer chopped off his mic. "He doesn't know Christmas from Bourke Street. Just wants us to lolly off in that direction."

"Groundhogs. Prolly think we can just chuck a yewy right here in space and run off."

"You got that right, nav. Put me back on."

"I'd be more than happy to help you, Lieutenant. I haven't calculated it but my rough out of the orbit puts us to Mars in about fifty-eight days, give or take."

"*Excuse me?*"

"What are you unclear about, Lieutenant?"

"*Two months?*"

"Yes. I could be off by a few days, but not more than that."

"*You can't go faster?*"

"How much do you know about orbital dynamics, Lieutenant?"

"*Nothing, Captain.*"

"Well, this isn't like a lift car that you just open the throttle a bit more. It must be calculated and very carefully matched with the mass we have available."

"*So anything shipped has the same problem?*"

"Shipping is even worse. They have to take the most economical way. Anything in shipment today you are probably looking at more like two years."

"*Can you intercept all the shipping going to Mars?*"

"Only if you have a fleet under your arm somewhere, mate."

"*Well then, I will have to get back to you, Captain. Thank you for educating me.*"

"No worries, mate."

The channel clicked off. "What a *drongo*."

*   *   *

"*Colonel Reed, this is Commissioner Krylov,*" came the thick accent over the field percomm.

"I recognize your voice, sir. What can I do for you today? We are closing in on the final few square kilometers of our search. I think I can finish this off in the next two weeks."

"*I need you to change your priorities. We have new data that gives us a new target.*"

"Before you go on, could you verify our private command code? I want to be certain that the enemy isn't playing communication games."

"*Absolutely, Colonel.*"

"My prompt is Tango, Nine, Echo, Echo, Eight, Foxtrot, Kilo, Zulu."

"*I respond with Three, X-Ray, Papa, Three, Romeo, One, Three, November, Charlie, Three.*"

"Thank you, sir. I'm awaiting your orders."

"*Remember that body count I didn't care if you went up to?*"

"I remember that conversation very well. A modified version of it has been given to all my commanders and senior noncoms."

"*Scratch it. I want you to go out and kill nils by the thousands. I want piles of bodies that I can see from my window.*"

"Sir?" Colonel Reed blanched to a pale gray that even his subordinates noted.

"*You did hear correctly. I need casualties in the hundreds of thousands. The gloves are off.*"

"Understood, sir. Will you authorize CBRN? That is the quickest way to rack up a body count. I think in this urban environment a heavier than air, non-persistant nerve agent probably would be the most effective way to kill almost exclusively nils."

There was a pause on the other end of the line. "*I didn't think of that, Colonel. That is why your uniform is a different color. I think we need this to remain conventional, Colonel.*"

"Probably a wise choice, if I might be allowed an opinion."

"*Yes, Charlie, I always want your opinion. I know such a slaughter is going to be hard on your troops but it will end this in hours instead of weeks.*"

"Yes, Mr. Commissioner. I can't say I'm going to like it but I will obey."

"*Good. Come in tomorrow about noon.*"

"Affirmative. I'll be there at noon with a BDA."

"*Excellent. Until tomorrow, Charlie.*"

Charles Reed broke his own personal rule by sitting down in front of his troops. He steepled his fingers together and stared at the ground.

"Colonel?" Several second later. "Colonel, are you all right?"

* * *

At one time Oaks Amusement Park delivered joy to thousands every year. Now it housed tens of thousands in the shells of the buildings that remained. In the deep darkness of the cloudy Portland night, one building stood nearly empty, surrounded by hundreds of those homeless, all waiting for what happened inside.

The metal floor and ceiling of the Cosmic Crash bumper cars had long ago been torn out and recycled. The wooden beams that had held them became cherished pieces of expensive furniture in some affluent corpie's home. The leaders of the CorpGov alliance sat in a circle on the cold dirt floor under what remained of the concrete roof. A small oil fire burned in a metal bucket between them.

"I'm sorry for the accommodations," Tony said. "The Oaks Park Pod offered us this space to meet. The National Guard cordon has made moving anywhere difficult. In fact that could be the first part of my report, if our moderator so moves."

"I do," Susan Tipton, president of the United States, said confidently.

Tony released Jamie's hand so he could talk, as usual, with his hands as much as his mouth. "We've been keeping close tabs on the sweep being made by the National Guard. It is methodical. Every building they clear sets the new perimeter, which includes anti-aircraft, anti-personnel mines, and locally-controlled synthetic soldiers.

"We've tested the barriers many times and they are tight. Any attack or breach of the line is immediate and never the same twice, so we can't provoke a known response and exploit it."

"Colonel Reed is a professional," Mr. Marks, the only member of the team still standing, said from behind Nanogate. His gaze didn't look at anyone but scanned the perimeter for threats.

"Yes, and a damned good one," Tony cursed. "Why couldn't we have drawn a moron like that Debnath fool in New York. Man couldn't find his ass with either hand, a GPS, and a flashlight. But one doesn't wish in a war. We have what we have.

"There is only one part of the cordon that Reed doesn't control… under the surface of the water. It's been so long since people have used submarines that they've forgotten them. In the end the *GAMS Blueback* will be our only escape. That end is near. I think we should leave in less than a week."

"Do we even need to vote on it?" Nanogate asked. Not one head nodded.

"Passed by lack of dissention," Susan said.

"OK. Everyone rendezvous at the Oregon Museum of Science and Industry docks at eleven twenty p.m., sharp. The *Blueback* will submerge at eleven thirty and anyone not on her will be left behind."

"Is there anything else?" Nanogate asked.

Tony warmed his hand near the fire in the bucket. "Not that I can think of."

"What about any offensive actions?" Susan asked.

"It's taking just about every person we have just to keep us out of Krylov's clutches, much less doing anything productive."

"What about Wintel?" Thomas Marks asked.

"That's a no-go. Christine and several of your people eyeballed that one for us, Thomas. Your people laughed at me. Christine said she could do it but it would cost her life. She waited calmly for me to give her the order. She would have done it, too. I sent her off on another mission instead. Besides, if we kill him now then we are the bad guys and our people will know it. I don't want to even try and predict what would happen then."

"Augie could do it," Jamie said optimistically.

"You know she hates it when you call her that."

"Yeah, that's why it is so fun to tease her about it."

"Well, you remember that when she drains the mob's entire funds and donates them to No Child Left Behind or some other silly charity."

"She wouldn't do that would she?"

"Ahem." Nanogate cleared his throat.

"Yes, quite right," Susan said. "As fun as this is, let's get back to the topic at hand. I agree we don't want to take any extreme action against Wintel, but did Christine find out anything else in her reconnoiter?"

"Only that he's singing like a canary and his new friends aren't completely trusting what he has to say."

"That's something anyway," Jamie added.

"A very small something," Nanogate said.

"Is that all you have, Tony?"

"Yes, that is all."

"Jamie, would you please report on our supplies, arms, and munitions sent away to Mars."

"Before I do that I'd like to share some of the conversations I've had with organizations who've been co-travelers with us."

"By all means, Miss Ardwin."

"I've had six conversations recently. We've lost the Teamsters, the Clerks, the Plumbers Union, and three major companies, including WalMaCo. All of these organizations have gone over to the Metros."

"Ouch," Tony said.

"'Ouch' is right. You know this is just the first trickle out of a busted dam. The Teamsters is the only critical one of the bunch. Without their support locally we can't shut off the National Guard or Metro supplies. The Teamsters can also aid their mobility and limit ours."

"Is there anything that can be done about any of these?" Nanogate asked.

"Not that I can see," Jamie said confidently.

"What can't be cured must be endured," Tony offered.

"Jamie, could you and Tony try to put your fingers in the dike by talking to our other folks?" Susan asked.

"We could," Jamie said. "But it would be more valuable behind the weight of the president."

"Good point," Susan responded. "Instead could you introduce me to anyone in the wavering camp, and we can try to hold back the flood as long as possible."

"Will do. Now I can report on the material shipment. I'll start by saying that I didn't really know this, but the shipments take upwards of two years to arrive. We can't move things that haven't arrived yet. I've sent a message to my colleagues in the dock workers union there and have arranged for them to be moved immediately on arrival."

"Does our problem with the Teamsters make that problematic?"

"Not at all. The Mars dock workers have their own union and are almost always fighting the ones back here on earth."

"So does the delay put everything we shipped at risk?" Susan asked.

"Likely. Our enemies can send the same messages we can. I don't know if they have anyone in place to do anything about it, though."

"Unlikely, according to my colleague MinInc," Nanogate interjected. "He controls much of what happens on Mars. He says that the Metro Police aren't getting any sympathy. There are only two warships in orbit. They couldn't control all the shipping if they wanted to."

"Well then, at risk, but not highly at risk. Any chance we can divert some of them? Better not to put all our eggs in one basket."

"I'll inquire, but based on the input I've received before it is unlikely."

"Very good. Summing up, we can't do much about it, so let it run its course. Now that brings us—"

"*Folks, I hate to do this but I need to interrupt your meeting,*" Augustine said over each of their individual percomms.

"Augustine, I didn't think we invited you."

"*You didn't, Madam President, but you all need to hear this. The National Guard is massacring nils. They are flooding ground level with everything they have and killing anything that moves. Pull up any local station on your percomms.*"

"We're doing it, Augustine. Anything moving in our direction?" Tony asked.

"*They started downtown and the Pearl District, areas with heavy concentrations of nils. They are sweeping east and west of the river, rather than south and north. You should be safe for the foreseeable future.*"

Tony flipped his feed over to CNI and paid the stiff charge for real-time access. "*…as you can see here, the National Guard is literally killing everything.*" The solido panned over a pile of bodies the size of a mansion. It zoomed in to show the body of in infant, still cradled in its dead mother's arms, with a ragged hole the size of a dollar coin in its head and two more torn through its torso. "*We can hear machine guns and heavy weapons going off further down the street. We can't get any closer as we've already lost our production manager to the Guardsmen's fire.*" Through the darkness, the infrared images picked up the shape of a tank floating along flanked by dozens of infantry. Bright flashes spurted from their weapons. The irregular chatter of automatic weapons fire interspersed with the ripping sound of Gatling and gauss guns. The solido image flared white briefly, followed by the boom of the tank's cannon. Bodies lay strewn about the street and hanging out gaping holes in the higher floors of buildings. The thermal imaging clearly picked up the oozing but rapidly cooling blood running from each victim.

"*We are urging everyone to get off of ground level immediately. They don't seem to be firing on anyone getting above the tenth floor that doesn't attack them first.*

"*We don't know what possibly could have provoked this attack. It might be in retaliation of the Terwilliger Curves incident where a National Guard unit was mobbed and destroyed after it shot an innocent young girl, Rebecca Young.*"

"*Sorry to interrupt, Mark, but we have three other centers of National Guard activity. We are switching you live to the area just outside the Lloyd Center, where, if you recall, it was the scene of a riot smashed by*

Metropolitan Police a little more than a week ago. Our reporter on the scene is Grace Belmont. What do you see, Grace?"

"Our remote cameras, just a few minutes ago picked up the National Guard rousting nils. This being nothing new, no one paid any mind to it until they were lined up against a wall and mowed down with a pair of vehicle mounted gauss guns. We don't have an accurate count of the dead, but as you can see the number is large." The scene panned to show a ceramcrete wall sprayed with blood and at its foot a slumping mass that could only have been bodies. The image enhanced to isolate one body with its head looking like a pumpkin after it had been dropped off the WalMaCo Tower.

"And apparently, that was just the start. They've been moving down Lloyd Boulevard killing pretty much indiscriminately as they go. No, that isn't right, Jake. It is too professional to be indiscriminate. They are exterminating anything that moves."

"Thank you, Grace. We have another—" Tony snapped off his feed.

"It's our worst fear," Susan said in a voice so low it almost mingled into the background noise. Her face grew lines of pain in the dancing firelight.

"What do we do now?" Tony mused aloud. Jamie just held his hand, her eyes cast down at the dirt floor.

"Well, our plan was clear," Nanogate responded. "We make our way off planet and capitulate, giving them no further reason to slaughter innocents."

"May I offer another option," came a high-pitched buzzing sound from beyond the firelight.

Like a choreographed motion, Mr. Marks drew his katana and leapt. He landed without a sound between the unseen speaker and the alliance heads. Muscles not normally seen stood out in sharp relief on his copper-colored skin, poised for instant action.

Jamie produced a gauss pistol from beneath her bodice. Tony leveled his left index finger in the same general threat axis. The president and Nanogate both stood but took no other action.

"Please," buzzed the voice in a high octave, "Be assured I mean you no harm. I apologize for startling you but I needed to be quiet not to arouse the cordon of people around the building."

"How did you get in?" Jamie demanded.

A low frequency tone rippled through the room. "Even nils

don't know all the hidden pathways in the city. We do."

"I think more reasoned questions are 'Who are you?' followed by 'What do you want?'" Nanogate asked with the tact of a lifetime of calm negotiations.

"Well, I have two designations, the one I was born with and the one you all gave us when you put me in this shell," the voice said again. A small silver box about the size and shape of a toaster rolled into the flickering light of the fire. A1412 stood out in relief on its side. "My name is Henry Royston."

Training

Abe's memories of the immediate past consisted only of those from like a hazy disjointed solido. First it was hearing gauss guns out on the MLK. Next, crying people raced by the School Pod's digs. Chips of stone sprayed in Abe's face as bullets struck just over his head before he even heard the cracks of the weapons

The entire pod scattered. The lucky ones went out the back. Abe, in the middle of the pack, watched Terri, Bob, Sasha, Carl, and many, many others fall. Sometimes they'd jerk, or thrash when down on the ground. They all screamed. He actually ran over the top of June as she just collapsed in a heap in front of him.

They tried to turn toward downtown at Grand but even more guns arrayed 200 m south of them. Tracers flew by him like laser streaks. He couldn't think. He could only draw in breaths as if they were full of glass and struggle to put one foot in front of the other.

The leaders of the group tried to turn them west on Halsey. Abe knew they wanted to climb the ladders all over the base of the burned out Spears Tower. They wouldn't make it if the National Guard kept advancing. He grabbed a rock and threw it at the gunmen. Danny'd picked up a rusted pipe and rushed the National Guard line. Abe watched his best friend suddenly stop and drop down face first onto the street. He'd gotten no closer than 50 m to the nearest enemy.

Halsey Street had nothing but bodies and blood. National Guard troops had come around the corner from Martin Luther King just 30 m away. Abe dove for the doorway of the Grand Street Market, crashing into fellow podmate Erin. Metal whizzed over their head, chewing twelve nickel-sized holes in the door.

They couldn't stop. He pulled Erin to her feet and they raced down Grand. For a moment he felt like he might get away until he tripped over a broken manhole cover. As he fell down he'd watched Erin's face turn into a cloud of red. Her headless body collapsed to the ground between him and the marauders. He snuggled up close to the body, both saying a prayer for his friend and for himself. Two bullets struck her corpse before he decided to move.

Sprinting around the corner onto Weidler, he was out of the direct line of fire. An alley to the Grower's Pod stood open. No one guarded the makeshift chain-link gate. Abe thought he might just have shelter. He darted inside, finding himself sloshing through as much gore as he'd ever seen. Bodies lay around bleeding out into the growing red lake. Moans from those only wounded begged him for help. He ran on, not knowing where the maze of plastic crate houses and dirt-filled pots led him.

Stopping, he bent over and held the stitch in his side. He stared at his hand when it came away red. Panicked, he grabbed at his shirt, yanking it open, wondering where he'd been hit. No injury marked his filthy body. Then he realized it had just been the cuddling up to a corpse that likely caused the wet stain.

When his chest filled with air again instead of glass, he continued to jog away from the sound of gunfire, deeper into the labyrinth—ducking in and out of small shanties or strings of hung laundry in his path. He'd made so many turns he couldn't even tell which way he travelled any longer.

Ahead Abe saw a group of people climbing two fire ladders against the old Wells Fargo building. He pushed himself to rush up to the group. If he got off ground level, he'd be safe. Ten meters shy of the ladder he heard a whine and rapid chuff-chuff-chuff of automatic weapons fire from above him. The climbers on the ladder exploded in clouds of red. Chunks of bodies fell like hail just before a tornado. A tank hung in the sky, lashing the tight groups at the base of the ladders with what looked like a solid stream of flame.

Moving forward meant death. Moving back meant death. He pulled himself against the wall and jerked his head around for an escape. Abe's eyes lit upon a street drain. After sixteen years as a nil, he was skinny enough he could probably fit. He did a running slide across the street. His momentum forced his hips through the narrow hole.

Falling, he tried to grab the ledge of the street but the slick, rain-wet stone offered no friction. His ass landed on something that cried out underneath him. Abe saw an assault rifle go skittering across the ground ending up with its butt sticking out of the muck in the center of the drainage tunnel.

Abe rolled off. He'd landed on one of the murdering bastards. He had to get the gun. He jumped up and grabbed it. Pointing it at the kid on the ground he didn't even hesitate to pull the trigger.

Abe jerked, but he didn't feel the lethal current passing through his heart from the anti-tamper device of the weapon. Smoking, his body fell to the earth without anima, yet one more datum for the massacre's statistics.

*   *   *

"Sir you asked to be informed when our ammunition fell below one week operational status," George Biggle, Reed's G-4, deputy chief of staff and logistics officer stated.

"Thanks, George. What's the full report?"

"This last push to increase casualties for the commissioner," George said with some contempt in his voice, "has been depleting stocks of small caliber ammunition." George made no secret that he disagreed with their mission as a whole but he was a consummate professional who wouldn't be put off by anything as small as distaste. "We have scads of heavy rounds for tanks and artillery. Our artillery isn't firing, although with the right spotters we could use precision rounds. We haven't been getting the small stuff. It's almost been like a conspiracy to deny us personal weapon ammunition."

Colonel Reed thought for a moment. "Can we get our people into the factories and escort them out under guard?"

"I don't have the people to do that kind of work, sir."

"How about enlisting some of the Guard forces in other states where they aren't as taxed as we are. And for that matter, why not ask them for supplies?"

"We've already depleted most of the stocks of other states. The U.S. Army, for all its clumsy ineptitude, seems to have been thorough in destroying or usurping most of the key logistics we need."

"Can we move to lasers? They don't control the power grid."

"I wouldn't be too sure about that, sir. Remember who owns the power grid."

"Fuck it all." Charlie seldom swore. "What don't they own? What about generators. We've got those by the space station full."

"Insufficient, sir. If we lose the power grid we will only be able to keep about twenty percent of the field charged. If that wasn't enough, we don't have enough lasers to equip everyone. Even if we did, I think you realize the problem with that option."

"Not enough suppression fire."

"Yes, sir. And laser wounds, while painful, are less debilitating because of the cauterization factor. We've the equipment to arm fifty percent with lasers. I personally wouldn't go over forty, but that's your call, sir."

"George, your recommendations are usually well thought out. This one is no exception."

"Thank you, sir. I also recommend the use of more heavy weapons. I say use what we have."

"Well, we've refrained to prevent mass civilian casualties in the past. Now we want casualties. I guess it makes sense."

"If we factor that, using forty percent lasers, always assuming we don't lose the power grid, we can extend our personal weapons by—" the major ran numbers on the combat computer on his sleeve, "—by about two weeks, maybe three unless we secure additional stocks. That gives us an operational timeframe of one month, sir."

"George, you're lucky I've never been one to shoot the messenger."

Major Biggle laughed. "Your right to shoot me if you wish, sir. But I appreciate the restraint and the bullet that we can use elsewhere."

"One month," Charlie said, with his hands on his hips. "God created the world in less time. Should be enough time to conquer a city."

* * *

"Mr. Royston, we have about a million and a half questions for you, but you specifically suggested a way out of our current dilemma. Could you please elaborate?" Nanogate asked, returning to his seat on the cold earth. Mr. Marks had moved to stand behind him. The bodyguard absently toyed with the hilt of his sword.

"Well, I would suggest that all the boxed join forces with your alliance," A1412 said in a voice that sounded like it came out of the rusted Tin Man.

"What could you do for us, wash our windows?" Jamie said with a snort.

"While I don't share my comrade's lack of manners, I do wonder what you could bring that would change our current situation," President Tipton said.

"We could bring two things you currently lack, heavy firepower—"

"Heavy firepower?" Tony interrupted with his eyebrows raised at least 3 cm.

"Quite right, Mr. Sammis. Do you remember the Miami disaster?"

"Who doesn't."

"Exactly. The news reported some heavy demolition equipment went berserk and destroyed four city blocks. Would it surprise you to learn that was the work of just four boxed? We slip on that equipment like you do your clothes."

"Those units are monstrous. They'd tear a tank apart like it was just toilet tissue," Jamie said.

"Quite right. Now multiply that kind of firepower by tens of thousands of us boxed."

Tony just looked on with a twinkle in his eyes and his mouth hanging open.

"I will grant you that point," Susan said. "But you mentioned two things."

"Yes, I did, something even better than firepower."

"I don't know, Mr. Royston, I think Tony is in love already," Jamie said. "I've only seen him that way when I take my clothes off."

"Hey, that isn't fair," Tony objected. Then with a smile he continued, "It's a different kind of lust. So what can be better than things that can shred tanks?"

"How about information?" Henry squeaked. "I can tell you exactly where and when any National Guard or Metro unit will be. I can tell you how many of them there will be and how they are armed. I can tell you the plans and intentions of your enemies."

For seven or eight heartbeats the only sound that came above the muted murmur of the city was the crackling of the badly distilled oil in the fire.

"And how can you do that?" Tony said, breaking the silence.

"We can and do go everywhere. Does anyone notice a service bot? How about a window cleaner? Do you notice the janitorial construct in the bathroom? How about the catering tray that glides into the room and sits while important meetings take place? We know pretty much everything about everyone."

"I think I can speak for everyone in saying, 'Welcome aboard!'" Susan said after looking at each member in turn.

"Hold on, one moment," Henry said. "I said we could do all these things, and we are quite willing to fight and die, if necessary, at your side—"

"I hear a 'but' coming," Jamie said.

"Quite so," Nanogate agreed.

"Yes… BUT we want our humanity back when we win. All of us. No matter our crime, no matter our indebtedness, no matter where we are. We are all to be returned to human bodies."

"But that must be hundreds of thousands of you!"

"As of this morning, four hundred, sixty-four thousand, six hundred three, Miss Jamie."

"Pardon me, but coming up with that many humans—"

"We accept," Tony said abruptly.

"The logistics doesn't—"

"I said, 'We accept,'" Tony said again, cutting off discussion. "If I have to accept unilaterally, then I will." He looked deeply in the eyes of Nanogate. As usual the man's poker face revealed nothing. Thomas Mark's eyes twinkled with the light of knowledge. Jamie squeezed his hand in, if not approval, then acceptance. Susan turned to him.

"You baffle me, Tony. I would like to know what's on your mind and how you are going to do this, but I'll go with you."

"As will I," Nanogate agreed. "I am puzzled as to how you intend to pay this debt."

"You aren't trying to get our help with a promise of something impossible, are you, Mr. Sammis? You are known for your honesty and square dealing, but even I'm curious now."

"Can you read lips, Mr. Royston?"

"One of the tricks we pick up, Mr. Sammis."

Tony turned away from the rest of the party and mouthed something to the boxed Henry Royston.

"I'm sorry my shell prevents me from smiling, Mr. Sammis. We would be happy to join your little adventure. Where do we start?"

*   *   *

The girl in the faded Greenpeace shirt and mohawk couldn't have been more than twelve. Johnson winced when Gohar grabbed her from behind by her rucked up hair and spun her against the wall.

"Hey, fucker." Her eyes widened when she took in their uniforms. "Sorry, sir. I thought you was one of my clannies."

Gohar didn't hesitate. His truncheon struck across her bare midriff. The air came out of her in such a rush it didn't even make a sound.

"Where can I find the Greenies, bitch?"

Tears ran down her face spreading black mascara and bright white foundation. "I... don't... know... nothing... 'bout...no Greenies... sir." She said gasping for breath between each word.

The truncheon came down again across her middle. Johnson heard the crack of bone. "I can keep this up all night, sweetie. Give up the Greenies and I'll go easy on you."

Yeah, you'll put a bullet through her head, Johnson thought.

A red froth formed on her lips, a distinct different color from her onyx lipstick. "He'p," she said, collapsing to the ground, "me."

The girl stopped moving after four more questions by Gohar. "Must not have known anything," he said, kicking her in the head.

Johnson wondered who he needed to blow to get a new partner.

*   *   *

Every charging booth held a boxed. The pathway ledges to the charging stations held them nose to tail. They stacked so deep on the ramps that rollers hung over the edges. The main floor couldn't fit an additional matchstick, much less more, yet they started stacking themselves two and, in places, three deep.

"Have you ever seen so many in one place?" Stephanie asked, her G996 shell pushing back against the rambunctious crowd. From the other side of the opening J112 jostled to hold his position.

"Nope. Hope Henry don't be gett'n stage fright," Ben Calwood said as he rammed the shell nearest him. "Stay back, buddy."

Henry was tired—a deep, weary fatigue of too many years. A1412 rolled up the ramp to the third level rim where his two best friends held an open space for him. The noisy crowd roared. The white noise threatened to overload his input so Henry dialed down the amplifier. He knew that he'd never get across to the crowd now so he set his mind at ease and shut down for five minutes.

Henry dreamed. All boxed dreamed. The dreams themselves meant nothing, no matter how wild they seemed. Up until recently dreams provided the only way to dispose of the emotional abuses they couldn't otherwise express.

He woke up to a crowd nearly as raucous as when he'd dropped off. As loudly as he could maximize his speaker, he said, "Please let me talk!"

Either his brethren didn't hear him or they didn't care. They got louder.

It took twenty-five more minutes before they quieted enough for Henry to be heard. "Brothers and Sisters, the Green Action Militia has agreed to our demands... YOUR demands!"

The mass of boxed people shook the building. It took another thirty minutes before they would let him speak again.

"Your humanity is within your grasp. All you have to do is WIN! IT! BACK!"

Henry got the two pieces of information out that he wanted. He knew better than to think he'd get another word in edgewise the rest of the night. He felt dizzy and tired. Let them party. The stress of waiting, of plotting, of keeping his own people in check, of meeting the CorpGov and GAM had gotten to him. He needed to rest.

He shut down with a timer set for four hours—a timer that would never go off. A weakened wall in his internal carotid artery burst. Henry Royston would never have the opportunity to reclaim his humanity.

* * *

"Welcome again to our staff, Colonel," Reza said, standing at the end of the table as usual for the morning brief.

"Thank you, Lieutenant."

"And as such I'd like to afford you the opportunity to start us out, hopefully with good news."

The colonel stood, his dark skin getting lost in the shadows near the ceiling. "I am not sure that the deaths of this many people constitutes good news but I've followed my orders.

"Commissioner, this is an official Battle Damage Assessment for the actions of January twenty-three.

"First we suffered only two fatalities in the entire action. An enemy dropped on one of our men, breaking his back. He died two hours later. One other of my men was killed by fratricide. We had fourteen lesser injuries, the most serious being two broken arms from thrown debris. We had one TSV that broke down in action but it is already back in service.

"Based on battlecams, hospital casualty and coroners' reports, and statistical analysis based on historical data, we estimate total dead of forty-eight thousand, four hundred. We approximate one hundred twelve thousand injured. We will probably have additional deaths in the injured by about twenty to thirty thousand due to the low medical capability of the nils."

"Exceptional news, Commander."

"Thank you, sir," Reed said in a low monotone. "I do have to report that we are dangerously low on ammunition. I've ordered a higher use of lasers that will give us another three to four weeks of capabilities but after that we will lose our ability to project force unless the logistics issues can be resolved.

"I have a team engaged in solving the issue but I'm not sanguine that it will be resolved positively. The issue seems to be a direct attack on the key point of our logistics chain."

"I'll let you handle those things. I'm only concerned about the big picture, Colonel," Krylov said with a grin that would look appropriate on a crocodile.

"Lieutenant, I want you to craft a communique to Nanogate. Require his surrender or the killings will continue."

* * *

"Baby, this is the first time I've had a chance to talk to you alone," Jamie said, cuddled up to Tony's hairy chest.

Cinnamon took the opportunity to climb up Jamie's leg and then jump across to Tony. She sat on his hip like queen of all she surveyed. Tony reached up and stroked the calico. She had almost lost the gawky kitten look even if her ears were still too big for her head. She closed her eyes and purred loud enough for a lion.

"Well, almost alone."

"What's up, Jams?"

"Have I told you how much I hate that nickname?"

"No."

"Well, I don't. I actually adore it. Use it as much as you want," Jamie said cuddling in closer. "Anyway, what did you promise that boxed thing?"

"I don't understand. Henry is a person just like us or at least his brain is."

"They always gave me the creeps. I never let them work in my place just because I kept expecting them to jump out of their shell and attack me. Irrational, I know, but they creep me out." Jamie pulled a sheet and a blanket up to cover the goose bumps all over her skin.

"Hey, now. No covering up the art," Tony said dragging the blanket back down to expose her body past the waist.

"I'm cold, you pervert," she said grabbing them from his grip and pulling them up even higher to her neck. "You want to see me then come under the covers."

Tony leaned forward and planted a kiss on her lips. "As you wish, m'lady." He dove under the covers. This dislodged Cinnamon, who squawked indignantly. She took up a new perch on the bottom corner of the bed.

"Hey, stop that. No tickling!" Jamie said, pushing and squirming away from her lover.

"Mrfmmpfm," came from under the covers.

"You didn't shave! Now that just scratches. Get out of there!"

"Spoilsport," Tony said, climbing out from under the blankets. "I guess the honeymoon is over."

"Oh, bloody hell. Do I have to fuck you every night?" she said with fake exasperation.

Tony made a production of looking up in the sky while stroking his chin. "Yes. And twice on Sunday."

Jamie hit him upside the head with a spare pillow. Cinnamon decided that her slaves were just being too rambunctious and jumped down off the bed. She found Tony's shoes and curled up atop one of them.

"And spousal abuse. This relationship isn't going very well."

"You bastard. Just for that I'm going to rape you seven or eight times tonight and you will be a quivering mass of protoplasm in the morning."

"I be skeered, worman. Git on wit' it then."

Jamie sighed and cuddled back up to Tony's chest. They lay quietly together in the dim light of only one small lamp. "Seriously, what did you offer Henry?"

Tony took his turn to be quiet before answering. "Jams, I don't ever want to keep secrets from you, but on rare occasions I need to. In this case I need to keep this from you so you will be able to do your job better."

"Is this something about me having the willies around the Boxed?" Jamie asked in an indignant huff as she sat up.

"No, honey, nothing at all. I'm keeping everyone in the dark, although I think Mr. Marks may have guessed. He is a very perspicacious person."

"You've been spending too much time with Nanogate. You're using big words again," she said going down for the third time to snuggle.

"Pshaw. You do too, wench."

"Only to intimidate people who don't have any education. Personally, I like simple words. 'Mr. Marks is observant.' Or how about, 'Mr. Marks sees things others don't.'"

Tony reached up under the covers and tickled Jamie's areola. "Fine. Mr. Marks sees how sexy my woman is. Is that better?"

"Still not going to tell me, eh?"

"Honestly, it is better you don't know."

"Well, you've left me no choice. I will have to use the woman's second most powerful weapon… I'm going to fuck you until you tell me."

"Oh, shit, it's to be torture," Tony chuckled deep down in his chest. "But if this doesn't work, what is a woman's most powerful weapon?"

"Not having sex."

*   *   *

"I'm sorry to hear that Mr. Roystor has passed away," Susan Tipton said to boxed unit G996.

There had been a problem with protocol as a boxed unit can't even get up to the seat of a chair, much less sit down. It didn't seem to be appropriate to look down on it on the floor. Susan had made the only decision that seemed to make sense. They all sat on the floor. Augustine protested her aging, brittle bones but she managed a full lotus position. Nanogate sat with dignity on one of the couch cushions he placed on the floor.

"He was our oldest and wisest leader. We will miss him and his guidance," came Stephanie Delfalkis's voice in a high buzzing pitch.

"So you were next in line of succession, Miss Delfalkis?"

"Please, it is Stephanie. Our leadership is nominally based on how long someone has remained boxed. I'm nowhere near the top. However, I'm the eldest of the people who have been with Henry since the beginning. I know every phase of our plan to help you. Because of that, the eldest moved that I am taken on as the acting leader during this crisis instead. I've been sworn in as the leader *pro tempore.*"

"Excellent, Stephanie. If we are to be allies we need to share. I have much to tell you…or if Henry was right, I have much to share that you already know. Did you have anything you wanted to start off the meeting with?"

"Yes, Miss President—"

"Damn it. If you insist on 'Stephanie' shall we please dispense with titles and protocol? It slows down meetings and gets in the way of real progress between friends."

"I think that is an excellent idea, Susan. As I was about to say we do have one problem that perhaps your friend Augustine might be able to help us with."

"Whatever I can do to help a friend, Stephanie," Augustine said, her smile brightening up her face under the unreadable, all-silver eyes.

Stephanie paused just a moment. "You know Henry and I envisioned this day many times. We had contingencies and backup plans based on the fact that we were forcing you to comply with our demands. I think we have misjudged you."

"I haven't done it yet," Augustine said with a wink.

"I think I already know you better than that, Augustine. Be that as it may, each of us boxed carries a tiny destruct capsule in our brain. The explosive is so small its force wouldn't even escape our brain even without the shell. They were added after the Miami rebellion. We have no way of even accessing the systems that control the signals that would kill us all in seconds."

"Give me a minute," Augustine said with her silver eyes seeming even more vacant.

"So while Augustine performs with her usual exceptional skill, shall we talk about the commissioner's communique?" Nanogate asked.

"I don't know what I have to say about it, Clarence. We are just the muscle and you're the eyes and ears," Stephanie said.

"Good grief, woman," Susan said. "You are the leader of your people. You have as much voice in this as anyone here."

"Thank you."

"For what?"

"For calling me a woman. I've not been able to think of myself that way in quite some time."

"Hopefully I can greet you as a fully functional woman sometime in the near future."

"My name is Stephanie Delfalkis," she whispered. "Absolutely, Miss...I mean Susan."

"Well, that didn't take much," Augustine said suddenly. "I guess no one thought anyone would zip in to undo the signals. To set them off would have taken much longer with a serious decryption team."

"Huh?" Stephanie asked.

"Oh, I went one further and left everything in place so anyone checking it will think they still have positive control, but the protocols to set off the devices are gone. And as subtle as they were, I doubt they could ever be reconstructed. I'd say less than one chance in a million."

"You mean that's it?"

"Yes, Stephanie. You and your people are free from the possibility of someone killing you one at a time or en-mass—at least that way."

"You did that all in less than a minute. Are you sure?"

"Stephanie, I know you don't know me very well. If I just thought I'd accomplished it, I'd've said so and give you my best guess as to how confident I was. I'll go even one better than confident on this action. I'll say that I'm certain. Not only did I get rid of that destruct device but the three backups they had in other systems."

Stephanie just sat. Her metal body couldn't betray her with expressions or body language. "We definitely were wrong not to come to you earlier... but then we only had one opportunity."

"Ladies, I appreciate how emotional this moment is, but could we please get back to the commissioner's demands and our response."

"Is responding with 'Nuts!' too strong?" Stephanie asked.

* * *

With January's cold and Columbia Gorge's prevalent winds, only three humans and a boxed occupied MillenniaLink's Multnomah Falls outdoor patio. A family and a pair of lovers watched the falls from the warmth of the observation deck but no one bothered them in the open. The falls itself provided a level of white noise perfect for a clandestine meeting, and the freezing mist prevented nanite surveillance.

Stephanie had secured a position as a food cart vending hot cider, hot chocolate, and warm Voodoo doughnuts. Wherever the mist from the falls struck it froze. A fine layer of ice covered the pavestones between the two high-rise buildings that flanked the Oregon landmark.

"One of the first things we need to do is take out that bloody drone facility in Kansas City," Jamie said, wrapping her hands around a steaming cup of cider. The one sip she'd taken proved bitter and sour at the same time. She still approved of it as a hand warmer.

"We can't take it from the ground without obvious help from the boxed. We aren't ready to tip our ace in the hole," Tony rebutted, his breath white in the air.

"Well, whenever I send my people out with you I'm sending 'With regrets' letters to the families and paying out death benefits," Jamie said.

"Hopefully with our intel your losses will be minimized, if not eliminated," Stephanie said.

"While I'll retain some reservations, I agree with Miss Delfalkis's assessment," Mr. Marks said.

"Please, it is just Stephanie."

"My apologies, Stephanie. It is a strong habit ingrained into the very fiber of my personality. In my training had I the temerity to call anyone by their given name I would have been beaten with a split rattan cane. I made the mistake only once and you don't forget again."

"I mean if you are more comfortable, go ahead. I just distrust formality."

"I'll do what I can, Stephanie."

"So what you are saying is that I shouldn't be losing any more of my people?" Jamie said.

"That is likely the case, Miss Ardwin."

"OK, well then I'll remove my request to hit KC."

"Oh, we'll hit it. We'll need to take it out—but later," Tony said. "I think the first thing we need to do is whittle down the National Guard, maybe even take them out as a player entirely."

"I never thought of this but what about going after the governor? He's the command authority for the troops," Jamie offered.

"Great thought, babe! We could wrap this all up in one raid."

"I'm sorry to disagree with you two," Mr. Marks said, "but I feel it won't produce the desired results for at least two reasons. First, to the people we will look like bullies, kidnappers, and extortionists. The people might just turn on us as one."

"Hmm," Tony mused.

"Second, Krylov and Reed are too far down the road to turn back now. What would happen if Reed shuts down? He'd likely face a war crimes tribunal for mass murder. He'd likely and correctly assume the order was given under duress and ignore it."

"Mr. Marks is right," Stephanie buzzed out. "I say go after him for other reasons. I think Jamie should keep planning for the snatch if we decide to go for it."

"That's interesting," Tony said. "Stephanie, my colleague Nanogate said you'd been tentative at your first meeting. I'm sensing anything but temerity from you."

"Oh, fuck that," the vending cart said. "I'm a girl of action, not diplomacy. I felt stifled at our first meeting. I want to do things, not sit around and talk about them."

"OK then, how do we screw the National Guard?"

"Optimally we'd exploit their reduced availability of ammunition," Thomas said.

"How about dummies that they could shoot at?" Jamie offered.

"Why would they shoot at targets?" Stephanie asked.

"Because they would think they were real people about to shoot back."

"I'm confused." Tony said.

"Don't worry, sweetie. I'll catch you up later with a little private tutoring. So could the *Blueback* handle a little cruise up to Vancouver?" Jamie asked.

"Sure. Morgan has it humming like a fine watch. Probably two days, just to be safe."

"Perfect. I've got a phone call to make. I know a guy in the film industry up there. Our army is about to grow."

"Oh, shit," Stephanie said as she caught up with Jamie. "That's brilliant! The best part is even if they find out we've positioned the androids around, they can't afford NOT to destroy them."

"I would have to concur," Marks said. "No trooper will hold his fire. In war it is kill or be killed. There is no wait for confirmation."

"OK. I get it now. So we can force them to spend ammo," Tony agreed. "What next?"

"If that fat tub of lard Krylov plays the way we expect, you won't have to do anything. He'll put those big bulbous man-tits in a wringer for you. All you need to do is make sure it gets turned... hard."

"Analysis based on input from the boxed on Krylov's behavior predicts an eighty-three percent probability he will order another wave of killing nils and blue collar corporate workers," Augustine chimed in.

"So we just need to see where he sends his troops," Tony said.

"And make sure we are there before he is," Stephanie heterodyned.

"So we need a fast response force set up as soon as possible, with as many as possible trained snipers," Tony concluded.

"All bodyguards have sniper training so we understand their constraints and can deal with them more successfully."

"Looks like you just got a job. Put together a team of forty. Jamie will provide the weapons. I'll get the transportation. Stephanie, you get the intel so we can vape these assholes.

"Oh, and Augustine, please shut down all the Guard's heavy weapons. I don't want a flaming steel enema."

* * *

Commissioner Krylov, we appreciate your offer to allow us to surrender, or just lay down arms and disappear to prevent further deaths. Unlike you, we have a duty to the people. We don't slaughter, maim, or use the deaths of the people to further our cause. Leaving you in power would be abrogating our responsibilities by allowing you to perform even more atrocities as you did the night of January twenty-third. We must bring you before the bar of justice. We must allow the people to have their day.

As much as we'd like nothing more than to lay down our burdens we must fight on—so much for the value of your vaunted traitor. I actually thank you for taking him from our ranks. It's been a chore keeping up the pretense of trusting the maggot. I hope you two are very happy in bed together, both literally and figuratively. Only a fat khuyesos *such as yourself could enjoy such a spineless* pisda.

Reza wondered if he should continue. Every visible centimeter of the big man's skin had the hue of a plum. Each fist balled up like the head of a mace. While he didn't move from his seat he vibrated in place, grinding his teeth loud enough it could be heard over Reza's reading of Nanogate's response.

I find my response to your request equals one of a general over a century ago. He was also fighting a larger force from an equally evil empire when given the opportunity to surrender. I can't state it more eloquently than he could. This is our final response to your vile vision of the future.

NUTS!

CorpGov Chairman CEO Nanogate.

"Colonel?" Krylov hissed between clenched teeth.

"He is quoting General Anthony McAuliffe…"

The entire room shook with the force of Krylov's fists as they pounded the table as one. Filmies danced in the air from the impact. Two cups of coffee tipped and poured out. The staff let the hot drinks pour onto their pristine uniforms rather than draw attention to themselves.

"I! DON'T! GIVE! A! FUCK!" Krylov launched into Russian with a growl, barking out invectives loud enough to rattle the windows.

Reza recognized several vile curses but couldn't understand the rest except to be certain that they probably followed similar patterns.

The tirade lasted nearly five minutes when suddenly Krylov stopped himself, closed his eyes, and took several deep breaths. "Colonel, I don't care who he was quoting. I want to know how soon you can kill ten times as many of those fucking nils, and two give me the head of that *predatel*. Oh, and why we are at it, I want that Wintel fellow shot."

"Sir," Colonel Reed said unfazed, "I can begin another campaign immediately. We are within two weeks of closing out Portland as a place for the CorpGov to be hiding. At this point I'd assume they have already fled so I can't guarantee that I can deliver Nanogate to your charge."

"Sir, and if I might," Captain Cohen added. "Killing Wintel would have just the opposite effect you want."

Krylov looked at Cohen as if she'd just grown a second head. He stood up and turned toward his office. "Take no action against Wintel, for now. Colonel, start immediately. If we haven't a nil in the entirety of Oregon when you are done, I'll say it is a job well done."

After the room cleared the boxed unit wearing a catering cart dutifully cleaned up the spilled coffee. It collected the loose filmies for destruction per Metro doctrine. It read them prior to shredding.

*   *   *

"Augustine, can we shut down the heavy stuff without letting them know we're tampering?" Tony asked to a rare physical meeting of the GAM action committee. The Pink Tulip, a competitor to the destroyed Wilted Rose, rented the banquet hall to the Stipland PTA, a dummy set up by GMa Ice, for a morning meeting without a question. Tony wasn't even concerned about the fact that these concerned parents looked uncannily like the fugitives on Portland's Most Wanted. Every employee was a member of Greenpeace. Tony owned just enough of an interest in the bar to influence hiring but not enough to have anyone poking their nose into the business.

"Not sure that we can completely keep them from knowing. But I can give them a convincing trail of breadcrumbs and let them decide if they want to follow. I'm thinking of the following scenario. Mr. Tank Gunner fires but instead of a grav dart, explosive shell, or antipersonnel bomblette, he just gets an inert mass. While still dangerous the projectiles, designed for something else, will not be catastrophically dangerous. I just deactivate the ammunition before it leaves the barrel. Afterward, with my help, they'll trace down 'bad ammo.'"

"Sounds great but doesn't sound like we can do it more than once," David offered.

"The second time they'd know they were an inclined plane wrapped helically around a shaft," Augustine said. Several people chuckled. As usual Christine just sat quietly. "However, what if I instead just tweaked their firing system to miss where they were aiming?"

"Lots of their weapons don't matter if they are on target or not, and they may be more dangerous to everyone else if we start fucking with it," David said.

"I have to agree with David on that one. Can you image a grav dart going through the Galleria, or maybe through the front door of a family home and ending up in a TriMet bus?" Tony said.

"Maybe not, but what if I could program it to only fire on their own people?"

"Zat vould be *vunderbar*, Augustine. Kill many, many more of zose *nutte*." Since his brother Joe's death, Wayne spoke almost as infrequently as Christine and usually only about killing.

"I have to agree with Wayne. I can't think of anything better," Tony said, nodding profusely. "But how would you be able to do that?"

"Oh, that's easy, boss. The tanks all carry IFF, identify friend or foe, modules so there aren't any friendly fire accidents. I'll just reverse it. Whatever coordinates they enter, the target selector will choose the closest IFF as a target. It's all 1s and 0s to the processors. And I'll also program it so that any fired manually will not arm, as before."

"But they could still use them as mobile pillboxes," Edward Longfingers said.

"True, but they have to expose themselves to do it. I don't mind one difficult target shooting an assault rifle as opposed to an impervious target shooting weapons that level whole blocks," David replied.

"Augustine, is there anything more we can do with them?" Tony asked.

"Actually there may be. The lift generators on most grav vehicles are computer controlled. I could play havoc with their ability to even move them until they rigged them all for manual control."

"Oh, shit. Can you do that for TSVs as well?" David asked. He winced a bit when he gesticulated with his left arm.

"I'm looking into it but they are from a different manufacturer who hasn't been forthcoming with access to their licensing data or their computer systems."

"Could you drop them from the sky?"

"Not on a real-time basis. I have the ability to preprogram them so I can't just say cause one tank upon your command to be wiped out, but I do have altitude within the set of available controls."

"OK. What if we program random units to drop out of the sky if they get over a certain height," Tony said, building on the work of the rest of the team.

"Yeah, and I think I can mask it so it seems like a manufacturing defect."

"Later we can talk about maybe just stopping them all together. For now I want them to think they have their vaunted tanks to protect them," Tony said with a smile.

*   *   *

"Private Simms," Colonel Reed said, not even out of his jump jeep yet.

"Yes, sir."

"I want my command staff assembled in command sim in three minutes."

Reed walked directly to his office, ignoring the salutes around him. Once inside he poured himself a very stiff drink. He knew the answer even before he downed the tumbler in a single shot. In for a penny, as the old saying went. He poured himself another lighter one and slammed it back as well.

He strode down the stairs to the command sim and climbed onto the combat couch. He ignored the sim personnel and the physical indignities they performed to jack him in.

Suddenly he loomed large over the state of Oregon. Three of his four regimental commanders were waiting for him and the fourth joined almost at once.

"Gentlemen," Reed started. He mused that the masculine terms remained in the military jargon despite the fact that the commander of 82nd Armored Regiment was a woman. "We have a new mission. It is very similar to our previous one. I want the 162nd, which is controlling the non-Portland Metro areas, to move immediately to Portland. Michael, contact Lieutenant Richards for FOB information."

"Yes, sir."

"Now for the 186th. Mitch, I want you to remain controlling the grid. Don't try to make any additional advances. By doing this you should be able to hold the lines we've already made."

"Yes, sir."

"And 28604th Infantry, it is time to do some more killing. Your soldiers up to it?"

"No problem, sir. We don't mind killing rag dolls," Lieutenant Colonel Richard "Rich" Holmes said, using the euphemism for nils.

"Well, make sure your men don't go soft on me. This is coming right down from the top. Take all four of your companies and make a sweep through the densest population. I've looked at the drone feeds and that will be in grid 142. Kill all you can find."

"Yes, sir. With pleasure, sir."

"Emma, while I'm not expecting serious resistance, we know they've found a way to bring down TSVs but tanks are another matter. Attach two platoons to Rich for his sweep. Get them moving now."

"Yes, sir."

"Get moving now, folks. We need another victory for the commissioner."

In one corner of the simulation room, a boxed worker repaired a power conduit that had mysteriously failed for the eighth time that week. It innocuously placed a recording device with a burst transmitter as well.

*   *   *

The owner of the disposable ring phone, Audrey Penn, only knew that her Greenpeace cell officer told her to keep the percomm with her at all times. When it rang she wasn't to speak. She wasn't to write anything down. Hell, he didn't even tell her the bloody thing's contact code. For weeks the ring phone didn't make a peep. She figured it was a fool's errand until it buzzed while she was in the shower. She opened the line. She almost said Hello but remembered at the last moment.

A gruff voice on the other side said, "Game time. Bring everyone. Whiskey India Two Three." The line went dead.

Audrey didn't know why she then made four calls repeating the message she'd just been given. Per her instructions she then removed the ring's battery then slammed the phone against the counter six times, and just for good measure she picked up her shoe and slammed the heel of it down against the thing. On her own initiative she took the broken communicator into the shower with her, cradling it against her bosom to collect more of the falling water against it.

While Audrey didn't know exactly what she'd just done, she did have a good memory for voices. When she'd been given her instructions she'd thought they were paranoia personified. Now she wondered if they were paranoid enough.

She was quite certain that anyone who'd received a call from Tony Sammis much less passed a message for him would be interrogated, interned, and/or shot. Now she wondered if she should dispose of the phone in different parts in different locations.

While she followed the GAM news voraciously she never did anything more extreme than being a member of Greenpeace. Even though she'd never done anything in the past, she'd wondered if she could be one of those brave extremists. She now had an answer good enough for her.

∗   ∗   ∗

Boxed EA332 replaced a cracked seal on a thirty-third floor window of REI Tower. It sent a message. "We have the entirety of the 28604th Infantry Regiment linked up at the Steel Bridge with fourteen TSVs. Somehow they have picked up eight Powell-3 tanks. They are moving out now. ETA your position is twelve minutes, thirteen seconds."

∗   ∗   ∗

Washing the windows of an automated U-Store afforded K1488L better seats than the courtside Trail Blazers seats Bronwen had at one time in her previous life. Maybe now that the deal had been sealed she could enjoy watching those big sweaty guys again. Right now she couldn't even work up a good fantasy as her only sex organs were a pair of microscopic capsules of mixed hormones flowing into her blood stream at a controlled rate.

Bronwen watched as the National Guard marched up cracked, disused Davis Street in formation with weapons safed. TSVs provided overwatch and trailed the column which numbered 604. A trio of flanking scouts in pergravs led the way. Narco sticks hung out of the mouths of dozens of the soldiers. One even had his assault weapon slung over his shoulder and did card tricks for his squad mates.

Bronwen's own tension grew as they approached the abandoned

bicycle manufactory, now open air market, at Davis and Ninth. She could see nils milling around ostensibly doing their daily shopping. People moved from booth to stall, but without the usual chaos. No children roamed wildly or anywhere in the market. Eyes kept flickering toward the corner, watched for their hunters to round it. Every single person down there was a volunteer. Most had already lost family members in the other slaughters. While they wouldn't kill anyone directly, they would play their part.

The front ranks of National Guardsmen slowed up enough to allow the second rank to comingle, creating an even denser front. Those with slug throwers chambered a round and clicked off the safety. Superconductive toroids on lasers and gauss weapons charged.

As one the dozen leading troopers rounded the corner, weapons up and ready. A second group of twelve soldiers advanced through them to take a station 3 m further. The next group advanced through both.

The bait in the market could ignore them no longer. Someone let out a shriek and pandemonium erupted. Nils ran as directly away from the soldiers as they could. Carts tipped over in the rush. Other items were crushed underfoot. A single TSV swooped down into the path of the fleeing herd of humanity, diverting the flow to one side. The way was blocked by yet another TSV. The troops marched forward.

"Here comes a train wreck," Bronwen said quietly.

The entire intersection of Davis and Ninth Street exploded. Based on the Claymore mines of old, Tony's improvised trap fired fifteen hundred 5 mm balls down onto the troops in the intersection. Only one of the thirty-six National Guardsman in the intersection lived beyond thirty seconds. A further twenty-two hundred balls and other shrapnel raced eastward up Davis. Two companies suddenly became one in a writhing mass of blood. Most of the injured and dead were head wounds from soldiers refusing to pull down face protectors. Screams replaced precision maneuvering.

Snipers in the twenty and thirty floor levels fired down onto the disordered troops. The extremely thin, long uranium darts they fired lanced through the soldier's helmets like a needle through tissue paper. Seventy-eight shots were fired and sixty-seven soldiers died.

The two TSVs herding the nils imploded as they each took direct hits from three of the four fired gravity lances. Each crumpled up like a tight tinfoil ball about the size of a medicine-ball. The two balls hung briefly in the air before falling to the earth to drive a hole

2 m deep through the already broken roadway. The blood of the TSV crewmen poured out into the holes before percolating away through the sandy soil.

The National Guard finally reacted. The remaining TSVs and the tanks surged forward. The huge guns of the eight tanks barked in a ragged ripple. At almost the same time, fronts of buildings tore inward but didn't explode. Bronwen couldn't see if they hit anything other than empty rooms except in one case on the opposite side of the street where the mulched lower half of someone's severed body fell from the jagged hole made by a tank's projectile. The dozen TSVs floated up and hosed the twenty level with automatic weapons fire.

Out of windows of ten different levels, behind the ambushed National Guards, eighteen more Unicorn grav lances fired at an even dozen TSVs. Nine of them scored direct hits, compressing them into additional spheres of scrap metal and human flesh. One TSV took two glancing hits, tearing it in half as a powerful gravity field formed on either side of the vehicle. Two others took partial hits, sending them spiraling down toward the ground only marginally in control. Two additional missiles finished the crippled pair a scant second later.

The remaining troops on the ground scattered like cockroaches in the middle of the kitchen when the light is turned on. They found cover in doorways, broken-out ground level windows, and behind their already fallen comrades. This didn't help twenty-two more as the snipers picked off those slow to react.

Tanks roared out another volley. Some sought out those locations that shot missiles and others aimed for snipers. Once again the ordinance fired from the cannon but didn't act as anything but a single large projectile. Bronwen watched as a shell penetrated completely through one building and then ricocheted down the parallel block, making red paste of several of the volunteer nils as they retreated.

The National Guard on the ground started laying down suppressing fire into the buildings surrounding them. It looked like there was order being established until an apartment complex's swimming pool, filled with improvised napalm, dropped from forty floors into the center of the street. The splash of flames filled the canyon. Scores of men disappeared in the vomit from hell. Even those she could see running only got a short distance before they fell, screaming with flesh melting off their bones.

Bronwen decided that while this show pleased her to no end,

judgment was the better part of valor. Just as the ambushers bugged out, she chose to move on.

*   *   *

"Colonel Reed, we have reports that the 28604th is engaged and taking heavy casualties."

"What? How can a handful of nils inflict casualties? Get Colonel Holmes on the line."

"*Holmes here.*"

"What's your situation, Colonel?"

"*Sir, we are currently combat ineffective. I'm trying to rally my troops but we've taken over seventy percent casualties and have lost all of our TSVs in a prepared ambush. The tanks are still in place but they report some type of ammunition problems and are only twenty percent combat effective.*"

"What is the enemy strength?"

"*Based on what I've observed I'd estimate we face a reinforced company of infantry. Enemy casualties are deemed light based on our inability to engage.*"

"Are you still under fire?"

"*Sporadically, sir. I request support to allow us to either push forward or retreat at your command.*"

"I'll send in the 162nd Infantry supported by the 82nd."

"*Very good, sir.*"

"Simms! Get Majors Smith of the 162nd and Sands of 82nd Armored on the line."

"Yes, sir."

"*82nd Actual,*" Emma Sands replied almost immediately.

"*This is Captain Yancy of 162nd Infantry. Major Smith is indisposed.*"

"OK, both of you link up at the Hawthorne Bridge asap. I want you in support of the 28604th Regiment who has taken heavy losses. Contact Private Simms for a transcript of Colonel Holmes's report. As you push forward, I want the answer to just one question. How do we remove the enemy force from the field?"

*   *   *

Several Metro lift vehicles moved out of the way so that the SWAT mobile command center could land on the roof of the eighty-sixth story of the Mercury Delivery Building. The old-fashioned ceramcrete/tar roof made an excellent parking lot for the dozens of vehicles. News crew vehicles, with solidographs mounted outside, crowded in close. All of the solidographs pointed at Clinton Memorial Hospital across the street.

"Who's in charge here?" Captain Hogan asked before his feet even hit the roof. He jumped off the command center deck to find his counterpart and to officially take command of the scene.

"That would be me," a lieutenant with the nametag "Harris" on his pristine tactical gear said from behind one of the Metro lift vehicles.

"What's going on? Central didn't have many details."

"Someone has taken floors eighty through eighty-five of Clinton Hospital. We've been in touch with them via remotes pinned to the outside windows."

"What's the count?"

"Based on what we've been able to determine, there are thirty-one terrorists, eight staff, and fifty-four patients. The hostages are on the eighty-third floor. The gunman are patrolling around but primarily here and here on the eighty and eighty-five with four controlling the hostages," Harris said, poking at a solido projection of the building blueprints.

"Do we know who they are?"

"They haven't said. They are demanding that we arrest the National Guard for crimes against humanity and convene a war crimes trib—"

"Don't care, Lieutenant. How many men do you have here?"

"We have eighty-one here and another forty controlling traffic and evacuating other buildings. The blue dots also represent twelve snipers."

"Excellent. I can use the snipers."

"What's the deal, Captain?" SWAT Sergeant Biltoff asked as he walked up in full urban tactical armor.

"I want surveillance balls tapping every floor from seventy-five to ninety. I want to know how and where to go in. Get the men geared up. I also want Joshua to take a look for a good sniper perch to overwatch as much as he can of the eighty-third floor."

"Roger that, Captain," the sergeant said, marching away to carry out his orders.

"You aren't going to negotiate?"

"Lieutenant, they are calling for you again," a patrolman said from his control pad.

"Do you want the honors, Captain?"

"Sure. I might learn something about them." The captain took the mic. "This is Captain Hogan. To whom am I speaking?"

"*Ya surely do talk purdy.*"

"That is immaterial. I'd like to know your name."

"*If you must know, my name is Tony Sammis.*"

The eyebrows on both of the Metro officers went up.

"You do know you are wanted for many serious crimes. If you turn yourself in I am sure we can find a way to negotiate."

"*Thank you for your less than sincere offer, Captain Hogan.*"

"Well, what do you want?"

"*First, I'd like an answer to a simple question, Captain Hogan.*"

"Go ahead."

"*I doubt I'll get an honest answer but I'll voice it anyway. Did you assassinate President Lopez yourself or did you staff it out?*"

"Excuse me? I didn't have anything to do—"

"*That's what I thought. It was just an intellectual question that will never be answered to historians' liking.*"

"I tell you I had—"

"*Just shut up, Captain. I'm done talking to you. In fact everyone is done talking to you.*"

The entire eighty-sixth floor of the Mercury Delivery Building exploded outward at nearly ten times the speed of sound. The pressure wave tore the lungs out of every person on the roof and then the ceramcrete shrapnel tore bodies apart more effectively than a blender chewed up overripe bananas. One unlucky policeman survived both, only to fall 250 m and become a permanent stain on the pavement below.

Eleven of the twelve snipers found they had inadvertently perched on a remotely detonated grenade.

Over one hundred Metros ceased to exist in a space of less than a second.

Sales Support

"I think it is my turn to thank you for attending this meeting," Jamie said as the Teamster's representative, Carol Coldstone, came into the banquet room of Super Buffet. The Chinese restaurant occupied a profitable niche in the lower income Mill Park between the Sleeptite bedding factory and the Mill Park High School.

"I'm taking quite a chance being seen with you, Miss Ardwin," Carol stated. Her squat form more than filled her seat.

"You weren't followed, and as you might suspect we control this area quite tightly."

"You had me followed?"

"Of course, Mrs. Coldstone. I'm a wanted person and I'm contacting a person of the loyal opposition. I might suspect that you would turn me in to even further prove your new allegiance."

"Hrumph. I wouldn't do that."

"I'm pretty sure of that now, but I didn't know an hour ago."

"So what's this cloak and dagger all about? The only reason I agreed to come here is that we've done very profitable business together in the past. You did say you would make it worth my while."

"I do acknowledge that, Mrs. Coldstone. I want to offer you an opportunity to rejoin our cause."

"I thought our membership had made it quite clear to you a while back, Miss Ardwin. We won't back a losing cause."

"Your message was clear, Carol. But situations have changed," Jamie said as a boxed-operated catering unit rolled up to the table.

"Changed?" Carol asked, dishing up significant portions each of Kung Pao chicken and beef with broccoli.

"Yes," Jamie said, helping herself to smaller portions. "We have a new ally that has already allowed us to make significant inroads against the National Guard and the Metros."

"Why haven't I heard about either the successes or your new allies?"

Jamie looked at her watch. "Well, the successes happened about fifteen minutes ago. You'll see it on any breaking news feed you might subscribe to."

Carol got a distant look in her eyes as she brought up the net feed. "Holy crap! You ambushed both the Metros and the National Guard?"

"Yes, and it will get even worse. Our simulations show that the National Guard will no longer be a threat within a week."

Another boxed serving unit rolled up with onion pork and chicken with pineapple.

"A week? Are you insane? Who are these new allies that they can wipe out the National Guard in a week?"

"Oh, it's not just the allies but a coordinated effort among all of us. They just give us the edge."

"Edge? Holy fucking god, woman, you'd need more than an edge."

"We pretty much wiped out one of Colonel Reed's four battalions with the loss of three of our own. That's one-two-three people of our own. We followed that up by wiping out an entire Metro SWAT Team and another eighty or so Metro officers without a single loss."

"But surely they will—"

"Carol, they don't have a chance in hell. We know what they do before they do it. We can position whatever ambushes we want."

"Drone strikes. Artillery. Tanks."

Jamie smiled. "I understand your reluctance. We have all but one of those things completely under control and the other will be erased by tomorrow."

"But what about the fifty thousand Metros? You still can't deal with all of those!"

"Just remember what I did with just a dozen of my own people against the McMinnville Police Station. We can take out most of the outlying stations. We have one tough nut to crack, however."

"Yeah. I don't think the main Metro Pyramid is going down anytime soon."

"That's where you come in, Carol."

"What? I haven't agreed to anything yet."

"You will," came a high, squeaky voice adjacent to the table.

* × *

"Thank you for assembling again so quickly," Colonel Reed said around a makeshift simulation with tables and chairs. "It appears that our opponents have removed a great percentage of the nil population from the downtown area."

"We have drone reconnaissance showing movement from downtown to Hillsboro," the avatar of Major Emma Sands offered.

"Excellent. How long to regroup and push to Hillsboro?" Reed asked.

"We can be there inside thirty minutes with a light force in TSVs with tank support, but we are limited in troop vehicles due to the losses downtown."

"No. I want a fist, not a jab with a finger. And a light force, if the opposition is prepared, could be rolled up."

"Agreed, sir," Major Smith's avatar said. "To bring a cohesive force will take seven hours by foot or we could move troops to intermediate positions with vehicles in rotation."

"Why can't we just commandeer lift-trucks?" Colonel Holmes asked, his person actually in the simulation room with Reed.

"Excellent idea. Get started on that, Rich."

"So I think I can scare up transportation in just an hour."

"In that case, sir, we can hit them in as little as three hours," Smith said.

"Good. Rich, are your people regrouped?"

"Yes, sir. We are now little more than a company. It might make more sense to merge what remains of my battalion into 162nd or 186th Infantry."

"I'll take it under consideration. For now you will be our tactical reserve.

"Emma, what in the flying fuck happened to our tanks?"

"Bad ammo, sir. We now know why the corps have been so benevolent in supplying ammo. It's all been cocked up. I've got our quartermaster running around checking lot numbers and reloading vehicles. We'll have everything squared away before we attack. While we were checking, we found a similar problem with the artillery. That will take longer to straighten out."

"Don't think we would use it in this urban a setting but nice to know that sometime soon if we need it, we can deploy it with confidence.

"All right. Three hours from now . . . Mark. Let's pile up some enemies, people."

The sim shut down. While the two people in the command bunker unhooked from their simulation couch, a moronic little listening device compared the parameters of the conversation it had just overheard against its transmit authority. Both CPUs agreed that it had authorization to transmit its recording. It waited to hear the mass of electronic signals that indicated that the room had been unsealed and it could be heard. Three seconds later it heard the heartbeat of its twin outside. The transmission burst lasted less than a millisecond.

"Sir, we have a breech!" Private Simms said, sprinting to the side of Colonel Reed.

"What?"

"We monitored a burst transmission from within the vault as it opened."

"Get a messenger to every unit to hold action and rendezvous at Grid TG 141 and stand by for further orders. After those revised orders go out, I want the command vault stripped to component parts if necessary to find the device that sent that signal."

Five minutes later, the twin burst both its information and that of the conversation it just heard to the ether.

*   *   *

"I don't think they will fall into another trap like the last one," David Swift offered. Out of his unruly red hair, he combed the cobwebs he'd walked through getting to this quiet little place under the Steel Bridge.

"No way and our guys don't have the ability to take on three battalions even if one of them is shooting at itself," Tony said. "I think we are going to have to give this one a miss."

"I believe I agree with you gentlemen as much as it pains me to say so," Mr. Marks said. "I suggest that we get the people moving in random directions. We will lose some but only a small segment of those there."

"Wait a moment. What if we are thinking about this backwards," Tony said. "What if we attack the troops left in reserve. Wouldn't that bring them back to reinforce?"

"I like the concept, Mr. Sammis; however, I am not sure it will work. I agree that we need to start forcing the action instead of being reactive."

"David, set it up. Looks like 28604th Infantry hasn't had enough grief for one day."

*   *   *

Jamie Ardwin didn't know WalMaCo but she walked into the office loaded with information. Nanogate had briefed her carefully on who she would meet.

"Miss Ardwin, what can I do to help you?" said the tall, gaunt woman whose ribs showed even beneath her tailored dress. The blue tattoo of a dragon on the left side of her bald head stood out. "Come over and sit."

For once it was a CEO's office that hadn't been designed to intimidate. An intimate seating area with a tasteful brown, designer sofa and matching wingback chair sat around a leather upholstered coffee table. Nanogate warned Jamie that WalMaCo tried to set people at ease before slipping the knife in their back.

"Thank you very much, WalMaCo."

"Oh, Diana, please. I've never cared much for the stuffy use of titles."

"Thank you. As you probably have already heard from your assistant, my name is Jamie Ardwin."

"A name I've only heard in whispered, water-cooler gossip. Are you truly the *Capa Famiglia* of the entire Pacific Northwest?"

"Yes, Diana, I am. In fact my influence actually stretches further than that. I have the ear of several other *capas* and most of the families trust me implicitly."

"Amazing. Well, I'm sure this isn't a social call. I don't have any union contracts to negotiate in the near future so can you please bring us to why you requested this meeting?"

"Yes, well it is about your break from the CorpGov and your alliance with the Metros."

"Purely a business decision. Coffee?" WalMaCo asked as a serving unit rolled into the office.

"No, thank you. Well, I'm here to try and convince you to get your board to change their minds."

"So the rumors are also true that you are in bed with the CorpGov and the GAM."

"Yes, quite true. I'm here to inform you that the CorpGov will win this conflict. It will be bloody and possibly long, but we will win."

"Quite unlikely, Miss Ardwin. Every simulation I've seen gives you less than a two percent chance to succeed and only a pathetic twelve percent chance to even survive in exile."

"Your simulations haven't taken into account several new key pieces of information."

"Oh, we've seen your recent successes against National Guard and the Metros. I applaud you on them, but they are irrelevant blips that just give you a momentary spur of hope."

Jamie sighed with her shoulders going up and down at least 5 cm. "I don't even know where to start to change your mind, Diana. The truth is that the days of Krylov are now numbered. Our 'irrelevant blips,' as you call them, will continue. We want you back in our fold."

"I'm intrigued. Please tell me more."

"Oh, and if you are merely placating me until the Metros can arrive, I assure you that we won't be disturbed. Your signals, primary and backup, have been silenced. They are not coming." WalMaCo's face didn't fall but Jamie thought she detected a slight increase in inscrutability.

"So you are going to threaten me physically while unable to call for help?"

"No, Diana. While I sometimes go in for those kind of tactics, our alliance does not. As a representative of the alliance I bring the carrot. Join back with us. We'll forget that you jumped ship and you can be in on the spoils at the end."

"You can't win. No simulation gave you even one chance in ten."

"Redo your simulation. We'll give you forty-eight hours to run them. Then we'll give you another twenty-four for your propaganda corps to come up with a public message to put the best face on things and publically announce for the CorpGov."

"And if I... I mean we... refuse?"

"Well, quite frankly nothing will happen now. But Nanogate and President Tipton have authorized me to tell you that WalMaCo will cease to exist. To use a war parlance, 'No two stones will be left standing on top of one another.'"

"That sounds like a threat to me," WalMaCo said with a frown crossing her face.

"No, ma'am. Prophecy."

                              *   *   *

"Bear this is the strangest duty yet."

"What's so strange?"

"All we have to do is follow this broad around and do what she tells us?"

"Not quite, Mickey. You heard the sergeant. We were all deputized as special federal marshals. This means that we are authorized to protect Mrs. Sanchez as she goes about her lawful duty and to assist her in the service of papers."

"Why does she need a whole bloody company of us with weapons?"

"Mickey, shut up and soldier. Here we come up on our first assignment. This could get tense so shut up and listen."

A black woman, no more than 160 cm high jumped down off the lead truck and walked straight up toward the landing pad surrounded by old-fashioned razor wire.

"Halt," a private said. "Identify yourself."

"My name is Maria Sanchez. I'm a special federal agent acting on behalf of the Aerial Fighting Vehicles, Incorporated to repossess thirty-six M1216 'Long Rifle' self-propelled artillery for nonpayment."

"Ma'am, I'm not allowed to let you enter our deployment area. Let me get the sergeant on the line and see if he can help you."

"You do that, Private."

"Sergeant, we have a woman here claiming she's here to repo our guns.

"Yes, Sergeant. I'll hold her here.

"Ma'am, I need to hold you here until the sergeant and the colonel arrive."

"I'm not going anywhere without my vehicles."

Miss Sanchez showed her military background by standing at parade rest.

Lieutenant Colonel Antares double-timed up to the guard post. His sergeant followed only a half-step behind. "What is going on, miss?" the Lieutenant Colonel asked with no introduction.

"Are you the commanding officer?"

"Yes, I'm commander of the 218th Field Artillery Regiment."

"Then I hereby serve you with these formal papers of repossession for vehicles with VIN numbers as listed on these documents. I've brought my own drivers. If you would have your men dismount, I'll take them and be on my way."

"Ma'am, I can't just let you take state property."

"These papers make it clear that they don't belong to the State of Oregon any longer. They have failed to make payments on these vehicles for the last two months and they now belong to Aerial Fighting Vehicles, Incorporated. I'm ordering you to dismount these vehicles immediately."

"Or what? Excuse me, ma'am, but I have a couple hundred troopers and armored vehicles. We aren't going to just hand you the keys."

"That's our cue, Mickey," Bear whispered to his friend.

"*Combat dismount*," came the order over the U.S. Army tactical net.

As one, the six lift-trucks disgorged one hundred sixteen U.S. Army soldiers with weapons readied and leveled at the National Guardsmen. In only moments crew served weapons were emplaced on the roofs of the civilian trucks.

"Captain Antares, these deputies of the U.S. government are armed with light anti-armor weapons and we have a number of heavier crew served weapons as well. However, I believe none of this is necessary because you are a reasonable man. Additionally, I can turn off your armored vehicles, all of them, by one percomm signal."

The captain looked at his sergeant who gave a millimeter of nod.

"Good, I see there is definitely some intelligence back there. I'll give you five minutes to remove your men from my vehicles before my deputies exercise their legal discretion all over your traitorous asses."

*   *   *

First Sergeant Pierson finished his check of the perimeter. Happy thoughts shied away from his dark mood. What battalion chair-warmer decided that an abandoned high school was a good place to establish a forward operating base? He'd rather be out under the stars where he could see trouble coming. Instead he had sixteen entrances and exits that he knew of so far. He knew he hadn't found them all. If he had been charged with attacking the place he could breech the walls just about anywhere. Morons.

But security was only the first of his unenviable tasks. Colonel Holmes had left reorganizing the mess of this morning's debacle to him. Oh, he'd warned Colonel Holmes that marching into battle in formation had all the hallmarks of those stupid English redcoats of the 1700s, but the colonel knew best. He'd reckoned that speed was more important.

"Pffa!" the sergeant said to himself before spitting his red chaw into what at one time had been a wastebasket. Keeping it in his mouth would've set a bad precedent. He marched into the gymnasium and called out, "FALL IN!" The men stopped an impromptu game that resembled basketball with a deflated ball and scrambled into formation. Obvious holes stood out in the ranks. Several of the soldiers were bandaged in one place or another. One stupid bastard even had a cast on his arm.

"Close RANKS!" The men stepped into one another filling the gaps.

"Jenkins, you have the honor of joining Hawkins' platoon. Billings, you get to show off your marksmanship, or lack thereof, in Montgomery's platoon. Move it. NOW!

"We are this brigade's tactical reserve. It is about time we start looking less like a gaggle of geese and more like the soldiers—"

"BOOM!" the building shook. Chunks of the ceiling tiles dropped on the half folded bleachers. The loud zipping of a chain gun came next.

"Report!" the sergeant said over the regimental net.

"*Attack, NE corner. Two IEDs destroyed the atrium windows. Fire coming from multiple sectors. One man took some glass shrapnel in his leg but no other casualties.*"

"Call out the 3Ds."

"*Estimated company strength, thirty meters in all directions plus or minus ten meters.*"

"And only one injury? Are they attacking with peashooters?"

"*No, Sergeant. Sounds like they are firing* Britva Thirty *assault rifles but in single shot mode. We don't even have the* Britvas *yet. These guys are well-equipped.*"

Donald Pierson's mama didn't raise no fool. The initial attack was a ruse. Single shot? Even an incompetent boob could have overrun that post. "Cummings, reduce return fire to lasers only unless clear targets present themselves."

"*Yes, First Sergeant.*"

"Lieutenant Montgomery, you are in charge with the colonel away."

"What do you suggest, First Sergeant?"

"I'd advise that Lieutenant Hawkins takes his platoon and reinforce the point of attack. I might also advise moving the three remaining platoons and using the abandoned bank ten floors up. You would have height and it is a tight, defensible position with good solid walls. You could get a tactical advantage on the enemy."

"Excellent suggestion, First Sergeant. Hawkins, make it so. The rest of you gather your platoons and follow me. We have some stairs to climb."

"Oh, sir, I might also suggest you report that we are under attack." The sergeant didn't think much of the officers left to him but he had to work with what he had.

"Good idea, First Sergeant."

*   *   *

Tony hoped he wasn't getting too sneaky with this one. With surprise and the National Guard's hideous defensive position the outcome was inevitable even with something as basic as a frontal assault. Tony's only concern was to limit the number of his friendly losses—and to try out his new toys.

About 40 percent of a laser beam's fire reflected off the dirty window he'd selected as his vantage point. Another 40 percent of the energy was absorbed by the glass shattering it. The remaining twenty struck him on his head. The bitter smell of burnt hair mixed with the dust and rat droppings of this unused tenement. Tony ducked down, deciding it was time for alternative viewing. With a mental command his replacement eyeball dropped out into his hand. It nauseated him just slightly looking into his own eye in his hand but he was getting used to it. Tony slid it into a mounting frame and propped it on the window ledge. Closing his real eye he could see everything as if his head were still up looking over the ledge without the risk.

"Everything set for Operation Q-ship?" Tony asked over his percomm.

"*Yes, Tony. The boxed are reporting that the Guardsmen are going right where we hoped,*" David responded from his own location kilometers away.

"Good, I would've hated to bring down the whole building just to squash some cockroaches. Tell q-ship to stand by."

"*Roger.*"

With his eye in position he could see right into the bank windows. The leading National Guardsmen took up positions behind the solid masonry wall and used electronic periscopes to check out the lay of the land. Tony zoomed in and could even see them talking amongst one another. He made a mental note to pick up the skill to read lips in the future.

"*The boxed—*"

"Damn it, they have names, just like us," Tony snapped.

"*Sorry, Tony. It is a new concept. I haven't wrapped my head around it yet.*"

"Don't tell me sorry, tell the person you've been insulting."

"*Y4494, also known as Jasmine, reports that all but a rear guard contingent is in the bank and that they are setting up some form of command post in the vault area. And she says it happens all the time.*"

"What happens all the time?"

"*People referring to them as just boxed.*"

"Well, we won't because they are people. I don't refer to you as a Yank, or a Cauc do I? Understand?"

"*Yes, sir, Tony, sir.*"

"Clown."

"*That's what my high school said. I was class clown.*"

"*Can we get to business here, folks,*" Augustine interjected. "*Lots of people are going to die no matter how this turns out. We don't have to make it playtime in the park.*"

"*Yes, ma'am.*"

"Yes, ma'am," Tony echoed. "David, get q-ship rolling."

"*Roger.*"

"*Shit. I need medical,*" Edward Longfingers called out.

"*Medical en route,*" said one of the GAM support people.

"You hurt, Ed?"

"*No, but Christine took a laser through the thigh. The smell of burnt meat is nauseating.*"

"Why didn't she call out?"

"*She's too busy still trying to shoot more.*"

"Leave it to Christine." Tony waited impatiently as he could see the National Guard preparing to engage. "All team one units hold fire and shift to alternate firing location. Once in place get your team two counterpart shifted as well." There was no response but the fire pouring into the front of the school dropped and then almost stopped. The National Guard in the bank open fired, streaming mass destruction into places from where Tony's team had been firing. A couple of calls for medical came across the tactical net.

"*Sixty seconds, Tony,*" David said over the command channel.

Tony took to the all-hands channel. "Q-ships ETA now sixty secs. All units take cover."

In Tony's spare time he had looked at the problem of fire support. His team with all of its auxiliaries were only light infantry at best. They were guerilla fighters, not a stand up army. They didn't have any tanks, artillery, or support vehicles. But they would have to fight regular army.

* * *

"Sarge. We just got a report of a GlobalD freight hauler and three smaller lift-trucks on an intercept path to this block," a bandaged Specialist Thorn, the communications lead, said.

"Wave them off." The sergeant popped up over the protective wall and snapped a shot into a window frame that had spewed a considerable amount of ordinance. He didn't know if he'd hit anything.

"Ground control tried but they insist on having a National Guard delivery one block over."

"What level?"

"Ten below this action."

"What did the lieutenant say?"

"Umm. Lieutenant Montgomery is indisposed."

"You mean he's pissing himself," Sergeant Pierson replied, popping up to take another snap shot. This time he heard the unmistakable ring of his armor-piercing bullets hitting something metal.

"I wouldn't be so indelicate, Sergeant, but I believe you have the gist."

"Any reason to believe these are hostile? I mean, they are just delivery trucks.

"Careful with your ammo!" the sergeant yelled when one man fired out a full clip on auto.

"They have the right delivery codes so I don't have any reason to tag them as hostile, but what if they had more enemy troops."

"Where in the fuck would they get more troops? And where are those tanks of ours. I'm tired of playing patty-cake with these bozos."

"Tanks are ETA two minutes, Sarg."

"Tell the inbound trucks that if they come within twenty floors of us we'll destroy them. They are nothing but bugs and we are the zapper."

"Rog on that, Sarg."

*   *   *

The huge GlobalD truck, normally used for international shipping, and its trio of relatively microscopic, local-delivery trucks descended ten flight levels to comply with the edict by the National Guard. David Swift didn't expect the added 50 m to be any problem for his christened q-ship, *Switchblade.* As the best with just about any weapon in the GAM, the job fell to him to perform.

"Stand by to fire." Just by eye, David lined up *Switchblade* perpendicular to the action above. "FIRE!"

The side of the hauler instantly had 20 skull-sized holes in the side. That same number of Unicorn grav lances raced up to the bank level. The shot wasn't as accurate as David would have liked. Four of the ground-to-air missiles raced into the sky never to be seen again. The other sixteen of them tore through the building's stonework and ceramcrete as if it were butter. Normally the lances would have detonated on the outside or flown through the building as if it were just thick air. These had a special arming trigger. Tony rigged a heartbeat sensor to each of the detonation warheads. The sensor had a radius of 3 m.

Fourteen of the warheads activated inside the bank. Miraculously, only ninety-four of the one hundred six soldiers compressed like goo in the massive gravity distortions of the missiles. Eight of the remainder had wounds that were as grotesque as they were debilitating.

The three smaller vehicles, *Puff, Mnementh, and Smaug,* halted their forward movement and raced directly upward. One took station outside the bank level and the other two outside the level of the initial attack. Their sides fell away to reveal a pair of vehicle-mounted chain guns in the back. They began immediately unloading a rate of fire that actually pushed the nonmilitary vehicles back against the building on the other side of the street.

An enterprising National Guardsman launched a *Robin Hood* ground-to-air missile. The missile reached its cruising speed in 30 milliseconds. It split into eighteen different spearlettes, each with a shaped charge on the end. The rolling crackle that sounded as it struck turned *Smaug* into falling scrap metal and killed everyone else, including the driver, by flying shrapnel.

For his trouble, the courageous National Guard private took the three rounds from one of the chain guns in the neck, effectively decapitating him.

*   *   *

"Ma'am, we've just received reports that action at 28604th FOB has changed. They are reporting that they are under heavy fire by improvised fire support vehicles and request immediate support. In fact their exact words were, 'We're getting slaughtered!'"

Major Emma Sands smiled. Air-to-mud operations were fine, but the opportunity to score some air-to-air kills made her grin. "Respond that we are only thirty seconds away from engaging."

*   *   *

"Here comes the cavalry," Tony muttered as the Powell-3s came around the edge of the buildings nearest the Willamette River.

"*Don't worry, Tony,*" Augustine said over the command net. "*I got this one.*"

"Who, me? Worry?"

"*You do every chance you get, lover,*" Jamie said from 50 km away. "*Looks like you have one success with that bloody missile behemoth of yours.*"

"It is all for naught if those tanks don't fall. I would say, 'No kibitzing from the peanut gallery,' but I'm so nervous a baby kitten would freak me out. Keep me occupied. How did it go with the

Teamsters?"

"We're back in. They want to talk about a long term contr—"

"Hold it…here it comes."

Sixty-three Powell-3s floated down the narrow skyscraper canyon that was Holgate Boulevard. The roadway only allowed them to array in a three-unit wedge, one up, two back, so they deployed vertically. Each platoon of three was separated by 20 m, forming a triple column over 400 m high.

The two smaller q-ships continued to rain fire down on whomever remained alive under the pummeling of tens of thousands of depleted uranium rounds. *Switchblade* tried desperately to turn off and run for cover.

* * *

"Weapons free," Emma Sands said over the regimental net.

"Ma'am, the auto-loader fed a heavy armor piercing round when I ordered high explosive."

"Never mind, Private Roach. It must be some kind of glitch in the loading program. It's good enough to take down those trucks."

"Yes, ma'am. I'll strip it down after we mop up these guys."

Again over the all-regiment net, Emma Sands gave her last order—ever. "Fire free. Engage at will."

"Ma'am, the turret is traversing away from targe—"

A HAP round, fired point-blank by one of Major Sands's own platoon, lanced effortlessly in through the rear deck of the tank. The armor, turned molten by the passage of the projectile, turned into a superheated fountain. The fiery metal incinerated every flammable and many inflammable materials in the main cabin, including the crew. The HAP's core shed the remainder of its fragmentation coat. One of the bits of shrapnel pierced the driver's compartment. The driver, who up to that point had only been burning alive, had his head removed by the irregular shaped casing. The tank round's core ripped a smaller, but still lethal hole through the ammunition compartment and back out the tank's side. The superheated air and metal cooked off the first stored round. The chain reaction exploded the Powell-3 tank in less than one second from the initial impact.

* * *

Tony watched twenty-six tanks explode into a vertical column of flame. Windows, façade, and even masonry on either side of the explosions shattered and rained down. Through the smoke and pouring debris, twenty or so more of the behemoths fell unceremoniously to forever cave in the street below where each of them landed.

As the smoke cleared enough to see, twelve tanks hovered unscathed and another five burned in midair.

"You broke them, Augustine. I see only a dozen left and they seem to be retreating!"

"*Give the order, Tony.*"

"We actually get to finish a fight as the last ones on the field," Tony transmitted to everyone. "All hands: ground assault from the bottom up. Try to take prisoners but don't risk yourselves. Good hunting."

* * *

"*Listen, you headquarters chair-warmer, we are dying out here. We need fire support.*"

"I'm sorry, but—"

"*Just let me talk to Colonel Reed.*"

"I can't do that without the correct radio procedures."

"*Look, you puke. Every officer in our outfit is dead. None of us has the correct radio procedures. This is FIRST Sergeant Donald Pierson. The daily challenge is Hotel Lima Mike and the response is Zulu Tango Uniform. Now get me the fucking colonel or, so help me God, lieutenant, if I survive this I'm going to shove a torc grenade up your ass and laugh as you melt from the inside out.*"

"Colonel Reed, I have someone on the net who claims to be First Sergeant Pierson from the 28604th."

"Why do you say, 'claims'?"

"Well, he says all the officers are dead and no one left knows the correct—"

"Let me guess, he threatened you?"

"How did you know, sir?"

"Because he was one of my platoon sergeants as I came up

through the ranks. Put him on."

"Yes, sir."

"Sarge, what happened at the Tyco Star in Luna City?"

"*Holy shit, sir. I had to drag eight strippers off you that—*"

"That's enough, Sarge. You are who you say you are. What's going on down there?"

"*We need air support immediately, sir. We've lost seventy percent of our remaining strength and dropping fast. The force engaging us have heavy weapons firing from mobile platforms. Not, I say again, not infantry.*"

Reed could hear the automatic and burst weapons' fire in the communication feed. "What happened?"

"*No one has told you yet, sir?*" A dull boom partially covered Pierson's last word.

"It's like a black hole down there. Report."

"*Fucking Commo idiots. We are under heavy attack by infantry and mobile platforms of approximately company strength. We were ambushed and have taken heavy casualties. They are eating our lunch, sir.*"

"What about the 82nd Cavalry?"

"*Sir, all those tanks fired on one another at point blank range. If there are any left I can't tell it, sir.*"

"You'll get what we can bring to bear, Sarge. Hang in there."

"*Yes, sir.*"

"Order in the drones," Reed said, his dark face fading to ashen gray.

"We'll lose our cordon, sir."

"I know it's your job to remind me of things, Lieutenant, but if we don't, those men die."

"Ordering drone strike now, sir."

*   *   *

Tony watched sixteen missiles or bombs, he couldn't tell the difference at this speed, fall out of a nearly clear sky. Twelve of them hit David's *Switchblade*. The vehicle evaporated in a ball of flame reminding him of a fiery Mount Hood. Five of the remaining six targeted *Mnementh*, one of the smaller q-ships. Another conflagration removed it from the sky. *Puff*, the remaining q-ship, took the remaining bomb as a glancing blow. The bomb didn't detonate due to a cable that had come loose in loading.

"*Drones!*" Tony heard over the net. He also heard the telltale buzzing of grav lances reaching up toward the deadly air power. He assumed the drones were all destroyed as he heard no further launches.

"Samuel," Tony said to one of Mr. Mark's colleagues, "take your team and check the wreckage for survivors. Everyone else stay on plan." Tony didn't wait for a response.

He'd picked David specifically to pilot the missile q-ship. He'd killed yet another friend. With his mouth in a tight line, he plucked his eye off the windowsill and with a gentle shove returned it to his eye socket.

*   *   *

First Sergeant Pierson had pulled the almost nonexistent remnants of the 28604th Regiment back in a fighting retreat six times. He didn't think he could lead them through another. Only twenty-one remained, barely a platoon. Only the n00b Fraiser still wasn't injured in some way or another. A single round had torn through the fleshy part of the first sergeant's calf. There would be no more retreat for him.

They holed up in what used to be the girls' locker room. He'd collapsed the main entrance from the hall and the door to the fitness teacher's office with a pair of his grenades. He arrayed his force behind a barricade of toppled, colored-concrete lockers. The fortified doorway looking out at the gymnasium.

He'd like to have said that he'd forced his enemies into a war of attrition but it hadn't worked out that way at all. Every time he'd put up a good defensive ring they used explosives in some unique way. Someone over there was a fucking genius with anything that exploded. In their last position the OPFOR had fired the school's water heater through their improvised battlements, breaching a hole 8 m across. The time before that they'd blown a hole right through the floor, taking half of his soldiers with it.

"Sarge! There is someone out there with a white flag," Private Desoto said, waving the Colt automatic back in the direction of the barricade. His other arm ended 10 cm below the elbow in an emergency amputation cap. The man was only on his feet because of some serious drugs the military kept to themselves.

"So?"

"He's walking this way."

"Don't shoot him, but don't let him come past the doorway. We don't want him seeing what we have in here."

"Fuck! It's Tony Sammis himself!"

"Is he carrying a gun?"

"No, Sergeant, only that damned white flag."

Donald Pierson stood up, the pain receptors in his body muted because of MilSpec 1499 Pain Deadener, Disposable Injector, Moderate. He still limped as the muscles didn't like to work the foot.

"Hello?" called out Tony Sammis from beyond the pile of lockers.

"We hear you, Mr. Sammis. Have you come to surrender?"

"I'd laugh at that if it were a laughing matter, but there is too much blood on the field."

"I won't deny that. Some of it is mine. What do you want?"

"Who am I talking to? I'd like to be able to put a name to the face."

"First Sergeant Donald Pierson."

"Thank you, First Sergeant. Are you the ranking person?"

"Yes, sir." Donald cursed himself for calling the insurrectionist "sir." The Army forced one to either paint it, salute it, or call it sir.

"I'd like to tell you that we've taken forty-eight of your people prisoners so far. They are all receiving proper medical treatment and are being handled in accordance to the articles of war."

"Assuming you are telling the truth, I thank you."

"I am. In a moment I'll bring forward some of the lesser wounded members of your team to corroborate my statement."

"That's nice, Mr. Sammis. Why?"

"Sergeant, we want you to surrender. There is no reason for the remaining twenty-one men to die, although from what I've been told one of your more wounded men, Villareal, just passed from this world."

The sergeant looked over his shoulder, and out of the line of sight of this interloper. The medic drew his hands over the eyes of Jose Villareal. He shook his head at the sergeant.

"How did you—"

"I'll play my cards face up, Sergeant. I don't need them hidden to win this. We have a real-time feed into your room. Sergeant, we have you outnumbered five to one." Tony gave a hand signal and two platoons of men popped up in just the gymnasium alone. "We have you surrounded. You are running out of ammunition. Even more important, I've got the outer walls of your fortification rigged to explode inward. If neither the overpressure nor the shrapnel kill those remaining, the area above this should collapse into the locker room crushing anyone left. All that being said, I don't want to kill anyone else."

Sergeant Pierson didn't need to look around at his people. He wasn't some idealistic butter bar. They were beyond any hope of inflicting additional damage. Holding out would do nothing but get them killed. "You'll let me talk to your prisoners to make sure they are being treated correctly?"

"Yes, Sergeant. We have no reason to want you dead, only not shooting at us."

"Assuming you are telling the truth about my men, I'll agree to surrender."

*   *   *

"Maxwell, I need reinforcements. I've got a full-blown insurrection on my hands and all you are doing is guarding the key intersections and level translators of Albuquerque."

"*Using New Mexico National Guardsmen in Oregon? Are you serious?*"

"I'm deadly serious. Portland is where the war will be won or lost. I need those troopers."

"*Why don't you just send in tanks?*"

"Tanks won't do this, Max," Reed lied. "I need boots on the street and as many TSVs that you can break loose."

"*Well, I can let you have one regiment, Charlie. They are green but ready.*"

"Thank you, Max. I won't forget it."

"*Just win this thing so we can get our country going the right way.*"

"Working on it." Reed shut down the connection. "Simms! Get me Colonel William Nelson of the 36th out of Austin, Texas. And while you are at it, line me up Lieutenant Pierre Giroux of the Third Saskatchewan Dragoons."

G3433 lollygagged in the corner, only pretending to work on the air conditioning unit. The fix to the temporary field building normally would take at most ten minutes. G3433 drug it out to two hours, thirteen minutes before Colonel Reed had finished his inter-brigade calls for help.

*   *   *

"Folks, the GAM, the CorpGov, and I need your help," Jamie said to a small group of nils called the Solver Pod gathered in downtown Vancouver.

"You got it!"

"Anything you want!"

"We're with you."

"When do we attack?"

"Quiet, please. Are there any of you with military training?" About three quarters raised their hands. Jamie smiled to herself. They really wanted to fight.

"Come on. I know that all of you haven't. I'm not recruiting a group to storm the Metro's bastions." Hands started drifting down. "Be honest. How many of you have military training?" The majority of arms fell but five hands stayed up. She had them step forward.

"What outfit were you with?"

"I'm one of the first of the first, ma'am. Ooohrah!"

"Why did you leave?"

"My sergeant decided that stealing booze from the Officer's Club wasn't a prank."

"Was it?"

"Yes, ma'am," the marine broke into a grin, showing two teeth missing, "a four hundred liter prank."

Jamie smiled. "What's your name?"

"Joe Biggle."

"Joe, you'll do. Stand over here."

The next man was mousey in the extreme but clean shaven and neat. "And you?"

"Third Supply Battalion. You really a mobster?"

"Yes."

"You look too pretty to be a mobster."

"Thank you. What's your name?"

"He don't talk much," the next man in line said after the little man didn't respond. The larger man, both wide and tall, stood out among the nils. His white face, bald head, and speech mannerisms all screamed yokel but his body moved like a cat. "We's calls hims 'Brain' cause he gots good ideas on how to fix things. Only be watching your womenfolk around him."

"Brain, can you tell me why you were mustered out?"

"I didn't want to kill anymore."

"That's better than many. What did you do with women?"

"I just love them."

The bald man behind him shook his head very slightly while looking into Jamie's eyes with something that screamed caution.

"Thanks very much, Brain, but we don't want any women loved. Go on back to your people and we will—"

The little man's right hand flashed toward her like the blur out of a cartoon. Gregori spun her away and out of range even faster. By the time she had turned back to survey the scene, Brain's hand lay on the ground, cut off at the wrist in a growing puddle of blood. The severed hand still held an ancient straight razor clenched in its fingers. Brain just stood there looking at his spurting stump without any reaction except puzzlement.

Gregori already had quick-drawn his massive Mauser 14 mm sidearm. Its single, mild pop understated its power as the back chest of the Brain ceased to exist in a cloud of pink spray. The gun automatically centered on the chest of the bald bumpkin before Brain even started to drop.

Jamie just caught the motion of the yokel hiding something back into his oversized clothing.

The rest of the nils had just caught on to the immediate danger and began fleeing. Even Mr. First of the First took off as the body of Brain slumped to the ground with little more sound than a rustle of fabric.

"I don't wants no trouble, boss," the bald man said, slowly raising his empty hands.

"Hold on, Gregori," Jamie said, touching her bodyguard's arm. "What's your name?"

Ever the consummate professional, Gregori didn't change his point of aim, but he did ease his finger back from the breaking point of the trigger. The grim line on his face remained.

"Lance, ma'am. I ain't got no other one 'cause she who birthed me died when I was a young'n. I never been knowing a dad."

"Why did you save me?"

"Who said I been doing that?"

"Lance, I've seen a monofilament whip used before but rarely so quickly and in such close quarters."

"It's nothing, ma'am. I couldn't let one of ours be hurt'n the good folk. We be let'n him live with us 'cause he figured out so much stuff, but we be keep'n him away from our womenfolk."

"Lance, why haven't you made a living with your whip? Assassins can make good money."

"I gots what I need. I don't want no high and mighty sky house or corp folks who lie to your face."

"I guess I can understand that." The smell of Brain's intestines really started to overpower everything. "What would you say to lunch, Lance?"

"Two conditions, ma'am."

"What's that?"

"First, you be get'n your man ta stop point'n his cannon in my face."

"Absolutely," Jamie signaled Gregori to stand down. Her bodyguard brought his gun down to his side, but didn't holster it quite yet.

"Second, you be pay'n."

Jamie laughed. "Of course." She walked over to the man and wrapped her arm around his waist before leading him down the street away from the growing pool of blood and offal. "We need you to gather a group of friends to guard some National Guardsmen we just captured. You think you can do that?"

*   *   *

"Sir?"

"Yes, Private Simms."

"Colonel Reed, I have Captain Tonga from the Third Quartermasters Corp to see you."

"I'm busy trying to salvage this cluster fuck. Tell him to come back some other time," Reed said as he typed orders.

"He said it is an Article 104, sir."

"Aiding the enemy? In my Brigade?" Reed stormed out of the

office to find Captain Oliver Tonga standing at parade rest in his outer office. "What the fuck is going on, Captain?"

"Sir, this morning I was conducting some morning PT on my personal time when I discovered three enlisted men loading light arms ammunition on the back of a truck. I had them arrested as I knew no shipments, especially of that type, were planned."

"We're very low on that type of munitions."

"Yes, sir, I know. I discovered that each of these men had twenty thousand dollars in cash in their barracks, and a quick check of their accounts showed they had amassed more than half a million dollars."

"So you are suspecting them of selling the munitions."

"Yes, sir."

"Do you have any proof?"

"Yes, Colonel. I have record crystals with both the video feed of them loading war materials over several months into trucks and manifests showing bogus deliveries."

Colonel Reed placed one of the record crystals into a portable player. The flat video showed three men loading a civilian lift-truck with his precious light infantry munitions. "Where are these men?"

"Outside, sir."

Reed marched out the temporary building's door to find three soldiers handcuffed and guarded by six MPs. He walked up to each one in turn, placing a freeze frame he'd blown up of the incident confirming the two men and one woman's facial features.

"Is this you?" he asked the first man. The accused chose to remain mute. "How about you, soldier?" he asked the female private. She also stood mute. "And you?" he asked the third man who followed his comrades' example.

"I find you guilty of Article 104, Aiding the Enemy," Reed said with as much emotion in his voice as a hunk of quartz. He drew his service pistol and put a hole in the first man's head the size of a quarter. Before either remaining prisoner could react, he pivoted and placed a controlled pair into the woman's head.

The remaining man turned to run. One of the guards leveled his assault rifle and squeezed off a burst. The prisoner fell to the ground, wounded. Colonel Reed marched up to the writhing man and put a single shot into the man's head.

"Sentence carried out. Captain, you may now return to your unit. And I expect to see a commendation and recommendation for promotion on my desk for that man," Reed said of the guard who had fired, "before morning."

*   *   *

"I want to start this war council of the CorpGov with a quick announcement," Tony Sammis said to the hodgepodge of members and invitees. Today had Nanogate sitting side by side with President Susan Tipton, with Mr. Marks and Connie Powell hovering over their charges. Morgan had parked, or whatever it was called, the submarine and joined them sitting next to Christine. She talked to Stephanie Delfalkis, a boxed with G996 etched across her toaster-sized, titanium casing. Cinnamon had claimed Jamie's lap as her throne for this meeting that was obviously in the cat's honor. Gregori failed to ignore Cinnamon and was petting her over Jamie's shoulder. Augustine sat alone, working some of her magic in the network, barely paying attention. Martin Fox, Edward Longfingers, and Wayne Weissmuller huddled together. It was a good group. He'd risk his life for any one of them and felt that they would reciprocate.

"I just received word that David Swift is alive."

If Tony knew nothing of David, the sigh of relief that ran through the room of dissimilar people would have told him how well respected and loved the man was. The GAM wouldn't be the same without his flaming red hair and mischievous nature.

"One of our recovery teams found him pinned in the wreckage of *Switchblade*. He is in bad shape and likely will lose both his legs, but he will live.

"So with that good news I want to admonish the lot of you." The room suddenly got quiet and looked at him. "We've won a battle, not the war. A good number of you took unnecessary chances in your approach to our meeting today."

"Thanks, Dad," Morgan said with enough sarcasm to sink her submarine.

"I'm deadly serious. One slip-up and this all could come crashing down around our ears."

"Sorry," Morgan said.

"Yeah, that and a fiver will get you a cup of coffee. Just don't let up your vigilance.

"OK, now that I've played the heavy, let's talk about the good stuff. We had our first ever standing fight and we took the field!"

The group burst into cheers, even from the normally staid Nanogate and Mr. Marks.

"You did it, Tony!"

"No, we all did it. And we paid for it in the blood of those of us who didn't come back. But we won! We even took prisoners. Mistress Tipton, could I press upon you to negotiate a prisoner exchange to get back your Army boys that surrendered?"

"Absolutely, Tony. It would be my pleasure."

"May I interrupt for just a moment?" Augustine said from her corner.

"Always, Augustine," Tony said yielding the floor.

"May I suggest that the president isn't the right person for this job? No offense, Ms. President."

"Augustine, the day I take offense with you is the day *I* join the nunnery. Oh, you already did that," Susan said with a smile.

"Cute. No, I just think we need a neutral party," Augustine explained.

"And where in the bloody hell are we going to find one of those? Everyone has chosen a side." Martin asked.

"I've got one who hasn't," she said cryptically.

"OK, Augustine, I'll leave it in your hands."

"Thanks, boss."

"So Stephanie, can you fill us in on your latest intel? I understand something important came up."

"Yes, Mr. Sammis," Stephanie said in the high, squeaky voice possible by her external speakers, "We learned that Colonel Reed has secured reinforcements from other states. Last count he was to receive no fewer than twelve regiments of infantry and six motorized companies, all with older stock tanks that don't have all the bells and whistles for Augustine to yank on."

"We are having trouble enough with his four. If he gets twelve more and heavy armor support, too, then we are finished here in Portland even with the heavy punch that our boxed friends bring with them. We could melt away and start up again in another place but Krylov wins if we do that," Jamie said.

"And the boxed would most certainly pay the price," Stephanie squeaked out.

"I agree," Nanogate said.

"So here we stand," Tony declared. "How do we keep those bloody infantry from getting here? I'm open to suggestions."

"How about ambushing them?"

"I like the idea, Edward, but it would only work two, maybe three times, not twelve."

"Vy not drop rocks on zem from orbit," Wayne offered.

"Orbital bombardments are weapons of mass destruction," President Tipton offered. "I gave my word we wouldn't use them even if we could mitigate the collateral damage."

"Wait a minute. I think I see where Wayne is going. Wasn't your promise not to use them on the Oregon National Guard?" Jamie asked.

"So now we are going to split hairs when we are talking about unleashing that kind of firepower?" Augustine argued.

"While only the president has the authority to release those weapons," Tony said with a nod to that worthy, "I am leader of our forces and I say that is not a viable option. I will authorize no weapons of mass destruction unless our enemies use them against civilians first."

The group got quiet. Chins got rubbed as people dug into their brains for answers.

"Augustine, I have a question," Susan Tipton said, breaking the thoughts. "You said the U.S. Army wouldn't fight the Metros when the fight is really between the Metros and the CorpGov, but what about someone else threatening the United States?"

"I don't understand."

"Well, speaking of splitting hairs, each of these troop movements is in violation of federal law. The National Guard is chartered to operate only in their state unless authorized by the sitting president, namely me. I didn't authorize the move. Would the U.S. Army follow my orders then?"

"I just ran a new batch of simulations and they say seventy-thirty. You could handpick units but you wouldn't have the general support you are requesting."

"Still, seventy percent of our current force is significant."

"Ve could combine ze two plans."

"What two plans?" Tony asked.

"Dropping ze rocks."

"I thought I made it clear—"

"Hold on, Tony," Jamie said, gently touching his arm. "Wayne, you have a sharp mind. What if we used a similar threat that we used against Reed on each of these forces? Bring handpicked units to block their move and tell them should they manage to win the battle that they will be considered troops of a rebel government and we will feel compelled to suppress them with any means necessary."

"It combines all the things I hate," Susan said. "WMDs and pitting U.S. troops against U.S. troops."

"But it will only have to happen once. Once they see we have resolve they will back down," Jamie evangelized.

"Brinksmanship," Nanogate said in his mellow baritone. Susan nodded.

"What's that?"

"Back in the twentieth century during the so called Cold War, countries kept themselves safe by threatening mutual annihilation of each other. They waved their nuclear bombs and missiles at one another and hoped no one would be insane enough to push the first button that would exterminate the human species. Brinksmanship. No one was safe. You are basing your plan on that same level of intent. Is Krylov sane?"

"But we control the orbital bombardment satellites," Edward rebutted.

"And he has nuclear weapons. How difficult would it be for him to get chemical, nanite, or biological weapons?" Nanogate said in as close to frustration as he'd ever shown.

"Don't get me wrong, I love a good argument," Stephanie squeaked from her speaker, "but if I might interject—"

"Please, by all means," Tony offered.

"I have a way to use all of these plans with little to no chance of CBRN."

"That's what we've been waiting for. Please share," Susan said.

"Tony, you said we couldn't ambush them more than once or twice."

"Right. They'll catch on."

"So be it. Let them catch on. We can take the rest in a stand-up fight."

"We don't have the people or the heavy armor they'll have."

"Oh? We talked about this before. Have you ever seen what a demolition bot can do? How about a drilling rig? Or a heavy earthmover? None of them are built for war but they pack a punch. And while our quantities of these are limited to a hundred or so of each, we do have any number of service droids. With just a little adjustment they can all be modified to carry just about any weapon a human can. Multiply that by our current numbers."

"Three hundred fourteen thousand, six hundred forty-two," Augustine offered. "In the continental United States alone."

"Holy shit," Tony said, verbalizing the silent opinion of everyone in the room.

"I hate to be a killjoy," Morgan tossed in.

"Uh-oh. You are going to burst my bubble, aren't you, Morgan," Tony said. "Can't you all leave me with a dream for just a few minutes?"

"We can't fight without close fire support. Also we would be fighting under their air support. With the drone facility in Kansas City and the other one in Benton, Pennsylvania, and yet another one in Havana, we would be fighting under their air cover. We'd get murdered."

"Kansas City is the key," Augustine offered, projecting a map of North America into the center of the room. Augustine painted overlapping circles of control from each of the drone facilities, each in a different color. "We've already taken out Anchorage." The light blue dropped from the screen. "If we take out KC," she said, and dropped the pink to show the West Coast as far inland as Arizona, Utah, Wyoming, Montana, and Saskatchewan was completely clear.

"And then we hit them as they crest the Rockies."

"That would be my suggestion," Stephanie said. "Now all we have to do is take out a heavily fortified bunker. Got any more of those captive particle accelerators?"

"Only one," Tony said. "And it's been damaged by some of the fighting nearby. I don't know if we can get it running in time. But if I can get just a couple of Mistress Stephanie's construction bots, I think we can put that bunker out of business in short order."

Production

"For someone who has been kicked out of the convent, you are increasingly a thorn in my side, Augustine," Prioress Hanna said, her brown hair sneaking peeks out from underneath her wimple. Her face could have been any woman from thirty to eighty in these days of DNA-based cosmetics, but her eyes showed a mature mischievousness that didn't come young. "And over unencrypted percomm. I feel honored."

"I'm sorry for troubling you, Prioress, but I need your help."

"I?"

"Well, we, Prioress."

"You know I can't get involved in your war."

"We aren't asking you to. Nor are we asking you to take sides."

"God forgive me but I am intrigued again. I can't think of anything you might need my help on that will fit all of those criteria. By all means, Augustine, explain. You were a truthful novitiate."

"Thank you, Prioress. We have some Oregon National Guard prisoners. The National Guard has some U.S. Army prisoners. We want you to arrange the exchange. It wouldn't violate any tenants of your oath to God or the Church. It is an errand of mercy to all of those men."

Prioress Hanna's eyes looked up into the sky. She genuflected. "I don't know how you always manage to catch me off guard, but you do."

"So you'll do it?"

"Yes, Augustine, I will. And while I'm at it, I'll bring Brother Adam and Sister Ruth."

"Well, I understand Brother Adam, being a former Metro, but why Sister Ruth?"

The prioress laughed. "The Metros aren't going to be happy with me butting in. And frankly, Sister Ruth could get a monk to laugh."

* * *

"Sir, we have a situation," called someone from the floor of the Fort Leavenworth Aerodrome.

"Who said that?" asked the supervising lieutenant from the raised dais.

"Station Four, outer Northwest perimeter."

"Yes, Four, what can I do for you?"

"If you'd jack into my feed I think it will be self-explanatory."

Lieutenant Greene had held his commission and his post for all of two weeks. He just remembered that E3 Erich Padwalah, who'd been a station chief at Columbia Drone Facility for the last four years, manned Station Four.

Michael Greene was still learning his procedures. It took nearly a minute for him to direct the feeds to his own solido tank. At first he thought he'd tapped into a civilian construction feed. He'd not yet memorized each of the camera locations and fields of view. Only seeing the scene through the chain link of the perimeter fence next to the primary defense tower gave it any context. Four demolition bots, each 50 m high, 80 across, and weighing close to 100,000 metric tons, scuttled toward the base perimeter like the six-legged crabs they were modeled after.

"Four, what is your assessment?"

"Sir, at first I thought they were just moving them to the big construction project on the east edge of Kansas City, but normally they give us notification and they rarely move them at night."

"Could this be an attack?"

"If it is, sir, it would be a very clumsy one. Demo bots aren't designed for digging and our upper structures are all nonessentials. On the other hand, having four bots all malfunction at the same time seems remote."

"Could they have all been programmed with the same commands, commands that were wrong?"

"Possible, sir."

"They are going so slow, let's try contacting the owners before we panic."

"Sir, should we put the standby birds in the air just in case?"

"That would be prudent."

"Sir?"

"Yes, Four."

"What would we do against them if we were to panic?"

"Remote kill switch would be my first option."

"I've actually already tried that, sir."

Michael paused to think. "How about an air assault?"

"Sir, those things are armored to withstand damage being done to them by toppling buildings. Oh, we could hurt them, but I don't know if we could stop them even with our heavy attack birds. They are just too massive."

"I don't think the brass would be too keen on us doing nothing, Sergeant."

"Wait a moment. I think this seals the deal, sir. Those bots are registered to Downput Demolitions, a subsidiary of Nanogate. Sir, I'd recommend that you wake up the general and activate the fast action teams."

"Roger to that, Sergeant. Now get every drone you can aloft. They may only be good to the end of their ammo and fuel but that's better than being destroyed in place."

"Yes, sir."

"Is there anything else we can do, Sergeant?"

"Sir, the launch site is two hundred kilometers away from here. Unless you want to grab your assault rifle and take a lift jeep out there, I think that's about all we can do."

Greene looked at the image again. It looked like an old horror flattie with giant insects against the hapless armed forces. "Sergeant, I think you're right. We can do much more good right here."

* * *

The fence didn't even slow down the construction bots' legs. There was a slight flash when they knocked over the communication's tower.

"Perimeter breached," Edward Longfingers stated. "Prepare to deploy," he said to his team. He wished David Swift were here. He would have enjoyed this. Instead, his brother in arms lay in a hospital bed after he'd been pulled from the *Switchblade*'s wreckage without his legs.

Edward watched a team of infantry set up in a hasty defensive position of light metallic-foam barricades. Two of the men actually fired off man-portable armor defeating (MPAD) missiles. They both easily hit the first, slow-moving monstrosity, but the MPAD had been designed to penetrate thick armor and devastate fragile equipment and personnel within. They barely scratched the workings of the demolition bots. Lasers lanced up from the ground. They had the same significance as a gnat to an elephant.

An eight-thousand-tonne manipulator from the lead unit came down on the scratch fortifications and crushed everything that could be broken and drove those few items that couldn't into the earth.

From other directions mobile firing platforms and infantry moved in and began to pelt the massive machines with firepower. With glee, Edward watched three platoons of tanks all but annihilate each other with Grandma Ice's electronic help. Only two remained functional. Apparently they had learned because they started firing manually as fast as they could. The leg his team was compartmentalized within shook in response to one of those shells hitting the metallic joint above them.

"Deploy," he said, triggering a false panel to blow out beside them. The team ziplined 5 m to the ground next to the gigantic leg. Their equipment landed about 20 m behind.

Ahead the multi-tonne armored doors flew open to release a swarm of drones before slamming closed again with a shock that could be felt even by units airborne.

"Lee," Edward said to the boxed unit controlling the machine.

"*Yes,*" H4435, Lee Popal responded over their communications net.

"Remember, just pull open the doors. We'll do the rest. You have no chance even against the relative gnats around you. They will find a way to get you."

"*Understood. These babies will be on automatic heading toward the control bunker before you can say 'Fake-out.*'"

"Let me guess, football player?"

"*Soccer, you heathen.*"

"Well, you'll be playing again before someone can say 'Goooooooooooooaaaal!'"

The boxed unit laughed in its high, shrill way.

"OK, team. Each pair has a single shaft. As soon as the door is off, everyone run like a maniac to the entrance. Don't be a hero. Just get your tube into the drone channel and hightail it to the rendezvous point."

Lasers and tracers gave the night some illumination. The bots, who had about as much chance of stealth as a rat in a cat show, had their construction lights on. Drones dropped munitions nonstop on the lead bot, eventually doing enough damage to the shoulder joint that the left manipulator fell to the ground. It caused a serious tremor in the earth. The damaged demolition machine paused, giving one of the fresh units the lead. It picked up the manipulator and flung it through the sky. The soaring arm knocked down two drones, a TSV, and smashed four soldiers to paste when it landed on them.

"Get ready," Edward advised.

The new lead behemoth reached the drone bay door. It grabbed on either side of the 130 tonne door. The manipulators tore it from its tracks and lifted it over its head like a giant looking to crush a mortal with a boulder. The modern day Goliath flung the door at one of the remaining tanks, swatting it out of the air as if it had never existed.

"NOW!" Edward yelled, picking up his end of a 10 m long tube with a bulbous head. The troop raced twelve of the fat spears toward the new opening. At least part of the plan was working. So much attention was being paid to the 800 kilo gorilla in the room, no one noticed the relative ants running along the ground. Four other teams, each carrying a dozen of the spears arrived almost simultaneously at the opening. Each team tossed their spear, point down into the 80 m silo.

"Fire in the hole," Edward said, setting off his twelve. "Move it!" The conflagration below sounded like a horde of kids with pop-guns. The spears were self-drilling explosive rings stacked up the shaft. As each ring detonated, the spear got shorter but the hole it fell into was about 8 m deeper. After each ring detonated, the central core of the spear horizontally launched thirty grenade-like projectiles. Many went nowhere in the hole, but on the levels where there were access halls, hanger bays, repair or storage facilities, they scattered. Five to ten seconds later the flung projectiles detonated. One of the submunitions found its way in a weapon's storage bay, setting off secondary explosions that jetted flame into the night sky. It even blew eight of the breaching spears from the silo where they vented the rest of their fury on worthless dirt.

But the breaching spears held their best for last. After digging down nearly 100 m, the upper end of the warhead, a 40 kilo-shaped charge of the best military grade explosives, detonated horizontally. This exploded a 30 m trench which undercut the silo's inner walls. It took twenty of the spears making their final suicidal explosion before the hole in the ground collapsed upon itself. The remaining explosive breaching spears only collapsed the debris further. It would take months, if not years of work before anything flew out of the silo again.

* * *

"Commissioner Krylov, I have come to report my failure to carry out your mission thus far, and to let you know how I intend to rectify this problem in the future."

Yuri had woken up on the wrong side of the bed. It hadn't gotten better with news reports of pitched battles all over the city. The opponents weren't supposed to have any force that could go head to head with his National Guardsmen, unless that *pizda* Susan Tipton lied and ordered the Army against them. Even then his own people in the Army should shut that down or at least warn him. He could feel the heat rising to his face.

"Go on, Colonel," he said, trying to keep his voice even and calm.

"Yesterday my troops were led into a three-pronged ambush. The first was almost to be expected with the explosives' skills of our opponents. This attack wiped out two companies of my force. This in itself wouldn't have seriously impacted our ability to continue. At the same time they used modern, man-portable ground-to-air missiles and reduced the close support fire platforms to nothing but wreckage. I'll note that they shouldn't have had these missiles, much less in such quantities. The U.S. Army doesn't even have them in more than handfuls."

"So where did they get these mythical weapons?"

"We believe the manufacturer made a special batch of them specifically for the CorpGov."

"So you expect they have more."

"Yes, sir."

"Do you have a counter for them?"

"Well, our normal counter for man-portable weapons is either drone strikes or artillery. As you know drone strikes are seriously hampered by the loss of our Fire Island drone facility. We now have reports that Kansas City's Leavenworth drone facility has been rendered inoperable."

Krylov could feel his blood boiling. He had to remind himself that killing this man would only be a momentary pleasure. It wouldn't give him what he wanted. "Go on. What about the artillery?"

"Well, in short, they were repossessed. The state somehow didn't keep up the payments. My troopers would have fought it but they were outnumbered and frankly surprised. They would have been slaughtered."

"So let me get this straight, you have lost aerial capability, your artillery, and got a portion of your troops ambushed?"

"That isn't all the bad news, Commissioner. Our tanks have been hacked. I lost the majority of an entire regiment of tanks because they fired on one another instead of the enemy. We've located the problem but disabling it removes the multiple capabilities of our weapons. We are reduced to nothing more than floating tanks with the equivalent of World War Two firepower."

"So you've lost more than half your vaunted force and still haven't put paid to those weaponless nil fuckers."

"Yes, sir. I agree with everything you said except the 'weaponless' statement."

Krylov fumed for several seconds while every pair of eyes in the conference room looked at him. "And tell me, Colonel, why shouldn't I have Sergeant Tolbert there pull his sidearm and kill you where you stand?"

"That is your right, sir. I have kept my deputy, Lieutenant Colonel Samuel Marley apprised on my planning. He should be able to pick up and carry on through to the end result you desire."

Krylov closed his eyes. He tried to control his urge to put this fucking dog down. It wasn't easy. He'd like to decorate the walls with the man's brains to warn others not to fail. Without opening his eyes he said, in a calm, unhurried voice, "So, Colonel, can you first tell me how it is possible that a handful of people can wipe out a vastly superior force?"

"The enemy used two different methods that together were devastating…"

A boxed serving tray rolled into the room bearing pastries, coffee, and juice.

"Who ordered that?" Colonel Reed asked.

"I did, Colonel," Lieutenant Narendra said. "The commissioner asked for refreshments this morning."

"I specifically requested no boxed units be present," the commander said.

"Please leave the tray here and then return to the kitchen," Reza ordered. The boxed unit did as it was instructed, rolling out of the room in less than thirty seconds.

"Why all the fuss over a boxed unit, Reed?"

"I was just getting to that, sir. If I may continue?"

Krylov just waved his hand dismissively as he reached for the pastries.

"Thank you, sir. The way the GorpGov were able to defeat us was three previously unknown capabilities. First they have mobile weapons platforms. These units are nothing more than converted lift vehicles and now that we know what we face we should have minimal difficulty with them.

"Second, they have the ability to net hack our heavy armored units. To counter this I've ordered some older tanks out of mothballs that don't rely on the same levels of network interaction. These should be here in about one week's time.

"And finally, and I think most devastatingly, a level of intel that makes me believe that they have been sitting in on our planning meetings and even were party to specific orders. In short, they knew *exactly* where and when to hit us and with how much strength."

"Are you saying that one of us is a traitor?" Krylov asked around a mouthful of bear claw.

"Not exactly, sir. It's the boxed. They go everywhere without rousing suspicion."

"Oh, now I've heard some whoppers in my time to get out of being blamed for something, but this is ridiculous, Colonel," Captain Cohen said.

"That's right, they can't even communicate to us except via programming interface," Major Broadsky added.

"I'm dead serious, Captain and Major. Furthermore, I have proof."

Krylov didn't say anything but waved his hands again.

"I suspected the boxed when the first trap happened. Only my battalion commanders and I knew our plans in time to create an ambush that quickly and that effectively. When I investigated I found out that a boxed had been repairing something that wasn't broken for the third time right inside my command simulation."

"That isn't proof, Colonel."

"Ah, but the attack on the Kansas City drone facility was spearheaded by four demolition bots run by boxed. They worked in concert with several bodyguards and GAM members. We weren't able to capture the boxed but one was killed as it abandoned its extensions. We have its remains." The room went quiet. Colonel Reed continued, "What this points toward, comrades, is that the boxed are also willing to fight and kill in their large machines as well."

"This gives the Corpgov a large army that have no reason to be in love with us," Captain Amber Cohen said, summing up the implications.

"Too true," the Colonel agreed.

"Then throw the kill switch on all of them," Krylov spurted out. "Wait a minute. What kind of impact will it have on us?"

"If you think about it, sir, the impact is already there," Reed said confidently as he'd already thought this through. "We will feel interesting pressures without the boxed to do our dirty work but whether we kill them or not we will feel those impacts because they will be fighting rather than working."

"We could negotiate," Cohen offered.

"With a bunch of boxed? The scum that couldn't make it as real humans? I don't think so. Terminate. Remove the filth from the face of the earth," Krylov said with all the remorse of turning a stray dog into a meal. "So you have a plan, Colonel? Please enlighten me... I mean, us."

"I obviously underestimated the enemy's capabilities. I will accept the blame for that. I've called National Guard units in every state that has declared martial law and that isn't pressed themselves. I secured the promise of fourteen additional *battalions* of infantry. With that and the two regiments of antiquated tanks we should crush the remaining resistance."

"When will you get these troops?"

"Over the next three days, sir. Each battalion will take one day to form up, and then up to two to travel from their respective points to here. And remember the tanks will take about a week."

"So maximum of about two weeks to wrap this up?"

"Unfortunately, no, sir," Reed said. "We have lost our cordon. From the time we can suppress the rebels it will take approximately two weeks to secure the rest of the city."

"So one month from now, or February twenty-sixth."

"Yes, sir, based on the provisos we have already discussed."

"I'll hold you to that, Commander."

"Excuse me, sir, but you have a visitor," Sergeant Witten, Krylov's aide-de-camp, said, as he stuck only his head through the door.

"Jason, we are in executive session."

"I understand, sir, but this may very well be important for all of you."

"Who is it?"

"Prioress Hanna of the—"

"Yes, we are familiar with the prioress. Send her in."

Instead of one person, three walked in. Krylov was familiar with the solido of the Prioress but the other two he didn't recognize. The male was physically fit under his habit. His eyes were hard even if the skin of his face were composed and still. The middle-aged woman flanking the prioress on the other side was plump and had that too-happy-about-everything look that just wanted to make Krylov slap it off her face.

"Prioress Hanna."

"Commissioner Krylov."

A message came across Krylov's in-desk computer from Lieutenant Narendra stating that the monk had been a Metro, Sergeant Adam Johns—an interesting datum that didn't change much. "What can we do for you, Prioress?"

"As a neutral party, I have been asked by the CorpGov to mediate a prisoner exchange."

"Neutral? Ha! You are a collaborator with the Greenies. I should have you arrested right here and now," Captain Lennart said halfway out of his chair.

"She didn't address you, fatso," the male novice said.

"Adam!" the prioress admonished.

"I'm sorry, Prioress. I told you I'd have trouble containing my emotions around that bastard after what he did to my brother."

"Try harder."

"Is that Adam Johns?" Lennart asked. "Your brother got everything he had coming to him. He took the decision to become boxed, not something I did to him."

"Prioress, may I have permission to wait outside?" Adam said, his eyes boring into the fat captain.

"No. Now I wish you to be silent."

Adam clamped his jaw shut but his eyes didn't stop burning into the Metro even as Lennart settled back into his seat.

"Well, getting back to the reason of my appearance, Commissioner—"

"I am sorry but in principle I agree with my subordinate. If it weren't for the fact that you have the protection of the pope, I'd just as soon throw you into jail for aiding and abetting Grandma Ice of the Green Action Militia."

"So should they have arrested me for taking in and treating your radiation victims from Mount Massive? Or how about the treatment of your National Guard wounded and disabled that we've done right here in Portland?"

Krylov thought about it for just a moment. "Even if we did accept you, there will be no prisoner exchange." He received another message, from Reed this time, asking to obtain more information.

"I am just here to reduce suffering, Commissioner. I have no ax to grind. If you don't wish to—"

"Maybe I spoke hastily. What is your... I mean what is the offer of the CorpGov?"

"They have sixty-seven living and two deceased from the 28604th Infantry. I was told that all of them are being treated with respect."

"Two deceased? How do we know they aren't torturing them for information?" Captain Cohen asked.

"I've been given permission to allow you to speak with the senior surviving member, a First Sergeant Donald Pierson, DNA coding 1449A—"

"I'm familiar with Sergeant Pierson," Colonel Reed said.

"Good. The CorpGov is also willing to accept a single person to go into the prisoner camp and report if you so wish."

"Let's talk to Sergeant Pierson first."

Ruth smiled, taking out a portable conference communicator and setting it on the table. She typed something into the interface before it came active. A sergeant with short, white hair solidified. He looked clean shaven, freshly showered, and appeared undamaged except for a single bandage under his right eye. Even his uniform was pressed.

"*I'm sorry, sir,*" the sergeant said upon seeing the image of Colonel Reed.

"Save that for later, Sergeant Pierson. Are you being treated well?"

"Sir, if you will forgive me, we are being treated better here than we were camped in Portland. These people have gone to extraordinary lengths to get us medical attention, food, and any amenity we have requested."

"Sergeant, forgive me for doing this but I have to be sure. I need to query you." The Colonel checked his sleeve computer before continuing. "I say, 'Horseradish.'"

"Sir, I say, 'Gypsum.' I am not under duress nor being forced to lie. We are being treated better than we had any reason to expect. They even went to full medical to save three of our wounded and even the two that didn't make it."

"How many of you are there?"

"Right now we are sixty-seven and two deceased."

"Thank you, Sergeant. We will do what we can for you."

"Thank you, sir."

At a nod from Colonel Reed, the female novice turned off the conference.

"So what is it that the CorpGov wants in return for these men?" the colonel asked.

"You currently have a pair of platoons from the Fourth 'Iron Horse' Division out of Fort Carson, Colorado, number seventy-three in all. They want all of those men returned. In addition they want the eighteen hundred plus noncombatants arrested in civilian riots released from custody."

"That's ridiculous, Prioress. Even you would agree."

"I'm not here to advocate any position, Commissioner. I am here to make a peaceful offer that will reduce suffering."

"No," the Commissioner said flat-out with an ax-like motion from his meaty hand.

"The CorpGov anticipated a rejection of that plan and offered their prisoners in exchange for the civilians previously mentioned."

The commissioner lifted his hand to make a similar response when the hand of Colonel Reed landed on his shoulder.

"Can we have a moment, Prioress?" the National Guard officer asked.

"Certainly," she said. She gathered her pair of support people and led them out the door. Lieutenant Narendra closed it behind them.

"Sir, I might offer a compromise. Give them back their soldiers in exchange for ours."

Krylov looked at Reed like he'd grown three heads.

"Bear with me, sir. The president has kept her word throughout this entire action. By giving her back seventy troops we've given her back people we don't have to care for, protect, and guard. They get nothing. The president has assured us they won't be used to attack us so they are relatively meaningless. The nearly seventy people we will get back are now hardened troops. We can use them!"

"I do see your point, Colonel. Call her back in."

Tolbert took the task and went out into the hall to retrieve their guests. When they had returned the commissioner began, "We reject the latest offer but have a counterproposal."

"By all means, Commissioner."

"We will let you have the seventy-three troops that surrendered to us in exchange for the sixty-seven National Guardsmen you have. Oh, and the two bodies. We must make sure they are given proper rites."

"Agreed, Commissioner."

"Agreed what?"

"I agree that they deserve proper rites and I agree on behalf of the CorpGov to your terms. Would it suit you to have me oversee the amenities of the exchange?"

*   *   *

Wintel's liftousine waited for him outside the main entrance of the Metro building. They wouldn't ever let him leave out of the VIP landing pad. Used and spit out, he thought. And they had the audacity to insist that he continue to do public appearances and tout their benevolence.

He climbed in the car, surrounding himself in the luxuries he so missed by being a fugitive and then a kept ally. His business suit was ruined after dozens of days in "protective custody." How can one expect a genuine Armani to withstand the crude devices of the Metro's laundry?

"Where too, sir?"

Wintel thought about that for a moment. Right now he wanted a shower and some good clean clothes before he got a handle back on his company. Rich Ramirez had made a capable caretaker in his absence, but Wintel needed someone at the helm who could drive successes instead of just maintaining the status quo. "My home is gone, so until I get a new one let's do the penthouse in Pleasant Valley."

"Sorry, sir. That was destroyed by a civilian riot four days ago."

"Hmm. OK then, how about my apartment in Oatfield."

"Very good, sir," Andrew said, putting the car in flight toward the luxury two-bedroom apartment in one of the poshest towers in town.

"I'm going to need Brandon to go do some shopping for me."

"Sir, Brandon quit a week ago."

"Really? That's disappointing. I guess I'll have to suffer with what I have at the apartment until I can get a new valet. Did he give a reason, Andrew?"

"Yes, sir."

"And?"

"Well, sir, there were many swear words and the kindest thing he said about you was 'traitor.'"

"I see. I guess he won't be looking for a reference."

The driver laughed. "No, sir, I don't believe he will."

"I have to say the thing I'm going to enjoy the most will be a soak in the whirlpool. The showers they subject you to are just murder. It's time to get back to the civilized world."

* * *

"Wintel is on the move," Christine said over her percomm. "Requesting permission to terminate." Her 3 cm, light, recoiless rifle, fitted with Mossberg optics tracked the liftousine.

"*Hold on, Christine,*" Tony replied.

"We have a limited window."

"*Hold fire, Christine. I'm putting Nanogate on.*"

"*Thank you for tracking him so diligently, Christine, but killing him now would be counterproductive. We would look like the bad guys. Besides, my son has a much more fitting fate for him.*"

"Standing down." Christine's rifle followed the liftousine, centered on the passenger compartment for seven more seconds before she pulled the trigger. The click on the empty chamber didn't satisfy her, but she'd have to live with it—for now.

* * *

Augustine Cordoba, aka gm4 1c3, received a priority interrupt from her network watch programs. She ignored her cookie dough and pulled up her HUD.

She smiled when she saw the telltale glowing red on her screen labeled, "Boxed Termination Signal." The signal's only effect was letting her know that someone on the other side had tried to pull the plug on her new friends.

They hadn't been able to remove the detonation capsules in every single boxed, but they had been able to change the input required to trigger them to become impossible to find. She'd spent two days, with three boxed watching over her shoulder, as she created a program that not only changed the input for each detonation device to be different for each boxed, but made the valid format for each member different. Only ten billion monkeys on ten billion typewriters could possibly find one of the signals, much less the right frequency and data rate. Finding more than one of them was statistically impossible.

"A mind is a terrible thing to waste, assholes," Augustine said as she went back to stirring her dough because sometimes grandmothers did bake cookies instead of helping international terrorists.

* * *

"I don't give a flying fuck what Sergeant Goody-Two-Shoes Tolbert has to say, Guppy," Debnath said in the runabout.

Johnson sighed.

"This informant knows what happens to my temper if she feeds me bum data."

Johnson imagined a flaming corpse and figured that was about what his partner would do to any informant stupid enough to lie to Gohar.

They met the middle-aged woman in the roof parktop of the middle-class tower of Banks Central. She didn't look like the typical low-life Gohar would normal run with.

"All right, Cynthia, give me the goods."

"You gotta promise me this is the last time," she said looking around nervously. "What I got is fucking gold. I can give you Jamie Ardwin."

"Incest is still a crime, you filthy cunt. Until you stop calling your brother your husband, I tell you when the last time is, not you." Debnath backhanded her across the face. She fell down into the bushes.

"You prick. I hope all you Metros rot on earth and then get puked into hell," she said from the ground.

"Moderately original but of no interest to me, Cynthia. You know what I'm going to do to you if you don't give me what I want. Remember the fireplace poker enema?"

"Oh, I remember every fucking thing you've done to me and my family, you ugly pig fucker."

"Good, so you remembered me taking your daughter's anal cherry. Pretty hard on a five-year-old. How old is your son? Not that I'd degrade myself by touching a boy, but I'm sure I can improvise something. You know how good I am at improvising."

"Go to hell," she said. She whipped an old-fashioned revolver from behind her back and fired point-blank at the detective. She fired the gun empty before Johnson could get out his Colt. Debnath went down in a heap, his vest smoking in multiple locations.

"Don't!" Debnath yelled at the Guppy. He sat up, his eyes watering from the impacts against his bulletproof vest.

Cynthia tried to crawl away from him but he caught her foot.

"This is going to be fun," Debnath said drawing his knife.

Phillip Johnson had never seen anyone take that long to die.

*   *   *

"Sir, there is a man approaching our marching route in a jump jeep. He's waving a white flag."

Major Dwight Eisenhower MacFarland looked over his combat solido. The Third of the Eighteenth Saskatchewan Dragoons had left Missoula 60 km behind an hour ago by roughly following the canyon of old state route 12. With no drone coverage he'd wanted to stay low and avoid detection rather than blaze over the mountains. They had planned to make the town of Lochsa Lodge their encampment for the evening. But where did this one guy come from and why? He obviously had access to military equipment or he wouldn't be in a jump jeep.

"Just one person, Private?"

"Yes, sir. He's about to pass the first scouts."

"Let him come in, but transfer him to another vehicle. I don't want someone driving a potential bomb into our midst."

"Yes, sir."

Dwight paced in his Trevor IV command vehicle. He didn't like unusual things. He liked his march to drill precision. He'd been assured that there was no opposition until they reached Oregon and then likely little nor no activity short of the Olympic Mountains. He was still over 180 km, as the crow flies, before he even hit the border. Had the battle lines extended this far out? Well, he had two battalions of infantry with two attached companies of light tanks. If they had stretched this far, any force was likely out of their league.

"Sir, may I introduce Tony Sammis, military commander of the CorpGov under a flag of truce," Private Falls said.

"That will be all, Private."

"Yes, sir."

"*The* Tony Sammis?"

"Yes, Major, I bear that onus."

"So what would stop me from just killing you and collecting the reward?"

"Because, Major Dwight Eisenhower MacFarland, husband of Patricia Marie, father of four, devout Catholic, graduate of West Point and Winnipeg College of War, both with distinction, we are both men of honor. I came in under a flag of truce. I know enough about you to know you will honor that flag until it has withdrawn."

"It seems you know more about me than I know about you. Would you have a seat?"

"Thank you."

"I'm afraid I can't offer you anything to drink. Since we joined with you Yanks we are as dry as the desert."

"Too bad. Would you be offended if I offered you a snort? I brought some Scottish single malt."

"You are a class enemy, mate. Sure, I'll take a belt with you before we get to business."

From a silver flask, Tony poured a double finger of the amber fluid in some disposable cellulose cups he'd brought. The major didn't hesitate. Closing his eyes he tossed the entire drink back. Tony took a good shot of his but couldn't get past the burn and stopped at half. He offered the flask again but the Canadian American waved it off.

"We probably had better get down to business, Mr. Sammis."

"Another time then," Tony said, slipping the flask down into one of the thirty-odd pockets that lined his jumpsuit.

"What can I do for you, Mr. Military Commander?"

"Well, it is quite simple. I'd like you to turn your vehicles around and return back to Saskatchewan where you came from."

"And why, in all heaven's name, would I do that? I have orders which put me in Portland tomorrow."

"Well, as to the why, we have you outnumbered. We have you outgunned. We know where you are and you don't know where we are. In my book that spells a massacre. I don't like killing people."

"It's funny that a terrorist would say he doesn't like killing people."

"I don't. If I never had to kill another then I'd be a happy man. However, there is a tyrant bent on taking our freedoms away so I must fight, and sometimes I must kill. This isn't one of them."

"You speak of a massacre when I have over two thousand men at my command. Last I heard you had like maybe three hundred and no air support. That sounds like outnumbered in the other direction."

"Would you please bring up your tactical map, Major? And I'll show you just a small portion of the iron I have in my fist."

The major punched a handful of buttons before the map showed the valley they travelled through. The map showed only his own units, all still loaded on transports although deployable in seconds.

"Watch closely. I'll huff and I'll puff," Tony said into his percomm.

Dwight's display lit up with thousands of unknown hostiles along the ridge above his position before disappearing. At least three of them must have been construction bots because they were so huge. He'd heard rumors that those had been used in Missouri.

"We would destroy your entire command inside three minutes."

"But how many of your own would perish? Overall we have many more troops than you can hope to muster."

"I applaud your bravery, but if I might offer one other deterrent, I have here a message from the president of the United States that I would like to play for you. Even better, I'll give it to you as I want you to share it with all the other National Guard units who might be thinking of sending reinforcements to the Oregon conflict."

Tony offered a single memory crystal. The major took it and slid it into his portable player. The image of the upper half of the president's body appeared on the table between them.

"I believe I am addressing Major MacFarland. If I am not, I apologize.

"My name is Susan Tipton and you should recognize me as the president of the United States. At this time we have an internal problem with the National Guard of Oregon and the Metropolitan Police Force of Portland.

"If any other state's police force or National Guard should disregard their charter and operate outside their state, then I will have to assume that there is a general rebellion against the United States Constitution. As such, I will act against the rebelling state with all the might and fury at my disposal, up to *and* including weapons of mass destruction. I bid you good day."

It had been a long time since Dwight had played poker. The president had just raised not the size of the pot but effectively put the entire national gold reserve on the table. The Metros had assured his commanding officers that they controlled the orbitals, but what about all the other weapons of mass destruction?

"The president has authorized me to inform you that nanite weapons have been deployed in the towns of Saskatoon, Moose Jaw, Prince Albert, Regina, Yorkton, Estevan, Swift Current, and North Battleford. Should you not heed our warnings and return to base, those weapons will be activated."

"That's an act of war!"

"Against whom? Our own country? Major, we don't want to hurt anyone; however, you and your troops represent a clear and present danger to the Constitution of the United States."

"I'll need to consult with my superiors."

"Your choice, but my orders are simple. Should you move even a kilometer further west, your force will be annihilated. Any other force moving west of 115.75 degrees west will cause its destruction. The United States Army will then attack directly the state which sent them."

*   *   *

"Sir?" Sergeant Tolbert said as he knocked on Reza's door, opening it simultaneously.

"Yes, Sergeant. What doom and gloom do you bring to me today?"

"I am something of a realist, aren't I, sir?" Tolbert said, falling naturally into a parade rest in front of the lieutenant's desk.

"Realist? Hmm. As your superior I refuse to comment and give you ammunition to take to a board."

"Do you think my attitude undermines my effectiveness, sir?" the sergeant asked suddenly serious.

"Hell, no, Sergeant. You natural pessimism keeps us flighty officer types from running rampant on wild goose chases."

Tolbert wrinkled his mouth but didn't say anything.

"Sergeant, you can speak candidly to me. I'm not Krylov who would more likely shoot you than listen to you."

"Yes, sir. I was thinking that this whole fiasco with the CorpGov started out because we couldn't leave the Greenies alone. I tried to be the voice of reason on that one, too."

"We're still going to win, Sergeant."

"Sir, I doubt it very seriously. We've been out-fought and out-thought at nearly every turn."

"Then why are you still here?"

"Because I'm a policeman, sir. I've been a policeman my whole life. And if we go down then I go down with us. You could say it's like a 'One for all and all for one' mentality."

"I can understand that, Sergeant. So what news did you bring me?" Narendra asked leaning back in his chair.

"Well, we are having a few problems with both supplies and maintenance."

"OK. Tell me more."

"Well, we are having the same issue as the military with small arms ammunition. While we don't use nearly as much as they do, our own supplies are starting to dwindle."

"Limit practice."

"Already done, sir. We also have lasers that we are training our new cadets on rather than projectiles."

"That should be fun," Reza said with a smirk.

"Yes, sir, and some will require remedial training after this is over."

"OK. What else?"

"Well, just like ammunition we are running low on parts to maintain equipment around the stations like computers, control assemblies, lift vehicle parts, pergravs, and even our combat suits."

"Let me guess, the corporations supplying them are experiencing some temporary difficulties in shipping."

"Yes, sir, or unexpected dip in stock, or excessive demand, or shortfall in production. You can pick your own excuse. I've heard most of them over the last twenty-four hours."

"Can we threaten them?"

"I could send squads of men over, but I don't think it will work. My guess is that they've already moved, destroyed, or otherwise made these items unavailable."

"Well, try that first. If they don't have them we will have to adjust."

"Yes, Lieutenant. I've already given a green light to reduce sim time and limit usage of all critical systems. With your permission I'd like to use the larger vans to carpool troopers to their beats."

"Approved on all counts."

"The one that bothers me the most is maintenance. We have contracts with many of the unions but they are refusing to honor the contracts claiming that the boxed have stopped reporting for duty."

"What about human workers?"

"Oh, they exist, sir, but we are told that they are committed elsewhere. Normally this wouldn't be such a problem but we have a serious sewage problem. One of our treatment plants is down and the other is threatening to fail so is only on half duty. This means that our storage is filling up at an alarming rate."

"Can we dump to the city sewer?"

"Normally, yes. But that is a big ticket repair item that has been cut out of the budget three years running."

Reza did a face palm. "Well, that one bit us in the ass," he said taking his hand down. "Limit showers?"

"As an initial action, sir. We may even have to go to flushing commodes only twice a day or so."

"That's serious."

"So I think a few squads of our troops need to track down the plumbers and explain just how bad this would be if we don't get it fixed. Explain it with a truncheon if necessary."

"So ordered, Sergeant."

*　*　*

"OK, Birddog to Rover. Birddog has the ball," Augustine said.

"Oh, knock off the silliness, Auggie," Jamie rebutted.

"I'll show Tony your baby solidos if you don't behave," Augustine said.

"Where in the hell would you get my baby solidos?"

"Where does everyone store their pictures? I think the one with you peeing in the middle of the—"

"OK, Augustine, you win. I'll behave."

"Or how about your fifth grade picture where you cut—"

"I said I give up. Can we please get back to the National Guard troops?"

"I'd be interested in those solidos," David said as the action committee, minus Tony, huddled around David's sick-bed in the Nanogate Prosthetic Division. "Purely as blackmail material, mind you."

Jamie turned toward him with a mock glare, "You can't run yet, mister. I'd be very careful."

"Point taken."

"I've split-screened the four closest troop clusters, Saskatchewan, Texas, Missouri, and Nebraska."

The flat view from various space stations and or orbiting satellites gave resolution enough for David to pick out individual troopers and weapon type, as well as determine sex and hair color/length.

The Saskatchewan troops were stationary in Idaho. Jamie prayed they wouldn't fight. She watched Tony's jump jeep zip westward and out of sight of the main troops before arching up and over the valley walls and backtracking to the mass of CorpGov troops.

"Please don't fight," she whispered. Grandma Ice took her hand and squeezed. Jamie wouldn't admit that she cared more for her lover Tony than the cause, but she did.

Jamie felt she could measure the speed of time passage as one minute of real time to six years of waiting. The boys broke out some cards and made a halfhearted attempt at a poker game using pretzel sticks as money. It went flat when Wayne went all in on a pocket pair of twos and lost to a pocket pair of threes. Morgan tried to lighten the mood by rubbing balloons across her frizzy black hair and sticking them in the middle of the wall that held the projection.

"What are they doing, debating the U.S. budget?" Jamie barked in frustration.

"Hold on. We are getting conflicting data," Augustine said. "The

Saskatchewan contingent is bedding down right in some farmer's field. Only the New Jersey contingent has turned back. The Texas contingent has actually sped up. My data says that the Texas forces will cross our line tomorrow morning at 0730 if they keep up this speed and don't camp."

Susan Tipton just bowed her head.

* * *

"Reed," Krylov said, striding into the colonel's command building.

"Yes, sir," the colonel said, not expecting the commissioner without a warning of some kind. He hadn't expected him today at all.

"As you have seen, the CorpGov is playing hardball with our reinforcements. I suggest we send a message of our own."

"I'm all ears, sir. What do you have in mind?"

"How about a fractional bombardment on the boxed recharging stations. Hit the ten most remote sites in the country and the one here in Portland."

"That would be dramatic, Commissioner," Reed said with a mental shudder.

"I'll go on the news programs after that and justify my actions to the people. It does two things. It gets rid of both nils and boxed all in one fell swoop."

"And no matter how careful and accurate we are, it will also kill quite a number of innocent taxpaying civilians, sir."

"Are you telling me this is the wrong action?"

"No, sir." *YES!* he mentally shouted. "I just want you to have all the data before you make your decision."

"Well, the other thing this will do is to show our resolve to those morons in the CorpGov that think they can wave weapons of mass destruction around and make people jump."

"It is your call, Commissioner, but I believe you should look at some simulation results before you make your final move."

"Fuck that. All those electron jockeys have done is give me bum data from the very beginning. This is the right thing to do. Make it happen, Colonel. I want impact at 0900 tomorrow morning."

"Yes, sir."

It was Philadelphia and Rodeo Cove all over again.

*   *   *

"*President*," Tony said from his command post in Idaho in overwatch of the Saskatchewan force. He rolled his neck to a chorus of popcorn snaps. He'd not spent a comfortable night in a sleeping bag on the ground. "*The Texas forces have passed Elko, Nevada. They are now in violation of the ultimatum.*"

"I know, Mr. Sammis. It's just all those boys and girls—"

"*President, in most wars the troopers on the ground have as little say in being there as a gun does in the hand of a murderer. This is the first war that I can historically think of where the individual soldiers have had more than one REAL chance to pick a side.*"

"I know, but I've never killed, Tony."

"*It isn't easy, Ms. President. I won't pretend otherwise. My first wasn't a picnic, either. But nothing I can say is going to make it any easier and nothing I can do will change the fact that this time it is your decision and only your decision.*"

"May God, in all of his infinite facets, have mercy on their souls for I certainly don't deserve any. Augustine, I authorize the three launches we discussed. Code Zulu, Bravo, Tango, One, Niner, Seven, Five, Lopez." The last three words came out through tears. Snot rolling down her cheeks. Nanogate walked up and put his arm around her shoulders. Jamie came up on the other side and took her hand.

"Code activated and sent," Augustine said, sliding controls in midair that only she could see. "Targets identified. Bombardment groupings beginning deorbit burn. Just now starting to get radar and lidar returns. No indication of detections.

"Correction: lidar hits. Frequency is French. African Union is now tracking. China just jumped their alert level as did Brazil. OK, too many signals to make sense of them. Impact on Texas troops in four minutes... mark."

"And to the other targets?"

"Four minutes, thirty seconds... mark"

"President, you have a percomm from the governor of Texas."

"Put it on speaker."

"Good day, Governor Markenson."

"*My God, Susan, what are you doing?*"

"I'll turn that around and ask, 'What are you doing, Governor?'"

"*You know we had no choice. We had—*"

"You had a choice. You know me better than most, Jasper. You knew I wasn't bluffing. I'm following through on an ultimatum."

"I'll turn the troops around. I'll order it now."

"I'm so sorry, Governor."

"But you are getting what you want! Abort those missiles!"

"I'm so sorry, Governor. I hope the death of those brave soldiers out there will prevent any further loss of life."

"Susan! I'm begging you. Stop those bombs!"

"I'll be honest, Jasper. If I had the chance to shoot you instead of killing those kids, I would."

Christine perked up from the other side of the room and then went back to practicing her smile.

The president continued, "Unfortunately I don't have that option. The rest of the governors have to learn what will happen to them when they violate the Constitution of the United States. Now you and I both have to live with the consequences of our actions."

Augustine began a countdown. "Five . . . four . . . three . . . two . . . one . . ." The projection of the troops racing along in the barren Nevada landscape was erased when the screen went white. The image from orbit pulled back to show the growing mushroom-shaped cloud, not nuclear, only the result of a horrific amount of kinetic energy released in a very small area.

"For all that is holy, Susan, call off your other shots. I admit I was wrong. I'll do anything you want... anything."

"Goodbye, Governor."

"You know if you do this you are forcing me to declare Texas independent. I'll have no choice."

"The Mexican states will love that, Governor Markenson. Goodbye. I don't think we will ever speak again."

"Susan, ple—"

"Counting down. Five . . . four . . . three . . . two . . . one . . ."

In the space of milliseconds, dozens of small, reinforced projectiles landed in a pattern that blotted Fort Bliss and Fort Hood from the face of the planet along with one hundred fourteen thousand, three hundred four souls.

"Folks, I'm getting a change on the inbound troops. Nebraska has turned around."

"Saskatchewan is packing up," Tony said. *"I don't know where they are going yet... wait.. we are seeing scouting units being sent back north*

and east."

"We have a reversal of course now on all the inbound National Guard troops. It's over!"

"'Nothing except a battle lost can be half so melancholy as a battle won,'" Nanogate said softly as he looked at the glowing red remains of what had been two major military bases.

*   *   *

Colonel Reed looked grim. "Set target package Yankee, Kilo, Bravo, One, Four. Break. Hotel, India, Three, Romeo, Six, Alpha. Break. Three, Foxtrot, Golf. Break."

"Launch control: We show message received. Keys are inserting. Keys have activated. We now have full control, Colonel."

"Thank you." Colonel Reed passed a memory crystal over to the fire control tech. "There is your coordinate package. All are stationary targets and need pinpoint control."

"Yes, sir. We are loading now. Eleven targets." A map of the United States materialized on the solido. The eleven targets lit up on the map as gross points with two in South Dakota, one in Florida, three in Montana, one in Washington State, two in Texas, one in Idaho, and the final one smack dab on top of Portland. The sky above the ground dots held tens of thousands of pinpoints, all in motion. "Time on target 0903 Pacific. Is this all correct, Colonel?"

"Yes, Sergeant."

"On your order, sir."

"By authorization of Commissioner Krylov, execute," Colonel Reed said.

"Launch control: Executing. First bird reports shroud deployment and now deorbit burn."

"Tracking: We aren't seeing any release."

"Launch control: Processing. I show deorbit burn continuing. All systems look go. Second unit releasing shroud. Deorbit burn commencing."

"Tracking: Negative. We show no relative movement by lidar or radar. Visual says they cannot confirm deorbit burn."

"Launch control: Are you on the right bird?"

"Tracking: Radar tracking relative motion of all vehicles shows two millimeter per day maximum differential. Visual and lidar focusing on bird Mike Mike Alpha Four. Bird hasn't moved out of original polar orbit."

"Launch control: Bird reports now eight kilometers from its previous course. Resetting telemetry. What the fuck?" the launch control officer said. His screen blanked out and was replaced by a solido of Commissioner Krylov. The man's right hand was against his forehead with the hand in a fist except for the index finger sticking straight up and the thumb at right angles.

The image flickered onto screen after screen in the control room. A crudely pasted together audio of Krylov's own voice said, "I... am... a... loser. I... am... a... loser. I... am... a... loser..."

Reed didn't know whether to be angry or relieved.

* * *

As usual the meeting room left everything to be desired. The only amenities were two plastic chairs that had seen better days. The damp from the sleet coming down outside seeped in even through the vacuum barrier clothing. Mildew blackened the walls in a creeping pattern down to the floor. The ceiling material lay scattered around the floor, leaving only bare ceramcrete joists and random holes in the next level's floor. Someone had made at least an attempt to push the debris away so they could walk and roll into the room comfortably.

Stephanie squeaked out, "We've posted guards around our remaining recharging facilities but we've lost eleven of them along with approximately sixteen thousand of us. Exact data isn't yet available."

"Fifteen thousand, four four seven plus or minus one hundred four," Augustine said. "That's based on those boxed plugged in or who had unplugged close enough to the explosion. Adding in an estimate of those coming to plug in based on past usage. We were fortunate that most of them were in low population densities: Billings, Helena, and Bozeman, Montana; Weston, Florida; Pierre and Edgemont, South Dakota; Pullman, Washington; Coeur D'Alene, Idaho; Midland and Temple, Texas."

"And of course the one they set off here," Tony said.

"Two-thirds of the casualties were here."

"Do we know how they did it?" Tony asked.

"They used bomb squad robots to bring in high velocity explosives and plant them at the base of the building. In the case of the facility north of Billings, Montana, they sent a message by using a pony nuke. All the inhabitants of the town will have to undergo radiation treatments."

"Don't forget that they learned they don't have control of the satellites anymore," Augustine said.

"So this may be their way of telling us that they won't stop and won't be intimidated?" Stephanie said.

"Sounds like what Krylov would do."

"Are there any shortfalls in charging capabilities?"

"All of our boxed units in Montana need to move because of the loss of the Coeur d'Alene power stations and the two in South Dakota. We are sending most of the boxed in Montana to North Dakota and Wyoming. South Dakota still has two charging stations that will allow us to share. None of the other locations has a problem transferring units to another nearby city."

"I'm sorry to hear about your loss, Stephanie," Tony said.

"At least they died for freedom rather than dying because they forgot who they were," Augustine said.

"I guess you are right. Does this give us any reason to change our plans?" squeaked Stephanie Defalkis.

"I don't see any."

"Neither do I," Augustine said.

* * *

"Commissioner, we have to face the fact that we will not be getting any additional forces," Reed said.

"Fucking cowards," Amber Cohen said.

"In essence I agree with you, ma'am, but that doesn't change the fact that we are going to have to fight without them."

"You said you didn't have a large enough force," said Major Broadsky.

"No, Major, but while I don't have a sufficient force, you do."

"What?" Krylov said.

"I had but a handful of troops compared to what you control. If I interleave your police into my seasoned soldiers I could have a force larger than I started with."

"And what, Colonel Reed, do I protect the people of this city with?" Krylov interjected.

"Sir, if you will forgive me, you haven't seemed interested in the people of this city."

"Not true, Commander. I do care. But I only care about those that matter. Nils and boxed are only to be used, not valued."

"I stand corrected, Commissioner. But five percent of your force would be double what I have available now. Ten percent would be quadruple my current troops. With a group of that size I could resume operations with a much larger deployable force as one of my battalions isn't useless armor. And I still have my own soldiers coming with armor that won't shoot itself.

"I believe we can still win this conflict."

"Of course we will, Colonel Reed," Krylov said, his chest held out and his eyes sharp and piercing on the military leader. "We are still facing only a handful of enemy troops, and if we can get their leadership we will win. I'll give you thirty percent of my available officers. Commanders, I want you to go cut out the absolute best officers to give to the colonel. Make it happen, now."

Sergeant Tolbert caught the eye of Lieutenant Narendra as they walked out. Tolbert didn't need to say a thing as his superior just nodded.

*   *   *

"We need to end this before they get their Metro reinforcements trained," Jamie said, sitting next to Tony at the kitchen table of a safe house just two blocks from the main Metro Pyramid.

"I'm less worried about those extra men than the armor they have coming," Tony lamented, puzzling over maps spread on the table. He took a squeeze of a beer pouch.

"They are training the Metros hard," David said, from his wheelchair. David could have had any off-the-shelf prosthetic legs by now. With the breathing room the CorpGov had achieved, he'd even been offered regeneration. Instead he requested something different. The cyberneticists were still working out the bugs. "They don't have nearly the proficiency of the Guardsmen but they are good enough to give us trouble."

"I believe Colonel Reed has learned his lesson," Mr. Marks said. "He isn't concentrating his troops at any time and place. We can only catch company-sized units in bivouacs around the city," he said, drawing circles on the map. "They train in platoon-sized units in real settings, even to the point of shooting nils if they find them."

"All of this would be excellent if we were still into hit-and-run guerilla tactics," Tony said with a smirk. "But we aren't. We need one big push to topple all of this over or we could be in a position to lose."

"I have to say this yo-yo thing is driving me crazy," Jamie said. "First we are losing and then we're winning. Rinse and repeat."

"That is a colorful, if mixed, metaphor, Miss Jamie," Mr. Marks said.

"Folks, this is a planning session, not a coffee klatch. Focus. Is there anything that would congregate those troops?"

"How about we attack the main Metro complex," David said, pointing out the window at the armored pyramidal monolith.

"That would do it," Tony said, "but it probably would also bring the other sixty thousand Metros down on us, too."

"Good point."

"Actually, if I might be given an opinion," Mr. Marks started.

"Speak, Thomas, speak! I'm not your boss, and I don't stand on protocol because we are all fucking amateurs at this. I have ideas. You have ideas. Just spit them out."

"Thank you, Mr. Sammis."

Tony sighed. It must be like asking a tiger to lose his spots...or stripes, or whatever a tiger used to have before they went extinct.

"I was saying that David might be very close to the right idea. What if instead of attacking the main Metro complex that we attack the National Guard's headquarters."

Tony pursed his lips and narrowed his eyes. "It will get ugly. They have so much anti-air around that place we are going to lose lots of equipment."

"We could mix it up. First a few unmanned suicide flights to take out some of the positions and follow it up with unmanned empty lift vehicles." David built on the idea.

"That's right, make them see what they want to see. It won't take long for them to empty their magazines. Then follow it up with the real stuff," Jamie added.

Tony thought for a moment. "Do we know where they moved

their headquarters to?"

"Yup, and it is in a very handy location for another reason," David said, pointing at the map.

Tony smiled. "Morgan, looks like you get the honors."

Deployment

Alarms sounded and Colonel Reed bounced out of his bed.

"Base one. Base one. We are under attack. I say again, we are under attack," came a frantic voice over Colonel Reed's percomm at the same time he heard his first explosion. The sky outside his tent blossomed with brilliant reds and yellows. He raced out the tent to see the dying fires on the rooftop of the building next door. Tracers fired up into the sky in streams that threatened to turn night into day. The yellow and red point sources of light glinted off hundreds of lift vehicles circled like buzzards waiting on a feast. Another explosion sounded to his left, creating another flash on top of Broadcom Tower across the street. For protection he threw himself behind a rooftop vent. The thin wind blew the exhausting sewer gasses in his face.

Something bothered him about the scene but he couldn't put his finger on it. He needed to get to the command center where he would have all the data at his mental fingertips. However, it was across most of the open rooftop and down two flights of stairs.

Reed's fingers jittered against the vent. He heard the zipper sound of auto cannons. He received repeating slams into his chest with the larger weapons firing off I-flak. The chuff and fizz of handheld missiles assaulted his senses. His mind screamed, "Only thirty meters to the next cover." His legs carried him without a conscious command.

He dove behind the electrical sub-panel. He peeked up to see a pair of lift vehicles explode in midair. Another trailed flame and smoke behind it until it landed on one of the anti-aircraft guns he'd positioned on the roof of the Versatile Building directly opposite.

A behemoth cargo carrier, even a bigger one than the rebels had converted to a makeshift battleship, swooped down toward the rooftop of his command center. Three of his soldiers each launched their handheld missiles. They buzzed up to meet the monster. All three hit: one centered on the cab, and the other two tearing holes in its cavernous belly.

Reed did a crouched sprint for the remainder of the hundred meters to the stairs. Climbing down partway he realized what was wrong. While his troops fired massive amounts of munitions, not a single enemy bullet landed anywhere he could see or hear.

He ran down the stairs, each foot touching only long enough to push him off to the next step. Private Simms, who must have seen him on the surveillance solidos, held open the baffle door for him as he ran in. Bent over he put his hands on his thighs and sucked in some air as he waited for the meter thick honeycombed door of the mobile combat-control center to close so that the double thick inner one would open.

He triggered the intercom. "Sam! What's going on!" The pressure of the closing door compressed his eardrums. He swallowed hard to clear them.

"We got more bogies than a body's got flies. They are stacked up over three kilometers deep and out as far as four," came the voice of his second in command over the static from the speaker. *"We're shooting them down as fast as we can but without resupply I don't know if we will have enough ammo."*

"Stop!" Reed yelled at the speaker. "Are they firing?" The inner door started its ponderous swing inward.

"No, but the first group suicided in on the anti-aircraft and the supply floor."

Reed didn't wait for the gentle entry to the command network. He shoved the cable right into his net jack. The nausea of wrenching his conscious directly from one reality to another folded his body up and left a sour taste in his mouth.

"Casualties?" Reed asked as he scanned a sky so full of vehicles that it must have overwhelmed the local traffic control by a factor of ten.

"Light. Mainly anti-aircraft crews."

"I want remaining AA moved off the roof and indoors. It will limit their field of fire but reduce vulnerability to suicides."

"Yes, sir," said Lieutenant Colonel Samuel Marley.

"What's our current ammunition availability on AA?"

"Not good," Marley said, sliding his slate of numbers over in front of his boss.

"Worse than I thought. New general orders: No firing on any air vehicle unless it is about to kamikaze in or it fires first."

"That will give them the initiative."

"Would you rather give them a free sky?"

"No, sir."

Reed pulled up his troop list. The 162nd,186th, and the reconstituted 28604th Infantry regiments were en route. The orders to attack the lift vehicles from above made sense so he let them go. To Reed, the sim flashed as the AI tried to get his attention. It highlighted a pattern emerging, too late to do anything about it. Reed kept telling the bureaucratic brass to upgrade the programming in these bloody things, but the money kept being appropriated on more sexy things like tanks and vet benefits.

The pattern was twenty-four pairs of lift vehicles, a 4 tonne followed by a 2 tonne, aimed at different points of the building and picking up velocity. As the trucks approached, the troops manning those locations fired heavy machine gun and light armor defeating rounds in abundance. Even the common soldier fired his assault rifles at them. Three times a portable ground-to-air missile launched. Two of the incoming pairs of kamikazes were destroyed in the air. Six of the remaining had the initial vehicle destroyed or pushed off target and the second truck heavily damaged.

The data flew across Reed's display, and he watched one entry point in real time. The initial lift-truck acted as a shield absorbing all the damage and actually exploded as it entered the building at a loading dock. The second vehicle stayed just beyond the blast radius and landed as chaos reigned. The sides popped off to expose hundreds of box-controlled, android forms packed in like sardines. Each of them had an assault rifle. Each of them shot immediately upon offloading. It took them only seconds to establish a beachhead in the chaos of the explosions. Multiply this disaster by the eighteen unhindered insertions he saw, and Reed knew he had a shitload of enemies in his rear.

Unbidden, an irrelevant thought flew across his mind. The great leaders of history like Napoleon, Rommel, and even Powell had it easy. They only had to think really in two dimensions. Oh yeah, Rommel and Powell had to think about air attack but not the vertical stacks of city height. Here he fought a true three-dimensional war.

"I want laser and auto cannons covering the stairwells.

"Get me Major Hendrix of the 186th Regiment."

"*Yes, Colonel,*" the 186th commander said almost immediately.

"We are being invaded by box-controlled infantry. I need your troopers to land on the roof and upper loading dock."

"*Yes, sir. Landing on the roof and upper loading dock.*"

"It's a hot LZ so watch yourself, Major."

"*We roger hot LZ. ETA four mikes.*"

"Major Smith."

"*Yes, Colonel.*"

"Coordinate with Captain Franks. She's new, running the 28604th Infantry. When you arrive I want you to take over all the adjacent buildings and put a fire platform on each level from eighty, up."

"*Sir, what about Broadcom Tower?*"

"What about it?"

"*It's scheduled for demolition. They've supposedly already weakened the structure.*"

"I don't give a damn. I want a place we can retreat to, a place where we can cover the outside of this building to prevent them from rappelling up, and provide fire support against any of those armed lift-trucks."

"*Yes, sir. We'll cover all seven of the buildings, sir. ETA six mikes.*"

"Make the fire teams small. I want the bulk of your force to move up through this tower from the ground up."

"*Aye, sir.*"

Reed took a deep breath. They couldn't possibly punch him out in the next six minutes. With his forces centralized he'd crush them like grapes between his two superior forces.

*   *   *

"Left standard rudder," Morgan said as she peered through the antiquated periscope. Her afro had started to unkink after all of her oil-covered repairs to the *Blueback* and being inside her moist atmosphere for almost two months running. It looked more like frayed dreadlocks dangling around her face. Pushing them back with one hand, she promised that as soon as this run was over, she had a long overdue appointment at a beauty salon—and Tony was paying.

"My rudder is left standard."

"Make turns for three knots."

"Three knots, aye."

Sliding a submarine into a ship basin underwater, at night, without a tug was for acrobats that could juggle with one hand and paint with other, all while maintaining their balance on a unicycle.

A sound like sandpaper ran through the ship as she dragged the bottom. "Up bubble one degree. Make your depth two zero meters."

"Making my depth twenty meters."

Morgan winced as she heard the chuff, chuff, chuff of the blades biting into the same bottom they'd just slid over.

"There is the bell tower on that bug-ugly science building Portland State University built. Looks like a hairball my cat threw up except it's purple and white," she said to no one in particular. "All stop."

"Engines answering all stop, Captain."

"On the one MC: Man battle stations torpedo. Man battle stations surface action.

"Communications. Send message to Tony Sammis: Ready, willing, and able. Message ends."

"Message coded and sent, ma'am."

"Torpedo room reports manned. Deck gun being assembled. Estimated completion one minute."

Morgan spun the periscope and centered it on Broadcom Tower, and waited. "Your move, Tony."

*　　*　　*

Jim Price, night watchman at the Port of Portland, did his hourly walk along the waterfront. He never had much to do except chase off the occasional nil that thought fishing the sewage-laden water was a good idea, run off the drunks that seemed to gravitate to the waterfront, or sometimes report a cartel drug run. All in all it carried all the excitement of watching snail races. He'd wanted to be a Metro and have a shiny suit of his own.

Metros got the respect and money. Unfortunately, his weight kept him from meeting the entrance criteria. Every year for the last fifteen years, just before the standard civil service testing, he'd cut back to almost starvation to try to lose the weight. The first few years it was 15 kilos. Then it was 20. Now he needed to shave nearly 35 kilos. It wasn't fat, he kept telling himself. His big bones and bulky muscles weighed too much. He never made the weight, but he kept dreaming.

Jim heard the sound of metal against metal somewhere in or beyond the Swan Island Basin. It couldn't be mistaken for any other sound. The dock lights had ruined his night vision so he pulled night vision goggles out of his pouch. He'd purchased them out of his meager salary to give him the edge when he needed it.

He took off his hat and slid the goggles over his eyes. The world repainted in pale greens. It took him only seconds to pick out the sail of a submarine in the basin. Someone had the nerve to drive a submarine up the Willamette and park it in his basin. And they were setting up a huge gun on the deck of the thing.

He drew his Colt automatic and worked the first bullet into the chamber. He'd show them whose waterfront this was.

A supersonic bullet entered the front of Jim Price's head within 5 micrometers of centered. It mushroomed on contact and splintered within the skull ricocheting more times than were necessary. The body that had been Jim Price crumpled to the ground with a wet sigh of his last breath. Both of his sphincters let loose, leaving him in a nasty smelling puddle.

On the sail of the *Blueback,* Christine scanned the waterfront with her sniper rifle for more targets.

*   *   *

"All enemy battalions are converging on University Park," came a report from somewhere south. Tony only knew it was human as it didn't have that high screeching quality of the boxed. Probably one of the Greenpeace they'd coopted for a noncombat position. Enclosed in a bulletproof pantsuit, Jamie looked at him and nodded with a smile.

From behind the window of the ninety-third floor of the Broadcom Tower in the heart of University Park, Tony marveled. He'd never had choices before. The situations had always forced his hand down a single path. He either did it that one way or it was over. Tony could win this battle any number of ways and couldn't lose it unless he surrendered here on the spot. As long as those troops continued to close, his opponent, Colonel Reed, had already lost and just didn't know it. Unfortunately, many more people would die before the colonel realized the trap he'd walked into. For his own conscience Tony had to reduce those numbers as much as possible. So it had to be all at once. The attack had to be devastating.

With a sigh Tony gave half a smile back to Jamie. He looked forward to the day when he wouldn't have to kill people.

*   *   *

"*Colonel?*" Major Mitch Hendrix said. "*We are landing now. How do you want us deployed?*"

"I got spotters on every other floor down to the eightieth," Reed said as he ordered more stores for this action with his hands. "I want you to reinforce each spotter with two squads. I want the bulk of the remainder of your men on the eightieth to get ready to push down."

"*Roger that, command.*"

His opponent might be good, but he'd just committed a major blunder. He let him consolidate his troops.

*   *   *

"*Morgan, I want you to stand by to fire. I'm going to take out any anti-air they have just so there isn't any chance they can stop our new little toy, and then you will get your shot.*"

"We'll be ready to launch in thirty seconds."

"*Remember, I want the eighty-third floor targeted.*"

"Yes, Tony. We'll give you a bulls-eye."

"*Thank you, Morgan.*"

"Fire control: Prepare two thermobarics out torpedo tubes for launch."

"Aye, ma'am. Two thermobarics to launch station."

"Flooding tubes one and three." Morgan watched the indicators light green. "Open outer doors."

"High pressure air to eject payload, tubes one and three." Morgan felt the shudder as two oversized torpedo-shaped weapons jetted 30 m forward before losing momentum and floating up gently to allow only the top 3 percent of the warhead to crest above the waves. They waited with the mindless patience of machines.

* * *

"*Colonel?*" Major Michael Smith said. "We have troops stationed on every floor of the surrounding buildings above eighty."

"And the remainder of your forces?"

"*In position to push upward. We have brought eight portable elevators to make our movement up easier and faster.*"

"Don't make any assumptions, Major. I want the ground floor and the stairwell swept for booby-traps before any force moves into them."

"*Already have my demolition units positioned, sir. We won't let you down.*"

The simulator had the whole building and the surrounding buildings in wireframes. The floors fifty through seventy-nine glowed red. Charlie Reed checked the setup of his troops in each of the buildings and the layout of his defensive location on the eightieth. Then he looked over at his second in command, Sam Marley, who flashed him a thumbs up and a huge Cheshire cat grin.

"Hendrix, get ready. Nothing gets past you."

"*Yes, sir.*"

With a deep breath in and out, Reed gave his order. "Major Smith, attack."

* * *

"*Tony, we have indicators on the ground floor,*" Augustine said over the network.

Tony meant for his explosives on the ground floor to be found. They were his tripwire. Jamie looked at him. Her face was calm, but her eyes darted all over him.

"*Now we are getting indicators in the elevator shafts. I have two, now five, eight. Eight indicators and holding,*" Augustine offered.

"Everyone stand by. We have movement. This is likely a general assault. All ground troops follow the plan. The boxed in the target building should be making their way to the seventy-eighth floor for minimum safe distance."

"*More indicators on same elevator shafts at level thirty-five, and now forty-seven. That's the last of our indicators.*"

"Just like we planned, folks. All ground personnel in buildings two through eight, execute on initial barrage." Tony turned off his mic.

"The end?" Jamie asked.

"How about the beginning of the end." He turned back on his mic. "Phase one, now."

*   *   *

Kilometers away, thirty-six repossessed M1216 Long Rifle self-propelled artillery fired, and using their multiple barrels they kept firing until they'd exhausted their basic load of twenty-two. They emptied magazines before their first shell landed. Their work in this battle was over.

"Phase two," Tony called out after a mental count of ten. He understood time-on-target but really didn't know how to achieve it perfectly with his crude weapons so he used the engineering method of WAG—wild-assed guess.

The night of the 4000 block of North Willis Boulevard became day. Anyone looking at Broadcom Tower would have been blinded. Eighty missiles and forty-six large caliber recoilless weapons fired simultaneously on the National Guard's newly relocated anti-aircraft positions. Within seconds the mass fire immolated fifty-nine of sixty-one remaining anti-air weapons.

Two seconds later the first of the simple explosive rounds of the Long Rifles landed on the roofs of all the buildings. Personnel and lighter weapons' emplacements evaporated in the flames and shrapnel. Over six hundred of the rounds landed on the National Guard's headquarters. Smoke and debris obscured the rolling explosions as the guns battered the reinforced building repeatedly.

"Tony to *Blueback*. Fire."

*   *   *

Reed had less than ten seconds warning. His AI noted the artillery launch but he didn't react properly. Where would these rebels come up with artillery? It had to be a malfunction.

"Sir, are you seeing this?"

"Yeah, but—"

The building shook but inside his protective, shock-dampened vault he barely felt a tremor. Green personnel telltales went black all over his map. Hundreds of his men and antiaircraft weapons ceased to exist.

Then his world shook hard enough to topple everyone inside. And then prone, they were rattled around again. And again. And again. And again. The primary lights went out but the pounding continued. Reed slammed into something hard. One hand got trapped between his body and the hard thing. He felt the bones in three fingers snap. He screamed out but the impacts were so loud he couldn't be heard even by himself. The emergency lights came on just as the impacts stopped.

"Bring up the backup sim!" Reed shouted as he looked at the fingers of his left hand pointing in the wrong direction. With a grimace he yanked them one at a time back into some semblance of their correct orientation. By the time he had them tied together, with some help of emergency Velcro lashings, the sim regenerated.

A quick glimpse showed the situation could have been worse but he didn't know how.

"Oh, shit, sir. More incoming."

"Launch laser countermeasures."

*   *   *

Jason Bale, also known as V33473, didn't have the ability to smile at the moment, but he did so mentally. People ignored things they expected to see. In an office building you expect to see an automated mail cart. You expected to see a janitorial floor scrubber. The trio of National Guardsmen setting up the crew served weapon in the window didn't break that rule. None of them even looked back as he and Terry Crowder, Q13B, quietly released torc grenades out of their service chutes. The grenades rolled into the room occupied by the National Guardsman and the two boxed soldiers rolled away.

They knew that most of their little ambushes would end up the same way—dead enemies.

*   *   *

"Fire as programmed," Morgan said, "and may heaven let in the poor bastards."

The two quietly unassuming torpedoes floating on the surface of the water lit off rockets in their tails. In less than a second the rockets burst out of the water and jetted off north by northeast. The fuel-air explosive missiles, FAE, travelled less than two seconds before closing on their targets.

Lasers bounced off the windows of the eighty-third floor, but eight hovering, spherical decoys shot out lasers directly at the two missiles as well. The first of the two projectiles got confused when one of the laser countermeasures hit on the right frequency. It rammed directly into the ball, shedding its vaporized fuel payload into the air as it travelled close to the speed of sound. A trio of carbon arc generators on the missile body ignited the flammable mixture. Salem, 60 km away, reported feeling the concussion. Locally, it burst the eardrums of eighty-two civilians. It burst every window in a 2 km radius and lit up the sky like a worm made from the sun itself.

The countermeasures didn't fool the tiny brain of the second missile. Oddly because it was fired so close, the accuracy of the missile was less than if it had been fired from hundreds of kilometers. Limiting the fuel gave the missile a larger payload so accuracy wasn't that important.

Plunging through the wrong window on the eighty-third floor, 2 m left of its aimed point, the vaporized liquid sprayed out like the water from a car wash on steroids. The weapon had released three quarters of its cargo before it burst out the other side of the building. The electronically generated arcs ignited the mixture. Being somewhat confined within the building made the detonation even more powerful than in the open air. The compression and shock wave removed the reinforced floor and ceiling of the eighty-third level, sending it as shrapnel into the eighty-second and eighty-fourth.

The blast wave destroyed every National Guardsman and Metro within five floors of the blast. Only one survived the concussion wave and the vomit of random debris but that unlucky individual had his lungs pulverized and died drowned in his own blood.

The pressure wave travelled with little hindrance through the six floors to pass over the boxed where they lay lashed to brackets in the floor and other immovable objects. In spite of their preparations six of them were ripped free and thrown out open window frames.

Eighteen boxed had flying wreckage tossed against them too hard for their android bodies to handle.

Forty floors below the pressure wave, much of it having escaped through windows, still knocked down two-thirds of the National Guardsmen. Three died from head trauma. Twenty-one suffered debilitating injuries preventing them from continuing.

Above the blast the shock wave forced all the smoke and dust from the artillery barrage to disperse like a smoke ring in a wind tunnel. Those few still alive after the concussion roasted in a growing heat as more of the building began to burn.

The roof and second floor down were gone in rubble from the artillery barrage. The self-contained command vault could actually be seen through the broken walls canted at a 10 degree angle like a ship threatening to tip over and sink.

The building itself now bulged out one side where the FAE had detonated. Smoke poured out the windows and the ruined top of the building. Left to its own devices the building would eventually collapse in upon itself.

Tony looked at the devastation. "This is over. Augustine, let's see if we can save any of those men. Work your magic and let's see if Reed is still alive over there.

"Just in case, let's get our air units down to cover the ground floor for any escapees. The rules of engagement haven't changed yet. Shoot anything that moves."

"*Got it,*" David said as he controlled his team of lift vehicles.

"Get the boxed moving on fire suppression."

"*We're on it,*" Stephanie whistled from her position on the seventy-eighth floor.

*   *   *

Reed picked himself up off the floor for the third time in as many seconds. He winced with every change in position. He felt unsteady on his feet until he noticed that the floor sloped. He couldn't imagine how something so massive and with its own gravity drives could be tilted. None of the emergency lights remained on but the still-working simulation sent out a pale light across the room.

Sam lay bent backward over a sim couch at an angle only

reserved for bending forward. Charlie didn't understand the heap at the far end of the room until a hand twitched on top. His three support staff had gotten tangled and slammed together. Captain Joan Gardner picked herself off the floor with the help of one of the sim couches. The swollen right side of her face kept that eye from opening fully.

Reed blinked hard and went back to work. He needed to be in control. The virtual rendition of the building showed partially why his command vault tilted. Most of the upper four floors of the building were just gone, as were the floors below him. Something blurred his vision. He wiped it away to find his own blood on his sleeve.

An attention light flailed in one corner of the display. The temperature in the room was creeping up. The sim showed the fire below him. He and the survivors in the room were in a pressure cooker in the most literal sense. Nothing he could do about it now. What about the rest of the troops?

The sim had a sea of red and black indicators above the eightieth floor of his headquarters building. Most of the other buildings where he'd stationed squads with crew served weapons showed black and red. Miraculously, two showed blinking green and yellow indicating they were in close contact.

His troops in the forties and below primarily looked green. He still had a fist, if not an anvil. The haze of enemies in between were unknown but the devastation left by the shelling and that FAE missile made him think they might have taken serious damage as well. He still had a chance, if only a meager one.

Another attention light flashed. He tapped it with his virtual finger and it showed a change in disposition in the circling air vehicles. Thirty-one of the small trucks now ran racetracks at the base of his building. Zooming in on them he could see the chain guns in the cargo compartments. These weren't decoys.

The virtual reality sputtered with static once, twice, and then went to snow completely. Colonel Reed started to shout at his simulation support staff but stopped when he realized they were likely all dead.

"Captain, see if you can get that back online." More blood oozing from a cut he didn't even know he had. It forced him to wipe it away again.

"Sir, I've already been trying. All our equipment is functioning correctly," the captain said, mopping the sweat from her forehead.

The simulation snapped back in place but with an addition. An avatar of Tony Sammis's real image stood in the middle of the virtual reality. "Colonel Reed?" The image turned and asked to someone out of frame, "Is this getting through?

"Colonel Reed, are you there?"

Charlie stepped further out into where the simulation lines provided more light. "I'm here."

"Oh, good. I was afraid you were dead."

"While I have considered that possibility myself, Mr. Sammis, can you tell me how you've linked up to a high security command vault?"

"I'll just say that I have a very good network worker and your systems are far from state of the art. But I didn't call to discuss hacking."

"I didn't expect you did."

"I called for you to surrender. I don't want to kill any more of your people."

"I think that probably is premature, Mr. Sammis," the colonel said stiffly.

"Right now we outnumber your remaining troops four to one and have you in a tactically disadvantaged position."

"My troops are veterans and that will negate both of your advantages." Reed knew that the statement was just bluster.

"Two-thirds of your troops are Metros with little to no combat experience. But I didn't contact you to debate the relative strengths of our positions. I hacked your system to save lives. Can I at least share a view with you?" Tony's visual disappeared and the look across a dark bay showed the sail of a submarine but focused on two floating torpedo-shaped objects. "Those are two more of those FAEs we used on the eighty-third floor. I'm prepared to launch those into the fortieth and twentieth floors. Either one will completely annihilate the vast bulk of your troops. Meanwhile you will cook inside your tin box." Tony's image reappeared. "I want your unconditional surrender now, or I will be forced to destroy hundreds of your people. It won't be a fight. It will be an execution. None will even see one of our people before their life is snuffed out."

Reed's mind fought with the humiliation. Somehow an untrained, middle-level manager with a handful of people had outfought him, a highly trained designer of death. He knew he was beaten. He couldn't send his people to die for no reason whatsoever. "I surrender to you, sir."

"Please give the order, Colonel Reed."

"This is Colonel Reed to all units. This is an order. Cease hostilities of any kind. Lay down your weapons. Do not fight. I have surrendered to save your lives."

"Thank you, Colonel. I'll have you know that my people already have the fire under control and should have it out in the next ten minutes. Halon is a wonderful substance for those who don't need to breathe."

"My people will be treated properly?"

"Yes, sir. In accordance with all the articles of war. I will talk to you in more detail soon, Colonel." Sammis's image faded out.

Reed, suddenly relieved of the burden of running a battle, went and checked on each of the members of the bunker. One of the three technicians still survived, a Staff Sergeant Fletcher. Reed sighed as he tied a splint on the man's broken leg. He felt he should do more but there was no more to do except wait.

Technical Support

"Sir! Wake up!"

The knife from beneath Krylov's pillow ended up at the throat of his aide, Jason Witten, belying the heavy man's sluggishness. With one of his boss's hands around his neck and the molyblade at his Adam's apple, Jason didn't move. The only way Jason would mess with that fire in Yuri's eyes was at the end of a sniper rifle.

"What do you want!"

The edge of the blade working against his throat, Jason answered with deliberation, wishing he'd brought good news. But then good news could have waited until the morning. "Sir, we have reports that Colonel Reed has surrendered to the CorpGov."

"Did the *khuyesos* just give up?" Krylov's eyes lost their wildness. He also released his grip on Jason's neck but continued to hold the knife defensively.

Jason eased back away eventually standing to his full height. "No, sir. There was a massive battle where the National Guard and our Metro reinforcements were mauled. At least that's the reports. I was ordered to wake you immediately."

Krylov looked at the clock. It showed a bleary three twenty-eight. "Tell the watch officer that I want senior officers in the conference room in fifteen minutes. Throw me some clothes."

* * *

Amber's hair imitated a harpy's nest and the dress she wore looked as if it had swum the English Channel by itself. Two of the staff were still in pajamas and Reza wore sweatpants and a sweatshirt. Only Major Broadsky and Sergeant Tolbert were fully dressed in uniform and looked presentable. Even Krylov addressed them in a track suit that needed to have been retired at least three sizes ago.

"As I'm sure you've all heard we have been let down by our allies, the National Guard." The dark look on Krylov's face spoke for him. "Those *lichinki.*"

"Are we going to surrender?" Captain Lennart asked.

"Are you insane, Captain?" Krylov said. "It just means we will have to do it ourselves."

Reza and Tolbert shared a very quick look but managed to retain their bland expressions.

"With the force they had, the National Guard surely inflicted grievous wounds on our *vragi.* We should just have to mop up what's left. But just in case let's do a few things to protect ourselves. Get out your pads and start taking notes. We have a lot to do in a very short time.

"First I want all of you to consolidate our Metro Police and families here in the main Metro Pyramid. We won't give them anything to hang over our head.

"Next I want us to gather hostages... and I mean a lot of them. I want as many of the Greenpeace organization as we can get. They have been helping the Greenies and the CorpGov. I want any families of the corporations. I want as many nils as we can get our hands on.

"Finally, I need three or four dozen snipers to set up in random apartments in the area. We are waiting for a shot on the key members of the CorpGov or GAM. Their instructions are to *lay doggo* until they have a shot on one of the leaders. They aren't to wait for approval if they have the shot. They are to take it.

"Anything in these instructions unclear?" There were many shaking heads around the table. "Then let's make it happen."

Krylov exited from the back of the room. The other staff members filed out the front door leaving Lieutenant Narendra and Sergeant Tolbert standing alone. They looked at one another. Reza started to open his mouth and the sergeant just shook his head.

* * *

The lift-truck hovered a meter over the rubble, closer than was really safe with all the sharp edges and heated materials. The boxed androids shined lights all around to augment the spotlight of the truck. Tony and

Jamie jumped down into a 3 m square spot that had been cleared by the boxed. The truck moved up and out but hovered nearby with its doors open. Close enough for a leaping escape should the worst happen.

In the light that the boxed panned around, Tony could make out the charred bones in the rubble—a crushed foot here, piece of a skull there, and a lone humerus. He put the death toll aside for the reason that he'd come for. The vault pinged and snapped as it cooled under the steady, cold, January sleet. The ice crystals melted against the residual heat of the rest of the building, preventing any snow build-up.

"The door was jammed so we're cutting through. We'd done most and left the last for your arrival, sir," squeaked one of the boxed who no longer rode his android body for some reason.

"Thank you—"

"Margie, sir."

"Bloody hell. I'm not 'sir.' I'm just Tony."

The giggle almost sounded like a little girl. Tony could see the dimples. "Yes, Tony. Miss Jamie, if you ever get tired of him, you let me know," Margie said.

"I've been getting that offer quite a lot lately. I think he is going to be tied down pretty well for a while. Maybe literally, if his eyes wander."

The giggle returned. "Better behave, Tony."

"Win a battle. Get abused. Sounds normal," Tony teased, lightening his own mood.

Laser torches burned through the outer door in seconds. The cut-out fell to the floor, sounding like a gong.

Colonel Reed walked out. His face had been wiped of blood but many traces of it still remained in splotches and streaks.

"Colonel Reed. It pains me to meet you this way," Tony said, walking forward and extending his hand.

"No more than me, Mr. Sammis." He took the hand and the two men shook. "For my formal surrender. I offer you my net jack." The colonel removed the insert from in the skin of the back of his head and handed it forth.

Tony took it and then handed it back. "Colonel, I've looked into your record and your life. You are a man of honor. When you say you've surrendered, you mean it. I don't think I need this."

"I appreciate your respect, sir. I am not so sure I would have been so magnanimous in victory."

"We serve different masters. Mine allows me to be merciful.

Yours on the other hand—"

"Yes, I should warn you about Commissioner Krylov. He is one dangerous son of a bitch."

"That much I think we gathered, Colonel."

"Please. I don't think I rate that title any longer. Just call me Charlie."

"I think you earned that title, Charlie, and the respect that goes with it. However, if you insist then you can just call me Tony."

"Thank you, Tony. What I meant by Krylov being a dangerous SOB is that he is likely to do anything at this point from nerve gassing the entire city to raping babies. He is just a bit on this side of sane leaning toward crazy... and leaning more every minute."

"So... like the tsars of old."

"Precisely. He's definitely one who would throw a child out of the sleigh if wolves were chasing it."

"Well, thank you very much, Colonel," Tony said stressing the title. "I would like to give you your choice of prisoner accommodations. Do you want your own cell or to be housed with your men?"

"May I ask a very large favor in that regard?"

"You may ask, but we don't necessarily agree," Jamie shoved into the conversation. "And as my partner has been so rude as to not introduce me, my name is Jamie Ardwin."

"Ah, the *capa famiglia*."

"Yes. And I liked the smile you made when you said that. Have we had dealings in the past?"

"No, ma'am. You just look exactly as I expected and very unlike those hideous wanted solidos."

"Yes, they didn't exactly ask me to pose, now did they?"

"No, ma'am, I didn't expect they did. But, Tony, I wondered if I could request that my men be housed separately from the Metro prisoners?"

"Well, they are easy to segregate and the additional guards shouldn't be a problem. May I ask why?'"

"Simple, si...ah, Tony. Many of the Metros are fanatics. They might see our losing this war as a reason to seek retaliation upon me or my folks."

"A valid request. I'll carry it out to the best of my ability."

"In that case, sir, I'd be more than happy to be billeted with my own men."

* * *

"Sir, there is a percomm call for you."

"You know what to do with that, Jason," Krylov growled as he shoveled in his morning meal.

"Normally I would, sir, but this man insists he is Tony Sammis."

"Woaat?" Krylov mouthed around his *kasha*. He hastily swallowed. "Transfer that call to me."

"Please hold for the commisioner."

"You have a lot of *zhelch'*, Mr. Sammis, if that is who this is."

"*Zhelch'? Oh, gall. Yes, I guess you could say that, Mr. Commissioner. And as a* mudak *you would know, wouldn't you.*"

"So you know some Russian, *pizda.* How do you know I'm not tracing this call?"

"*Well, more to the point, Commissioner, I don't care if you do or not. We are past the point where you can make us dance to your tune, sir. You don't have the capabilities to do so any longer. To prove my point, I'm currently in the penthouse of Roy Towers at Twenty-Second and Glisan. I've even activated my locater for you. Send as many of your goon squads as you want.*"

"What is your point, Mr. Sammis?"

"*My point is that you have lost, Mr. Commissioner. In spite of my recent past, I'm not a violent man. I don't like to see people die, especially in a lost cause. I'm asking you to surrender.*"

"You are having delusions of grandeur, Sammis. We still have the upper hand and you will soon be on trial for your life." Krylov didn't hear anything for several seconds. "Are you there or did you wet your pants?"

"*I'm here, Commissioner. I'm just having a bit of difficulty believing anyone could be so nearsighted and so stupid. Well, you have my word that I will do everything I can to reduce the body count of your Metros but I won't risk even one of my people to save yours. Maybe after we've killed enough Metros the people under your command will see the futility, even if you don't. Goodbye, Commissioner.*"

"Jason, get a message to Captain Cohen. Tell her to trace the percomm from Sammis and see if we can get one of our snipers in place to take a shot."

* * *

Ty Brown shuffled down the busy hallway, his gait defined by the shackles on his legs to the person in front and behind him. Metros in full body armor paralleled them. Women, men, and children ran about the hallway unchecked, moving boxes and setting up pallets in very small barracks style rooms lining the path.

Last Ty remembered he'd been loading clips of ammunition in the Greenpeace headquarters and one wall had exploded inward. The big knot along his head explained some of the lost memories. He'd woken up just in time to see the paddy wagon take them into the massive pyramid that was the main Metro facility. His fellow prisoners had managed to fill him in on the raid that had gathered them up with a whole passel of nils.

He didn't know why he was here with nils. He'd done nothing against the law, even though he was pretty sure that the ammunition was to be used by the Green Action Militia.

"Quit dawdling!" one of the faceless Metros barked from behind his reflective black faceplate. As a group the chain-gang shuffled a bit faster when the Metro snapped a rubber truncheon over the back of one of their number.

Some of the bystanders had stopped in the hallway to watch their passage. It only takes one in a mob. That one started a chant. "Scum. Scum. Scum." Soon all the people that lined the hall joined in until they shook the hallway with their derogatory song. A cauc woman drew her two waist-high children closer to her as they shuffled along. One of the brats actually peeked out from behind her skirt and stuck his tongue out at the passing captives.

Something burst in Ty's emotions. He roared at the woman and children and then lurched at them to the end of his short chains. The mother squealed and yanked her children back into their small room as Ty toppled. He landed on the floor with his hands outstretched toward them.

He didn't see the butt of the gauss gun as it came down and struck the back of his head. Ty didn't see anything ever again.

* * *

"Let's start with the good news," Reza said. Krylov didn't react. "We have consolidated the entire Metro force here and the ninety-eight percent of dependents that have requested relocation."

"There were some that didn't?" Cohen asked.

"Yes. It was a very small percentage."

"Thank you."

"You're welcome, ma'am. We've compressed enough to fit everyone in. We are in very tight quarters with all the single men hot bunking. Families of as large as eight are bedded down in a double room. No room has fewer than five."

"That's good news, Lieutenant. That eliminates a large weak spot we have."

"Thank you, sir. Next item of good news is that we have detained eleven thousand nils and members of the Greenpeace organization without a single Metro loss. We have them crammed into the holding cells and a couple of the empty storerooms."

"Good. Did we get anyone on the special list?"

"Yes, sir. We got the families and partial families of twelve large and midsized companies. The most notable of them are the families of General Electronic."

"Really. Very nice. Who do we have to thank for that?"

"Debnath, sir," Sergeant Tolbert offered.

"How many bodies were left on the ground?" Lennart asked with a sarcastic tone.

"One friendly and eight others," Tolbert said.

"At least they were mostly others," Cohen said with raised eyebrows.

"Continue, Lieutenant," Krylov said, "we have a lot of ground to cover."

"Yes, Commissioner. In all we lost six troopers on the actions."

"*Dulce et Decorum Est,*" Krylov said, showing off his classical education. "Thank you, Lieutenant. What else do we have?"

"On my own initiative I had a sweep performed of our building defenses. We have now had ninety-four percent of our defenses online, up from less than eighty percent. I hope to be up to ninety-seven percent before the end of the day. We also discovered three breeches in our armor."

"Exceedingly well done, Lieutenant," Krylov said with a rare compliment. "That we were that open concerns me. What else might we have missed? I want you to continue your efforts. If you need more bodies you can recruit among the families. I'm sure there are some competent adults there."

"Very good, sir. I will. On to our next topic."

"Per your request we have gotten forty-three snipers out with your explicit instructions; however, only nineteen have responded now that they are out."

"Dead?"

"Unknown, sir. The real options include communication failure, death, and desertion. Statistically it is unlikely that they have all experienced comms failure. Your guesses are as good as mine."

"All right, Lieutenant, you began with the 'good news.' I suppose we also have some bad news to go with it?"

"Not much, sir. We have a supply problem. We now have one hundred fourteen thousand, six hundred and eight souls in this building. We are hard pressed to feed so many mouths. Right now we have enough stores for only twenty-seven days."

"Are you counting the hostages?"

"Of course, sir."

"Well, don't. Let them starve," Krylov said. Even Captain Hardy looked askance.

"Sir?"

"Oh, not the family of our corporate heads but the nils and Greenpeacers. Let them starve. That should give us a little breathing room."

"Uh—" Reza began, looking at the other staff members for some support. They all looked away at their note systems. "Very well, sir."

"Continuing on the subject of less than stellar items, we still have a serious plumbing problem. We've been unsuccessful at getting or coercing anyone to deal with our treatment plant. Add to that we've added sixty thousand plus souls to the mix. Even if we get the second plant online they won't take the full load."

"We could just vent the raw waste," Lennart proposed.

"Would take some work but I think it would work. It will be a hell of a mess to clean up later. It may even cause some health issues if this goes on very long."

"Do it. We will have plenty of time to clean up anything after this is over," Krylov said, ending the discussion.

*   *   *

Diana Malcomb, Di to everyone who knew her, got a charge out of the fact that she finally had some decoration. Di used to have two rooms dedicated to clothes and held six makeup subscriptions before she ran afoul of the Metro's accounting system. The colors of her urban camouflage might not be flashy, but the blue-gray and black represented a change from her dull titanium shell.

Di rolled her V1244 box past the main boxed entrance of the Metro Pyramid. Those moronic Metros still hadn't figured out that their automated defenses were programmed to ignore boxed units. The CorpGov knew the main boxed entrance had been sealed. Tony wanted to see if any of the other lesser known entrances were still open. Diana was to scout as many as she could.

At the ground speed of the basic box it would be a long day for her and her four sister scouts to circumnavigate the base of the Metro Pyramid. As target four rolled into sight, she didn't even need to roll up the ramp. It was as inviting as a whirlpool bath, something she longed for. She could almost feel the body she would receive. She fantasized about how much fun she would have again with the feel of silks and satins against her skin and the smothering feel of old-fashioned lipstick.

Twelve more targets.

* × *

"I have to say it's nice to have our pleasant surroundings back for a change," Nanogate said to the rest of the CorpGov council and his four guests, President Susan Tipton, *Capa Famiglia* Jamie Ardwin, boxed spokesperson Stephanie Delfalkis, and Green Action Militia leader Tony Sammis, de facto minister of war.

"Just don't let it go to your heads, folks," Tony said. "We are still at war. Just yesterday a sniper took a shot at Nanogate and probably only missed because a lift-truck got in the way. We've taken out over thirty of those bastards and I figure that is only about half."

"We won't forget, Tony," BeringC Protein said in her furry soprano. "We are just so happy to have a positive outcome. We'd all planned for the worst."

"It has been a joint effort, ma'am, and it is too early to be patting one another on the back."

"I couldn't agree with you more," Nanogate said. "So may I ask what you've called all us together for?"

"As you know, when we first realized all the Metros had pulled back into the pyramid our plan was to starve them out. There seemed to be no need for speed or risking even one additional person. But we have another problem, one brought to my attention by President Tipton." Tony nodded at his friend and gave her a hearty smile. Susan was hard not to like with her bubbly personality and intelligent insight. They'd spent many an evening debating governmental styles.

"We are facing an issue not here in Portland but rather all over the country. If we don't get a handle on things very quickly then we will be faced with dozens more despots that we are going to have to defeat one at a time. Krylov has made us look weak and now he makes us look ineffectual."

"Would you be having a proposal now, Mr. Sammis?" Royal Petrochem asked.

"We all know they have taken close to ten thousand hostages. None of us wanted them hurt and any assault would hurt the hostages as much as our enemies. I really hoped someone here had a brilliant idea, because I only have two left."

Nanogate looked around the table. He even looked at his bodyguard, Mr. Marks. He saw nothing but blank faces. "All right, Tony, let us hear our options."

"Ms. President, you have told us how critical this is. The first, and least palatable option is the one we've had all along. We can crush the pyramid in a number of ways, the least damaging, oddly, is an orbital lance—one single guided projectile. We will have to deal with the fallout both literal and figurative. We'd have a radiation cleanup of the Metro's nuclear reactor and the emotional loss of the hostages. The president has already told me that she's had to send troops to deal with another tin-pot dictator in Northwest Territory. It was crushed quickly but at the cost of a bit over twelve hundred lives. Multiply this by hundreds of even worse problems all over the U.S. alone, not counting other countries, and perhaps the ten thousand are an acceptable loss as martyrs."

"Tony, I appreciate that we would prefer not to use option one. Let us have our other options," Nanogate prompted.

"I say option two is marginally better. We have found places where the boxed can still get into the pyramid. We could mount a two-pronged attack. The first prong would be to destroy the Metro's foodstuffs. The second prong would be to try and release the hostages. Because they would have to enter in their boxed form without any attachments, our allies infiltrating would have limited carrying and weapon capability. This plan is no better than a suicide mission. While Stephanie assures me otherwise, I've seen the building wireframe."

"It will be no picnic, Tony, but I think my people can handle it," Stephanie squeaked.

"Stephanie, I believe very strongly that they would succeed. I just have no faith that they would return."

"It is our war, too. We have been risking our lives for decades. What is one more risk? I have over six hundred volunteers out of the first eight hundred I asked."

"How many would you need for the mission, Tony?"

"I'd send three hundred—one hundred after the foodstuffs as they don't shoot back and the other two hundred to release the prisoners."

"Would more be better?"

"Augustine has run the simulations and the more troops we send the earlier the alarm sounds. I'd use seventy-five percent as my nominal force with the remaining twenty-five waiting to support wherever needed.

"But I have to emphasize that if this doesn't work we are down to only option one if waiting isn't good enough."

"I'd like to propose something else built off your options, Tony. You may be too close to the problem." Nanogate said.

Tony nodded. He hadn't slept more than thirty minutes at a time since the hostages had been taken. "That's what I'd been hoping for."

"I'll call this option three. Why don't we just go after the foodstuffs? We limit the number of boxed at risk to one hundred. If it works we get the hostages back anyway."

"That's fine by me."

"I've received my orders from the council in silent ballot. I'd like to pursue option three. What about the other leaders?"

Jamie smiled weakly when everyone looked at her. She'd done not much better on sleep lately, trying to support Tony and to reconstitute her own organization. "I also vote for option three. No more boxed at risk than those necessary to the key mission."

"Mr. Marks, what say you in your role as spokesman for your guild?" Nanogate asked.

"I'm afraid I see life a bit different than the rest of you. I would vote for option one. My brethren, however, have requested that I vote for option three with a quick statement to our boxed brothers that we wish we could go in your stead."

"Thank you for that, Mr. Marks," Stephanie squeaked. "We vote for option two, but will support option three if it will break a tie."

"Ms. President?"

"While I don't like ordering death, I think we will be forced to option one anyway. But if there is any way out of it, I'll clutch at those straws. Option three."

"That leaves you, Tony."

"As long as every boxed has full disclosures of the simulations and is a volunteer, then I say option three."

* * *

"I know this is mundane, Commissioner, but these issues are important."

"I don't see how a toilet paper shortage should be an issue for the senior staff."

"After just one week we are now effectively out of toilet paper. We didn't notice the lack until too late to start any rationing."

"Boo-hoo!" Krylov said. "I had to fucking eat Fruity Circles in milk this morning. That is a real crime. Do people actually think there is nutrition in that sugar-fest?"

"My apologies, Commissioner. Perhaps we can find something a bit more suitable to your digestion," Captain Lennart, food rationing officer, said.

"Damned right, Captain. Now about this toilet paper—"

"Sir, the only reason I bring it up is as an example of the problems we are having. People have been stealing anything that isn't nailed down. We are almost to the point of needing to patrol our own families and this is after only a week."

"If you feel you have said enough on this topic let's move on, Lieutenant," Krylov snapped.

"May I make one more suggestion, sir? How about looting parties? Send large and small groups of armored troops out of the pyramid to bring back foodstuffs and other items. I mean we'd pay for it, but—"

* * *

Tony basked in the simple act of taking a percomm without worrying about it being traced. He didn't even look to see who called as he answered, "Sammis. It's your nickel."

"*One day perhaps we can sit down over some beer and you can describe to me the etymology of that phrase.*"

Tony didn't recognize the voice. Polling his percomm log he saw the name "Michael Beckman-Ford."

"Perhaps. It would be nice to have a beer buddy again."

"*I'd like that. People in my position too often only have toadies and 'yes-men.' From my side it would be nice to have someone whose opinion wasn't to curry favor of some kind.*"

Tony laughed. "You know, there was a time in my life where I would have been that simpering jerk looking for the next rung in the ladder. I think I've shattered those chains."

Michael laughed in a mellow baritone that he obviously inherited from his father. "*Oh, I think you could say that and more, Tony.*"

"So what can I do for you, Michael? You didn't comm just to discuss beer or my less than normal career path."

"*Ah, yes, business. Do you remember all of those shares of Wintel I asked your people to purchase for me?*"

"Certainly, but honestly I'd forgotten about it until you just reminded me. As you can imagine I've had other things on my mind."

Michael gave another light chuckle. "*Yes. Well, I wondered if I could get you to transfer the shares to my new corporation. I've named it Némein.*"

"I'll make it happen as soon as I get off the phone. So do I get any hints?"

"*I'm disappointed, Tony. With your Greek ancestry I thought you would have picked up on that right away. Until next time, Mr. Sammis.*"

* * *

L9843 was unusual among her kind. She couldn't remember her name and was glad. When asked her name she just said, "Ellie Nine." She'd worked hard to erase all her memories from before boxing. She'd gone to such lengths as to spend her free time practicing memory washing techniques. The only thing she'd chosen to retain from before was to marry intelligently and not go looking for memories of her past.

None of this made her anything but a patriot. She wanted a human body again to start over. She wanted to prove herself capable of making a good life. For now this meant paying the piper. She'd seen the simulations and knew her odds of returning from this mission weren't promising. She told herself that if she failed they'd remember her name as a martyr to the cause. Maybe they'd name an online school after her or she'd make some obscure reference that college students would study intently for a dissertation on the battles of the Metro Wars.

Ellie had two tasks for her mission. Primarily she was to tote equipment needed by others. As such she pulled a small sled with a combination of explosives and a tool that looked like a cutoff saw.

Entry point Omaha was a half-meter, rough oval that had been formed where some conduit had passed through the armor of the building in the distant past. Whatever had been there now no longer existed. Some enterprising boxed units had built a tiny ramp up to the hole with dirt and gravel. The going gave slight traction issues but nothing serious. Infrared showed plenty of heat escaping the hole into the Portland winter night. The heat gave her clear vision even in the pitch black of 3:00 a.m.

Third in line for the entrance designated Omaha she moved slowly along with sixteen more of her kind following. The first of her team rolled up to the hole. If there were alarms or active defenses they were to drop their loads and scatter. P6509 got to be the first trooper on the beach. It pushed an array of sensors in front of it. They all got relayed the take from the instrument package. No lasers. No nanites. No electric, magnetic, or gravitic fields over background noise. No visible weapons or sensors. P6509 rolled forward through the irregular opening.

Ellie mentally released her breath when her compatriot didn't explode or get cleaved in two. While she had intellectually accepted her death, she wanted it to mean something more than what happened to those poor bastards at the Bay of Pigs. Complete the mission first. Then she could die, if that was her fate.

U69, Mike someone-or-other rolled in next. Ellie skirted over the lip and onto a grouping of pipes. Her rollers slipped down into the area between two of them but it didn't hinder her. She slid through the tight tunnel for several minutes until the convoy stopped.

She'd thoroughly studied the layout of the building, especially around Omaha. The group had stopped because of a door. P6509 had tools to open it.

Suddenly the darkness of the tight space exploded with searing light. Her thermal optics overloaded as intense heat of over two thousand degrees filled the space in milliseconds. She couldn't move forward or back through the narrow tube as the mass quantities of liquid iron from the thermite fire above her poured over the shells of all the volunteers.

Ellie's box softened. She mentally screamed as her speaker had disappeared several instants before. The heat turned her brain to ash more effectively than a crematorium.

*   *   *

Leave it to the fucking Metros to screw up a sure thing, Wintel thought as he bustled around his office. He had to get certain things in order before he bolted for his last resort. He needed another two hours to finish. He'd be beyond touching at that point. He owned that entire country. They would protect him better than a mother lion defending her cubs. Now where was that power of attorney?

"Sir," his admin said from the doorway, "I have a gentleman here to see you."

"I don't have ANY time to see anyone, Joyce. Get rid of them," Wintel said not looking up from the stack of filmies on his desk.

"I tried, sir, but he wouldn't go away."

"Well then call security and make sure they are rough on him. I don't have any time for nonsense. Have you seen the Vanderbilt power of attorney?"

"But, sir, security came with him."

Wintel looked up with one eyebrow lifted. "What?"

"Enough of the preliminaries," said a blond young man with a strong chin as he pushed open the door. The man would be nondescript in any shopping center or bar in the world but he reminded Wintel of someone. The man continued, "Make sure the admin doesn't touch her computer, nor does William Trager." He directed his comments to the half dozen Wintel-logoed security guards arrayed behind him.

"That's Wintel to you, youngster."

"Not anymore, Mister Trager," the well-dressed man said emphasizing the title. The blond wore a Harvard class ring with a diamond of *cum laude* and a real silk tie. Lightning gems studded six places in each of his ears and must have cumulatively cost the same as a liftousine with all the options.

"So why do you keep saying that? I am the president of Wintel and will continue long after you are ground up for recycle."

"I say this because the board of Wintel, in a secret session this morning, agreed to the merger with my company and the removal of you from any relationship… other than as stockholder."

"You can't do that, whoever you are. As president and the owner of the single largest block of stock in the company I would have to approve such a move."

"No, sir. You used to have the single largest block of the stock. My company, Némein, now controls over one third of the voting stock. This was enough to convince the other large block shareholders to throw in with me."

"Nonsense. I would have seen you acquiring the stock."

"Fortunately, I have lots of friends buying small blocks of stock. The final transfer to my account happened last night after midnight," the man said in a butter mellow baritone.

That voice! It couldn't be! "Joyce, get me the stock report!"

"Don't let her touch anything," the man said to the security guards. "I have here a certified report that was good enough to convince Wintel security. Now, Mr. Trager, if you will be so good as to let these men escort you from the building we can save a great deal of unpleasantness."

"I will NOT go. I own this company. What gives you the right to barge in here like this and perpetrate such a charade?"

"I guess it is going to be the hard way. Gentlemen," the young man directed to the security, "I'd like you to escort Mr. Trager to your security center. There I'd like Chief Goodings to show him the reality of his situation as a civilian no longer associated with the company, both in a documentation form and with something a bit more stringent."

Two of the physically-augmented security guards flanked the former Wintel and clamped their prosthetic hands on his arms. A third took up station behind the other two with a neural amplification baton. Without too much trouble they duck-walked him from the room.

"Who are you!" the man cried out over his shoulder.

"Hold on just a moment."

The guards turned the man around.

"The name is Michael Beckman-Ford, but from now on you can call me Némein. Just as an aside, the U.S. government has already frozen all of your onshore and offshore accounts, including those of that island nation you own. Your passport has been revoked and you are now on the terrorist DNA list so you can't travel. I believe the IRS is preparing a multi-year audit against you, and several large companies are looking into your business practices and preparing lawsuits against you personally. Wintel has started repossession on the houses it helped finance on the ground you violated the moral's clause of your contract." Nanogate's son stood there with a gleam in his eye.

"What about me, sir?" the admin asked.

"I'm sorry, darling. I have nothing against you but I can't risk having you here any longer. You will be given a generous severance package and recommendation to any other company you wish to work for but at a significantly lower level than you are working now."

"I understand. Thank you, sir."

"Thank you for understanding. If you would go with these gentlemen they will gently escort you from the building. Anything personal you have here we will get to you before tomorrow." Némein turned to see Trager still standing there. "Are you still here, maggot? I know you won't learn from being stripped to a nil, but maybe one of your colleagues will. Don't fuck with us," Michael said.

* * *

"Sir, I've come to report on the supply situation and other actions," Lieutenant Narendra said.

Krylov looked with disdain at a doughnut that had the appearance of having been mutated by one too many doses of radiation. "Go on, Lieutenant."

"We've analyzed the results of those suicide raids by the boxed. It has left us with only three days of viable foodstuffs."

"WHAT!" Krylov actually jumped to his feet with his entire face assuming the color of powdered cayenne pepper.

"We have been lucky we salvaged that much. Had we not destroyed two of the forces *in toto* we would have lost everything plus whatever other mischief they had in mind. Based on camera footage we destroyed all but four of the eighty boxed units that came in."

"Get back to the food," Krylov demanded as he sat his solid bulk back into his chair.

"Sir, we have two ideas that could stretch the food. The first would be to send out our noncombatants under a flag of truce. That would roughly double the length of time."

"Unacceptable."

"I agree," Reza continued, "but I don't think for the reason you do, sir. The retention rate and effectiveness of the troopers whose families have been turned out will decrease."

"Excuse me, retention rate?"

"Sir," Amber Cohen said, sensing another explosion. She didn't want to see the lieutenant choked to death by Krylov. "We've had a number of desertions. They sneak out through the defenses and surrender to the enemy."

"And when were you going to tell me about this?" Krylov said, steepling his fingers together.

"The numbers were so low as to not even be statistically valid until this latest raid," Reza said. "We've lost only one hundred twenty-two."

"Over one hundred cowards! I want orders to shoot anyone caught outside the pyramid without my permission."

"Commissioner, I consider that unwise," Captain Hardy said. "You taught us never to give an order that won't be obeyed. It waters down all our other orders. This one won't be followed."

"There must be something we can do to discourage them!"

Tolbert offered, "Sir, I believe we could set the automatic defenses to fire on any unauthorized personnel in the cordon around our base or in the air."

"Do that. And for now there are NO authorized persons, including those fucking boxed.

"Now what are we going to do about the food."

"First thing is rationing. We can stretch the food out to three or maybe even four weeks if we ration well."

"How do we get more provisions? Rationing is a stopgap!"

"We've sent out seven different scavenging parties. Only one of them made it beyond the clear zone between buildings. That one was just that, a single lone man who is adept at sneaking around. He returned with about forty kilos of foodstuffs, not even enough to make a statistical blip in the overall situation."

"So our scavenging parties were turned back?"

"No, sir, they were destroyed with zero quarter offered. The actions were over so quick and from multiple sources that sometimes it was hard to determine what the causes of their deaths were."

"Not good. Did they take any of their troops with them?" Amber Cohen asked hopefully.

"As far as I can tell of the one hundred six men sent, only two actually used their weapons. We can't tell what, if anything, they hit but it wasn't significant."

Krylov pounded the table. The doughnut and its plate jumped 5 cm. "This is ridiculous. We have thousands of men. Why can't we overwhelm them?"

"We could try, sir, but we aren't a military force. We have trained for riots against poorly armed civilians. We don't have the tactics to go toe to toe with another armed force."

"Neither do they!" Krylov shouted back.

"But, sir, we would be attacking a fortified position," Tolbert offered. "The attacker always takes a disproportionate number of casualties. We have no artillery, which they obviously do, and we are likely outnumbered. Even if we dealt one-for-one casualties, unlikely with a frontal assault, we would lose."

"I have to agree, sir," Major Broadsky said in an uncharacteristic offering of something the commissioner didn't want to hear. "I believe conventional warfare is not an option."

"Then we will have to be unconventional."

$$* \quad * \quad *$$

Tony walked into the room with a bandage across his left cheek.

"What the hell happened to you?" Morgan asked.

"You know I'm really tired of getting shot," Tony said.

"Sniper?" David asked. He now floated on his new "legs.". Three pergrav lift units had been mounted in a triangular base where his thighs had been. With a slight shift of his weight he could start moving in that direction. He'd already demonstrated his new speed and maneuverability, both horizontally and vertically by ramming at high speed into the duct work of the large open space. He hadn't quite gotten down the balance yet.

"Yup. That's the fourth this week. Those bastards are really starting to bug me. They picked off Joe Roberts this week with an almost perfect headshot. He looked quite a bit like Nanogate. The sniper must have thought he had the gold ring when we sent him to hell."

"Bet the devil had a good ol' laugh at that one."

"But Joe didn't," Jamie said in uncharacteristic melancholy.

"True," David said, changing the subject. "So, illustrious leader, what are we here for today?"

"To plan the destruction of the Metro Pyramid and everyone inside."

"Shit," David said.

"Too true," Augustine added.

"But before we go there is there anything I've overlooked? Any possible way we can get in and save those hostages?"

"Could Augustine hack into the defenses and then we storm the place just with overwhelming numbers? With all of our new recruits we have to have them outnumbered five to one," David said.

"No good," Augustine said. "Their defense computer is not on the net. It is intentionally separated just so that it can't be hacked."

"How about an EMP like we did with the cabal?"

"Sorry, Morgan, but they are shielded; but I like the thought."

"Well then, how about firing one of those fuel-air explosive missiles right at the upper half of the building? That was fun launching those bitches," Morgan smiled.

"We don't know where they are holding the hostages. And something massive enough to pierce the armor will likely be no better than an orbital bombardment. You saw the damage done in University Park."

"True. Well, I'm all out...anyone else?"

Tony waited several seconds. "I'm out, too, people, so it is the time we all dreaded. What is the best way to take out the pyramid, with everyone inside?"

"Orbital bombardment," David offered.

"NOT a nuke," Augustine said.

"I think that is taken as read, Augustine."

"Gas," Christine said. "Burn them out."

"What did you say?" Tony asked.

"Burn them out."

"No, the other one."

David got it too. "We'll still lose people."

"But at least it gives us a chance. That's all I'm asking for."

"I think I fell behind," Jamie said.

"Don't worry, baby. You make up for it in other ways," Tony said playfully.

* * *

"Sir, you have a percomm call from the commissioner," Williams said with his usual dearth of emotion.

Nanogate waved the call to him. "Good morning, Commissioner. What can I do for you on this fine day?"

"*You can surrender.*"

"If that is a joke, Commissioner, it is in very poor taste. We have the upper hand and we will keep it until you are captured and held accountable for your crimes."

"*Well then, if you would do me the favor of turning on your solido to the Metro channel? We still control that one.*"

"One moment. There it is." The channel had no talking, only showed the Metro building and zoomed in on one of the executive balconies.

"*Now if you will watch, Chairman.*"

A fat Metro in a captain's uniform walked out, leading a very thin young woman. Her eyes were sunken and she barely struggled against her captor even though she wasn't bound.

"*This is on your head, Nanogate,*" yelled the fat man as he pushed the girl over the railing. She grabbed the ledge as she fell, screaming for help. The heavy Metro kicked her fingers until she couldn't hold on any longer. The station let the audio of her thin shrieks run unedited. The solidograph followed her fall until less than four seconds later she smashed into the side of the pyramid, leaving behind a red streak and echoes of her screams.

"*Nanogate,*" the commissioner said over the percomm, "*that is just the first. We will execute one hostage every hour until you surrender, and each one of them will be broadcast on the Metro channel for everyone to see.*"

* * *

"Chairman, we have a plan. It will just take a day or so to get the key ingredients together," Tony said to the collected war council.

"Having my name associated with at least twenty-four more deaths doesn't seem like a viable solution," Nanogate stated.

"Chairman, I can speed that up somewhat," President Tipton said. "Make it twelve hours from now."

"And what do we tell the people out there as hostages die? I strongly urge us to bomb them now. One single horrific finale will be acceptable. This slow torture is not."

"Folks, I think the chance of saving nearly ten thousand lives is worth the small risk in public opinion. Nanogate, isn't it for the greater good?"

"Yes, Tony, but this could easily backfire. We could lose in victory."

"Then let me go in and talk to the Metros. I'll offer to negotiate," Tony said.

"NO!" Jamie exclaimed immediately. She realized her mistake and modified her tone to merely horrified. "And give them a high-level hostage?"

"I should be able to at least slow down the executions to give you time to run our plan."

"And who actually leads our attack? You are our general," Susan Tipton asked.

"Let David do it with Morgan, Marks, and Augustine as his lieutenants."

"I don't like it, Mr. Sammis," Nanogate said. "It seems like we are sacrificing our queen for a bishop."

"But this should put them into checkmate, if we are going to continue the chess metaphors."

"But you are risking your life."

"I'm not sure that even Krylov is stupid enough to abuse a flag of truce."

"I'm not that sure," Jamie said.

"I echo your partner's sentiment," Mr. Marks said.

"I have faith in our plan," Tony said, "and barring being shot outright I should be safe."

"I won't forbid it," Nanogate said.

Tony said, "So then, let's make this happen and lose the long faces."

* * *

Christine had the Metro channel on the solido. The only thing shown was "Next Execution for Aiding and Abetting the Outlaw CorpGov: 0:00:34," and the timer ticked down. At ten seconds the image changed to the same balcony.

Punctuality and consistency must be a class taught at the Metro Academy, Christine thought.

Captain Hardy, the fat Metro, walked out onto the balcony with another teenage girl. If the prospect of being thrown to her death wasn't enough, she'd been stripped of her clothing to abuse her dignity even more. This girl thrashed and fought the Metro, trying to claw at his face. Hardy clubbed her with one meaty fist. The girl went down in a heap. He picked up the girl over his head. *"Nanogate, this girl's death is on your head."*

Christine feathered the trigger, feeling the instant it broke. She didn't feel the recoil. She kept her eye on the scope to see Captain Hardy's head explode like an water balloon pierced by a needle. The girl dropped to the floor like a limp sack over the body.

The Metro channel cut the live feed and the signal on the channel returned to "Next Execution for Aiding and Abetting the Outlaw CorpGov: 0:59:55." Christine didn't notice. She just kept her eyes peeled through her scope.

The balcony door opened. The people retrieving the hostage and the body kept low, but the people back in the room weren't so smart. Christine got two more idiots before they all got down, closed the door, and pulled the blinds.

Killing with a gun wasn't as satisfying as with her knives but it did feed her demons, and a Metro captain, no less.

* * *

Tony walked between Jamie and David. Jamie had her hand in his, interlacing their fingers. She squeezed so tight he felt she must be hurting herself.

"David, you will be in charge as soon as I get into that jeep. I don't give all that many orders around here, but I'm going to give you two."

David nodded solemnly but said nothing.

"I'm going to go into that rat's nest knowing that I may be killed outright, flag of truce or not."

Jamie squeezed his hand even harder.

"Order number one. Unless I come back, you are to go with the attack as scheduled exactly on time. If they torture me I should be able to hold out at least that long."

"Yes, Tony."

"Order number two. Should the attack not succeed in effectively breaking the Metros, you are to pull back your remaining forces and bombard the site from orbit. If the president won't pull the trigger, use every conventional weapon you can lay your hands on and reduce the place to rubble."

"I will, Tony. I won't like it, but I'll do it."

"None of us likes killing people, except Christine. Not even Christine wants to be responsible for the death of friends. This is one of those cases where it is imperative."

"Oh, I understand, Tony, I just won't like it."

"Good. Now I want to give you three code words if we get to communicate after I'm inside. 'Paint' means the gas attack is likely to fail and you should go directly to order two, but you must decide. I'm only giving you information. 'Negotiate' or 'negotiations' means that I'm under duress and 'spare' or 'sparing' means that I'm not. But you should assume that I'm being coerced no matter what and ignore any order or request that I make."

"Yes, Tony."

"Now get back and start setting up your plans. I don't want to know what they are in case I might give something away."

"Righto, boss-man. We'll make you proud."

"You better or I'm going to come back and short circuit those hoverlegs of yours."

David leaned forward too far and his "legs" jerked forward, standing him upright again. He gave a wry smile and tried again. This time he did better and managed to hover back the way they'd come to leave the couple alone.

"I know what you are going to say," Tony said.

"No, you don't. I'll bet you don't have a clue."

"Well, I was going to say, 'Don't try to convince me not to go.' This is important. I —"

Jamie flowed up against him and silenced him with a kiss. "I am afraid for you. I'm afraid for what I will become without you. But I knew you didn't know what I was going to say. 'Come back with your shield, or on it.'"

*   *   *

Reza sat in his office trying to think of a way out of the cluster fuck the Metros found themselves in. Krylov wouldn't listen to even his senior staff's recommendation that they surrender. Instead now they were murdering people, although he had to be honest that the sniper bullet that killed Hardy did everyone a favor. *But now we are murdering people*, he thought again. *This is what we are supposed to fight against, not do!*

A commotion started out in the wardroom outside his office. The police officers clustered around a solido tank in the middle of the room. A large round of cheers rang out before one of the younger patrolmen, who was from another station, ran up and knocked on his door. Reza waved him in.

"Sir, you have to see it. Tony Sammis is on the solido getting shot at!"

"Huh?" Reza responded less than brilliantly.

"Just come look, sir."

Reza walked out. His short stature wouldn't have gotten him attention but the sight of his lieutenant's bars did. Slowly the crowd parted. The solido showed a hardtop jeep flying in erratic patterns. As the camera zoomed in he could see Tony Sammis's face and the huge white flag he had flying from his vehicle's aerial. As he watched, a projectile embedded itself in the ballistic glass of the jeep.

"Why are we shooting at him? He's carrying a white flag." A spark flew from a divot that materialized on the hood. "You there. Get down to defense control and tell them to stop shooting!"

"I'll do it, sir, but that isn't autogun fire. Those are sniper shots."

"Oh, fuck," Reza said. He dialed a number known only to five people in the world. "Cease fire and relocate," Reza told his sharpshooters.

The fire in the solido stopped but the jeep kept jinking.

"Now go order the landing lights lit on the executive pad AND turn off our automated defenses. All defense personnel on high alert for any action OTHER than that jeep landing on our pad."

*   *   *

"Why didn't you just let the snipers take him out?" Krylov demanded.

"Sir, he was flying a flag of truce. Besides, all that would have happened as they fired on that lightly armored jeep is to get all of his friends to kill our snipers."

"Bah!"

Reza didn't have a good response that wouldn't get him punched on the spot so he chose discretion as the better part of valor.

"I might suggest, Commissioner, that the lieutenant acted correctly," Captain Cohen said.

Reza looked at the captain. She'd never been his ally before and people just didn't stick their neck out for no reason.

"Well, what does the fool want?" Krylov asked ignoring the lieutenant.

"Perhaps he wants to surrender," Major Broadsky said, occupying the deceased Hardy's chair.

"Why not call? They have our percomm."

"Honestly, Commissioner, we don't know, but we will in just a few minutes. Sergeant Tolbert and his squad will be bringing him down."

"Here they come now," Lennart said.

Four troopers formed a diamond around Tony Sammis with Tolbert marching to one side. "Detail halt."

Sammis had a smaller version of his white flag tied to his arm.

"I assume this traitor has been frisked?"

"I did it myself, Commissioner," Tolbert said, remaining at attention. "I scanned him for explosives, nanites, and even plastic weapons. I removed his prosthetic eye, removed the firing pin from the crude flechette gun in his finger, and the power pack to his prosthetic hand. Other than his clothes he carried only this," Tolbert said, holding out a standard memory crystal.

Reza noted that Sammis's eye socket was empty.

"Looks like at least one of us got a good shot on you," Krylov taunted.

"Yes, Commissioner, they did."

"So what did you come here for? To surrender?"

"Ah, that is a fine joke, Commissioner, but I came to ask for your surrender. If you will place that recording crystal in any portable solido I'll show you a few good reasons why."

"Might as well do what he says," Krylov said with a wave of his hand while he rested his chin on his other palm.

"Based on the income tax records we have, we assume you have fifty-one thousand, eight hundred fourteen officers. This first solido shows your current position with our positions around you. This satellite photo was taken three hours ago and all of our positions have changed but if you look you can count a good portion of our troops. Even a quick count will find our numbers over two hundred thousand. We have artillery, heavy weapons, heavy construction equipment that can turn tanks into doughnut holes."

"So what do you offer?" Amber Cohen asked and then suffered under the withering glare of Commissioner Krylov.

"We only offer the ability to live. We demand unconditional surrender, and we promise only that none of you will be put to death during your war crimes trials."

"I'm sorry, but despite your heavy weapons we are holding a large number of hostages."

"Yes, Commissioner, and you are killing them claiming a halo for doing the deed. You are then trying to place their deaths at our feet. With that choice, the CorpGov has allowed me to tell you that at twelve minutes past three p.m., that is six hours and two minutes from now, this building will be destroyed by an orbital strike."

"They wouldn't dare. The death toll would be horrific here and that doesn't mention the collateral damage, nor the fallout from our nuclear reactors. It won't happen."

"Sir, I am the head of the allied forces. I gave the order before I left. The only thing that can counter it will be the surrender of your forces."

"*Chush' sobach'ya*! Do you have anything else you *bolbo yeb*? You are all bluff and no play."

"Sir, my only reason in coming here is to protect as many of the hostages as possible. I will admit if it weren't for them your vaunted pyramid would have been destroyed long before now. I'm afraid I have limited sympathy for you and your brethren."

"HA! We defeated your little brain boxes and all your sneaking around does you no good. Do you have anything else to offer us?"

"On the memory crystals you might find other items which may or may not matter to you, Commissioner—our force structure, our armaments, a list of your sniper dead to this point, Metro and National Guard prisoner lists, and even a list of your defectors. I invite you to review it. You can surrender up to ten minutes till three p.m. After that time the orbital bombardment will strike this building, killing everyone inside."

Krylov jumped up, grabbing the crystal from the machine. He threw it to the floor and crushed it under one of his heels, grinding the pseudo-glass into the tile. "*Lozh*! Lies! These are nothing but lies."

"I see I've wasted my time here. There can be no negotiation. If your men will escort me back to my vehicle I'll return to my people with only failure."

Krylov took a deep breath as he settled. His unibrow wrinkled in the middle. "I don't think so, Mr. Sammis. It seems that you are a traitor and thus the cloak of truce doesn't apply to you."

"The cloak of truce is irrelevant to any criminal status, Commissioner. If I don't communicate with my people the three p.m. deadline will be moved up."

"They won't kill their beloved leader. Sergeant Tolbert. Take him and throw him in with the rest of the scum."

*   *   *

Tolbert accepted the good with the bad as a Metro. As a rare almost straight cop, he'd rolled with the corruption as best he could to perform the work police always were there to perform—protect and serve.

This order he'd been given weighed on his soul. To throw a man under the flag of truce into a prison cell he didn't agree with, but it was the commissioner's call. To order him to form a detail and shoot a prisoner, a hostage, on live solido was wrong. He didn't really think he had much choice, however.

Fortunately, he had five Metros that had close family that had been devastated by the conflict. They would like nothing more than to get some of their own back from the scum that were the nils. He marched them down to the holding cells in the lowest basements. A pair of solidographers followed the small troop.

The guards near them acknowledged the senior NCO. He received a knowing nod at their mission. A mass of humanity milled tightly behind the heavy wire mesh. None of them looked in good condition. Over a week without food will make even the most robust person seem to have a pallor of failing faculties.

"Cover me." The five men aimed their weapons casually at the prisoners. Tolbert opened the cage and stepped inside. The prisoners shrank back, glaring at him. None showed fear, only the rage of someone who has no chance to fight back. Tolbert grabbed the arm of an older man whose rheumy eyes indicated a deeper problem. He had to help the man to his feet. "Come with me."

"No!" came a clear interjection from deeper in the crowd. Tony Sammis stepped forward. "If you have to take someone, take me."

Tolbert just looked at the man. Tony's eyes managed to convey both a peace within himself and a disgust for what Tolbert was about to do. Tony exhibited no hatred or fear—more like a sadness.

"No!" another from the crowd said, stepping in front of Tony.

"Not him, me!" came another. And another. And another until the entire room raised the ruckus to a level of mob.

"STOP IT!" Tolbert yelled in his loudest drill-sergeant voice. The crowd noise ceased.

"Seriously, Sergeant, I'd rather you take me than this man," Tony said once again stepping out from the crowd.

"Mr. Sammis, I can't. I don't know what the commissioner has planned for you and your premature demise would cause additional problems."

"Mr. Sammis," said the feeble old man Tolbert still held. "If someone has to die, then this... uh, person, has picked correctly." The old man coughed three times with a wet mucus sound deep in his chest before continuing. "I don't know if he does it out of kindness or cruelty, but I'm already dead. The doctors give me maybe another month. Let my life save someone else."

"Old timer, what is your name?" Tony asked.

"Art Wilkie."

"Art, do you have any family?"

"Naw. I'm alone, but if you would remember me on All Saint's Day I'd appreciate it."

"Gentlemen, I do have a time limit here."

"Thank you, Sergeant Tolbert, for being gracious. Art, we all will remember you."

Tolbert had no difficulty getting out when just moments before he'd wondered if he would be torn into tiny bits by hands alone. "I'm sorry, Art," Tolbert whispered to the old man as he stood him up against a wall. The man with the camera was waving for him to hurry.

"Art Wilkie, you have been convicted of conspiracy to commit murder with special circumstances, accessory to murder with special circumstances, and further numerous crimes. Your sentence is death. May God have mercy on your soul.

"Ready. Aim. Fire." The multiple gun reports rolled over them like physical impacts in the enclosed space. Tolbert unsnapped his holster, drew his side-arm and went over to the twitching body and delivered the *coup de grâce* to the biological heap that had once been a man.

* * *

Reza edited his percomm list carefully. There could be no toadies. There could be no boot-lickers or brown-nosers. Fortunately in his position he knew most of them and a few judicious inquiries found those in stations he didn't know. He didn't want yes-men or those he liked. He need a good representative sample to let him know what he already believed.

Tolbert guarded the weapons' locker where Reza made his private call without anyone overhearing. His percomm opened a one-thousand-person teleconference. "Gentlemen and ladies of the Local Three of the Law Enforcement Fraternal Union, I am in desperate need of your input at this time. I have only one question to ask, and then you can get back to your duties.

"'Should we surrender or continue to fight?' Please indicate your answer now with one being surrender, two being fight, and any other key undecided."

Reza came out of the vault less than two minutes after he entered. "Eighty-nine, four, seven," he said, giving Tolbert the percentages.

* * *

"*Commissioner Krylov?*" came a voice over the speaker that none of the staff had heard before.

"This is he. Who am I addressing?"

"*This is David Swift of the alliance. I'm calling after Tony Sammis. He was to have checked in by this time.*"

"I'm sorry, Mr. Swift, but Mr. Sammis has been arrested on the charge of treason."

"*Even though he came under a flag of truce?*"

"It doesn't protect a traitor. I'm sorry, but that is our interpretation of the applicable laws."

"*Well, he had considered this possibility. It is my duty to inform you that in three hours, sixteen minutes, I will be hitting the pyramid with enough firepower to leave it nothing more than a depression. I just haven't decided if it will glow in the dark or not. You see I have lots of options.*"

"Go back and suckle your mother's breast, little boy," Krylov taunted. "Let us adults take care of this problem." Krylov terminated the connection smiling. "If that is the best they can come up with we should be in power by this time tomorrow."

Reza chose that time to speak up. "Commissioner, you may not be aware of this but the union has voted over twenty to one to surrender."

"When did that take place?" Krylov growled.

"It was a private survey."

"Then it's skewed. We are winning and all my people know it. I think your attitude isn't right for this meeting any longer, Lieutenant."

"Very well, sir. I'll bow out now and allow you to pick a replacement."

"Oh, Lieutenant, please don't get so stiff-necked," Krylov said. "I was kidding. I don't want myself surrounded by yes-men, or at least not all of them," the big man said looking at Major Broadsky.

*   *   *

"Ms. President. You heard the commissioner," David said in council with the leaders of the alliance.

"He almost bragged about having arrested Tony under a flag of truce," Jamie said. "David, you had better kill that man dead or when I get my hands on him he'll beg for something as gentle as torture."

"Honey, we are all worried about Tony," Augustine offered.

"If we could get back to the subject at hand," Nanogate suggested.

"What are you asking from me, David. Please be clear so there is no ambiguity."

"Quite so," Nanogate agreed.

"Madam President, I am about to go into battle where I might be hurt or killed. I promised Tony to call down an orbital strike if our assault fails. I would like to put the strike in now for a future impact, more precisely for impact at 1500 hours local time on top of the Metro headquarters."

"Why not do it after the assault?" Susan asked.

"Because Ms. President, I won't be here to convince you later," David said floating comfortably lower to the floor so he was eye to eye.

"But what if I choose to shut it down while you are away."

"That is your prerogative; however, I believe that you are a woman of your word. If you agree to do this now you won't be tempted to turn it off unless we win."

The president sighed. She closed her eyes. "You know this means the death of thousands of innocent lives?"

"Yes, ma'am," David said. "But if you don't it will cost more lives as we do it the conventional way."

"I know this isn't a responsibility that can be shared, Ms. President, but it's the correct thing to do," Mr. Marks said.

"Is there even one dissenting voice in the room?" Susan asked. No one responded. "Augustine, you heard what was said. Would you please program it for me?"

"Already got it, Ms. President. All I need is your authorization code."

Susan shook her head. "Alpha, Kilo, Bravo, Lima, One, One, Juliet, code word fallen angel. Execute."

*   *   *

"Reza, could you call Sergeant Tolbert. It is time for another of our object lessons to the weaklings out there. Just one or two more and then we'll put Sammis up there. That, if nothing else, will get them to surrender."

* * *

Sergeant Tolbert's conscience burned brighter the closer it got to the top of the hour. He cursed Tony Sammis but the man had only triggered what he himself knew was right from wrong. He also knew all the gray murky areas between that the Metros trampled through regularly. He'd wrestled with his moral sense many times and convinced it that what he did overall was for the best.

This didn't reconcile. This couldn't reconcile.

"*Sergeant, it's time,*" Reza said over his percomm.

He already knew what he had to do. Moving over in front of a mirror he straightened his tie and flicked off a spec of lint. He straightened his decoration bars. He checked his side-arm to make sure it was loaded and chambered. Clicking on the safety he returned it to his holster and snapped it shut.

He marched out and down the hall. He counted each measured step to settle his mind. He walked into the senior conference room. "Sergeant Tolbert reporting as requested. Give me an order, Commissioner."

"Go down and execute another of those miserable curs."

Two decades as a soldier and another three as a Metro had drilled Tolbert's motions into muscle memory. He wasted no efforts. From attention he flipped open the snap of his holster with just his thumb. His right arm drew the gun on the way up. At the same time he took half a step forward, his left hand cradling the butt of the pistol into a perfect Modified Weaver stance. The heavy pull of the double action of the uncocked trigger gave him zero difficulty after so many years of experience. He felt the break of the trigger release at almost the same instant a red hole blossomed in the center of Krylov's forehead. The explosive tipped bullet blew the back of his target's head off. The bark of the weapon sealed in this little room would leave everyone's ears ringing for hours.

No one else in the room reacted before Sergeant Enrique Tolbert hit the decocking lever and set the gun on the table, pointing and threatening only the body. Tolbert stepped back out of reach of the firearm and waited before even the first reaction of the audience.

"Holy FUCK!" Lennart shouted.

"Jesus!" Cohen exclaimed.

"What the hell!" Broadsky yelled.

To Tolbert all three reactions seemed like hours after the shots. They say that even professional soldiers often take several seconds to react to something unusual.

Cohen finally drew her sidearm and pointed it at Tolbert. Broadsky grabbed at the automatic on the table. Lennart just stared at the carnage.

Other than Tolbert himself, Reza seemed the only person nonplussed. He looked at the body. He looked at Tolbert.

Maintenance

Geared and ready to assault the pyramid in twenty-five minutes, David sat in front of the Metro solido channel with the allied council and the rest of the CorpGov. Every hour, the group joined to watch the gruesome spectacle. They all felt it their duty to watch those sacrificing themselves to make time to get all the pieces of their assault in place.

As usual there was the "Next Execution for Aiding and Abetting the Outlaw CorpGov" counter ticking down. Everyone had settled in their seat and all talking stopped by time it reached one minute. Each second the attendees wished they could somehow stop it. The same inabilities frustrated them every hour. They just told themselves that the next hour would be different.

But this hour something different happened. The counter went to zero and held without the picture changing. Nanogate and Susan looked at one another.

"What's going on?" Augustine asked.

"A couple of seconds doesn't make any difference," BeringC Protein said.

"They've always been so punctual," Jamie added.

"Not this time," Mr. Marks offered.

"What does it mean?" David asked.

"How the hell should I know what it means," Connie Powell said from over the shoulder of the president.

"Please settle down, people. Focus," President Tipton said.

"But what—"

The solidograph changed. It showed an executive conference room with Commissioner Krylov at the head of the table, leaning back in a chair. Behind him blood, bits of bone and brain matter, painted the wall, still oozing down. The hole in the body's forehead spoke volumes.

A short, middle-aged man, whose ancestors came from the subcontinent of India, moved slowly into the frame from one side. "*My name is Lieutenant Reza Narendra. On behalf of the Local Three of the Law Enforcement Fraternal Union we surrender to the CorpGov.*

"*To show that we have in fact surrendered, we are releasing Tony Sammis and all the hostages. We have already turned off all automated weapons and are in the process of sealing all other weapons in secure vaults to prevent any accidents. If you will give us fifteen minutes to complete this action we will then open all doors and comply with any commands you give us.*"

"Augustine, please cancel the planned bombardment," the president said.

"It could be a trick!" David said. "Hold on until—"

"Augustine, please comply with my order."

"Done, ma'am."

"If we need to, David, I'll turn it back on."

*　　*　　*

The ground-level, armored gates of the Metro Pyramid hadn't been used in at least five decades. They screeched as they crept open, spraying dust, dead insects, and paint chips as they did.

Prisoners spilled out as soon as a crack developed wide enough to fit a single person through sideways. The crowd spread outward away from their place of captivity. Some jumped for joy. A few kissed the ground. One man grabbed a random woman and gave her an embrace so passionate that in most societies in the previous centuries meant a wedding. Many of them got to a point of safety and just stopped, unsure what to do next.

Tony carried one woman whose feet had developed chancres. He was met by David and more members of the GAM, Greenpeace, and bodyguards than he'd ever seen in one place. One of them took the woman from his arms and put her on a gurney. She tried to protest and thank Tony. He just smiled and waved.

"I've got food carts inbound," David said. "If the conditions in there were as bad as I've heard—"

"Worse," Tony interrupted.

"Well, food is coming. We've got all the volunteer doctors, nurses, and paramedics that I could round up… which I think is practically all of them in the greater Portland area. I've got mental health workers that will be here within the hour."

"You've got this handled. Who are you sending in to wrap up our friends?"

"The boxed, of course. Less chance they can be hurt and they won't take any crap."

"Good. So when do I get to thank Christine?"

"Huh? For what?"

"Well, they wheeled a solido tank down there for us to watch. Unless they did makeup magic or some serious retouching of that footage, someone whacked our friend the commissioner."

"How does that tie in with Christine? She didn't shoot him."

"Well, who did?"

"I have no clue."

"Well, find one when you go in there."

* * *

"*Excuse me, ma'am?*" said a stout, well-dressed, young man through the solido.

"You heard me correctly, Mr. Attorney General," President Susan Tipton said from in front of her seal of office.

"*Susan... I mean, Ms. President,*" William Lueke, attorney general and friend, said, "*there is a question of constitutional law here.*"

"Yes, they broke it. They committed conspiracy, sedition, and treason."

"*I mean, ma'am, that their office protects them from—*"

"Nothing, Bill. Remember my background in constitutional law."

"*Are you expecting my marshals to go up against possibly dug-in National Guard troops?*"

"No, Bill, I'm not. I'm giving you the Army."

"*Holy crap, Ms. President, that is going to break about three layers of the constitution itself.*"

"Barak Obama signed Directive 3025.18 stating that the military can be used against U.S. citizens and on U.S. soil during times of unrest. It has never been revoked."

"*Its constitutionality has never been challenged.*"

"Trust me, Bill, it won't be."

"*Hell, if I was one of their defense attorneys that would be my first line of attack.*"

"They will beg us for a plea bargain to save their lives. These are slam dunk cases. Now are you going to carry out my—"

"*Ms. President, I'm sorry if I gave you any reason to believe I wouldn't do as you asked. I was just trying to instruct you on a point of constitutional law. I think this is going to blow up.*"

"I want them all arrested and charged."

"*Yes, ma'am. Who shall I liaise with in the Army?*"

* * *

"Never thought I'd be wearing corporal's stripes," Mickey Andersen said. "And look at you, Bear, a sergeant."

"Yeah, now I don't have to threaten you with the sergeant because I am he. Now shut up. If you mess this up you are going to be dreaming of getting back up to a private's stripe."

The convoy of eight TPVs landed on the well-manicured lawn and shrubbery. Even in February the grass remained green in Salem, Oregon. Bear's squad ignored the state of the landscaping, tearing the soggy wet earth to shreds as they deployed.

Seven Metro Police guards quickly realized they had zero opportunity against the light company with fire support and put down their weapons. Even the gunners in light assault cannon in the turret of Mahonia Hall stood down.

Mickey and Bear flanked Marshall Brad Watkins to the front door of the Governor's Mansion. They pounded on the door until a slight asian man came to the door. "What is this outrage about? Why are you crushing—"

"Governor Paul Nguyen?"

"Of course!"

"I have here a federal warrant for your arrest on the charges of conspiracy, sedition, and treason against the United States."

* * *

"Governor Glenna Sarrong I have a federal warrant for your arrest on the charges of—"

* * *

"Governor Thadius Polk?"

"Who wants to know."

"I'm a federal marshal. I have here a federal warrant to arrest you on the charges of sedition, conspiracy, and treason."

"I don't recognize your authority to arrest me, young woman."

"Listen, Governor, those eighty men toting machine guns behind me is all the authorization I need; however, the law grants me the power to arrest even a governor if he is suspected of treason.

"As such, you have the right to remain silent. You have the right to an attorney—"

* * *

"Why did you do it?" Tony asked of a shackled Enrique Tolbert. They sat across a table in an FBI high-risk interrogation room. Both knew that a solidograph recorded everything that took place in the room.

"My name is Enrique Tolbert. My badge number is—"

"Sergeant, I'm not angry with you. I'm not happy with you. I'd just like to understand."

"Why? You are going to kill us all anyway."

"Is that what you think, Sergeant?" Tony reached out and rapped the window. A young black woman with curly hair came into the room and unlocked the Sergeant's hand and leg cuffs before leaving the room. "I think you have been listening to your colleagues too much. While we will be executing some, of that I have no doubt, you are not in danger."

"Why? Just because I'm more useful alive as the man who murdered your enemy?"

"Actually because a young Metro named Frances Fischer mentioned your name several times as being an honorable man."

"Frances was a good girl caught up in an ugly world."

"I don't disagree."

"So you intend to use me as a propaganda toy."

"Sergeant, I don't give a flying damn about propaganda now. The war is over. I won't argue if the right side won or lost as the victors always write the histories. But I just want to be that one person who really knew what happened."

"You want me to tell you that Krylov was an evil man?"

"I want you to tell me why you pointed a gun and pulled the trigger."

The sergeant didn't hesitate. "Because I'm a patriot. That man would have killed every single Metro for his ego. I couldn't allow that."

"Thank you, Sergeant. Your act may have indeed saved many thousands of lives. Remember the old saw about if you could go back in time and kill Hitler? I think you just did. In return, would you like me to set you free?"

Tolbert snorted.

"Was that a yes or a no?"

"I belong with my brethren. I don't deserve any special treatment."

"I say you do. But how would you like the opportunity to help your brothers in arms one more time?"

"How would I do that? Sounds like you still want a propaganda toy."

"No, Sergeant Tolbert, I'm looking for a judge… or to be precise one of three judges."

"I don't follow."

"Sergeant, I will not kill your people off in job lots nor let the CorpGov do the same. However I'm sure you agree I can't just set your people free."

Enrique snorted again.

"Exactly. So I have an exceptional solution for them but I need a good man to make sure it isn't being abused, as is the wont of victors."

"You want me to judge my fellow Metros? Do you want me to be forever a pariah?"

"No, I want you to be a patriot," Tony Sammis said.

Tolbert could see why people followed this man. Honesty and integrity shined out from every corner of the man's soul. It is said that no organization is any better than its leader. Tony could lead a group of pacifists against the gates of hell itself. Enrique felt the pull of the man's charisma himself, and it frightened him.

"First tell me your solution."

* * *

Without any fanfare, Susan Tipton walked up behind the podium in front of the Presidential Seal. "I appreciate how patient you all have been with me in hiding. I ask just a bit more indulgence to let me give you my statement before asking questions.

"The United States still stands. We are still free.

"The leader of the rebellion, Yuri Krylov, was killed by one of his own people at 1051 hours today within his own stronghold. The remainder of the Metros unconditionally surrendered. They were all taken into custody with no additional injuries or loss of life.

"Other ringleaders of this attempted coup on our way of life were arrested. These included any governor who declared martial law and called out National Guard troops to control the populace. Seventeen of these warrants have been issued and suspects taken into custody. One governor, Uther Brown, of Alabama, has gone on the lamb. We don't expect he can stay hidden for long.

"In short, we are back to the business of the people of the United States. I'm sorry to say that as of this moment I'm reinstating all taxes I suspended earlier."

This drew a few chuckles.

"Now I'll take a few questions. Margret."

"Ms. President, you said only seventeen governors were arrested. What about all the others who declared an emergency?"

"Good question. The governors who declared martial law and never called up the National Guard are not subject to arrest warrants at this time. It will be up to the attorney general to determine if any laws were broken, but hazarding a guess I would say no. It is the governor's privilege and sometimes duty to declare martial law or an emergency in their state. The law is clear on that."

"But not use troops?"

"No. Not against the expressed desire and order of the president. Next question. George."

"So who murdered Krylov?"

"I could give you a runaround about that, but instead I'll say that it's classified."

"But you are sure that it was one of his own people?"

"Yes, George. We have a confession. Anne?"

"During your, uh, absence, there has been a great deal of other unrest in the country. With the government out of money how can you possibly respond?"

"One miracle at a time, Anne. I'd like to say I have all the answers, but I don't. I'll pull together the best team possible to come up with the right course of action."

"Follow up: Would some of those teams be part of the GAM or the family?"

"If that is where I find the expertise, then yes. I won't avoid anyone because of his background. I judge a person on his abilities."

"Madam President, what about the devastation of your use of weapons of mass destruction on Texas and Nevada?"

"Are you asking about the political ramification or the cleanup?"

"Well, both, ma'am."

"The cleanup has already started. I've ordered National Guard troops from nearby states, the correct use of National Guard troops I might add, to aid in dealing with the disasters that have come from the orbital bombardment I ordered. FEMA is also en route.

"As far as the political ramifications, I, as president of the United States, alone have the power and responsibility of unleashing those horrific weapons. I will bear the grief of the lives they took. I will rejoice in the lives they saved and the freedoms we retain. Only the people will decide if my actions were appropriate.

"Next question."

"Ma'am, can you answer to the rumors that you are dismantling the Secret Service?"

"Nothing can be further from the truth. The Secret Service will remain in operation for years to come. However, I think your rumor came from a very correct source that says that the Secret Service will no longer guard the president. As of today I've signed Executive Order Sierra Tango 3343, which states each president is responsible for her own personal protection.

"And before you ask: Yes, the GAM will be providing mine in the foreseeable future."

* * *

For the first time in over a week, the Metro staff was in the same room as Colonel Reed. All were well-dressed, even if it were civies. Reza, in spite of his lowly rank seemed to dominate captains, majors, and even Colonel Reed. They had been asked to wait to talk to the leaders of the

CorpGov. For some reason his people had decided to stand and wait instead of sitting.

The imprisonment so far had struck Reza as odd. Their captors hadn't been harsh but rather fair and firm. They'd provided every reasonable request their prisoners made, including conjugal visits with spouses. The prison felt more like being confined to building in summer camp than a stringent lockdown. There were no beatings. No rapes. No killings. It really shocked Reza.

Even with the soft treatment, the prisoners felt like the niceness akin to a last meal. They all expected to die.

Tony Sammis came into the room, followed by President Susan Tipton, the chairman of the CorpGov, Nanogate, his bodyguard, and, as a supreme shock to all, Sergeant Enrique Tolbert carrying a boxed with the designation G996.

"Please, folks, sit," Tony said, gesturing to the seats on the other side of the table.

The boxed and the sergeant took a seat at the end of the table. Reza watched the sergeant's eyes. They didn't seem happy or sad.

"We are here to talk about disposition of the prisoners," Tony said. "If we could just return to the world before this all started... but we all know that is impossible."

"When are we to be executed," Lennart said, full of confidence in his assessment.

The president interrupted. "We are sorry to disappoint you, Captain, but that isn't what our goal is here. It may still happen but that is not the disposition of most of our prisoners."

Lennart raised an eyebrow as if to question her lie.

"Gentle beings, first each prisoner will get a trial," Nanogate interjected. "All the laws of the United States will be used as will the courts. Every single one of you will have a lawyer and a trial."

"I know you are thinking it will be a kangaroo court but it won't," Tony chimed in. "Each and every case will have a three-judge panel who will rule on the guilt or innocence of each accused."

"We have actually already seated the first trial. It has been conducted and its sentence begun."

"Who was executed?" Reza asked, looking at Tolbert.

"No one died, Lieutenant," Nanogate said.

"Then why wasn't anyone called as character witnesses?" Cohen asked. "Are these proceedings going to be in secret?"

"No witnesses were needed. The prisoner denied calling witnesses and requested that his hearing be in private. The president, Nanogate, and Tony Sammis acted as his judges."

"Who?" Colonel Reed asked.

"Why Sergeant Tolbert, of course," the president said.

"The prosecution asked for a suspended sentence but the defense, Sergeant Tolbert himself, would have none of it. His sentence began this afternoon and will run until two years after the last trial has been completed."

"But Sergeant, you don't seem harmed or imprisoned in any way."

The boxed unit G996 rolled out onto the table and squeaked, "Not exactly imprisoned."

Reza looked at Sergeant Tolbert, who finally spoke. "I always wanted to be a man, but I had to take the cards dealt to me by genetics."

"I'm confused," Amber Cohen said.

"Enrique Tolbert has been boxed in the capsule G996," Tony said. "We will not call him such, as that was part of the cruelty heaped upon the boxed, but rather call him by his name. His body has been taken by the young woman, now man, formerly known as Stephanie Delfalkis. I'd like to introduce you to Stephan Delfalkis."

A stunned silence followed.

"So you intend to box us all and give our bodies to your allies?" Colonel Reed asked.

"Each prisoner will be dealt with on a case by case basis. Only in the most serious of cases will the prosecution request the death penalty. Our primary punishment will be boxing," Tony said. "So I guess the answer to your question is yes."

"So you are going to keep us forever?" Reza blurted out.

"No, sir," Susan interjected. "Unlike the past Metro controlled system, this one will be fair and unbiased."

"Pffag! Unbiased. Probably like your tribunals," Broadsky scoffed.

"Actually," squeaked Tolbert from his new prison, "I think it is. You see I will serve on the tribunals and as head of the newly formed Federal Commission on Indentured and Punished Persons."

* * *

The open bar, and camaraderie after the last tense weeks led to many different activities in Nanogate's luxury penthouse in Crawford Tower smack in the middle of trendy Kelso, Washington.

If Tony were being honest with himself, he'd taken part in one too many toasts over the night. Sitting off to one side and watching the revelry die down, he didn't know how to feel. Jamie's hand felt good in his. The Metro War was over and they'd won. But once again too many good people died. There was no doubt he had a talent for leading people into combat but what a horrible gift to have been given.

George Orwell once said, "People sleep peaceably in their beds at night only because rough men stand ready to do violence on their behalf." Tony wondered if he was one of those rough men. What chose him to pick up the gauntlet? Could it have been nothing more than random chance?

Connie danced with the president of the United States to something vaguely resembling a polka. Edward was passed out on the floor, his blond hair still immaculate even after one too many tequila sunrises. Augustine argued something technical over a chessboard with David floating on the other side. Michael Beckman-Ford, aka Némein, necked with Morgan on the loveseat against the windows.

Wayne, paler than usual, chatted quietly to Christine on the couch. What impressed Tony even more was she talked back. Tony would like to have been a fly on that wall.

Nanogate stole away with the curvy, Cuban woman, Janet Prieto. Both looked like they had taken more than their share of liquor and intended to share something else. Who was Tony to judge? He couldn't even judge his own actions

Mr. Marks, almost aloof to the foibles of mortal mankind, watched over all of them in case they'd somehow missed an enemy.

"Only one more," Tony said cryptically.

"What, baby?" Jamie asked, more than half asleep against his shoulder.

"I made a promise not to let Sonya's dreams die."

"She was a good friend?" Jamie asked, implying more in the question than just friendship.

"She was only a friend, but 'only' seems to downplay it somehow. I think she honestly was my first real friend. I knew I could ask anything of her and she could ask anything of me."

"You miss her?"

"Every day, baby. Oh, I'm not pining for lost love. I'm missing something that I had never had until she filled the void. The closest friend I'd had before that sold me out without blinking. Sonya's friendship wasn't for sale at any price."

"I can understand. Being brought up in the family you never are quite sure what anyone else really wants. That's why you are such a find. Maybe you were her first friend, too?"

"No way, baby. All of her Greenies were her friends, faults and all. I think she loved them more for their foibles. Hell, it sounds like I'm describing Jesus Christ instead of the leader of a terrorist group."

Jamie gave a soft laugh. "I know what you mean. I enjoyed my time with her, too. You don't have to worry. She was no saint."

"No. I can honestly say she was no saint." Tony fell silent for several seconds.

"What were her dreams that you promised not to let die?"

"First was to make sure that the people were cared for instead of abused and bullied by the corporations. I think the CorpGov is the right ve…vehi… oh, the right thing for that.

"The second is only one more thing," he said, the liquor clouding his brain a bit.

"What's the one more thing, honey?"

"I gotta save her magic. She wanted someone to carry on her magic."

Cinnamon took that moment to jump up into her slaves' laps. Everything was all right as soon as they adored her—everything.

Author's Note

I hope waiting for the end of the two-book Metro Wars has been worth it.

Thanks again for coming along with me on this ride of the *CorpGov Chronicles*. With the completion of *The Bleeding Edge*, I will be taking a pause in this series. Please don't despair, because I have many more books to write in this universe, including Tony fulfilling his promise to Sonya, quelling the violence in America, a witch hunt, a family member of the cabal seeking revenge, and more!

Unfortunately, with my current obligations I'm only able to write about one book per year and next year's schedule has on it the long awaited sequel to *Toy Wars* entitled *Toy Reservations*.

The Bleeding Edge's basic concept from my twisted mind—a guerilla war translated into a war of equals. You already knew that the concept of the Metro War was coup on top of the previous GAM coup. This book explores how a war can go from very lopsided to even and then tipping the other way.

The title for this book seems to scream out "obvious" with all the people dying for their cause, but there is a hidden meaning as well. In business, the bleeding edge is the very forefront of technology. It also indicates the hemorrhaging in the pocketbook that the company goes through in order to stay in the technological lead. In *The Bleeding Edge*, that leading edge is the social reform that is required to make Metros once again viable to the mass of humanity.

I want to apologize to all the folks who speak the languages that I've butchered in this book, especially those who speak Russian. I have no great talent for languages, other than a smattering of Spanish, but I tried to do my research. If I've messed up something, please let me know and I'll fix it in future versions of this novel, giving you credit for pulling my *cojones* out of the fire. Oddly enough the idea for adding a smattering of another language came from an ex-girlfriend who was a second generation Polish immigrant to the United States. I was pleased to see the word *pizda*, which I learned from her, was the same in Polish and Russian.

I thank you all for making this journey possible. Without your support this would be nothing more than a vanity press run amok. As it is, TANSTAAFL Press is a growing concern with fans all over the U.S. and will be growing by adding more titles and almost certainly multiple new authors in 2015. Please let us know if there is something you want to see or a way we can better serve you!

Glossary

ambi: a flamboyant homosexual or bisexual man or woman.

arbeit macht frei: roughly translated to "Work makes you free," the slogan over the entrance to Auschwitz concentration camp.

avatar: an alternative image, chosen by the user, to represent themselves in virtual reality, usually matching emotional or desired traits.

bagbiter: a program or part of a program that makes you think it isn't working in order to make you either change to an alternate or to allow it to do something else while you aren't paying attention to it.

blow queen: a term for an unlicensed prostitute, sometimes used to indicate a person that is sexually easy.

BOWMI: Broad Off-World Market Index similar to the Dow for off-world investments

boxed: individuals who have had their brain removed from their body and sealed into a breadbox-sized metal prosthetic. They have been indentured because of poverty or by conviction of a crime.

bucky string: a device that replaced the venerable but outdated door chain. A "bucky" chain of carbon molecules that is nearly unbreakable.

burn: a term for a drug addict, usually one who has had their mind altered to a point where they can no longer think straight.

cabal, also Corporate Cabal: the irresponsible group nominally operating as an over-government prior to the Green Action Militia coup.

capa famiglia: an honorific given to the head of a crime family. Sometimes shortened to just *capa.*

Catholic Reformation and Catholic Schism: Catholic sects that split off from the main faith but who still consider the papacy to be the primary interface to the Almighty. Each has a large following but each has taken slightly different spiritual stands on issues such as alternate sexuality, birth control, and other key items.

cauc: a shortened form of Caucasian

CBRN: chemical, biological, radiological, nuclear—also known as weapons of mass destruction.

ceramcrete: a substance with the same purpose as concrete, but adding ceramic, bucky strings, and mono molecular mesh to a concrete mix makes this a significantly more durable substance.

cohab agreement: a legal agreement that could be thought of as a short-term marriage contract or an agreement to live together as sexual and monetary partners for a predefined term.

CorpGov: a new over-government that has arisen from the ashes of the old Corporate Cabal.

corpie: an employee of a megacorporation.

raid: a coordinated attack on a network location by multiple net jocks.

daemons: a background program, often critical to the prime function of the system.

data jack, also neural jack, personal neural interface, or PNI: a neural-electrical interface that allows sensory data (visual, text, olfactory, auditory) to be transmitted directly into the brain without using the direct senses.

drop-chute: a high-speed, emergency evacuation method from super-high buildings involving a biodegradable cocoon.

Duolon rounds: armor-piercing, jacketed ammunition.

EMP, also electromagnetic pulse: a high-energy electromagnetic signal, originally produced with nuclear weapons and later by other means. This signal usually will destroy unshielded electronics within several kilometers of the source.

Faraday cage: a metal cage made of either solid conductor or conductive mesh invented in 1836 by Michael

Faraday. Electronic signals cannot penetrate the cage, depending on the size of holes and the frequency of the electronic signal.

flimy: plastic sheet filling the same niche as current day paper.

flatie: any two-dimensional image such as old style television, pictures, or movies.

floatboard: a skateboard-like device with a lift generator attached instead of wheels. These are very dangerous and difficult to control.

gauss gun: an assault style weapon that uses magnetic induction to fire vast quantities of metal shards at extreme velocities. Very effective against unarmored targets.

gimu: roughly translated this word means duty or obligation. It is the word used for the yellow tights worn by a member of the bodyguard guild, or the code of ethics the bodyguards assume when they join the guild.

gm4_1c3: net slang, or l33t for Grandma Ice.

Greenie: a derogatory term for a member of the Green Action Militia.

Green Action Militia, also GAM: a radical offshoot of the Greenpeace movement initially intent on returning the future earth to a green and viable ecosystem. Slowly this morphed into an organization that wanted to remove the irresponsible Corporation Cabal. Their prime mission is to make life better for the vast dispossessed on earth.

ground level: a slum area inhabited primarily by nils and welfs and the place where most illicit trafficking takes place.

hacker, also hack: a low grade version of a net jock. Usually people with these skills get weeded out by ice before they become proficient.

ice, also black ice: anti-intrusion software on a network. Terms coined by Tom Maddox and made popular by William Gibson.

implants: either neural, or physical, bio-mechanical devices that are attached to a person's body usually in place of similar items removed (e.g., a prosthetic arm, or an artificial retina that shows more data).

jacked: plugged into the network.

Jupiter Cloud: a street drug in concert with electronic signal inputs through neural interface, which is characterized by the mental impression of floating.

kinetic strike vehicle: a device floating in orbit that is designed to deorbit and impact as a bombardment vehicle. Its destructive power is entirely because of its mass and its speed upon impact.

life capsule: a part of a system to allow egress of super towers in times of emergency. A biodegradable, sealable capsule just large enough to encompass a single person that absorbs the shock induced by massive acceleration and deceleration.

liftousine: limousine that has antigravity capabilities.

lift-bus: antigravity bus that with the ban on personal vehicles provides the mass transit network.

megacorps: corporations so large that they can dictate terms to governments rather than being under any control.

memory crystals: removable mass storage similar to USBs, or CDs.

Metro, also black, black suit, black shirt: Any member of a Metropolitan Police Force.

molecular explosives: very powerful explosives using molecular bond strengths rather than chemical interactions.

monofilament wire: a wire that is a single molecule wide. Used as an antipersonnel barrier and/or held taut to form a bladed weapon.

nanites: microscopic machines programmed to do specific tasks.

nano: prefix for very small, usually microscopic machines known as nanites.

nano-blocked: someone who has nanites injected into the brain to prevent them from revealing specific bits of information without a specific keying phrase or image.

nano curtain: a constantly flowing stream of nanites similar to an invisible waterfall. This barely tangible field samples atoms on anyone or anything passing through it. Normally used as a security device to make sure weapons aren't being carried.

narco stick: future version of "electronic" cigarettes that dispense various drugs.

net jock: a professional who is proficient in making the network do exactly what they want, regardless of any safeguards. Usually used to obtain information that its owner doesn't want disseminated, to control computer-operated machinery, or to remove safeguards.

net cradle: some network operators (net jocks/hackers) use an antigravity cradle that allows the body to float as it is connected into the network. This is thought to assist in removing the distraction of the physical body while concentration is totally within the network.

neural amplification device, also NAD: a weapon that causes no physical damage but can, at range, cause the specific neurons that cause pain to receive very high-level stimulus, causing excruciating agony and most often incapacity.

neural reconstruction: a procedure that takes the brain from a cadaver and draws the memories of the person out. It is only possible within a very short period after death.

news chips: key news items compressed onto a disposable and biodegradable transport media.

nil: a person who has no legal standing of any kind, usually because of illegal immigration or by sentence of a court.

nultruck, also lift-truck: antigravity version of a panel van or semi.

nymthol: an unregulated street drug.

psychic overwhelm: a method of forcing the brain to reveal information even if programmed against it. This requires a court order to perform legally.

percomm: a future version of our modern day smart phones that is embedded in the skin (usually under the ear). These can use speaker phone, or be totally private. They also allow the retrieval of email, etc. Usually linked with data jack.

pergrav: a personal antigravity device that is notoriously

cranky, requires maintenance, causes poor stability, and is often dangerous to the user. The only group that uses them regularly is the Metros.

poly boards: analogous to modern day circuit boards

Purple: an unregulated street drug.

rag doll: a euphemism for a nil referring to the fact that nils often bundle up in multiple layers of clothing to keep warm and dry.

RPV: a remotely piloted vehicle.

solido, also solidocast, solidography, solidograph, etc.: a three-dimensional image generation (*solid*-ography) that replaces television, pictures, and movies.

stunbag: a large, nonlethal projectile usually fired from a grenade launcher with the intent of rendering a person incapacitated. Usually a bag filled with sand.

tattoo girl/boy: a prostitute. Called tattoo girl/boy because of the required state tattoo showing that person has been licensed and inspected.

token girl/boy: the lowest level of tattoo girl/boy who will accept food tokens or tube hotel tokens in lieu of cash.

TriMet: mass transit in the Pacific Northwest, originating in Portland but traveling as far north as Vancouver, BC, as far south as Redding, CA, and as far east as Boise, ID.

TSV: Troop Support Vehicle analogous to the Armored Personnel Carriers of today.

tube or tube hotel: a hotel room that is about twice the space of a coffin, 2.5 meters long, 1.5 meters wide and a meter high. Contains all the needs except bathroom and shower, which are usually communal in nature. Used primarily by the indigent, the poor, and traveling salesmen.

United States of America: has grown to contain the Canadian provinces (at their request), the Mexican states, and several other countries within Central America to a total of ninety-seven states. Hawaii has declared itself independent and has stopped at least two attempts to return them to the fold.

vape: short for vaporize—verb meaning to kill.

vidow: a video imitation of a real window usually on interior flats.

virtual reality, also VR, vir: a personal sensory representation of what is happening within a network or computer system. A net jock's skill at defining, being able to absorb and manipulate those representations determines their overall success.

welf: a person subsisting on welfare and often supplementing that meager income with petty crime.

yellow jacket: a derogatory term to indicate a member of the bodyguard guild, primarily because of their requirement to wear bright yellow tights.